EST 1923

LUCK

THE BAXTER BILLIONAIRES

by Daisy Allen

Copyright © 2023 by Daisy Allen

All rights reserved.

No part of this publication may be reproduced, distributed, or transmitted in any form or by any means, including photocopying, recording, or other electronic or mechanical methods, without the prior written permission of the publisher, except as permitted by U.S. copyright law. For permission requests, contact [include publisher/author contact info].

The story, all names, characters, and incidents portrayed in this production are fictitious. No identification with actual persons (living or deceased), places, buildings, and products is intended or should be inferred.

Book Cover by Daisy Allen

Editing by Rick Rollins

1st edition 2023

Contents

Dedication	VII
Prologue	1
1. Kiara	3
2. Kiara	12
3. Kylian	21
4. Kiara	29
5. Kiara	36
6. Kylian	41
7. Kiara	46
8. Kylian	48
9. Kiara	62
10. Kylian	68
11. Kylian	71
12. Kiara	76
13. Kylian	79
14. Kiara	94

15.	Kiara	98
16.	Kylian	109
17.	Kiara	115
18.	Kylian	129
19.	Kiara	140
20.	Kylian	144
21.	Kiara	147
22.	Kylian	162
23.	Kiara	178
24.	Kiara	182
25.	Kylian	197
26.	Kiara	210
27.	Kylian	217
28.	Kiara	225
29.	Kylian	229
30.	Kiara	239
31.	Kylian	255
32.	Kiara	262
33.	Kylian	275
34.	Kiara	296
35.	Kylian	301

36. Kiara	307
37. Kylian	320
38. Kiara	334
39. Kylian	342
40. Kiara	344
41. Kylian	347
42. Kiara	354
43. Kylian	361
44. Kiara	371
45. Kylian	382
46. Kylian	386
Epilogue - Kiara	390
Also By	395
Acknowledgements	397
About The Author.	399

*This one's for the girlies who like a little sunshine with their spicy men. Who want the golden retrievers, and to be the grumpy one in the relationship but still loved all the same.
For the ones who want to be fought for.
And to be told, that nothing else matters but them.*

Thank you for my manperson for putting up with me while I wrote this book. Your endless support is the reason I feel like I can do absolutely anything.

And for the person who gave me the K name; who was nothing like the K male in this book but just as memorable and made me realise what I did and didn't want. But I probably wouldn't be doing this writing thing without you.

Prologue

"WHO ARE YOU?" THE little girl peeking at me from behind the fridge says. I almost can't even see her eyes, they're so hidden behind a thick black fringe. But I can feel her staring.

"Hi. I'm Kylian, your brother's friend. What's your name?"

She ignores the question. "Which brother?"

"How many do you have?"

"Just one." She shrugs as if she thinks I'm an idiot for asking.

"So why did you ask which one?" I ask, confused by this strange little girl.

"Why not? Anyway, he's never brought any friends home before. He must like you."

The comment almost makes up for her teasing me. "I hope so. I like him a lot."

She continues to stare. It shouldn't be unnerving considering she's so little. Or maybe that's exactly why it's so unnerving.

"Kylian." She says my name like she's trying to figure out if she should waste time trying to memorize it, if she'll need to know it some time in the future. Do you want to play cards sometime?" she asks, holding out a deck of cards.

"I'd love to. What do you want to play? Go Fish, maybe?"

Her face rearranges into a disgusted expression. "Go Fish is for babies. I play poker."

"Aren't you too little to play poker?" I regret saying it as soon it's out of mouth.

She splutters as she glares at me, squares her shoulders, and straightens her back until she's almost a whole inch taller. "I'm not too little. And you just don't want to play because you're afraid I'll win."

"I'm not afraid of that at all. In fact, I bet I'd really like being beat by you."

"You're going to be sorry you said that to me one day."

I lean in and say with a wink, "I look forward to it."

ONE

Kiara

London

"Kiara! Is it just me or are your fucking tits out!"

I flash a grin at my best friend, lifting my Long Island iced tea in a boozy toast.

"I fucking hope it's not just you!" I shout, barely audible over the thumping music in the club. "I didn't buy this new bra for no one to notice!"

She laughs, shaking her head as she grabs my hand and leads me back to the dance floor where the rest of our group of friends have congregated. There's something about the smell of fresh, sweat, cheap alcohol, 90s RnB, and my shoes sticking to the floor with every step that brings out a primal instinct in me.

"You make me wanna..." we shout along with Usher, bodies contorting and writhing along to the lyrics about a guy wanting to cheat on his girlfriend. The irony seems lost to us that we're all actually out tonight to help a friend get over her betrayed, broken heart.

The female mind is a complicated place.

And tonight, mine is a drunken, messy, convoluted landscape as I try to forget for just a moment why I'm back in London in the first place.

Once the song is over and another Usher song comes on, I step off the dance floor for a moment to take a breath. Downing the rest of my drink before placing the glass on a nearby bar table, I glance around the club. It's dark inside; I can barely see more than a few feet in front of me except where the disco lights shine.

We'd stumbled upon this club after our group had been kicked out of the previous one when I'd kicked a guy where he deserved to be kicked because he wouldn't take my friend's no for an answer. I didn't take fifteen years of Taekwondo at my brother's dojang to watch a drunken sleazebag put his hands somewhere they're not wanted.

The short rest refreshes me, and I'm welcomed back into the dancing throng by my friends' outstretched arms glistening with perspiration and dollar store body glitter.

As one song fades out and a new one in, the beat slows.

Suddenly, there's a wall of heat behind me.

A chest has moved in close, into my space but not quite touching me, moving left when I move left, right when I move right.

I lean forward to see what happens, and the body follows.

There's the softest touch of a large palm against my right hip, neither moving me closer nor pushing me farther away—just there.

I feel no need to brush it away; instead, with eyes closed, letting the music lead me, I lean my head back, and it meets a shoulder. Another palm comes up to rest on my other hip, letting me guide it as I twist at the waist, the music driving my body to drop closer to the ground, my movement slowing, becoming more fluid and sensual.

"I love the way you dance," a voice, low and husky, growls into my ear.

I don't reply, but a tingle creeps up my spine as I press back against the chest, and it rumbles with approval.

Trickles of sweat slide down from between my legs all the way down to my ankles as I drop my hips a little more, drawing circles with my ass, purposely pressing back against the stranger.

"Careful," he warns in a way that sounds more like a promise against my ear.

"Careful... or what?" I finally say, reaching up behind me, fingertips grazing against the stubble on his cheek.

"You don't want me to get any ideas."

Something about his words ignites a fire somewhere deep inside me. The mystery, the intimacy, with a stranger whose face I haven't even seen yet. My neck pivots, so my mouth is closer to his throat, and I purr, "Maybe that's exactly what I want."

He chuckles. I feel it rather than hear it, a rumble that vibrates from his ribcage and against my shoulder blade. "Maybe you should just tell me the ideas that you're having, and I'll tell you if we're on the same wavelength."

"Now, what would be the fun in that?" I whisper, my mouth so close to his skin I can almost feel his stubble against my lips. Almost.

His hands that had barely grazed me on either side suddenly grip my hips, and he pulls me in closer, his legs pressing against the back of my thighs. There's hardly a spot along the back of my body that isn't touching his, and it's making my pulse quicken with every second.

We dance the rest of the song in silence, although calling it "dancing" is a blatant exaggeration. I'm barely moving, his hands keeping me rooted to the spot and joined to him, my ass against his groin.

There's no question about what ideas he's having.

Because they match mine.

The four or five Long Island iced teas along with the two rounds of shots we'd had as soon as we arrived at the club have drowned any inhibitions I might normally have had and, as my friend pointed out, my tits are out... for a reason.

And it seems as though they have done their job.

The lyrics of Silk's "Freak Me" thump around us, low, slow, sensual, the music expressing the things I inexplicably want to say and do to this stranger. This stranger about whom I know nothing except that his fingers digging into my hips feel like they know how to do things to me. Things he could probably talk me into doing—almost anything—right here on the dance floor in that husky voice of his.

Through hooded eyes, I look over to see my friends grinning at me, one throwing a none-too-subtle thumbs up, but I barely notice them.

His breath is hot and sweet against my cheek.

"Let me buy you a drink?" he whispers as the music slowly fades out.

"I'll let you buy me two."

"And then what?"

"And then maybe I'll let you show me about these mysterious ideas you've been having."

"I hope you have all night."

Hands on my waist, he spins me around just as the club's spotlight washes over his face, illuminating his light cornflower eyes.

Eyes I've seen before.

Oh, my god.

The shock on his face mirrors mine, and the mouth that had just been whispering dirty promises to me drops open as my entire body alternates from icing over to burning hot.

"Kiara?" he shouts.

I just nod numbly. Mutely.

"What are you doing in London?" he shouts, the surprise and confusion in his voice doing nothing to calm the storm building inside me.

I can't tell him.

I can never tell him why I'm here. Not now.

"Hey, Kiara, who's your hot friend?" my friends shout, circling around us.

His name stumbles out of my mouth, as if I haven't whispered it a thousand times before, "Th-This is K-Kylian. Kylian Baxter. He's my brother's best friend."

Kylian's hand is tight around my wrist as he drags me off the dance floor and out of the club into the still warm London summer night air.

"Let me go!" I yell as soon as we're a few feet away from the club's entrance.

He spins me around so that I'm facing him. "Kiara," he hisses, anger spilling from every pore. "You shouldn't be here. I'll let you go when I get you—"

"Get me where? Home?" I yank my hand out of his hold. "I don't have a home here, remember?" I yell and try to ignore the way my voice sounds bratty, even to my ears.

He looks down at his hand as if he hadn't realized he was still grabbing me and then scowls, reaching around to rub the back of his neck. "What the fuck are you doing here?"

I meet his scowl with one of my own. "I am—ugh, I *was* enjoying a night out dancing with my friends."

"I mean, what the hell are you doing in London? I thought you were in the U.S. at college."

"I. Just. Told. You. What. I'm. Doing," I spit out. Why is he being such a dick? If it's because he's embarrassed about what just happened, that makes two of us, but at least I'm making an effort to be civil.

My eyes shoot poison-tipped daggers at him at the same time as they take in a view that I haven't seen in three years. The last time I saw him was the day after my high school graduation when he came to say goodbye to my parents. They were moving away from London and returning to Hong Kong where my father was from. I would spend my summer there with them before going to the U.S. for college. Whatever I thought might happen when I came back for a visit to London has fled from my mind. As it stands now, though, I want nothing to do with Kylian Baxter.

He sighs long and slow as if the entire world is weighing on his shoulders, then pinches the bridge of his nose, no doubt thinking about what he's going to tell my brother. I've heard that sigh before. Most memorably, I'd heard it when he caught me cutting class in grade ten. He'd come to visit London during his spring break from college, and after running into me in town with a bottle of bourbon in my hand at 11 a.m. on a Tuesday morning, he had sighed just like he was doing now. I'd begged him not to tell my brother, and he'd finally conceded but only if I'd let him take me home. I'd agreed but only because my friends were looking at him like he was an ice cream sundae, and they either wanted to be the topping dripping down the sides or to swallow the sundae in one big gulp. At the time, I hadn't understood what the appeal of Kylian Baxter was.

His sigh finally comes to an end, and he reaches out for me.

I take a step back; the last thing I need is for him to touch me. Again.

A frown ripples along the tanned, smooth skin of his forehead, almost imperceptibly. "Come on, let's go. Do you need a place to stay? Nathan is going to go fucking psycho if he knows you went to a club like this. I'll give you a ride." He walks off, then turns when he realizes I'm not following.

"I'm twenty-one, Kylian. I'll get a ride when I'm done dancing. You can't tell me what to do. You're not my brother."

My words must strike a chord because before I know what's happening, he closes the gap between us and my back is against the wall with him towering over me. With his back to the streetlight, I can't make out anything but the shadows of his infuriatingly handsome face. I lift a hand to shield my eyes, but he grabs it and holds it over my head against the wall.

"Yes, you're right. I am not your brother. And don't you ever forget it," he says in a voice I've never heard from him before. Dark. Husky. Dangerous. Taunting.

The breath sticks in my throat like tar. My eyes flick upwards and directly into his eyes.

I've never been so close to him that if there were light, I'd probably be able to see my reflection in his irises.

"I..." My voice sticks in my throat just as my breath did, and the corner of his mouth lifts into a smirk.

Something has shifted, seismically, in the last few seconds. I've gone from wanting to slap him to... I don't know what. That's a lie. I know exactly what I want him to do. It's what I came to London for. I just hadn't expected it to happen like this.

His breath is hot against my cheek as he leans in closer to whisper, "Kiki, I didn't know it was you when I... I've never seen you dance before."

The image of him watching me dance sears into my brain. "N-No?"

His head shakes once. In the headlights of a passing car, I can see the corner of his mouth lift into the smallest smirk. "Not like that, anyway."

My tooth digs a little too hard into my lip, and I let out an involuntary yelp.

"Careful," he whispers, his thumb running along my bottom lip. It takes everything I have not to buckle at the knees. And then he leans forward until his lips are half an inch from mine.

Time stops, the earth freezing in her orbit as I wait for him to close that last breath of space between us. Waiting for the one thing that I've been wanting since the first time my brother brought him home to visit almost thirteen years ago. His scent infiltrates every one of my cells, and I feel my lips part, wanting to breathe in as much of him as I can.

And just as quickly as all this happened, it's over.

"Fuck!" he shouts as he pulls away from me, his fist meeting the wall behind me with a sickening crunch. "Fuck. Fuck!"

"Kylian!" I hear myself shout as he cradles his hurt hand, his face scrunched in pain.

"I'm fine. You... you need to go back inside," he says, avoiding my eyes.

"You're not okay," I whisper, laying my hand on his back. The way he instantly recoils feels like a punch landed in my solar plexus, and I'm suddenly gasping for air.

He turns at the sound of me struggling for breath, his face instantly flooding with concern "I'm sorry. I-I'm sorry. I shouldn't have..." he growls.

But he's hurt me, and I'm not going to hide it. "Shouldn't have what? Pushed me away or almost kissed me? Which one?"

The wince at my words almost makes me regret them.

"Both," he admits. "I don't know what came over me. Your brother would rip my throat out if he knew..."

"What the fuck does Nathan have to do with anything?" I shout louder than I mean to, but the last thing I need to be thinking about right now is my brother. The tequila in my blood seems to be rallying and loosening my tongue. "I wanted you to kiss me. Me. This has nothing to do with my brother. This is just about us."

"Kiki..." His voice fades to nothing, his eyes fixed on my lips.

My stomach lurches at the nickname he gave me all those years ago. The name I won't let anyone else call me. "I wanted you to kiss me. And you wanted to kiss me, too. I know you did."

"Maybe." He drops his hurt hand to his side and lifts his other hand to my face. "Maybe I did."

I grab his hand and push it to my cheek. It's warm and strong against my face. My breath stills as he lowers his palm down to my throat, my pulse quickening under his touch. I feel my body inch closer to his until his breath is hot against my forehead.

"You did," I breathe out.

His eyes lock on mine as if seeing me for the first time.

"I can't do this, Kiara. Fuck," he curses under his breath. "But dammit I want to." His hand closes more tightly around my throat, and I feel like I'd collapse if the wall wasn't holding me up. "What do you think is going to happen if we kiss right now? What do you want from me?"

"I don't know. But I want you to kiss me."

"And I want to kiss you. What the fuck is wrong with me?"

He shakes his eyes, but the desire in his eyes doesn't change. "I can't, Kiki, you're just a—"

I cut him off. "If you say child, I will knee you so hard you'll be choking on your own balls."

A smirk spread across his face. "Feisty." Something about the realization makes him serious again. "Do you really want me to kiss you?"

"Yes." Decisive.

"You might regret it."

"Not as much as you'd regret it if you didn't." Where this bravado comes from, I don't know. Maybe I just know that it's now or never.

This time he smiles in response.

And then sighs, his hand falling from my throat.

I almost whimper in disappointment.

"I can't. As much as a fucking asshole I can be, I don't want to be that way with you. So I'm not going to do something that we're going to regret when we are both sober."

"But..." I start, he cuts me off with a look.

"Do you know Bottle in Soho?"

I nod; it's one of the hardest bars to get into in London and is owned by his brother, Kingsley. "I think so. Why?"

"I'll be there tomorrow afternoon. If you... if you still feel the same, be there at 6 p.m. tomorrow."

What? What is he saying? I shake my head to clear it. "You... want... me... to meet you at Bottle tomorrow?"

He leans in and presses a kiss to my forehead like he's done to annoy me a hundred times before. But this time it feels different.

"I want you to if, and only if, you want to, okay?"

My chin dips in a single nod.

He gives me one last look.

And is gone.

Two

Kiara

Five Years Later — Hong Kong

There's a little beep as I press my key card against the security pad and my door unlocks.

A quick glance up and down the hallway satisfies me that I'm alone, and I slip into my apartment.

The cool air instantly envelops me, an audible sigh slipping from my lips, and then I take what feels like the first full breath of air in hours. The Hong Kong climate is cursing me with its record humidity this year. Hot days followed by barely cooler nights followed by even hotter days and stiflingly humid nights. Whoever tells the visitors that they'll get used to it is lying; I was born here, am cold-blooded, thriving in the heat, and still some days I can barely survive the humidity here.

I push the front door closed, making sure I hear the click of the latch mechanism falling into place before I drop my ace of spades keychain into the dish on the stool by the door. The leather couch sinks under me as my Tony Burch bag slips off my shoulder onto the floor at my feet.

It's been a long day.

Productive.

Lucrative.

But long.

Reaching for the locked black pouch from my bag, I give it a little shake before unlocking it with the key on my charm bracelet. I pull out the neat stacks of money that fit comfortably but heftily into my hand. One, two, three, the cash gets separated into equal piles.

One stack goes back into the pouch to take to the bank, one into the hidden safe on my bookshelf, and one into the disguised plant box by my bed. Repeat experiences with my apartment broken into have taught me to never leave it all in one place.

Granted, I'm no longer living in the kind of place that could, and would, be easily broken into, but old habits and learned-the-hard-way life lessons are difficult to unlearn.

The city's bright night lights flicker in front of me as I slowly strip out of my black bodycon cocktail dress. The simple lace detail around the hem tickles as I slip it down my body and step out of it. The dress is only one of many of my little black dresses, or my "uniform" as my girls call it. I take one last glance out the window before I pull the curtains closed and make my way to the bathroom.

The bathwater is shockingly hot when I slide my body into the tub, causing me to hiss as my muscles seize before slowly relaxing, the hard warm water jets kneading the soreness from my body. Once the water has cooled enough, I massage a handful of shampoo into my hair, and then, holding my breath, sink under the water, swirling my long black locks around my head. I'm still as amused by the foaming sound of the lathering suds dissolving into the water as I was when I was little.

Only a lack of oxygen prompts me to finally emerge, my hair slick against my head following the curve of my neck and all the way down almost to the small of my back.

I lean back and close my eyes.

There's nothing but the sound of the occasional dripping of the tap and my breath in the room, just the way I like it at the end of the day. If I listen hard enough, though, I can probably still hear the echoes of the music blaring in the club, the traffic on the car ride home, and the sound of street food vendors selling their wares.

Silence is what I'm craving.

As if on cue, a shrill ring echoes around the tiled bathroom, and I pretend for just a second that I'm going to ignore the call. It's a little gift to myself, a moment of hope that I'm only minutes from bedtime and rest. But then reality hits, and I reach for the Bluetooth earpiece on the edge of the tub and slip it into my ear, absentmindedly playing with the bubbles in the water.

"Yeah."

It's noisy in the background with the music thumping, and there's some fumbling before a voice finally speaks. "Kiara? Where are you?"

"Home."

"It's not even 2 a.m." The voice sounds surprised.

I shrug. "I thought I'd have an early night."

"Lazy cow." It's a joke, and we both know it.

"What do you want?" I ask, already reaching for the towel by the tub.

"I have someone here you might be able to help. She really needs it, Kiara."

I swallow the sigh and push myself to my feet. "I'll be there in ten minutes."

"How was your week?" my dad asks at lunch about ten hours later as he reaches across the table to top up my wine. He's just finished telling me a story about a funny run-in with a former business partner's wife at the country club. My father, still incredibly handsome while newly retired and newly widowed, is what the women at the country club call "prime real estate." As always, location is key, and the view from the seat beside Dennis Yin and his billions is pretty good.

I reluctantly returned to Hong Kong from New York City before my mother passed away a little over a year ago and decided to move out on my own instead of staying at the family home. It caused a bit of a ruckus in the family, and after a series of heated arguments between my father, my brother, and I, that looked like they'd never be resolved. But my father finally agreed to not hire bodyguards to shadow me over everything if I promised to have a weekly lunch with him. Something about being able to see with his own eyes that I was okay. Sometimes we would go for a walk or try a new restaurant, but most of the time I'd come and see him at Amber, the family's cognac and cigar bar, my father's passion project.

"My week was okay," I answer as I pick up a piece of chicken from my platter and pop it into my mouth. Maybe if I'm chewing, he won't ask me any more questions.

The answer I do give him is far from the answer he wants, too short and uninformative as always, but he also knows it's the only answer he's getting. We've done this weekly dance enough times now for him to know that I consider my business mine alone and something I keep close to my heart.

As for his business, well, frankly, I don't give a damn about it. Something he seems to conveniently forget every time we meet.

"Kiara, my girl..."

My hand snaps into the air, stopping him before he can continue. "No, Dad. We're not doing this today. Please. I'm too tired; I didn't sleep much last night, and I'm not really in the mood to rehash the same conversation we have every week."

The sigh is short and accompanied by a drop of his shoulders, a sign of concession that doesn't come easily to a man considered a giant in his industry.

But the boardroom is one thing, conversations with his daughter are another.

I give him a smile and pat his hand, giving it a gentle squeeze out of sheer gratitude.

"Anyway, Dad, Nathan has everything under control," I say. "The last thing you need is the directors interrupting your retirement by constantly reporting to you that your two children are squabbling in the boardroom."

He grips my hand; his aging hands feel softer and smaller and less sturdy than when he used to lay them on my head every night before I went to bed. "I can't protect you forever, my girl," he says.

"I love you for always watching out for me, but I'll always be okay, Dad. Or have you forgotten how many times you had to come down to my school after I got into a fight?"

My father lets out a loud guffaw. "How could I forget? Your mother used to joke that the road from our house to school was worn down from her having to drive there so often to pick you up after you'd caused some mischief."

A warmth in my chest spreads as I hear him laugh at my story, and I silently kick myself for not being a little more open with him. Would it hurt to let him into my life a little more?

Before I can answer, my brother appears, interrupting our conversation.

"What's so funny?" Nathan asks, strolling in from the back room of the bar, newspaper rolled up in his left hand, briefcase in his right, looking like he was born with them attached to him. He takes off his tailored suit jacket and hangs it over the back of a bar stool, smoothing out an invisible wrinkle with his hand. Something about the movement makes me scowl. He's always been such a tightly wound control freak. Sometimes I've wondered if one day his head might just pop right off from the stress of being Nathan Yin.

Or maybe I'm just frowning at the intrusion.

I specifically picked this time of day for my meetings with Dad because Nathan is usually busy at the office during the day or having on-site meetings. I suspect the reason my lunches with my father over the last few months have lasted without too many problems is because there were just the two of us. I love my brother, but the journey he's taking with his life is very different to the one I'm on, something he refuses to acknowledge.

Dad waves him to our table. "Oh, Nathan, your sister and I were just reminiscing about her school days."

"You mean about the time she got suspended for starting that gambling ring?" Nathan reminds him, smirking.

My father almost falls off his chair guffawing. "Oh, I forgot about that. Made quite the killing betting on the school team's soccer games, as I recall."

"Some things never change, hey, sis?" Nathan reaches out as if to ruffle my hair, then pulls his hand back, seeing the look on my face. "Dad, you know she won every time because she was always flirting with the captain of the soccer team to see if she was in good form or—"

He stops ten seconds too late at the sight of the vein popping on my forehead. At least he can take a hint. Must be something he's picked up in the last few years.

Nathan is five years older than me and, having just turned thirty-one, seems to think that he is wiser than Solomon. As the current CEO of our family's company, Yin Tech, he will inherit the bulk of Dad's stake and control my stake as well. Nathan is richer than God and acts like it.

But he's also been my protector from the day I was born, so me now choosing to live my life out of the family fold (and checkbook) is the perennial thorn in his side.

And if I'm honest... maybe one of the reasons I do it.

Maybe.

Okay, definitely.

"How's your week been, Keeks?" he asks, plopping down on the seat across from me and nodding a thank you to the server who appears with a glass of whiskey and lays out a plate and cutlery in front of him.

"Fine," I shrug. "Busy."

"Well, that's more than she told me, Nathan," our father teases, giving me a wink. "What are you doing here? Shouldn't you be in the meeting with Tareen Enterprises?"

Nathan spoons some soup into his bowl and nods. "I was. They didn't have anything to tell me that we didn't already know, so I left. Waste of our time. Their books are in shambles."

Dad frowns but doesn't say anything. I know it's coming, though. He only retired a year ago, weighed down with the burden of mourning our mother. He thought it was the best time to hand over the reins, but I imagine that it's been hard to step back from the day-to-day running of the company.

If I know anything about my brother, though, it's that he'll do right by my father's legacy and take the company into bigger and better things. And as long as they don't involve me, I believe in him 100%.

Sensing my father's curiosity, Nathan gives him a quick report of his day, and I sit back, arms folded, closing my eyes, letting the business talk fade into the background.

I can't help but think how things have changed since I moved back to Hong Kong after living abroad since I was eighteen. Almost eight years on my own, away from friends and family. There were times I would've given my right hand to sit in this bar with my brother, reminiscing about the old days and holding my own as he teased me. But then I'd remember what had driven me away in the first place, and I wonder if I'd have been able to really enjoy their company again unless I'd spent that time away.

Not to mention the distance I needed from a certain someone...

Life gives you choices, but it never tells you what the other roads might have led to.

"Keeks, you're snoring," my brother shouts at me after who knows how long.

"Shit." I startle awake. The table has been cleared, and my father is nowhere to be seen. "What time is it?"

Nathan gets up from the table, pulling on his shirt sleeve to check the time on his watch. "Time to get some sleep. You want to stay at the house tonight?"

"I'm fine. Just resting my eyes."

"You been sleeping enough?"

"Yes." No.

"You sure? Do you need some money?" His eyes bore into mine. Earnestly. Annoyingly so.

"Ugh. See ya, Nathan," I huff and jump to my feet.

He frowns and rubs his temple. "Wait. Geez, I was just asking."

"Well, stop asking!" I struggle to keep my voice low. I know he's only asking out of concern, but I haven't given him any reason to think I can't take care of myself. "I don't need money. I have a job."

"Kiara. It's not a job."

This time, I have to bite my tongue to stop from shouting. I count back from five before I speak. "Nathan, it's not a job that you would want to do, maybe. But I do, and I make more than enough money to support myself." I stop before I start an argument worse than the one we're having.

He mutters something under his breath, rubbing his temple even faster now. "You'd make more money working for us. I need someone—"

My hand comes up again for the same reason. "Stop. I didn't want to have this conversation with Dad, and I'm certainly not going to have it with you. Why can't we have just one conversation where you two are not trying to force the company on me?"

His eyes narrow, and he bangs the table, his hand a fist of white knuckles. "Dammit, Kiara! When are you going to realize this is the best thing for you? What is the point of all this? Everything that Mom and Dad did, everything that I'm doing, if it's not to take care of all of us? At what point are you going to realize you're making us sick with worry?"

I lean over the table, my voice low. The words slink out of me, slow, deliberate. "I never asked anyone to worry about me. Never. Not once have I asked you for your help, have I?"

He doesn't say anything, just pulls back, dark eyes locked on mine.

"Have I, Nathan? Name one time," I press. He stays silent. "Yeah, that's what I thought."

He shakes his head. "Just because you haven't asked for it doesn't mean you don't need it. I know one time when you should've called us. Or at least me."

The reminder cuts and leaves a scar that I'll have to close later when I'm alone. I step away from the table. Away from him. Away from the past.

The bar is starting to fill up with customers, so I try to keep my voice down as I pick up my purse from the back of the chair. "You can tell Dad you tried. I'm going."

"Keeks," he says, following me toward the doors. "Stay. He just went to take a call. He'll be right back."

"Tell him I'll see him next week," I say, sighing. The last thing I want is to fight with Nathan. Despite all the disagreements, he has always been there for me.

"Keeks," he says again, this time touching my shoulder, his voice softened. Given in. For now. "You know it's just because I love you."

His words squeeze my chest. And I nod; I nod because I do know; I do know that he loves me. I'm probably the person he loves most in the world. More than our mother, certainly more than our father, more than himself. Even when it made me hate him, I know he's always loved me most. And maybe that's why he does so much to protect me. But that's not the way to love me, and he should know that by now.

"Get some sleep, okay? Stop going out at 2 a.m. every night," he says with a teasing shake of his finger.

"Yes, 'Dad,' I'll try," I say, brushing a kiss against his cheek and getting a smile. "Love you, Nath-ey."

"Oh, fuck off," he chuckles and pulls me in for a quick hug before shoving me playfully away.

I drape my jacket over my arm and turn toward the door to leave just as someone steps over the threshold, raising his hand in a greeting.

And the world gets pulled out from under me.

My brain freezes in place, and before I can think of a quick getaway, a voice, *that* voice, says, "Hey, Kiki. Miss me?"

Three

Kylian

The last person I expect to see when I arrive at Amber is Kiara Yin. Stupid, considering it's her father's cigar bar, but I haven't run into her here, or anywhere, even once since Nathan told me she moved back to Hong Kong over a year ago.

Maybe if I had preempted it, I would've come up with something better to say other than "Miss me?" because based on the look on her face, if she'd been holding any kind of sharp implement, she would most certainly have not missed me. That spear/bayonet/dagger/shiv would've stabbed right through my heart.

"Goodbye, Nathan. I'll see you later," Kiara says, completely ignoring my smooth opening line.

My best friend grins and tilts his chin at me. "You're not going to say hi to Kylian? You probably haven't seen him in eight years since he came to the airport with us when Mom and Dad moved back to Hong Kong."

I flick my eyes toward her to see her jaw tighten at the mention of it having been eight years since we last saw each other. Apparently, she'd told her brother as much as I had about what happened five years ago in London. Not a damn thing.

Her chest puffs out, chin slightly tilted at the ceiling, her eyes staying locked on Nathan's. To stop her looking elsewhere? Something in the depth of my stomach tickles at the thought.

"Huh, has it only been eight years?" she says, her voice completely lacking in any emotion. "Time sure does fly when you're not in the presence of a prickwaffle."

Nathan slaps me on the shoulder and chuckles, not at all surprised that she's acting this way toward me. As her older brother's annoying best friend, he'd only ever seen us insult each other.

I can't help but grin at her words, which only serves to make her even more angry. She growls, finally turning her eyes to me for the first time, and blurts out, "What the hell are you two laughing about?"

"Oh, so she can see you! Here I was wondering if I was back to my imaginary friend phase," Nathan jokes. "In fact, I wouldn't actually mind if you really turned invisible sometimes. It would definitely help me out when we're trying to pick up women at clubs."

Nathan prattles on in the background, but I can barely make out a word because I'm otherwise preoccupied.

Busy returning Kiara's gaze.

And it's knocked every breath, every thought, every intention, every memory out of my body.

All but one.

I don't know what I expected to happen when we'd inevitably run into each other again, but it wasn't this.

She looks different to how she looked in my memory. Older, yes. But I'm not sure that's the right word for it.

Mature. Confident. Adult. Self-aware.

Grown into one of the most beautiful women I'd ever seen.

I can't help but wonder what I look like to her, but I'm about to get my answer.

"Ugh," she grunts, apparently free from all the feelings that have flooded me, and gives me a glare that feels like she definitely is hoping I'd be invisible. "Has it only been"— she emphasizes the next word — "eight years since I last saw you? Life treating you a little bit harshly, Kylian?"

My name coming out of her mouth is like a shock to the solar plexus, and the tickle in my stomach has done a full-blown somersault. I take a breath, and then, again, I do what I know is going to annoy her most. I grin at her.

"You're kidding right? He looks like he's still twenty-five," Nathan says, apparently oblivious to the point of this diatribe and to his baby sister's aggravation.

The point, of course, is for Kiara to make it blatantly clear to me that she hasn't forgiven me for what happened last time we saw each other.

"What can I say? Maybe I've been packing on the pounds," I sigh, gently patting my six pack.

"Kylian! My boy, you are looking well," Nathan and Kiara's father, Dennis, shouts, stepping in behind Nathan and giving me a firm pat on the back. "Kiara! Isn't it lovely to see Kylian? You probably haven't seen him in years!"

She gifts us another eye roll and leans over to give her father a kiss on the cheek. "Yes, Dad. It's about as lovely as having my left pinky toe slowly removed with a pair of rusty hedge clippers and fed to me on the end of a dirty fork, dipped in a sauce made of mushed up eyeballs." She gives me one last look, filled with all things synonymous with pure hatred, before turning to her father. "I'll see you next week, Dad. Hopefully without unwanted interruptions." This time her brother gets part of the glare as well, and she walks away before she's forced to be in my presence for another second.

We turn, watching her practically run out the door. My feet itch to follow, and I would have, had her father and brother not been looking at me, wondering why I am staring out into the street.

"Thank you for coming, Kylian," Dennis says, taking my arm and leading me over to their table in the corner. "I know you're a busy man."

"Never too busy for you, sir," I say, my voice full of affection for the man. For a long time, Dennis Yin was more of a father to me than my own father. And while I'm now rebuilding my relationship with my dad, I won't ever forget the man who was there when I needed a father most. "What can I do for you?" I ask and hope he knows there's nothing in the world I wouldn't do for him.

He sighs, and there's a heavy seriousness in his face that I've rarely seen before, so I make sure to show that I'm listening.

Nathan returns from the bar and hands his father a glass of water. He takes a long sip before he says, "I'm worried about my daughter."

"Kiara?"

A chuckle. "She's the only daughter I know of!"

The joke lightens the mood.

"I'm worried about her future. She doesn't want to come work with her brother. She's made that very clear."

"I don't know why. I'm delightful," Nathan quips.

"Yes, well, whatever the reason is, it's still keeping me up at night." Dennis's voice drops as his chin does, and he looks older in this moment than he's ever looked.

"I can talk to her again, Dad."

The older man opens his mouth, and Nathan clamps his mouth closed. Nathan may be the CEO of a Fortune 500 company, but he's an obedient son first.

"No. I've made my decision. If she doesn't want to work at Yin, then that's her decision."

I nod. Coming from a family company myself, I know what it's like when someone decides that it's not the right choice for them. When it's time to let go and support them. "What can I do to help, sir?"

Air fills his lungs, his lips tightening against his teeth. He's about to ask me for a favor, and it's killing him.

"Sir? Please, you were a father figure to me, gave me a home when I needed one, offered me guidance all along the way. There's nothing I can do that can ever repay you. But please let me do something to show you how much I appreciate everything you've done for me."

His shoulders slack as he gives me a grateful smile.

My shoulders, however, tense at what he could possibly want.

"I would like... I need you to give Kiara a job."

"Dad—," Nathan gasps and is silenced with a look.

"If she's not going to accept the security that her own family can give her, then Baxter Enterprises is the next best thing. I know... I know you'd take care of her."

I open my mouth. That wasn't what I'd been expecting. I thought he needed me to take out some business man's daughter or talk to the authorities about getting a permit for another warehouse. I hadn't expected... Kiara.

"You... want me to offer her a job?"

He nods. "She's a very clever girl. I'm sure she will be an asset to your company no matter what she does."

I blink.

Kiara.

Working with me.

If she's going to be based in Hong Kong, it would be hard to completely avoid her if she's going to work in any of our companies. I make it a point to know everything that is going on in my organization or, at least, in my region. It's why I'd just come back from Singapore and from Vietnam two weeks before that.

But isn't that what you want, to get to see her? a niggling voice in my head taunts. Isn't that why... I mentally shut down the thought before turning back to the conversation.

"Sir, I have no doubt that she would excel at anything she wanted to, but... I'm not sure that working for Baxter is any better than Yin. She hates me even more than she hates him," I say, jabbing a thumb at Nathan.

Nathan grabs my thumb and twists it around, sending a sharp pain that strikes up my arm, and he only lets go when I kick him in the shin.

"See?" I say to Dennis. "Do you blame her for not wanting to work with this monster?"

The corners of his mouth twitch. "You young boys, trust me, she'll work with you if you offer her something. Anything, please. It will really help me stop worrying. It's taken my whole life to get this clown set up"—he waves at Nathan—"I can't help thinking I've let my daughter down by not providing her the same security."

His words feel like a poker in my heart.

"I will have to talk to my brothers first. This is somewhat of a special circumstance because—"

He cuts me off. "Of course, she'll have to sign an NDA. Don't want you thinking we're stealing your ideas."

My ideas aren't what I'm afraid she'll steal from me. Not that there's anything left of me for her to have.

"I have one more thing to sweeten the deal," Dennis says, interrupting my thoughts.

"Sir, that's not necessary!"

"Hush. Consider this a thank you for helping me. My son tells me that you have a special interest in the joint venture you two share and that you might have your eye on buying him out."

Nathan and I share a look.

"Watch?" I confirm, naming the streaming service that Nathan and I started a few years ago.

"Yes. It's doing well, yes?"

I nod. "Very."

"You've both worked very hard on it. I'm not surprised it's doing so well. If you can get Kiara settled somewhere at Baxter Enterprises in six months, Nathan will sell Watch to you. That's what you want, isn't it?"

I don't know how he knows that, but he does, and there's no point in pretending it's not true. "Yes, sir, it is."

"Then you can make an offer. As long as it's reasonable, it's yours. If you decide you don't want it, Yin Tech's 50% stake will go on the market anyway. But this way you will get the first offer."

The saliva dries in my mouth, and judging by the way Nathan is downing his glass of Remy Martin XO, he didn't know about the deal either. But the Yins are a traditional family in many ways, and if there's anything he's going to say to his father about their business, he's going to say it in private.

"I don't know what to say, sir."

Do I really want to be spending time trying to get Kiara to accept a job from me? It sounds like a complete waste of time; she's more likely to work on the docks selling lollipops to the sailors than work with me. She made that abundantly clear ten minutes ago, and I don't blame her. That was how I'd meant for her to react after all. But even so, the lure of having her close by is almost too tempting to resist. And Watch, even if it's not the main reason to do this, is a very delicious, lucrative icing on the cake.

Dennis stands up and offers me his hand.

"Believe me, getting Kiara to come work for you is not going to be as hard as you think," he says with a twinkle in his eye. I wish he'd share the secret with me, but I know better than to even try to crack that nut.

"Sir, I am doing this because you asked me. Not any other reason."

He puts one hand to his lips as he reaches into his pocket with the other and pulls out a folded piece of paper and pushes it into my palm. "Call this number. They might be able to give you some insight into what Kiara is doing right now. And what she might be able to offer you at Baxter."

He shuffles away without another word, leaving his son and I to stare at each other.

"He's wrong, you know," Nathan says, sitting down again. "About Kiara. She's not going to make this easy for you."

"Agreed." I nod, watching the older man brace against the wall as he turns the corner. He's looking older than the last time I saw him just a few months ago and makes me wonder why this is all happening now. "He must know that I'm going to do this with or without Watch. I'd do anything he asked of me." The thought of how this deal affects Nathan weighs on me. "Did you know he was going to offer Watch?"

The thinned lips are all the answer I need.

"And do you really think he'll convince the board to sell even if I don't buy it?" I ask even though I know the answer.

"Tell me one time my father has ever said he's going to do something and then doesn't. Not when he promised to take me to the movies, not when he promised to spank me when I wasn't sleeping, not when he told my mother she would not leave this earth without him holding her hand. Not once."

"Fuck. So I guess I'd better find your sister a job. If I don't want your half of Watch going to some other degenerate who'll outbid me and burn the thing to the ground."

My best friend shrugs; he looks like he has as much to think about as I do. "I'm sorry. I might be the CEO of Yin Tech by name, but you know as well as I do that while he's around, he's still going to be the one who calls the shots. I should've done what you did and bankrolled my investment in Watch myself."

"Ha. Ironically, I want to move it under the Baxter umbrella, so maybe I'll learn the hard way as well."

He shakes his head. "No, your brothers aren't the same. The company will do well under Baxter Industries. In a way, this is the best compliment he could give you, cutting off a piece of himself and knowing you'll take care of it."

For a second, I'm not quite sure whether he means the company... or Kiara.

"Blackmailing me into giving his daughter a job?" I say, only half-joking. As much as I love and admire the man, he is a bulldog, and I wouldn't have expected him to do any differently to get what he wants.

I turn the scrunched-up paper in my palm, looking at her name scribbled in Dennis's hand and sigh. Getting Kiara to forget that I'm her mortal enemy is going to take more charm than I currently possess.

And for the first time in a long time, I don't know what to do.

Four

Kiara

Every little thing about this club makes me want to retch, from the location to the humidity to the smell of stale beer and untreated mold rising up the walls hidden behind chipping paint and flashing lights.

The hostess leads me through the throng of sweaty bodies, and I bite back a yelp as a clammy hand brushes against the bare skin of my thigh at the same time someone else stomps down on my foot. My hand itches at my side not to slap the grin right off the stomper's face.

Gritting my teeth, I focus on the bobbing high ponytail on the hostess's head as she nears a side exit.

"In there," she yells, barely audible over the thumping music, pointing to a dark hallway covered by a tattered bead curtain.

I'd be wary if I hadn't walked through a hundred such hallways before.

It's just a part of my job now.

Part of my entire identity.

I slide a tip into her hand; she bows a thank you, and I wait until she's gone before I slip through the curtain. If the owners knew the real reason I was here and that the hostess helped, she'd be out of a job. Not that I'm really sure she knows what she's doing other than showing me to a hallway, but that's okay. The less she knows the better.

Part way down the narrow corridor, I find myself at a door, grimy and paint chipped. I rap three times on it, pause, and then two fast knocks. It's only a few seconds before the door opens and I'm yanked inside.

It's a janitor's closet, and inside stands a young girl dressed in a skirt so short I can see the fire engine red lace hem of her panties. Her makeup is smeared from tears, and her smoke-ringed eyes are red from being rubbed. Standing next to her is my friend Jimmy, the janitor, the one who called me here.

"This is Miss Kiara, she is going to help you," he says to her in Cantonese. "You can trust her. She is safe, okay?"

She nervously looks at me and then back down at her hands. I notice her nails are torn to shreds.

Jimmy turns to me. "Her name is Shi Lei. She's only been here for a few days, but... she's not cut out for it."

I nod and pull out a packet of clean tissues from my purse that I hand to the weeping girl.

She looks over at me and then back at Jimmy who gives her a reassuring nod. Her trembling hand reaches out for the tissues just as her face collapses again, shoulders shaking.

Her fear is palpable, thumping in the air like the bass shaking the walls.

I kneel, making sure not to touch her.

"You are okay now. You don't know it yet, but you can trust me. I'm here to help you. Jimmy's a good guy, right? Ugly and could use a bath, but good," I gently joke and am rewarded with the faintest glimmer of a smile. "Do you have anything you need to get before we go?"

She looks up, startled. "Go?"

"Yes, I have a car waiting outside. Jimmy will help you out the side door, and I'll take you somewhere safe, okay?"

Shi Lei grips the sides of the chair. It's nothing I've not seen before. Whatever's happened here, she knows she's survived it. Who knows where this stranger might take her, what might wait there?

Jimmy leans in, keeping his voice low and even. "She has a bag in the office. The boss makes them all leave them there when they come in for the night."

I hold the urge to curse the fear tactics used to exploit these poor girls. "Can you get it?"

His face is serious as he shakes his head. "No. Maybe in the morning when he's not here."

My hand finds Jimmy's in the dark to give it a squeeze to let him know I would never want him to put him in more danger than he is willing to risk himself.

"Shi Lei," I say, addressing the girl. "I don't think we can get your bag tonight. So you can either stay here tonight and try to get it at closing time, and I'll come get you tomorrow before your shift. Or you can come with me now, and Jimmy will try to get the bag later." While I prefer to take her as soon as possible, the last thing I want is for her to feel like she doesn't have control of her own life.

"No. Miss Kiara. Please, don't leave." She stands up, unsteady on her six-inch platforms. "Please, I will go with you."

The fear emanating from her isn't any less, but now it's at the thought of having to stay.

These poor girls. Their stories are all different, what they've endured is all different, but none of their stories are invalid. And if I can help them even only one at a time, then that's what I'll do.

Making it clear I'm about to pat her on the shoulder, I reach for her, slowly. She lets me and exhales, slowly and deeply when we make contact.

"Okay, I am going to go and will be waiting for you outside in five minutes, okay?" I hold up five fingers.

The clear, simple instructions seem to help. Her eyes grow wide, but she nods her understanding.

"Same place, Jimmy. Five minutes, okay?" I whisper to him as I leave, tucking a few hundred Hong Kong dollars into his pants pocket. He doesn't do this for the money, but it can't hurt. I don't know why he does it, to be honest. We've all come at this from our own different paths, and he's done nothing but show me he's to be trusted. "Be careful."

Four minutes later, I'm parked in the alleyway next to the club, the car doors locked as I watch for the side exit to open.

Breath held.

At five minutes on the dot, the door opens and Shi Lei, leaning on Jimmy's arm, emerges. Eyes wide, pupils large, a deer in the headlights.

The car doors unlock, and I jump out, running over to her.

She's trembling in my arms as I guide her to the car.

"Go, Jimmy. Go back inside, quickly!" I usher him. I can't be worried about them both. I need him inside, undetected, so I can concentrate on her.

He nods and gives Shi Lei one last look before he pulls the heavy metal door closed behind him.

The horn of a passing car startles me, and I slam the passenger door a little too hard, making her jump.

"I'm sorry," I tell her as I slide into the driver's seat. "Are you ready?"

In the dark, I wonder if I just imagine the nod of her head, but I don't have time to ponder on it. The gas pedal slams to the floor of the car, and we screech out of the alleyway toward safety.

I'm barely half a block away when I feel a sudden grip on my arm.

It takes everything within me to not slam on the brakes or sharply swerve off the road, sending us into a late night dessert stand.

Keeping the steering wheel steady, I glance down to see Shi Lei's hand gripping my arm so tightly. Her fingers are bone white, while my forearm has already started turning purple. I flash my eyes to her face, and it's as white as her knuckles, her teeth chattering. She's so scared her entire nervous system must be running on nothing but pure adrenaline.

"It's okay, Shi Lei," I say, trying to keep my voice calmer than I feel. I ease off the gas, hoping her heart beat might mirror the slower pace of the car. "It's okay. You're okay now. I'll take care of you," I gently repeat.

The girl nods and sinks lower into the passenger seat, her hand still gripped around my arm.

"It won't take us long to get to a safe place, and then you can get some rest, okay? I'll tell you more about it when we get there. Is that okay?"

She swallows. "Y-Yes, Miss Kiara."

"Okay, good. There's some water there on the side of the door and some snacks. You can help yourself."

She lets go of my arm and leans her head back, letting her eyes close after a few moments.

At the next red light, I sneak a peek at her; there aren't any track marks or scars on her skin. She looks around nineteen or twenty years old at the most, and the darkness around her eyes looks new. She got out of there early, thanks to Jimmy's vigilance.

Twenty minutes later, I turn into an underground parking location, then help Shi Lei out of the car and upstairs.

Before we can even step into the apartment, four women swarm around us, gently helping Shi Lei from me and into the shared bathroom. They chatter, asking her how she is, friendly questions about her clothes, her family. When she turns to look at me, her eyes are filled with tears, grateful ones, the fear visibly receding from her face.

It's 2 a.m. Most of the women have probably only just returned home as well, if their discarded bags and shoes in the living area are anything to go by. Half-eaten to-go boxes are strewn all over the coffee table, and the TV is on, blasting the latest streaming episode of Britain's Got Talent.

The House, as the women and I call it, is one of three apartments I have set up in the city, each housing up to eight to ten women. Safe houses. Places they can recover from their life and possibly start a new one. One I can help them with if they want.

Ananya Lim, the senior in the house, sinks into the couch next to me, giving me an update.

"Shi Lei's okay, already giggling about something. Apparently she went to school with Davina's cousin."

"That's nice. Good that she knows someone. Might make it easier for her to trust us."

Ananya makes a grunt of agreement and drops an envelope into my lap, letting out a laugh when I just let it fall to the floor, exhausted.

She picks it up and lays it against my stomach and then lifts my hand to hold it in place.

"Everyone's got their cut?" I ask.

She nods.

"And it was enough?"

"Of course. Gave them a little extra."

I nod and open the envelope, then split the contents in two and hand Ananya one of the stacks of money. "Use that for Shi Lei. Whatever she needs. You know what to do. Let me know if you need more." I glance at the stack in my hand, approximating the amount and hand it to Ananya. "Actually, here. Take this as well. She might need a phone and some extra if Jimmy can't get her bag."

Ananya doesn't say anything, just tucks it into her pocket. She does know what to do. She's been with me for almost a year now. This is as much her operation at this point as it is mine.

In many ways, more.

I fold my arms and let myself sit, eyes closed for a few minutes, enjoying the happy chatter coming from the other room and the glorious harmonies of the choir singing on TV.

Over the last three nights, I've barely had any sleep, maybe a whole ten hours in total.

I'm looking forward to getting home and falling into a deep, deep sleep.

I barely have time to properly enjoy the thought of sliding into my Egyptian cotton sheets and enjoying the silence of my apartment when—*Buzzz!!!* My phone vibrates in my pocket.

At two in the morning, it can only be one thing.

I heave myself to my feet even before I check the message.

"Set up another bed, Ananya. I think we're going to need it."

And I slip out the door, giving myself the luxury of one long satisfying yawn.

Night's not over yet, Kiara.

The elevator takes me down to the first floor, and I look around, making sure there's no one lurking in the darkened lobby before I slip through the door and make my way to my car parked around the corner.

But it's not there.

You've got to be fucking kidding me.

I look around; there's no sign to say I can't park there, and I look back at the parking spot. Still no car.

Where is my fucking car!

I ball up my fists again, punch the wall behind me, and let out a pained shout that isn't as cathartic as I'd hoped it'd be,

"Fucking shit bag of fucking shitty fucks!" I yell again at the empty parking spot.

I'm barely two seconds into what I'm hoping to be a very long and satisfying tantrum when I feel a hand against my shoulder.

Hot, large, firm.

I spin around, curses still spilling from my mouth as I swing my purse at my assailant.

He ducks out of the way.

I steady myself and get ready to swing again.

"Get off me!" I scream, suddenly understanding how Shi Lei had felt, adrenaline screeching through my body.

"Whoa. Whoa. Easy. It's me, Kiara," a deep voice says.

I pull my hand back, ready to swing again.

Wait.

Did the attacker just say my name?

I look up through the hair plastered to my forehead, focusing on the figure in front of me.

No fucking way.

I almost wish it was a stranger attacking me now.

Anything has to be better than him.

The very last person I ever wanted to see again

Five

Kiara

"Kiara."

He says my name again with that fucking lazy smirk plastered on his face. Really? Two run-ins in the space of less than twelve hours? The universe is really testing my ability to hold back the urge to slap his stupid face.

Ignoring the stupid face, I'm careful not to touch him as I brush past him to step out onto the road, as if hoping my car will materialize out of nowhere, driven up by my own imaginary private valet.

Unfortunately, all that appears is a cab that swerves out of the way just in time. A hand, tight around my forearm, yanks me back as the car disappears into the night, horn beeping angrily.

"Hey, Kiara! Be careful!" he says, his voice filled with concern.

I yank my arm out of his hold and swing around, facing him. And do the thing I'd wanted to do back at my family's bar. Swear at him. "Kylian Baxter, what in the flying bag of fucking shitballs are you doing here?"

The smile on his face doesn't fade; if anything, it widens a little. His cornflower blue eyes, bright even in the dark, twinkle infuriatingly at me. The jerk looks like he's sailing a yacht in a perfume commercial while a narrator recites random words as he looks out into the beyond. Now that I'm not trying to avoid looking at him, I can see his hair is even lighter than I remember, and it just makes him even more devastatingly beautiful. Less like a caricature of a preppy frat boy, and more... manly.

All man.

It makes me hate him even more, and I didn't think that was possible.

"What in the flying fuck am I doing here?" he says, and it's hard not to think that he's mocking me. "Saving your life, apparently," he answers. "Aren't you too old to be crossing the road without checking both ways first?"

If I hadn't just slammed my hand against the wall, his face would be a pretty good candidate for the target of my palm.

I glare at him instead. "I wasn't crossing the road, I was looking for my car."

"Oh, the valet is bringing it?" he asks, eyes widening, glancing behind me at the darkened apartment lobby.

"Ye-es," I lie. That's just going to have to do, I'm not about to admit that my car is probably in ten different parts at this point.

"Kiara?"

I really wish he'd stop saying my name. I don't like how much I like how it sounds. Much, much, too much.

"What?" I snap.

"There's no valet here, is there?"

Shit.

I square my jaw and set my face while waving my hand in the air. "Oh, that's right. I must have parked it in the parking lot down there. I guess I'll be seeing you," I say as nonchalantly as I can.

I move past him, walking confidently toward a parking lot that doesn't exist.

He falls in step beside me.

My feet stop once I realize he's following me. "Um, where are you going?"

"I'm walking you to your car, of course."

"I don't need an escort!" Not one with crystal blue eyes, in a tailored navy suit, and called Kylian Baxter, anyway.

"It's no problem." He leans in and gives me a wink. "Think of it as a favor for an old friend."

My eyes narrow. "We're not old friends."

"I meant your brother, Kiara."

That's the last thing I want to hear. "Ugh! Then I definitely don't want you following me."

For some reason, that makes him grin. "Why not? You fighting with Nathan?"

"No. I just don't need him knowing my business."

Kylian pulls an invisible zipper across his lips. "I won't say a word."

"I have an even better proposition for you."

"Let's hear it."

I point to the spot where he's standing. "How about you stay right here? Me, I walk to my car, alone. And you just tell Nathan you walked me to my car. Everyone's happy."

He frowns and tilts his head, pretending to be deep in thought. Then he shakes his head. "No deal."

"Kylian!"

"Hey, I never take the first offer," he drawls.

A groan slips out of my mouth, loud and annoyed. The thousands of times I've heard my father and Nathan say the same thing.

"Geez, is that in the How to Be a Cliché Businessman Handbook or something?"

He shrugs. "I don't know. I must've skipped that class. I wasn't very good at school."

That makes me guffaw. Kylian was valedictorian of both his high school class and his undergraduate class. How do I know? Because Nathan was in those same classes and never forgave Kylian for beating him both times.

If it had been anyone but his best friend, Nathan would probably have had him secretly shivved in a dark alley or something. And I'm only kind of kidding. Nathan does not like to lose and isn't known for being gracious about it.

But I'd rather be caught dead wearing an Oompa Loompa costume than admit that I know Kylian Baxter is as smart as he actually is.

"Look, it's clear that you're not the brightest bulb in the pack. I mean, you don't seem to be able to grasp the very simple concept that you're not walking me to my car."

He chuckles and just shrugs again before turning serious. "Forget Nathan. You know as well as I do that I can't let you walk there alone at this time of night. It's not safe, Kiara. Not just for you, for anyone," he says, leaning in, his voice utterly sincere.

But I know better than to believe a damn word that comes out of his mouth. That's not a lesson anyone who has learned forgets.

I take a step back and cross my arms across my chest. "I'm not just anyone, Kylian."

He steps forward, filling the space that I vacated, and turns his head so that his lips are dangerously close to my cheek as he whispers, "Don't need to tell me that."

I pull back immediately, his voice swirling in my head as well as the faintest whiff of his Maison Francis Kurkdjian cologne. All this time later and he's still wearing it.

Classic. Clean. Elegant. And the very reason I can't stand the scent of vanilla.

"Good night, Kylian," I say, short. Time to stop this... whatever this is... "Thanks for the offer, but I honestly don't want nor need you to walk me to the car." And not only because I have no idea where my car is.

To my surprise, he straightens up, looks at me for a second, shoves his hands into his pockets, and nods. "Okay. Good night, Kiara."

I'm a little taken aback at his sudden change of mind, but I take it.

Before he can change his mind, I spin on my heel and almost run around the nearest corner, stopping as soon as I'm hiding behind a building wall. A quick glance at my phone tells me it's almost 2:15 a.m.

I'm going to have to flag down a cab soon; if I wait for much longer, it's going to be almost impossible to find one. Despite my bravado, hanging around this dark street corner for too long probably isn't a good idea, no matter how good I am with my purse swing and fifteen years of martial arts training.

I jog back to where my car should've been and wait for a cab to drive by.

Ten minutes and ten occupied cabs later, I start to feel a little anxious. It's not too late yet that I probably won't be able to get one to stop, but you just never know in Hong Kong.

Two more taxis whiz by, both filled with passengers.

Shit.

The roads are already starting to clear.

It's almost five more minutes, an eternity when you're waiting, before a car turns into the street, its headlights bright in my eyes.

I wave a hand in the air, letting out my held breath when it slows.

It's not a cab, though; it's a convertible. Silver Jaguar, F-Type. Top down.

And it slows to a standstill three feet from me.

From the driver's seat, Kylian Baxter smiles that fucking smile at me again before he says, "Finally ready to admit you need a ride?"

Six

Kylian

When I called the number on the paper Dennis had given me, all they'd told me was the address of this apartment building. No amount of cajoling, threatening, bribing, and flat-out blackmailing got me any other information. I'd gone to dinner, responded to some emails, and gone to bed, with nothing else on my mind.

At 1:50 a.m. I'd jumped in my car and driven here. Other than the dark residential apartments, there wasn't anything to give me any clue as to what it could mean. I'd gone for a walk around the block, and when I returned, I'd been greeted with the sight of Kiara yelling at an empty parking spot. I guess it was a good thing I was there.

She hadn't seen it that way, though, so I let her go to pick up her imaginary car and gone to grab mine, hanging around the corner and making sure she was alright until it looked like seeing me again was going to be a relief and not an annoyance. I might've been a little too optimistic on that.

Somehow she is still hesitating taking up my offer for a ride, though, as if she's actually considering being stranded in North Point on a Tuesday night rather than sit in a car with me for ten minutes

"Offer's time limited, Kiara," I say when she hasn't replied after a few silent minutes.

Kiara glares at a point about two inches from my forehead, still avoiding my eye contact, and I can see a flash of white where her teeth are digging into her bottom lip. "Fine," she finally huffs as she opens the car door and slides into the passenger seat.

"Where to?" I ask.

I wait as the last remnant of hesitation fights to leave her body before she opens her mouth and says, "Fong Bar."

My hands don't move on the steering wheel while I wait for more information. None is forthcoming. "And where and what is a Fong Bar?"

Her tired eyes lift, staring directly at me, almost in a challenge. "It's a strip club. In Wan Chai."

I feel my eyebrows lift and fall as she holds my gaze, daring me to comment.

Wan Chai is the infamous red light district area of Hong Kong that is now home to dive bars, wet markets, amazing, authentic Chinese restaurants, and... apparently, strip clubs.

We drive for two minutes in total silence before the curiosity threatens to actually kill me. "Not that I'm not totally thrilled to be going to a strip club with you but why are we going there exactly?"

Her eyes stay trained on a spot two feet ahead of us, but she answers. "Work. I'm going there to work."

Without making it too glaringly obvious, my eye flick down to her clothes. Miniskirt, short, white crop top, knee high stiletto boots.

The picture painting in my head of what her work there involves is making it even harder for me to hold my tongue. But my need to satisfy my curiosity is not so important that I will risk making her flee like a baby deer at the first sign of discomfort.

We arrive in a few minutes; the area is almost empty with a few stragglers stumbling out of nearby bars. Come the weekend at 2:30 a.m, the streets will still be teeming with bodies. Many of my weekends when I'd just moved here had been spent in this area finding new friends I still see now. No one ever feels lonely in Wan Chai on a Friday night. Kiara points to the side street along a building with a flickering sign in front.

"Park there," she says, her voice hard, nervous. She hasn't exactly been a ball of sunshine since she saw me at Amber earlier today, but she wasn't on edge like this.

"Where are you going?"

"Inside." One word. She rubs her arms as if psyching herself up and then climbs out of the car. "Wait here."

"Kiara, are you okay? Do you want me to c—"

"No!" she yells and then glances over her shoulder as if looking out for someone before she lowers her voice. "Stay here. And do not get out of the car. I will be right back. And leave the engine running." She must see the concern on my face and probably considers what I might do if she doesn't reassure me and says, "I'm fine. I won't be too long. Just have the car ready."

Something tells me that I'm supposed to listen. That she's not kidding, and me sitting here is more important than going with her inside.

To work.

Whatever that means.

So I wait.

And I wait.

Until it's too long to be "not too long."

It's been over fifteen minutes. The skin on my legs is tingling like an entire colony of fire ants is negotiating a trail up my body, just waiting to sting me.

Everything's not okay. I need to get inside.

My hand reaches for the door handle when a side door I hadn't even noticed bursts open. A young woman is pushed out and falls to the ground. Behind her Kiara follows, backing out from the door, shirt ripped, hair a mess, in her hand a weapon, pepper spray, maybe. Her arm is outstretched as she steps toward the young girl still crumpled on the ground and gently weeping.

"Kiara!" I shout, and she turns to me as if just remembering I was waiting all along.

And it's a mistake. In that split second of losing focus, a behemoth appears out of the building and charges at her.

My entire body ices over with fear.

Somewhere, something, some *god* gifts me with temporary Herculean speed and strength. I leap over the side of the convertible and sprint toward Kiara.

I'm just half a second late, though, and he's already grabbing her by the shoulders when I reach her. He yanks her away but is still unbalanced from the momentum of charging at her. I take advantage of it by ramming my whole six feet five inches at him, every cell in my body jarring from the effort, but it works. He stumbles to the side, letting her go. I have to force myself to focus on him and not checking up on her; there'll be time to do that later.

"Grab your friend, and get in the car!" I yell and only hope she listens.

"Kylian!" she shouts from somewhere behind me, but through the thudding of my pulse in my ears, I can hear her shuffle to her feet and yell to her friend to get up.

Behemoth regains his balance and swings back to face me. His bald head is sweating, and he grins as he lifts his fists, pulling his feet into a fighting stance.

A few years in Nathan's Muay Thai class isn't going to cut it against this walking boulder. My hardest punch is probably going to feel like a tickle to his abdomen.

I take a step back, lifting my own fists, ready to protect my face and my sides.

He sniffs, rubbing the back of his hand across his nose and then lunges toward me.

I jump to the side and then toward him, catching the side of his chest with a swing punch that hurts my arm more than it hurts him. But there's no time to recover. I swing my knee forward with every ounce of strength I have; it catches his groin, and he falls to the ground like a landslide. I shove him, so he's all the way down, the adrenaline pumping. A flash of him grabbing Kiara plays on a loop in my mind, and I pull my leg back, ready to land a kick to the side of his head.

"Kylian! He's down, let's go!" Kiara yells from the car.

Somehow her voice penetrates the anger, and I lean over him as his face is scrunched up in pain.

"What made you think you could put your hands on her? You tell whoever sent you that if I ever get even the slightest sniff that he's thinking about her, I will come up and burn this shit pile to the ground. Do you hear me?" I grab his sweaty face and force him to look at me. "I said do you understand?'

Once he grunts, I let go and run to the car, jumping into the driver's seat and pulling out into the road.

No one says anything for almost a minute.

"Are you okay?" I ask, and she nods. "And... your friend?"

"Li Fern. I think so. Maybe a little in shock."

Hands on the wheel, I ask, "Okay, where are we going?"

"Back to where you picked me up. Please. I'm going to drop her off there."

I nod.

There is going to be time for questions. Now isn't it. Because I can't trust myself not to do something drastic with the man who just roughed her up. Something... that we might not be able to come back from.

I breathe, feeling the fear and adrenaline subside. My fingers itch to reach across and touch her to know for myself that she's okay, but that might be another one of those things I will live to regret.

Her face is pale, her honey brown eyes bright, fingers fidgeting with the pepper spray in her hand.

It's hard not to wonder what would've happened if I hadn't been there.

Seven

Kiara

"Thanks, Ananya. Call me in the morning tomorrow," I say and close the door behind me, leaning against it for a moment with my eyes closed.

I am so tired I could fall asleep right here in the hallway and not wake up for a week. But there was still one more thing to do.

Two things.

And I didn't want to do either of them.

The elevator arrives, and I climb in. My shoulders lift as I test my injuries; they're still a little sore from that security guard grabbing me. I make a point to not make any movement that might raise suspicions with Kylian. Something about the way he'd fought the guy that was almost twice his size tells me he will probably go back and finish things if he knows I'm actually hurt.

I ignore the urge to feel a sense of… flattery? To see him get so riled up over me being in danger, but the rational side of me knows that it was probably nothing but him having a testosterone flare.

He's waiting in the apartment lobby when I get down there. Hands in his pockets, looking toward the elevators, waiting for me.

Somehow he doesn't look anywhere nearly as affected by the incident as I am, which is too bad. Even in the dark, his eyes hit deep inside me and stir up feelings I thought I'd squashed years ago. The smart thing to do would be to turn around and walk away. Unfortunately, I'm not done with needing him yet.

"Where to now?" he asks with a smile.

"Police station," I say. "I need to make a police report."

"You got it," he replies, without even an ounce of annoyance that he's suddenly my chauffeur at 3 a.m. in the morning.

I don't even know what he's doing here, but for the next hour, I'm not going to worry about it. He appeared when I needed someone. And I wasn't going to look a gift horse in the mouth.

We get into the car, but we don't speak for the entire drive.

Eight

Kylian

"Your hot water, sir," a friendly voice says in Cantonese about fifteen minutes later.

A mug has appeared on the table in front me as I sit at an empty desk at the police station. Smiling, I respond with a thank you in the same language. When I'm in Hong Kong, I speak in Cantonese, and some choppy Mandarin if the occasion requires it, as much as I can. I'm an Englishman in their country; I shouldn't be expecting them to cater to me. My Cantonese is not perfect, and I make mistakes that I often get roasted for by my employees for weeks, but it's worth it for all the richness learning the language has given me.

Kiara had given me a very pointed look when we'd arrived at the station, which I'd taken to mean that I was to leave her to her business. That was after she'd given me a withering look when I'd parked the car and followed her inside instead of just dropping her off as she'd explicitly asked. It was the same look that I used to give my older brothers when we were children and they'd tried to help me with things that I knew beyond a shadow of a doubt I was better at than them. It hadn't worked on them, and Kiara's look wasn't working on me now. But I agreed not to say anything, to sit in a corner and be quiet, and I intend on sticking to my promise. I won't say a word... unless I feel I need to.

For the time being, though, I'm happy to sit at the neighboring desk, just listening as she tells the police officer what had happened with her car.

I tear open a small paper packet I've pulled from my pocket and pour the contents into the mug. My older brother Damien's fiancée, My-Linh's family owns a tea store, and she mixed up a concoction that was meant to cool my blood after I'd told her I've been getting nose bleeds whenever I return to Hong Kong after being gone for a little while.

The dried leaves slowly sink to the bottom of the cup, coloring the water, the fragrance already lifting me. She added something to relax me, knowing the lifestyle all us Baxters live. I smile, thinking about the way she'd reminded me to drink it every night. I miss her; over the course of only a few months, she's become like a sister to me, and my brother is lucky to have her. The hot water burns my tongue in a satisfying way that I've always enjoyed, and the drink instantly relaxes me.

I let out a satisfied, "Ahhhhh."

"Smells good," the uniformed cop who'd brought me the water comments. "Not as good as San Miguel beer. But good."

I laugh a little too loudly and elicit a scowl from Kiara from her seat ten feet away for interrupting her.

"Oops, we're in trouble," I say, dropping my voice conspiratorially, and the cop's eyes widen a little before he backs away. Probably wanting to put some distance between himself and the scary glare-y lady.

Smart.

Hooking my arms around the back of my head, I stretch my long legs out in front of me, trying not to appear like I'm following every word that Kiara is saying.

After not seeing her for five years, it's hard not to compare the woman who is sitting near me to the girl I knew before.

She's speaking in Cantonese, and I realize that I had never heard her speak the language before in London. Both she and Nathan had always stuck to English. It was a little thrilling to experience this new side of her. Her voice is a few tones lower; she speaks slowly, clearly, incredibly articulately. Considering she's here to report a stolen car, she's almost emotionless, her voice steady, her face barely changing in expression. After each question the police officer asks, she pauses for a moment, then gives a short, succinct answer.

Physically, there's no denying that she's matured in her body. The last time I saw her, she had just turned twenty-one. Her mother's pale English Rose genes mixed with her father's darker Chinese tones meant that her skin was swirled with equal parts opaque silk and translucence. She was probably on the taller side for most Asian women, and she'd always been slightly awkward in her frame as if not really sure what to do with her arms and legs.

That isn't the same woman I'm seeing tonight.

The black leather miniskirt she has on cinches at her tiny waist and stretches over curved hips, just a little tight so that when she sits down, it rides up her thighs, which I'm trying not to stare at from my position. Her white midriff top with puffed sleeves shows off the silky-smooth skin of her back, and leather boots are zipped all the way up to just below the knee. She looks ready to dance a night away at a club. And command every single man's attention in there.

Definitely not the same little KiKi I saw peeking around the corner when I would visit the Yin's Hong Kong residence during summer vacations, and not the Kiara of five years ago in London. Who knows the things she's experienced in that time. The places she's been, the work she's done... the men she's been with.

An invisible vice tightens around my lungs, and I have to press a hand against my chest to massage the breath back into my body, my eyes boring into the side of her face.

She suddenly looks over, and I squeeze my eyes shut, hoping she didn't catch me looking at her. After a few seconds, I peek out under my eyelashes to see a frown immediately crack across her forehead before she turns her attention back to the police report.

I don't blame her.

Me staring at Kiara Yin and contemplating her womanhood is not going to end well for anyone.

A few seconds later, though, my eyes are drawn back to her.

Sitting with her back dead straight in what could fairly be described as one of the most uncomfortable chairs ever constructed, arms in her lap, she's composed, almost regal, and holds the policeman's attention, looking serious but not unkind.

She's not showing any sign of any adverse effects from the incident at the club; I don't even really know what happened inside the club, but she doesn't look shaken or scared as I would reasonably expect any person to be. I don't know if that's a good thing, that it's not affecting her because she's immune to it now. Something tells me, though, that even though I haven't seen her in a long time and she could have changed in so many ways, the thing about Kiara is that she always felt everything deeply. No matter how often it happened. If she's not showing anything now, it's because she's holding it in to get the job at hand done.

I feel a flash of pride as I can't help but notice how the police officer is hanging off her every word. When she sat down fifteen minutes ago, he was watching YouTube videos on his phone, taking a swig of his Coke can, and making no secret of the fact that he was not happy about being interrupted at this time of night.

Now, he's leaning so far across the table his chest is almost touching it, his pen poised over the form, his eyes almost never leaving her face unless it's to make sure he isn't writing on the table.

Knowing Kiara, she would've made it a point to keep her name and face out of the Hong Kong papers. He probably doesn't know that he's sitting in front of one of the heirs to a billion dollar fortune and estate. No, she's commanding his attention based on nothing but the way she is carrying and conducting herself.

Like I said, pride.

Not that I have a damn reason to feel any ownership over who she's grown up to be. I'm nothing but Kylian, Nathan's annoying brother who eats too much, listens to horrendous old people music, embarrasses her in front of her friends when she's cutting school... and the person who... the person who turned out to be a complete and total asshole five years ago. She hasn't come right out and said anything about how she feels about what happened, but considering that she looks at me as if I served Tofurkey for Christmas dinner, I can hazard an educated guess.

And even when I was hanging around Nathan's house all those summers, I hadn't ever spent much time alone with her.

Nathan had made it clear that his sister was out of bounds, and after seeing how he reacted when he'd found a photo of Kiara with a boy's arm around her shoulder when we were in our senior year and she was only twelve years old, I'd be surprised if she's even mentioned a male in her life ever again. Probably not if she wanted him to live.

If anyone has ever seen Nathan train for even just five minutes at his Muay Thai club, they'd make it a point not to piss him off in any way. And now that I think about it, Kiara used to train right beside him. That might explain the tone of her legs and the slight curve of bicep.

The sound of the metal chair leg scratching on the linoleum floor draws me out of my musing about her body, and good thing, too. My body is starting to respond in ways I hadn't expected.

The police officer who took her report says, "We will call you as soon as we have any news. But... as I told you..."

"It might be very likely that I never see my car again," she finishes for him.

With their conversation coming to an end, I stand up, stretching my legs and shaking out the stiffness from the horrible chair.

The policeman turns to me, almost as if he's forgotten that I've been there the whole time.

"Kylian," I say, reaching over and offering him my hand. "Baxter. Thank you for your help with Miss Kiara and her car. If you don't mind, I'll take her home now."

He bows slightly and then takes my hand.

Kiara ignores me and says to the police officer, "If you will get me a taxi, please."

My hand keeps a grip on the cop's hand, and I stare directly into his eyes. "Please, don't trouble yourself. I will drive her home."

He swallows and nods.

I let go of his hand and turn to Kiara who looks like her glare could cut through a six-inch thick titanium wall. "You don't want to burden the officers any more, do you? I'm sure they need to get right on finding your car." While my tone is joking, the smile on my face is wide and genuine, but it doesn't have the desired effect, and the respectful attitude she had graced the police officer with has quickly faded.

"Never mind. I will walk," she hisses, picks up her purse, and storms out of the station.

"Please excuse her, she has had a very rough night. Thank you for helping us." A quick nod to the two policemen and I'm striding after her.

When I reach her, she's glaring at the empty parking spaces in front of the police station. It seems to have become a favorite pastime of hers.

"My car's over there," I say, pointing to where I'd parked it.

"Good. Now go over there, get in it, and drive off," she replies.

"Sure thing!" I say cheerily, "After you, milady." I bend at the waist and gesture to the car.

Her eyes harden into dark marble, and her lips silently move as if she's trying to conjure up a taxi out of thin air. That or cast a curse over my nether regions.

"Kiara. Come on. It's almost 3:30 in the morning. You'll be out here a while. You must be tired. Just let me take you home. I won't make you answer any questions about what happened tonight or tell any of my famous dad jokes," I promise.

The sharp exhalation of air out of her nostrils tells me she's not convinced.

"How far do you live from here?" I ask.

Reluctantly, she names the neighborhood; it is, at most, eight miles from where we're standing. I'm surprised to hear it's not closer to my home and the Yin residence in The Peak, the most exclusive residential area in Hong Kong. Had she really not accepted any money from her family at all, at least for a safe place to live? It's hard not to have a little admiration for her commitment to doing everything on her own. Except that it's the reason we are both standing on the side of the road in the middle of the night.

My hands splay out in front of me, palms up, a sign of transparency and surrender. "Come on, it's a ten minute ride. I'm exhausted, and you know there's not a chance in hell that I'm going to leave you here. So get in the car, I'll drive you home, keep my mouth shut, and even let you slam the car door when we get there. Deal?"

I walk over to my car and slide into the driver's seat as she stays rooted to the spot, staring at the potholes in the otherwise empty road. The car roars to life with a push of the button, and I drive over to her.

"I'll even let you choose the music. No DJ Tiësto, I promise. And I also won't sing along to whatever you choose," I call out to her.

Something I say penetrates the armor, and there's a little puff of her chest as if she almost lets out a laugh. Then, without a word, she finally agrees, opens the car door, and slides into my convertible.

"So what'll it be?" I ask, flipping through the pre-programmed channels on the radio. "Beatles? Top 100 hits? 90s RnB? Some Usher?"

Her head whips around, her hand instantly on the door handle.

"Um, okay, no Usher... Got it."

"No music," she grumbles.

"Yes, ma'am."

I turn into the road, enjoying the breeze of the open top through my hair, cooling the sweat on the back of my neck.

We drive in silence for a few minutes before she shifts, getting comfortable.

"You can adjust the seat," I offer.

Her arms fold over her chest. "I'm fine."

The streets pass by us for another silent minute; I manage to keep my mouth shut as I imagine she prefers. The wind picks up as I speed along on the empty streets, and I almost regret it. The air smells like jasmine and chamomile and roses, just like the shampoo she used and apparently still uses. It should be overpowering, suffocating me, but I'm taking great, big gulps of the air like I haven't breathed in a year. Images lift from the annals of my memory of us in the dark, her body moving along with mine, my face in her neck smelling of soft blossoms. Fresh and soft and her. Something from the memory pulls to the forefront of my brain, the song we were dancing to: Usher.

"Fuck," I say before I can stop myself. How could I have forgotten? Now, when I remember the way she looked at me when I suggested the music, something presses against my throat like a metal wire, sharp, painful. Suddenly, I can't breathe.

She turns and looks at me, an eyebrow curled at my sudden outburst.

Despite the ache spreading like a ripple on an undisturbed pond all over my body, I try to flash her a weak smile. "Do you want some water?" I ask, trying to distract us both from the thoughts in my head.

Her mouth clamps shut.

Oookay, I guess not.

Another minute of silence and I steal a look when we're parked at a red light. She's hugging her purse close to her chest, and there's a line of goosebumps up her forearms.

Shit.

Stupid Kylian. I may have a low tolerance for the heat, but not everyone is like me.

Pressing on the button to close the roof of my convertible, I lean between our seats to reach for my jacket. Being closer to her has only exacerbated the smelling her problem. Against my better judgment, I take such a deep breath, feeling her scent permeate my cells, I'm almost dizzy. Intoxicated.

"Here. Put this on," I say, dropping my jacket in her lap as the light turns green.

She frowns and just stares at it, pulling her arms tighter around her body. "I said I'm fine," she says, her mouth set in a straight line.

Checking for traffic in the rearview mirror with one hand on the steering wheel, I swerve hard to the side of the road, tires screeching on the asphalt.

"Kylian! Are you fucking insane?" she yells, bracing one hand on the glove compartment, one hand on the door.

"Not in the slightest," I say, ignoring her look of utter 'you total ballwallop, you almost got us killed.' "Now, I'm going to ask you again, and if you lie to me, I'm going to make you regret it. Don't you dare fucking lie to me. Ever. Got it?"

She gives me the smallest nod I've ever seen, her eyes wide.

"Good. Now, are you cold? I can see the goosebumps all over your arms and your... um, your neck." I gesture awkwardly to her bare neck.

She nods a little, the movement even more minute than before, her eyes wider.

"I'm sorry. The car will warm a little now that the car roof is closed." I turn up the heat with a push of a button.

She doesn't move this time because there's no question to answer, so I busy myself with draping my jacket over her, pulling the collar up to cover her front and tucking the sides around her arms. As I lean over to reach over to her far side with my torso grazing her lap, her breath is shallow and hot against my face as she sits rigid, teeth digging into her bottom lip.

Once I'm satisfied that she's sufficiently covered, I reluctantly sit back up.

"Better?" I ask after a few seconds.

A third nod.

"Good." I swerve back onto the road. "Sorry about that, I forget that not everyone has a permanent body temperature of 100 degrees."

She doesn't say anything, but out of the corner of my eye, I see her pull the collar of my jacket up higher so that it's flush against her chin. The ridiculous thought of being jealous of a jacket almost makes me laugh out loud so instead, I ask what I've been dying to ask since I saw her shouting at the road. "So... what were you doing out there tonight, anyway?"

A scowl flashes across her forehead, and she snaps, "You said no questions."

"Actually, I said you didn't have to answer any questions. I didn't say that I wouldn't ask any." I take my eyes off the road for one moment to give her a wink.

"I forget that you went to law school," she grumbles.

"Then you probably also forget that I was asked to leave law school. Multiple times."

She turns completely in her chair to look at me, mouth agape. "I didn't know that! I thought you just left because you got bored."

I nod. "I did. Get bored, that is. That's why I caused so much trouble I was asked to leave. Either way, going to Wharton turned out to be a much better fit for me. I didn't want to study law and have the joy taken out of arguing, anyway." I unashamedly laugh at my own joke.

She still looks shocked. "I always just thought you and my brother couldn't handle being away from each other, so you both chose Wharton for your post grad to continue your bromance. Who was Valedictorian of your year anyway? I know it wasn't either of you because I wouldn't have heard the end of it."

I guffaw at the bromance comment. It's not the first time I've heard my friendship with Nathan described that way. Even my brother Damien had shown a little jealousy when he'd seen how close I was with someone who wasn't one of my brothers.

Unlike my brothers, Eton had not been the school for me. Without telling anyone, I'd applied and was accepted into St. Paul's school the year I turned twelve and basically informed my grandfather that I was changing schools. He'd just laughed and held out his hand for the admission forms and warned me that one day my intelligence was going to get me in trouble.

He had no idea.

I miss him. It's been a hard few years without him. And sometimes I don't know if I'll ever really get used to him being gone.

The sigh that I think was just in my head must've come out louder than I'd thought because Kiara finally speaks without prompting from me. "You didn't answer, who was Valedictorian?"

I just smile and say, "Someone who deserved it way more than your brother or I did."

She seems satisfied with that and sits back in her seat facing forward. "Where did you go just then?"

"Hmm?"

"Just then, it looked like you disappeared somewhere in your head."

I blink. I hope she can't read my thoughts. Then I remember what I was thinking about. "My grandfather. I was just thinking about something he said to me once."

"Was it, 'why do you talk so much?'" she says, wryly.

I let out a little chuckle. The heat in the car seems to thawed her out a little, and she sounds like the Kiara I've known all my life. That was, in fact, something that not only my grandfather but pretty much everyone in my life has said multiple times. "You think I talk too much?" I tease her.

Her shoulder lifts in a 'what can I say?' fashion. "My brother is hardly the silent type, but when he's with you, he can barely get a word in edgewise."

This makes me roar with laughter, my hands slapping against the steering wheel. This is true. Nathan is certainly no wallflower, but he has nothing on me when I'm on a roll. I will talk him deep into the ground.

"It's just part of my charm," I say, taking my eyes off the road for a second to flash my brightest, most disarming smile at her.

She just stares back at me.

Utterly uncharmed.

"Wow, tough car."

That draws the tiniest chuckle from her, a single contraction and rise of her chest and twitch of the corners of her mouth. I'll count that as a win, which makes me wish I could keep her talking forever.

"And now you're the Director of the Asia Pacific region for Baxter Enterprises?"

I guess Nathan had shared that with her. "I am."

"Do you like it?"

"Yes."

"Are you good at it?"

"Yes."

She doesn't argue. "What are you working on now?"

"Well, a few things. I'm working on a submission to Lim Tech for their Heracles chip. And then our entertainment division has a big project. We're opening a casino in six months. We've almost finished outfitting the inside, but there are a few things still to be done." I glance over at her. "Including staffing. So I answered a crap ton of questions," I say as she gestures to turn at the coming intersection. "Surely that buys me one answer."

I expect her to immediately refuse, but she thinks about it for a second and then shrugs.

Not one for many words, I guess, but that's okay, I have enough words for the both of us.

"What were you doing at that apartment building tonight?" I ask again.

She doesn't answer right away, but her eyes show that she's thinking. I like that. As much as I talk, everything that leaves my mouth, I've thought about, even if only for a split second.

"What were *you* doing there?" she asks.

Shit. I hadn't even had a chance to think of an answer to the question that was inevitably going to be asked. The only thing to do is deflect. "I already answered a bunch of questions, remember? It's your turn."

Her shoulder drops in a sigh. "I was working, okay? Sometimes... I have to go to a club... for work. And the apartment... it's part of my work, too." She glances at me and then rolls her eyes at the way my eyebrow rises. "Not in that way. Geez. I don't care about anyone who is a sex worker, but it's just not for me, okay?"

I force myself to let out the breath slowly and steady, so she doesn't know my heart almost jumped out of my chest.

The GPS speaks, and I turn into her street.

"A little way down," she says, pointing to an apartment a few hundred feet down the road. "I... help some of the girls who work at clubs. The ones who want out. And... the apartment... it's one of the places I've set up for them to stay."

This answer is almost as surprising as the possibility of her being a sex worker. Nothing Nathan had told me had given any indication of this. I wonder if he even knows. He must. He knows everything. Especially when it comes to his little sister.

"Oh. Wow. That's incredible."

She just shrugs.

"What... do you do exactly? I mean... how do you help them?" I ask, trying not to bombard her with questions, even though I want to know everything.

"I have ways! I'm not just some spoiled little rich girl!" She raises her hand, not to hit me but as if she is trying to make herself bigger, more menacing, instinctive.

Whoa. I touched a nerve. I pull up in front of the building she pointed to and park, giving her a moment to calm down before I address her again.

Once her arm is lowered and her breathing settled, I turn to face her. "Hey, Kiki, I have never thought that of you." It's the truth; Kiara had always shown contempt in her position in society, seeing it as a curse rather than a blessing. "Remember that time you gathered up all your makeup and clothes and disappeared and everyone was sick with worry? And Nathan found you at the local school giving out all your things to the girls there because your driver had taken you by there and you'd noticed how they were dressed in worn and tattered clothes?"

She frowns and lifts her crooked finger to her mouth, nibbling on the knuckle of her index finger. A habit from birth. "You remember that?"

"Sure! It's one of my favorite memories of you."

"What... else do you remember?" she says, still nibbling.

I grin. "Everything. I remember that you like eating your cereal dry with a glass of milk. The only person in the world I know who does that and makes me question your sanity."

She laughs. Really laughs. "Goodnight, Kylian. Thanks for the ride."

I shrug. "No problem. I'm used to being the neighborhood hero."

I catch a sign of her rolled eyes as she gets out of the car, but before she closes the door, she says, "I don't like seeing people suffer. These girls... I can't imagine anything worse than being stuck in a place like that, if you don't want to be there. I have a business that I train them to work for; it's not an easy job, and they have absolutely no obligation to stay. Sometimes they stay, and sometimes they don't. It's not easy helping them, but it's the most important thing I've ever done in my life."

And there's not a doubt in my mind that every word she just said is true.

I feel my eyes flooding with warmth and admiration for her as I say as earnestly as I can, "I believe you, Kiara."

With that, she gives me a half smile and closes the car door.

I watch as she slides her card through the security device and goes inside, and I wonder if she's forgiven me enough to accept a job.

I know I wouldn't.

Nine

Kiara

It's not until I'm back in my apartment, leaning against the closed door, eyes adjusting to the dark, do I let out the breath I feel like I've been holding since I climbed into Kylian's car.

Any lies that I've told myself over the last five years that he's out of my system have made it clear that they were just that, lies.

What was he even doing there tonight? Of all places, of all times. Why had it been when I'd been in such a vulnerable position? Why couldn't I have been running him over with my car instead of needing him to do me a favor? And if I know anything about Kylian Baxter, the ruthless businessman behind that charming smile, I know that he always calls in those favors. Intelligence, charm, money, and ambition is a dangerous combination.

And I've been burned by Kylian Baxter before.

I slip into the bathroom, turning the tub faucet on to fill the tub, catching my reflection in the mirror.

Shit.

I'm still wearing his jacket.

And for just a moment, I let myself bury my face into the collar. His scent envelops me.

"No!" I throw the jacket across the room. "Kiara. Don't be fucking stupid!" I brace against the basin, staring into my own eyes in the mirror. "Repeat after me: I hate Kylian Baxter."

And by the time the tub is almost full, I almost have myself convinced again.

Almost.

I sleep through the alarm.

Twice.

The extra exertion of the previous night sent me into a fitful sleep filled with weird dreams of dark night clubs and cornflower blue eyes unnerving me, and although I wake up at almost 9 a.m, I'm even more tired than I was before I fell asleep.

My lit-up phone screen tells me the incoming call alert is probably what woke me, and I sigh seeing Ananya's face pop up. She'll text until her thumbs fall off before she'll make a phone call, so it must be important.

"Yeah?" I answer.

The noise in the background tells me everything I need to know. One voice is screaming while a bunch of other voices are trying to calm the screamer down.

"Shi Lei is freaking out. She wants to go."

I sit up, rubbing my head. I don't blame her. She probably doesn't trust anyone right now.

"Okay, well, try to calm her down, but if she really wants to leave, tell her you'll call her a car to take her wherever she wants to go. And give her some money. But make sure you get the address for wherever she goes from the driver. I'll be there as soon as I can."

I hang up the phone and am ready to leave in just five minutes.

Halfway out down to the lobby, I remember that my car isn't waiting for me in the parking garage.

"Dammit!" I yell just as the elevator doors open.

"Hi," a deep male voice says, and the face it's attached to is grinning at me, holding out a coffee.

"Ugh," spills from my lips before I can stop it.

"Good morning to you, too," he says with way too much cheer. "Black, no sugar. And here's an extra cream and sugar packet for when you decide you hate taking coffee black and plain."

In my surprise that he's gotten my coffee order spot on, I take the cup from him, the silent question lingering between us.

"I told you. I have a good memory," he adds with a smug smile that's just itching to be slapped.

"What are you doing here?" I snap, taking a sip from the coffee, wincing when the bitter taste hits the back of my throat.

He points toward the building's glass door and waggles finger.

"Use your words. I know you know how to talk, Kylian!"

He chuckles, his eyes annoyingly sparkling.

"Why are you laughing? I'm insulting you," I hiss. What the hell is wrong with this man? Is he permanently high or something?

"I know. It's cute."

I growl, only stopping when I almost choke on my mouthful of coffee. I hate to be called cute. Cute is for puppy dogs, or baby sloths, or... or... *Kylian Baxter*, a niggling thought in my voice traitorously cackles.

"I'm here for that." He points again toward the street.

"I'm in a hurry. Please, I'm begging you, get to the point."

He rocks back on his heels, crossing his arms. "You're in a hurry? What for?"

"For... none of your business!"

"Okay. And how are you getting there exactly?"

Shit. Running into Butthead Baxter had totally pushed the memory that I'm currently car-less out of my head. "Cab."

"I can do you one better. I'm here to chauffeur you for the day."

"What? No. Nuh uh. Absolutely fucking not." I reach into my purse for my phone.

"Good luck getting a cab; it's morning peak time. But that's fine. I can sit here with you until a cab comes. Don't want you to be lonely."

I grit my teeth. He'd do it, too, I know he would. I need to get to The House before Shi Lei leaves. Once a girl leaves, it's just that much harder to get her to come back, even if she wants to. Shame does crazy things to a person. And if I'm ever going to jump into a car with Kylian again, this is as good a reason as any.

"Fine. But not the whole day, just drive me to the apartment we went to last night. And then that's it!"

"Yes, ma'am!" He follows me out, bouncing on the balls of his feet like a golden retriever and jogs ahead a few steps to open the car door for me. Why is he so peppy? He probably got even less sleep than I did, considering he had to drive home after dropping me off, and he already looks like he's had a whole day before he came here.

I get settled, the leather feeling new but soft. The sign of the absolute top of the line interior. I take another sip of the plain black coffee and curse him under my breath for knowing that once I'm out of his sight, I'll be putting that cream and sugar into the cup.

"Ready?" he says, sliding his sunglasses down from his head. My own reflection stares back at me, and she looks grumpy. And, frankly, ungrateful, considering he's done nothing but help me since we ran into each other last night. I try to mold my face into a less bratty expression and take another sip of my coffee as he joins the traffic. It shouldn't be too hard to sit and not talk for ten minutes. Unfortunately, as he'd pointed out, morning peak traffic in Hong Kong is a gridlock.

We're surrounded by bus and car horns and people yelling. But somehow it feels even more chaotic in this car with us in the silence. My heart beats against my chest almost audibly. I blame being out of breath on walking the thirty feet out to the car. Hardly feasible but it was going to have to do. I don't want to think of any other reason my body might be reacting like this.

His fingertips on the steering wheel thrum to a beat only he can hear, and I realize it's a core memory from when he used to drive Nathan and I around London all the time. What is he doing here? What was he doing there last night? What's going on?

"Are you trying to kidnap me?" I shout, surprising myself. The voices in my head must be taking control over my mouth.

The question lingers in the air for a few seconds before he even reacts, other than the small jump when I'd startled the both of us.

"Would you like that?" he smirks.

Asshole.

I can't see his eyes through the sunglasses, which is probably the only silver lining about this moment. It's hard to concentrate when he's looking at me with those eyes.

"Ugh, no. I guess I was just wondering what you're doing here. You didn't tell me why you were at the apartment last night either."

He sighs and shifts the car forward five feet and then puts the car back in neutral.

"Firstly, I came this morning because I figured you could've used a ride. I was actually going to leave the car for you, but then... you looked so flustered I didn't really want you driving like that."

"Thank you." The words slide out before I can stop them. His Adam apple bobs, and then there's a tip of his head in acknowledgment. "And last night...?" He's better at avoiding question than I am.

Another sigh. He should get them trademarked as his signature expression. I get the distinct impression I'm not going to like what is about to come out of his mouth.

"Last night, you said something about having set up a business. What is it exactly, can you tell me? "

The question comes out of nowhere and catches me off guard. "Why?"

"You can trust me. I just need to know..."

I don't really see any reason to hide it, other than a sadistic satisfaction in being in control of the conversations for once. But either way, I'm sure Nathan will tell him, if he hasn't already and he's just pretending not to know.

"I... run an agency providing poker prop players to some private poker clubs in Hong Kong and casinos in Macau." Beside me, I feel something strike the air, interest maybe. And he's listening... and not judging, so I continue. "The girls who stay with us, I train them to play, and if they're good, then they're paid a retainer for the nights they work and get 70% of their winnings. They can stay with us as long as they need to. Usually what happens is they make close friends here, and after a few months, they move out together. Some stay and mentor new girls, and some move onto other jobs. I help them find those if they need it."

He doesn't say anything for the longest time.

And then finally, he turns around, pulls the sunglasses up onto his head, and looks at me with an indecipherable expression.

"Kiki, do you believe in fate?"

Ten

Kylian

The drive from Kiara's apartment home last night after I dropped her off from the police station was one of the most confusing fifteen minutes of my life.

Her bombshell about her business of rescuing girls in jobs they hated cut and healed me all at once. As I'd told her, it shouldn't have been surprising, considering what she was like when she was a child, but it was. I hadn't wanted to show that surprise because I imagine that's the usual reaction she elicits from people she tells about her job, especially the ones who travel in the same circles as her family did.

For all the money in the pockets of billionaires, many of the ones I'd met didn't really have a proclivity for sharing it. I more or less expected that from those who'd been born with platinum spoons in their mouths, but that selfishness showed even in those who'd scraped from humble beginnings to now sit at the top of the food chain. Instead of trying to make it easier for those like them to succeed, they carried this chip on their shoulder about how "if they could do it, anyone could."

Money does things to people's brains and morality.

It's a drug, a poison. One that I have to check every day, that it hasn't infiltrated my brain and turned it, changing what I view as right and what is wrong.

But when I'm in Kiara's presence, it's clear that line is blurred.

Last night, I'd waited for almost ten minutes outside her building, just in case she came back, having forgotten something... or forgotten to say something.

But she hadn't, she'd returned to the life that just a day ago, didn't have me in it.

A life where she's doing more with her life than I could've imagined.

As a child at school, she was barely ten years old before she organized competitions for her classmates, marble games, running races, hopscotch tournaments. The teachers wrote home about how resourceful she was, great at rallying her friends, a leader. What they hadn't known was the sheer amount of candy that was changing hands in the school yard. Kiara had set up a gambling ring that remained undetected until one of the mothers found her child's hidden candy stash and asked where it came from. The gambling ring was dismantled... temporarily. The pattern continued well into high school. And now she'd turned it into an outlet, a living, not only for herself, but for those needing a fresh start in life as well.

In this moment, it was the best thing she could have ever told me.

"Kiki, do you believe in fate?"

Her left brow turns into a question mark, curled into a mix of curiosity and confusion. I'm not going to let her wonder forever.

"Do you remember I told you about opening the casino last night?" She nods, almost scared to. "Well, we're looking for staff right now. Among them, croupiers, dealers, and of course, prop players. Most importantly, for our VIP rooms. There's a lot of money that's just begging to be lost. Would you be interested sourcing my casino with your players? Whatever deal you're looking at with your other contracts, I promise you, I can top it."

Her jaw drops. And then everything happens so fast, I can't react.

She reaches over and slaps me across the cheek, flinging her car door open and runs out into the traffic.

"What the...?" I shout, still reeling from the slap.

My eyes still blurry, I hear a car horn ahead and look up to see she's running between the columns of cars.

"Fuck!"

I kick my car door open, just as the cars start to move, and jump out right into traffic. Thank fuck no one's going anywhere fast. Except Kiara.

Ahead of me, she's reached the curb, out of imminent danger, and I follow as fast as I can, ducking and dodging between the rows and rows of cars. There's no room for me to cross the bumper-to-bumper lanes and over onto the curb.

Almost sick with worry, I just close my eyes and jump over the hood like I'm a fucking action movie star. A horn deafens me as I feel my leg brush against the headlights of a car.

"Kiara!" I shout.

But she doesn't turn around.

She's still running.

I don't know if I'm going to be able to catch up to her.

But I'm going to try.

My legs burn as I push, arms pumping at my sides, everything passing me in a flash.

In the distance, I see her figure turn a corner. How the fuck is she running so fast?

"Kiara!" I shout again loudly, frustrated by the effort of projecting her name as far as I can.

I round the corner, never slowing down, but she's gone.

The search for her continues down alleyways and across main roads until I'm miles from where we started.

Eventually, I have to give up. She's gone. And I've lost her.

Eleven

Kylian

Five Years Ago – London

The whiskey burns as it slides down my throat.

"What the fuck are you drinking?" Damien asks, picking up the bottle that's slid out of my hand and is spilling on the floor. He screws his nose up at the label. "Did you pick that out of a hobo's pocket? You know, about three feet from where you're sitting is a drink cart with about fifty thousand dollars worth of top shelf cognac and whiskey on it, right?"

"I don't want to drink any of that. I don't deserve it," I splutter as I snatch the bottle out of his hand and tip it into my mouth.

"Ahh, I recognize this. This is because of a girl."

I growl and try to train my eyes on him. Well, one of him, there are two Damiens standing in front of me right now

"You're such a know it all, which is interesting considering you're the dumbest out of all of us." I know I'm going to regret goading my older brother like that, but I'd happily take a punch in the head to distract the thoughts running through my mind.

"I'm smart enough to not be drinking myself into a stupor with cheap liquor over a woman," he says, not rising to the bait.

"We're not counting Mom, right? Because I remember dishing you out of a dumpster only a month ago after she called wanting you to send her some more money."

This time, there's no way he's going to ignore me.

I feel my body pulled to my feet and my body rammed against the wall.

"Sober up, you fucking twit. Before you say something this fucking stupid to someone who isn't going to be so nice to you." There's a dangerous tone underlying his voice that cuts through the dense fog around my brain.

He lets go of my shirt, and I fall to the ground in a slump.

"I fucked up, Damien," I slur after I pull myself into a sitting position, leaning my back against the couch.

"We've all fucked up. You wouldn't be a Baxter if you didn't. And if I think about it, this probably is your first time. So what did you do?"

I shake my head and pretend I can't hear a sloshing in my brain. "It's a girl. A woman."

"I know that. You're in a special kind of hell. What did you do? Hit on her sister?" He laughs, no doubt conjuring up the time he actually did that.

"No. Her brother."

Damien whistles. "You hit on her brother? That's new."

"No! Her brother is my best friend."

This time, the sounds that comes out of Damien's mouth is a curse. A string of them. "Shit. You hit on Nathan's sister? Does he know? Of course not. Your head is still attached to your body. How did that happen? When did that happen? She's not in London, is she?"

"Too many questions."

"Yeah, but you better have some answers. I'm going to ask the only thing that matters. Are you willing to lose Nathan over a fling with his sister? Because I'm telling you now, that's what will happen. I'm not saying not to do it. But... make sure you know what you're doing before you do it."

I arrive at Bottle half an hour early. I want to get there before she arrives, and according to Nathan, she's always been a stickler for time. Something about respecting someone else's time.

I nod to Marcus, the bartender, who flashes me a grin and reaches for the bottle of Hibiki Japanese whiskey I keep behind the bar and pours me a drink. He slides it across the polished bar to me, but the smell makes me swallow down a gag as soon as the scent reaches my nostrils. After I'd woken up with my head in an ice bucket, it had taken me about half a bottle of Tylenol, a long hot shower, and a five-mile run in to push back the symptoms from my bender last night.

There is nothing but a bunch of blurry images and a note from Damien that says, "If you don't die, I'll see you on Sunday for dinner." I reach for the jug of water at the end of the bar instead and down a whole glass, but it does nothing to wet my dry mouth. Another glass helps a little, but I forego a third and check my watch.

Twenty minutes to go.

I can't believe I'm about to do this.

But I can't think of another way to make a clean cut with her so that it's clear there will be no chance to pick things up again sometime down the road.

A tall blonde that looks like she breathes fire waves to me from the entrance, and I gesture at Marcus to pour her usual drink. My assistant Odette, my partner in crime. The one who came up with the idea in the first place. She joins me, flirting with me, and with everyone at the bar, man, woman, young, old. Marcus is the only one she ignores. And he her. He's been down this road with her before and came out missing pieces of both his body and soul.

The next twenty minutes feel interminable.

The second hand on the clock on the wall feels like it's going backwards, and finally I take Odette's hand and pull her into my private booth in the back of the bar, yelling to my bartender, "If anyone looks for me, I'm in my booth."

We settle into the booth, my hands shaking. Something screams at me that if I'm this nervous, then I'm doing the wrong thing.

"You ready?" I ask, my voice shaking

"Always." Odette winks, drapes her arms along the quilted leather edge of the booth, and lays her head back, giving me another wink.

I move in closer, brushing her hair aside, leaning in and pretending to whisper silly nothings in her ear.

In the corner of my eye, I see someone enter the bar, hair piled on top of her head in a perfect bun that shows the length of her neck. It's like every hair has been sculpted into place. I force myself to focus on the woman sitting next to me, but she has to grip my chin and turn it toward her.

"You're blowing it," she hisses into my ear.

"I know. Fuck. I'm trying. She's here."

"Fine, let me help."

She takes my head and shoves it into her lap as she leans back and lets out a soft, slow moan.

Something in my stomach lurches at the thought of how Kiara is going to react when she sees me, and I don't have to wait too long.

There's an audible gasp.

"Kylian?"

I swallow down the bile and sit up, pretending to wipe my lips on the back of my hand.

"Oh, hey, I didn't see you there," I say, casually leaning back against the back of the booth. "This is my best friend's little sister, Kiara. Kiara, this is Odette." Every single part of me yells that I'm making a mistake and aches to jump out of the booth and tell her it was just a joke, but Odette grabs my hand and pulls it into my lap, anchoring me. I don't know whether to thank her or kill her. "What's up?" The words sound callous. And it shows in the way her face crumbles.

"Um... uh, I'm... I th-thought..."

"You th-thought? What did you th-think?" I mock her, and Odette laughs cruelly beside me.

She gives me a look that screams of the pain streaking through her body and mind right now.

And then she turns and runs away, taking every little inch of my self-respect with her.

Twelve

Kiara

Present Day

Shi Lei is rushing out the door when I arrive at The House, and I catch her in my arms just as I step off the elevator.

"Shi Lei! It's okay... it's okay," I say, holding tightly onto to her shaking body. Ananya had texted me as I was in a cab on my way here and told me that Jimmy, the janitor from the club, had dropped by with Shi Lei's purse and told Ananya that the club owner was furious that she'd disappeared. He'd vowed to find her and make her pay. Unfortunately, Shi Lei had overheard, and she was apoplectic with fear.

Holding her tight is for her own good as I try to keep her from shaking in my arms. I gently whisper comforting noises until her body slackens and her sobs fade to the occasional hiccup and sniffle.

Her fear is still palpable; my whole heart breaks for her and those in her position. No one should have to feel this scared at the mere mention of an employer's name.

My hand strokes the side of her head, patting her hair.

"Better?" I say once she's breathing normally, and she looks up at me, giving me a small nod. "You are going to be safe here. We will keep you safe and will not let anyone hurt you again."

The way her eyes flick side to side tell me she's not so sure, but maybe she'd be willing to give it a try.

"Come on, come inside, and we'll talk."

I take her hand and lead her inside as the other women empty out one of the three bedrooms to give us some privacy.

After spending an hour answering all of Shi Lei's questions, I help her into her bed, pulling the curtains shut and blocking out the harsh morning light. I sit by the bed, holding her hand until it grows limp as her exhausted body falls into sleep. I don't leave immediately, not wanting her to wake up to see me gone. Finally, her breathing steady, I gently tiptoe out of the room and see Ananya sitting in the living room with tea waiting for me.

"How did it go?" she asks.

"Okay, I think she's going to be okay; she's really scared, though. She says... the club owner knows where she lives, so she's scared to even go there to grab her stuff."

"We won't let her go alone."

I nod. "Apparently, when he hired her, he promised her all sorts of things. How much money they would make, how much they would have to... do with the patrons, what their hour would be. But it was all lies. As far as she knows, there are new girls coming every day."

Ananya swallows. No matter how many you help, you can't help them all. "Jimmy will be busy."

"I don't know if we can keep putting him in this position. Sooner or later, they're going to find out he's helping."

She shrugs. "He wants to help."

"Maybe we can find him a job doing something else."

Ananya says out loud the words I don't want her to say. "But we need someone to help there."

"But that doesn't mean we can put our friend in danger."

We both have the same thought at the same time and blurt out, "We need more security."

I add, "And we need a bigger place, somewhere we can house the girls in one place, it's easier for us to keep them safe."

"What did you have in mind?"

My back straightens as I tell her what I had been planning when I was sitting with Shi Lei. "Renting a place where we can fit forty or fifty girls. Maybe a whole floor of apartments so we can keep them altogether, and security will be easier. We'll keep the apartments we already have so that when they girls are ready to move out, they can move into these apartment before moving onto other places if they want with their friends." I take a breath. "All this is going to take money."

Ananya sighs. "Money, money, everything takes money. We need more work. There's just enough to go around right now but not for another twenty girls. Not without getting more work from the casinos in Macau."

A certain blue-eyed blond's face grins at me inside my head, and I wave a hand in front of my face, trying to shoo him away.

Ananya frowns as she watches my antics. "What are you thinking about?"

"I don't want to tell you."

"Why?"

"Because you're going to tell me it's a good idea, but trust me, it's not."

She resettles, folding her legs under her, her face filled with interest.

I'm about to regret what I have to do.

Thirteen

Kylian

Almost four years ago, my grandfather passed away, leaving his entire 60% stake in our company to my three brothers and me. We've spent the years since his death getting situated in all the regions that Baxter has a presence: the Australia and Oceania region is headed by Damien, Kingsley in Europe, Matthias in the United States, and me in Southeast Asia. My grandfather made a deal with the company's board before he died for Kingsley to take over as CEO once he turns forty-two at the end of this year, just in time for the company's centennial. For the time being, however, our Uncle Gerald is interim CEO, as well as the utter bane of our existence. We know he's trying to find a way to oust all of us so that he can eventually be voted in as CEO instead of Kingsley. So far he's been unsuccessful, but there's no telling what plans he has.

Each Wednesday, the four of us have a standing appointment to check in with each other about any topic, business or personal. My brothers call it the "catch up" hour; I call it the "Pick on Baby Brother" hour.

But I still show up every week at 1 p.m, Hong Kong time on the dot.

The secret room on the company's server shows that one person is already in there when I log in. There's an image of an empty leather office chair and the sound of someone caterwauling in the background.

"Matthias! Seriously, grandfather did you and, frankly, the rest of us, a big favor when he pulled the funding on your singing lessons," I yell, covering my ears.

Matthias's face appears, so close to the camera that I could count the pores on his nose if he didn't spend a not-so-small fortune on the esthetician he has based in Baxter's headquarters in New York. Matthias pulls back far enough to open his mouth so wide I can see his uvula. He's the one who picked the time, so he can't complain. As the biggest playboy out of the four of us, I guess he figured that by 1 a.m. he'd be done with his "business" with whatever the girl of the day's name is and he'd be hyper for another hour before bed.

"Myy heeeaaart willlll goooo onnnn," he croaks at the top of his lungs with a flourish.

Kingsley enters the chat with his hands clasped over his ears. "Dear lord, I thought torture had been banned by the Geneva convention of 1949. Who is skinning a live husky!"

"I'm pretty sure the saying is "skinning a live cat," Matthias stops shrieking long enough to say.

"Fuck that, no cat makes that noise. Only a husky can howl like that."

"We've got to be talking about Matthias," Damien says, the last to join the chat as usual. Time is an elastic construct in Damien's head. One that revolves around him.

"Hey, guys!" a sweet female voice with a slight Australian accent pipes up.

"My-Linh!" I say, waving to Damien's fiancée, by far one of my favorite women on this earth. "Did you get the spices I sent you?"

"Hi, My-Linh," Matthias and Kingley pipe up just as she opens her mouth, cutting her off.

"Guys! Let the woman talk," I growl. Other than Damien, I'm her favorite Baxter, and I don't take kindly to my other brothers trying to vie for her attention.

"Hi, Matthias! Hi, Kingsley! How are you two doing?" she says with a big wave. "And, yes, Kylian, I got the spices, and my mom sends you a *huge* thank you. It was exactly what was missing from her dish. The Szechuan pepper we get here just isn't as good."

"No problem, just let me know if I can send you anything else. Like me, for example," I tease her.

There's a distinctive Damien growl, and he pulls her into his lap, glaring right into the camera. She giggles and wraps her arms around his neck, giving his cheek a big kiss.

I make a face and lean close to the camera as if telling her a secret. "I'm just saying, My-Linh, once you get sick of that buffoon, maybe you can move onto one of the more good-looking Baxters,"

Damien growls, his blue eyes darkening as he holds her tightly around the waist. He can take a joke about pretty much everything but My-Linh, and I don't blame him, considering he almost lost her once before.

My-Linh reaches down and squeezes his hand and whispers something to him. He visibly relaxes and meets her lips in a gentle kiss before she hops off his lap. "Gotta go, boys, I just wanted to pop in and say hello. I hope that's okay!"

We all reassure her that we'd much prefer to see her than Damien and wave as she disappears from the screen.

"You realize that any day now she's going to leave you for someone who actually deserves her?" I ask, already missing her. As much as I tease Damien about stealing her, I love My-Linh as a sister. There isn't an ounce of romantic feelings between us, which is probably for the good if I don't want my brother to skin me alive. She has proven time and time again that she has what it takes to love my brother the way he's needed to be loved his whole life.

I expect him to shoot back a sarcastic retort; instead, he just smiles and says, "I know. But I'll enjoy every moment I have with her until then."

"And then again, after you bury him alive."

We all laugh.

It's a joke, but Damien is the only one of us who has ever had the kind of relationship he has with My-Linh, and if he didn't murder the person who got between them, one of us would.

"Anyway, enough of Damien and his sappy love life, what's going on with you, Kingsley?" Matthias directs at our eldest brother.

"Fuck all. I've been wading in paperwork all week. I miss the sun."

"It looks it," Matthias chuckles. "There's such a thing as spray tans, Kingsy," Matthias says, using the nickname that makes Kingsley punch him if they're on the same continent.

"I'd prefer to not hog the benefits I provide for my employees, Matthias," Kingsley shoots back. As the one destined to be CEO of Baxter Enterprises in a year, he's had to deal with pressures the rest of us have only heard of. From the moment he was born, he has carried all of our futures and those of thousands of employees on his shoulders. I wonder if that's why he's the grumpiest among us, although Damien used to give him a run for his money. Apparently, the grumpiness gene skips a child as well as the chatty, hyper genes.

The few times Kingsley lightens up is when we're all together in person. Probably because he can make sure that we're all okay. He's always been the one that has ridden our asses the hardest while being our most fierce protector. He folds his arms across his chest as if to say that that's all he's going to say right now, and it doesn't take long for Matthias to jump in, talking about his new car.

"My Jag got towed," I cut in once I realize Matthias is not going to stop talking on his own.

"What? Why? What happened?" they all shout at once. They know how long I've been waiting for that model to come off the ship.

I take a moment to think about what and how much I'm going to tell them when Damien says, "Stop thinking about how much you're going to hide from us. You know we're going to find out anyway."

"Fine. I... left the car somewhere."

Kingsley gives me a look. "Why did you leave it there?"

I shouldn't have gone down this road. I'm either going to be yelled at or roasted, neither of which is going to help my mood. "I... was chasing... someone..."

Matthias grins proudly. I should've known he'd pick up right away what this is all about. "Was she worth it?"

Yes. "I didn't say it was a woman."

"Who was it, then?" Kingsley asks, rubbing his forehead, already tired of our weekly meeting.

I flick my eyes to Damien, then away almost immediately, but I know that it's enough for him now. He swears under his breath and rubs his forehead like Kingsley does. "You're kidding me. This again?"

"What?" Matthias shouts, jumping to his feet. He has never liked being out of the loop. "What is happening again?"

I glare at Damien, although it's my own damn fault. I should've known that he'd figure it out. He's always known me the best. "You tell them."

"Well, I don't know what's happening right now, but a little while back, baby brother lost his mind over a woman. And apparently, she's back again."

"Whoooo?" Matthias yells, shaking his speakers.

Damien shrugs and says matter-of-factly, "Oh, you know, just an heiress to a certain Hong Kong fortune."

Matthias's eyes bug out, and he sinks back down into his office chair. "Duuuuuuuude."

"What?" I snap.

"You're fucking Nathan's sister? He's going to skin you like the proverbial husky."

Damien snorts and then covers his mouth when he sees the look on my face.

"I'm not fucking anyone," I protest.

"That's too bad," Matthias interjects, entirely unhelpfully.

"Shut up. You know what I mean."

Kingsley cuts in, "I think you mean that you've got some crush on your best friend's sister and one of our biggest allies."

"That... is pretty much it, yeah. Fuck." My head falls into my hands. This is the first time I've said any of this out loud. I hadn't expected to be the center of attention today, but here we are. And to be honest, talking it out hasn't helped much at all.

"What do you think, Damien?" Kingsley says.

He holds his hands up and shakes his head "Hey, I've already gone through this once. If he's back in this situation, whatever I had to say didn't stick. It's in your hands now."

I roll my eyes. "He's exaggerating. I was fine."

Matthias takes a sip from his beer bottle and jumps up, finger pointed to the ceiling. "Wait! Is that when you fucked up the Henderson account?"

I cringe. Dammit. "Yes."

Matthias winces. "Ah. Okay. Shit. Yeah... he's in trouble if we're in for a rerun."

"I'm fine! Look, I haven't seen her in five years, and trust me, she is not in any frame of mind to be seeing me because..." My sentence trails off as I hear a commotion outside my office.

Julie, my admin assistant, can be heard shouting "No! Miss, you can't go in the—"

My office door flies open, and Kiara storms in, her face set in a straight line.

"Kiara!" I ignore the nosy faces on my screen and jump up, shouting, "What are you doing here? Where did you go before? I was worried sick!"

She ignore my questions by strolling over to my desk and slamming her purse down and folding her arms, her chest rising and falling with heavy breaths.

"Mr. Baxter, I'm so—" my assistant starts.

I wave her apologies away. "It's fine, Julie. I can take care of it from here."

A glance down at my laptop shows my three brothers glued to their screens, mouths wide open. They might as well be shoving popcorn into their gobs. I slam the top of my laptop down, and my three brothers with it, knowing that in less than a minute, my phone will blow up with texts, and no doubt, I'm going to be the topic of conversation for the rest of their meeting.

"I need to talk to you about something." She sounds a lot more calm than her storming in here suggests.

I swallow, gesturing to a chair. "Sure, have a s—"

She cuts me off. "Were you serious? About hiring my poker agency for the casino?"

That's an easy question to answer. "Yes. I don't make business offers I don't intend on following through with."

Her head shakes while her eyes lock on me, angry... hurt. "But how are we supposed to work together, Kylian? How am I supposed to believe anything you say? Trust you? Do you have any idea what you did to me?"

Every word cuts me.

But I can't tell her it was all a ruse, that it was all set up to make her hate me. All because at that point in my life, I couldn't bear the thought of losing her brother as my friend when I had so few people I truly trusted in my life. But that now that I've seen her again, I know I made the biggest mistake in my life.

"Kiara, I'm not the same person I was. I have no intention of screwing you over, in business or otherwise."

The answer seems to anger her even more, as if the reminder of past me stirs the hurt up into a dust storm in her eyes. She throws her hands up in the air. "It was a mistake coming here. Forget this happened. I don't ever want to see you again, Kylian. Stay away from me."

I run over, blocking her exit with my tall frame and grabbing her wrists, the touch of her skin against mine a thrill I've never experienced. "Don't go. Please. Just talk to me. Tell me what I can do to make it up to you. Just don't go."

Her eyes spew viciousness as she rips my hands off her and makes a run for it. But this time, I'm prepared. I chase her all the way to the closed door and push her up against it, pressing my body against her so she can't run away again. I grip her chin and force her to look at me.

"Kiara." Her name comes out in a shallow breath. "Would you fucking stop running and just look at me? Why did you run out into traffic? Did you know how fucking sick I felt, wondering if you've gotten hurt?"

She struggles against me, her hair from her ponytail coming undone and framing her face in angry wisps. Her cheeks blaze red, and her eyes are wild as they lock onto mine. Pupils dilated but raging as her top row of teeth crushes down on her bottom row before she hisses. Primal, like a cat in a cage. "What the fuck do you care about me getting hurt? You've never cared before. In fact, I think you get off on it."

I recoil at the words. They weren't what I'd been expecting, more hurt than fighting, but my hands are still gripping her chin. It takes a beat for me to recover from the question, but when it's my turn to speak, it comes out even more hurt than hers. "Do you really think that? Do you really imagine that I'd get off on your pain? Do you really not know me at all?"

She hisses and wrenches her face out of my hand and raises her hand like she's going to slap me again, and for a second, I ponder letting her do it again, just to let her frustrations out. We both know what sparked her anger, and I'm surprised it's taken until now for her to bring it up. But for all of my reputations for being all sunshine and fucking rainbows, I have never taken lightly to someone slapping me, so as her hand swings down, I catch it at the wrist and push it hard against the door over her head.

"We're going to talk. I'm going to let you say anything that you need to, but we're not going down the road of violence. Got it?" I growl against her. "Whatever's happened between us, it's not going to come to that. Nod if you agree. And it'll do you well to."

Her eyes narrow to such thin slits I can only just see her pupils pointed directly at me. Her chest billows in and out quickly, just as mine is. I blame it on struggle rather than the memory that this is how we stood outside the club in London that night.

And how I think about it almost daily.

And what it's done to my life since.

"Let. Go. Of. Me," she finally responds in a whisper so low I can barely hear it, but her lips spell it out for me.

"Not until you agree that we're going to talk about things as civilly as we can."

There's a microexpression of anger, then it fades. I can only guess how hard she's trying to hold her emotions in. And the anger I'm seeing is the spillover.

It's a lot, and it's warranted.

There's another moment of internal tug-of-warring as we stare at each other, and then I pull her hand down and let it go, watching her carefully the whole time. Instantly, she raises her other hand and swings. I catch it an inch from my cheek. And now she's not the only one angry. I grab her shoulders, spinning her around so that she's facing the door and press her against it, lifting both of her hands and pinning them over her head.

"You had a chance to agree, and now there are no more chances. You want to do this the hard way? Don't say I didn't warn you."

"Fuck you, Kylian."

Every single cell in my body shakes with need. It feels like the arousal came out of nowhere, but I know it's been simmering under the surface for so long, and the second my eyes fell on hers in Amber, the thin veil of indifference that I built stroke by stroke was torn down. And now, my body against hers, her scent in my face, her anger burning into my skin, there's nothing left but sizzling, unadulterated need for her.

She fights hard, but I have twelve inches and seventy pounds on her.

Not to mention five years worth of late night fantasies that have left me drenched in guilt and frustration. Never fully satisfying but that's never been what it was about. It was just about pushing back those visions of her face, her body, her sweet breath against my cheeks that night so that it wouldn't come to this, me pinning her against the door in my office, ready to give anything to taste her.

I lean in, my hips pressing against hers, and I wonder if she can feel my hardness. I want her to know what she's doing to me.

My lips brush her cheek as I whisper into her ear, "Are you mad at me for what I did in London? Or are you just mad that you're jealous I wasn't doing it to you?" My free hand reaches down for the hem of her dress, bunching it into my fist at the waist. "We can change all that now. Is that what you want?"

A shiver travels down her body.

She doesn't say anything, and the struggling has stopped for the most part. There's occasional twisting at the waist, but I'm not sure if that's to get a good look at me. It sure doesn't feel like she's trying to get away.

My hand drops under her dress, a finger tracing the skin of her thigh so lightly I'm not sure she can even feel it. But then the shiver travels up her leg and back to end at the top of her spine, telling me she does.

I'm so hard I feel like I'm going to burst out of my own skin.

I trace the skin all the way to the hem of her panties, and it makes me want to drop to my knees so much right now and see what she's got underneath the dress, but this isn't about me.

This is about her.

And showing her how much I've regretted what happened that day.

My finger lines the seam of her panties, and I reach around to her front and brush along the slightly raised softness of her pubis.

Her knees sag a little, her body held to the door by mine, my hand still holding both of her wrists over her head.

"Sweet, sexy Kiara..." I murmur against her ear as my fingers runs over the fabric covering her pussy.

"Oh." She lets out a single stifled sound, and it threatens to undo me completely.

It takes everything I have not to tear down those panties and drive myself into her.

"What is it, Kiki? This is what you wanted, isn't it? What you've wanted all this time?" I growl into her ear, my fingers lingering, playing, teasing, making her guess when they're going to push aside her panties so that we're skin on skin.

"Fuck you, Kylian," she chokes out and turns her face toward me. Face flushed with arousal.

"Soon, sweetheart. Soon..."

She's not fighting now.

Not when I slide my finger under her panties to run along the gap between her pussy lips. Soft. Warm. And already wet.

"Kiki, I'm not even inside your pussy yet, and you're already dripping for me."

She hisses, but the sound gets interrupted by another gasp when my finger dips deeper, the tip finding the entrance to her pussy. "Oh god..."

"I'm sorry, what was that? Were you asking me to stop?" I say just as my finger slides deep inside her.

Her response is nothing but a pushing down with her hips, swallowing my finger even deeper, right down to the hilt, that finally drags a whimper out of her. Her obvious need lights a spark in me, and I withdraw my finger until it's just at her entrance and ram it deep inside her again.

"Fuck..." the soft moan leaves her lips.

What I would do to hear my name on those lips.

"So wet," I mutter as I fuck her pussy with my hand, her wetness coating my fingers and dripping down my palm. "Such a needy little pussy. Have you fingered yourself like this, imagining it was me?"

The moan sticks in her throat this time, making her body vibrate under me.

I drag my finger out of her and play with her lips but am careful not to touch her clit just yet.

Not yet. But soon...

I draw a wide circle, traveling from the bottom of her pulsing pussy all the way up to graze the seam of her lips. I circle one way, and then the other way, drawing the circle smaller and smaller.

Each time, I feel her body tense as she waits.

Her hair tangles itself against my face as I growl into her ear. "Now is the time to tell me if you want to stop, Kiki. Because once I touch your clit, that's it; I'm not going to stop until you come. Do you hear me? Nod if you want me to continue."

I expect her to swing around and kick her leg back. Instead, there's the slightest dropping of her chin in a single nod.

"Good girl."

Before she can react, I drag my fingers over the curve of her clit. Not once, not twice, but over and over. She squirms, the moan stuck in her throat freeing and filling the air around me. "Ohhh fuck..."

Fuck is right. My cock twitches at the sounds.

Down boy.

This is about her.

It's always been about her.

Softly... slowly... the tip of my finger runs up and down over her clit, and then I'm flicking it from side to side.

"Oh god..." she murmurs; it's like a symphony of desire, and I'm already drunk on the sound.

"That's my girl... just relax... don't think about what I'm doing to you. Just enjoy it. We've both been thinking about it for so long now, haven't we?"

My confession spills out before I can stop it, and her body contracts, doing the one thing I don't want her to do. Think.

My finger flicks her clit harder, banishing the thoughts right out of her head, and the moans come one after the other, and she tips her head back, touching mine.

Her guava shampoo swirls around in my mind, the same one even after all this time. Sweat blooms on her forehead, and I lean down and drop a single kiss on top of her head.

She doesn't move, her eyes drawing closed as my finger maps out the terrain of her clit. It's about the same size as the tip of my pinky. Probably normally soft, but right now, hard, engorged, pulsing... and I ache to run my tongue over it.

Now.

I spin her around and drop to my knees in front of her, pushing her dress up and her panties aside in one movement as I drag my tongue in one long, slow lick from the base of her pussy to the tip of her clit.

She tastes like fucking heaven.

"Oh my god," she shouts, all inhibitions gone, her hands coming down to tangle in my hair.

Fuck. I almost come feeling her touch me of her own accord.

But there's no time to fist my own cock right now.

I lick her again, my tongue lingering on the dip of her pussy. God, she tastes just like I thought she would—sweet, dark, slightly salty against my tongue, making me want for more.

Her clit trembles as it feels my tongue flicking against it.

I nudge her legs open, wider. I look up, and her eyes are on me, lidded as she widens her stand, her soft thighs on either side of my head.

Something about the way she wants to watch sparks the last unlit flame inside me, and with my eyes trained on her, my tongue flicks over her clit, over and over and over.

Her chest rises and falls to the rhythm of my licks.

With each one, there's a flash of something... intense pleasure or pain over her face. The sheen of sweat on her face makes her glow.

I want to kiss her.

I want to kiss her so badly, fill her mouth with the taste of her own cum.

My cock strains at the thought.

I move my finger down to pump in and out of her as I lick.

"Ohhh, fuck... oh fuck... oh fuck..." she moans without end.

She's close.

Behind the door, there are voices, but she either doesn't notice or care.

That's my girl.

I pull my mouth away for just a second as my finger continues to slide in and out of her pussy.

"You are so wet, you taste so good, I can't get enough of you."

The air empties from her lungs, and I feel like I breathe it in. Then there's nothing to do but make her call my name.

The pad of my tongue presses against her sweet little spot, hard and rough as I move my head in a circle, pressing harder and harder, spurred on by her nails against my scalp.

A shiver emanates from her clit all the way up to her eyes, the lids fluttering for a second as I pull away and flick the tip of my tongue over her. Once, twice... countless times.

The flush climbs up her neck, and just as her mouth starts to form a silent O, I pull away.

"What?" She looks down confused, angry.

I smirk. "I'll let you come on one condition... you call my name out while you're doing so. Like I know you've done so many times before. Except this time, I'm going to hear it."

Her eye lids narrow but this time, not from want. From pure hatred.

That's okay. I'll deal with it later. Right now, I'm dealing with her need to come.

To remind her what's she's missing, I reach forward with my finger, pressing it gently against her clit. The anger flees from her eyes, and she leans back against the wall, moaning.

"Call my name or else I'm not going to continue," I growl into her ear.

She grits her teeth, pressing down against my finger. I pull away just enough to be making the slightest contact against her.

"Fuck... I hate you, Kylian." she groans.

"That's a good start. But next time, I want you to say it while you're coming." Then I drop, and her clit is against my tongue, licking it harder and faster until her breath trickles out of her throat in an unending moan, her hands against the back of my head.

When she hisses through her teeth, her feet arching up on tip toes, I know it's coming.

My finger pumps deeper into her, and it's all that she needs to fall over the cliff.

"Oh fuck... oh god..." she moans as her body squeezes in orgasm.

"Come for me, sweetheart," I murmur against her clit as I continue to lick her, pushing her higher and harder over her climax.

"Oh fuck! Oh, Kylian... Oh god, Kylian..." she moans, barely coherent.

It's me. It's my name. I'm the one making her come, and she's reminding herself, reminding me, as my name spills uninhibited over her lips.

"Oh... don't stop, Kylian... please..."

It almost sounds like a surrender.

I keep eating her, even though all I want to do is get up and drive myself into her, coming deep inside her and making her mine.

She keeps moaning, her eyes closed, her head shaking from side to side as she comes again... letting me take her over the cliff again. I could watch it forever.

Finally, when the breathing slows and her body stops shaking, she pulls her hands away and brushes me away from her sensitive clit. I give her one last long lick, collecting as much of her cum on my tongue as I can, coating my mouth like a reward.

Brushing her dress down as I stand up, leaning into her, my face buries in her hair.

I take this moment of stillness to say, "You are so fucking beautiful."

She pulls away, brushing the wayward wisps of hair stuck on her damp forehead away, so her eyes are locked on mine. "Really?"

"Yes. You've always been a pretty girl, but now... just now... you were one of the most beautiful things I've ever seen in my life."

And I lean in, ready to kiss her for the first time.

Fourteen
Kiara

It's been over a year since the last time I kissed someone.

A kiss carefully constructed to appease an angry man, to give in for just a moment to say a much belated farewell. A kiss that marks a beginning as well as an end. A kiss to start a new era of me. One where I do not need a man in my life.

And now, Kylian Baxter is about to rip it all away from me.

Before his mouth can come down to touch mine, I place my hands up against his chest and shove him so hard he's almost pushed back three steps before he catches himself. The look of surprise on his face would've been a satisfying sight if I couldn't feel the wetness between my legs, reminding me what I had let him—what I had been begging him—to do to me.

My head and heart feel like they're split right down the middle between the elation and crippling shame about what just happened. They pull me in opposite directions, tearing in the middle. But it's not a clean cut, it's a jagged, splintered split, with the shards nicking the raw exposed ends where the utter confusion lies.

"Woah!" he says. "What was that about?"

"What the hell did you think you were doing?" I shout, clutching at my arms, trying to forget that he just saw me at my most vulnerable.

He frowns. "I'm pretty sure it was clear what I was doing."

"I mean, what did you have to do that for?"

"Because"—he frowns, scratching the back of his head—"it's what we both wanted?" Is he starting to sound a little unsure?

"Was it? Or was it just you doing what you wanted?"

"Kiki, you know that you were in that moment as much as I was." Not so unsure this time.

My mouth clamps shut. Because he's right. There isn't a single thing or single person who could've made me stop letting him touch me that way.

He nears me again, and the look in his eyes eclipses every thought, every emotion, every memory in my body. There's nothing but the two of us standing on an empty plane, his hand about to cup my cheek.

"Do you regret what happened?" he asks. "Because all I can say is that I'll remember that moment for the rest of my life. I've been waiting forever to taste you, Kiki. The thought of your body hot and naked against mine haunts me. The sound of your soft moans is going to be the soundtrack to every single one of my fantasies from now on. And when I'm thirsty, the taste of your cum on my tongue is the thing that will quench my thirst, my never ending thirst for you."

Every word perforates my brain like a braille paragraph, forever to be read by anyone who can read my thoughts, and that person right now is him.

"I hate you," I say, the only thing that makes sense to me, the truth since I last saw him in London.

A soft smile tugs at his lips, and he leans in, his breath carrying the soft tang of my wetness on his lips. "That's okay, I hate myself, too, for waiting so long.'"

"Why did you wait so long?" I ask, even though we both know the answer.

A darkness seeps into his pupils, and he pulls away.

The action has the effect of breaking the seal on a vacuum, and the outside world floods into the space where only he and I existed, even if it was just for a few minutes.

His hand runs through his hair, and it's like déjà vu.

We've been here before, but last time, we had the presence of mind to stop.

"Nathan," we both say at the same time.

We've always known what it was. Who it was.

"Kiara," he says, sounding tortured. "Fuck..."

I sigh and nod. "I know. My brother will kill you."

He nods, staring at a spot above my shoulder as if he's picturing Nathan seeing us right now.

"So what?" I hear myself say.

His gaze drops down to meet mine. "What?"

"So what if Nathan found out? I'm an adult. I get to decide what I can or can't do... and with whom." My orgasm has apparently turned my head. I've lost my fucking mind.

"You know it's not that simple."

"I know. But what I'm saying is... so what? He'll get over it."

The laugh he responds with is hollow. "You mustn't know your brother very well."

"You'd be surprised."

He smirks and tries to rub it away with his hand. "So you know that he punched Simon Waterville when you were in grade ten when he found out that Simon was the one who sent you that secret admirer card on Valentine's Day?"

"What?" I never had found out who was the person who sent that card to me. But I did remember that Simon had come to school with a black eye the next day and had never spoken to me again. "You're kidding me."

"I never kid when it comes to how protective Nathan is of you, Kiki." He sighs and runs a finger down my cheek. "And who can blame him?"

The words have no effect on me. My brother's protectiveness of me is nothing to admire. Especially in this moment. "Me. I can blame him. You don't know what it's like to have a guardian angel who is the national champion of Muay Thai flying over your head when you're just trying to go to a school dance."

He frowns and studies me for a moment. "Is that why you don't want to work with Yin Tech?"

His words are like a splash of cold water over my whole body. And I'm reminded how we got into this situation to start off with. Him offering me a job with Baxter. "What do you know about that?"

His shoulders lift in a single shrug. "Doesn't take any professional sleuthing. Your family is the majority shareholder of the fourteenth largest company in Hong Kong, and yet you're out there saving wayward women and giving them a new life. As far as I know, and correct me if I'm wrong, I don't think that's a department of Yin Tech that I haven't heard of."

"And is that why you offered me a job?" I fold my arms.

He shakes his head. "That's not about them. It's about me. I think you could help me out with my new casino. Am I wrong? Couldn't you help even more people if you knew how much demand for prop players we have? We could retain all of your prop players and more. Isn't that what this is all about? Helping as many people as possible?"

His words strike a match inside me; he's right, and we both know it.

But that doesn't mean that this is the right decision for me.

Eighteen hours ago, he didn't have a place in my life, and I'm not sure that that isn't the place we should return to.

"Kylian. I... I don't know what's happening here. I don't know what you're doing back in my life. I don't know what you want from me. And I don't know that I can work with you. I've worked very hard to try to forget you ever existed. And this has just taken me by surprise."

He nods and reaches down, and I hold my breath, wondering what's about to happen, but he just picks up my hand, laying it on top of his.

"I know. I don't know what's happening either. Just that I think we can do a lot of good between the two of us. And that, despite a certain Nathan-shaped hurdle... now that I'm back in your life, I don't want to leave."

Fifteen

Kiara

After Kylian makes his declaration, I don't give him another chance to say anything more. I grab my things, and I run out of his office, jump in a cab, and hide in my bedroom for the rest of the day until it's the next day. Nothing stops me from reliving the moment I orgasmed with his mouth on me, every single part of my body wanting it to happen, except my brain. The only solution is to get out into the world and hope something distracts me. I'm texting to tell the driver I called for that I've reached the lobby and will be right out when I hear a chipper voice say, "Hi!"

I freeze in my tracks, and the coffee sloshes in my cup, almost spilling over the sides.

I glare at Kylian as I hold the cup at arm's length, waiting for the liquid to settle. "What are you doing here?"

He's leaning against the front door, hand in his pockets, giving me a lazy grin. "Has anyone ever told you that you have a very unique morning manner?"

It's too bad I'm already glaring because this would be an opportune time to express how much I don't appreciate a analyzation of my morning mood. "It's not unique. It's normal. Most people aren't perky before 9 a.m."

"Wrong! And I am proof of that," he says, pushing off the door and stepping closer to me, holding his arms out as if to give me a hug.

The way I step back clearly expresses the likeliness of that happening. My body is still tingling from what happened in his office yesterday. And I'm still not sure I know how we're supposed to move on from here. So I do the only thing I can to get him to stop thinking about touching me. I ask him a question. "What are you doing here? Again."

He stops. "Well, I assume that you haven't heard back about your car."

A white-hot pain slashes through my chest. I loved that car. It was the first big purchase I'd made after moving back to Hong Kong. After living in New York City for four years, the thing I'd missed most was having my own car.

"No. Nothing," I admit.

"Then you need a ride."

"And... you're going to give it to me?"

"Why not? I was in the neighborhood."

I shoot him a wary look. "And why were you in the neighborhood?"

He grins. "In case you needed a ride."

The chuckle that comes out of me is loud, unexpected, and unwanted, and I swallow it down as fast as it had come bubbling up. He really is charming. A jerk, but a charming one. But he doesn't need to hear that from me.

"So where to?" he asks, holding his arm out.

I ignore it as I walk toward the front door. "How about you show me this casino that I'm supposed to be working at. Make sure it's worthy of our time."

He doesn't even try to hide the look of surprise on his face and then follows me out, holding the car door open for me. The half empty coffee cup gets plucked out of my hand, and he throws it into a nearby trash can.

After he climbs into the car, he hands me a coffee tumbler with a lid he pulled from the drinks tray. "For you. I already put the sugar and cream that you don't want into it. Don't want you spilling hot coffee on you while I'm driving." He gives me a wink and takes off.

And something tells me, by the end of the day, what little resolve I have left to keep him at arm's length is going to be gone.

And for the first time in a long time, I'm not running away.

We drive over the bridge to Macau making teeny tiny talk. Hong Kong's laws are such that casinos aren't allowed, so casinos are run on cruise ships that can float out to international waters or open over the bridge in Macau.

A while after we enter Macau, Kylian pulls into a covered car park under a large complex. The outside of the building is still covered in some scaffolding, and the landscaping has only just started with a deep fish pond being built in front of the grandiose entrance. I follow him silently from the carpark up a service elevator that opens up into the back of a large kitchen.

He holds the door open for me. "This is going to be the kitchen for Grace, the restaurant that our friend Jax runs. If you're around in a month, he's going to do a tasting to finalize the menu. He's going for a Michelin star in the first year. Can't say I wouldn't be happy with that. Some of my brothers are going to come over for that. And Damien's fiancée, My-Linh. You're going to love her. As for Damien... er, maybe not so much, but that's okay, he only has eyes for My-Linh anyway."

He chatters away as he leads me through a wide hallway decked out in a plush red carpet, golden ornate but modern light fixings that give the effect of burning oil lamps on the walls. A drop chandelier that looks like it has over a thousand crystals on it hangs in the middle of the hallway, and empty shops line each side.

"We've got about thirty vendors coming in. Louis Vuitton, Prada, Tiffany, all the luxury brands, and six of the positions that you see at the end here will be for pop-ups of local businesses from Macau and Hong Kong. We're renting them out for free for six-month leases, and they'll pay us 25% of their net receipts. No point letting the big names scoop up all the casino winnings. We've been looking at applications for the last year of so, and some of these designers and products give the luxury brands a run for their money. It's actually how we found the designer for those lamps you see along the wall. Almost all the materials and decor that you'll see in Jade Bay comes from local businesses."

Touched and impressed at the attention to detail, I nod as he leads me down another hallway with more store spaces. Already I'm seeing the scope of this building; it seems to go on forever. The interior is coming together, and everything feels rich and opulent. This isn't just any casino. This is gunning to be the best casino in Macau. And I've been in enough of them to know that he just might have a shot.

There's a swelling of pride somewhere in the side of my ribcage.

Even without telling me, just from his voice, I can tell he has lived and breathed this project.

Kylian leads me into one of the main game rooms by descending into a stunning grand staircase.

"Wow, this is like something out of—"

"Titanic?" he finishes with a grin. "Thanks for noticing."

My mouth drops open. "You modeled it on that?"

"Let's just say it was inspired by it. It's almost twice as wide, we have a little more room than a cruise ship, and about one-and-a-half times higher."

"I feel like Kate Winslet descending to meet Leo," I say with a nostalgic sigh.

"I would've thought you would have preferred to be Kiara meeting Leo. As I recall, you were a little jealous of Ms. Winslet in your teen years."

I press a finger to my lips. The crushes of our youth should not be brought up in our adult years.

He stands on the middle step of the staircase and pulls his phone out, showing me the layout. "So this is the main games floor. No special memberships or VIP levels. Machines over there, game tables along this side here, and in the middle of the floor, we'll have the displays for our machine jackpots."

I nod. It sounds about standard, but there's something different about the layout. It takes me a moment before I pick out what it is. I peer again at the blueprint on his phone to make sure.

"Are those machines in the... shape... of...?"

He grins. "Of the number nine?"

I stare at him open mouthed. "That's brilliant."

In many Asian cultures, the number nine is lucky. And Asian people like to enjoy their gambling with a healthy dose of superstition.

He jogs down the stairs into the still empty game room, holding his arms out. "The machines and tables will be in at the end of the week." He closes his eyes as he says, "Kiki, can you hear it?"

"Hear what?"

"Close your eyes."

I do as he says and stand in the silence for a moment.

"Can you hear the sound of the roulette wheel being spun, the pill racing along the edge before it bounces on the number, the machines beeping away, coins clinking as they fall into the buckets. The cheers and laughs of big winners!"

I peek out of one eye to see a smile spread wide across his face, his arms up in the air as if the cards he's been dealt show Black Jack.

"Can you?" he asks again.

I don't, but I come over and pat him gently on the shoulder. "I know you do, and that's what is going to set this place above the rest."

His eyes flutter open, and when he looks at me, it's with such intensity that my feet itch to flee. But they don't. I just stay and stare back at him.

"Wanna see the VIP room?" he finally says. "It's where most of your employees will work, but we'll need some players for the main gaming room as well, if that's okay with you."

"Absolutely, we can put the training ladies out here."

I'm led through an almost invisible door near what appears to be the row of cashiers and to another hidden elevator. A sly smile covers his face when the doors open, and he takes my hand to push through a velvet curtain and into a gambler's paradise.

And my breath is taken away.

"Wow."

This room, unlike the other one which is still completely empty, is almost fully set up. With the highest end tables surrounded by chairs and stools that must've cost a thousand dollars apiece. I run my finger along the edge of one of the poker tables. "BBO?" I ask, naming one of most luxurious gaming table brands.

The grin I get tickles me. "You know your tables."

"This mahogany finish is one of my favorites. So nice to play on. But I don't recognize this design.'

"That's because it's custom."

I'm truly impressed. "You have expensive taste, Mr. Baxter."

To the side along one wall sits a full bar already stocked with every top shelf liqueur I can name.

"I call it The Light Room. Other than our three other VIP rooms, this is our VVIP room."

"Ah yes, your Very, Very Important Players."

He nods. "Whales. Cash in is a minimum of two million U.S. dollars. We will have ten poker tables, serving ten players on each. Depending on how busy we are, we'll have at least one prop player on each table. We will also have three Black Jack tables, one Baccarat, one craps table, and two roulette games running. The other rooms have the same amount of tables as well."

I walk over to one of the tables, settling on the stool, and run my fingers over the plush lining. I couldn't hear the sound in the main game room, but I can hear them here. It's quieter, the sound of ice melting and clinking in glasses, the shuffling of cards and rearranging of chips. The soft banter and trash talk, the dropping of bets into the pot. This is my arena. And while I'm playing poker, I am a puppet master.

"What do you think?" he asks as he watches me look around the room.

"I think I might be playing here more than my employees."

He throws his head back and laughs. "You have a standing invitation. Let me know if you need a line of credit. I know Nathan's good for it." He takes a beat and then asks, "So... are you in?" with more insecurity in his voice than I have ever heard.

I'm hesitant to give him his answer just yet. "Is there somewhere we can go and talk?"

Five minutes later, we're standing in a private room on the highest level that overlooks the entire main game room floor. It's still mostly undecorated and unfurnished, but the potential is clear.

"This will be my private salon. Not for entertaining. We have a similar room on the other side. Just me and family."

"Not an office?" I tease him.

He smiles. "I don't intend to be doing too much of the daily running of this place. I'd only screw something up! Accidentally set the roulette machine to always come up black or something."

I settle on a leather couch, and he takes a chair facing me. My eyes avoid his for a while as he stares at me, waiting for me to speak. Why is he so unnerving?

My throat croaks the first time I open to speak, so I try again. "If we're going to do this, we need some clear terms."

"Yes, ma'am."

"Firstly, I need you to sign a six-month retainer. If you pull out, you pay the remaining amount in a lump sum with the minimum of two months payout. I can't play around with this. These women deserve stability." I place a folder on the table and push it across to him. "Here's the contract starting with five prop players and then the fee for each subsequent player you keep on retainer. If you want to start the retainer for ten prop players, I can give you a better deal."

He slides the piece of paper across the table but doesn't bother looking at it before he answers. "Is this what your deal is with your current contracts?"

"It's 6% more. The main reason is because we are trying to spend more on their accommodation, security, and training. I can negotiate if you want."

"Nope. Sounds good. What other terms?"

I frown. Is he playing? "Aren't you going to look at it?"

"Do I need to? Is it in fact 500% more than your current contacts?"

"No. I wouldn't do that."

He tilts his head to one side and studies me for a moment. "I know. So no, I won't look at it. My lawyer will draw up the contracts, and we'll both look them over before we sign, okay? So, like I said, what's next?"

I eye him for a moment before I move on. "I need security for the girls. A lot of them have come out of very dangerous situations that continue to be dangerous for them."

"You'll have security here. They will meet the women at their cars in the staff car park and will be walked back out when they're done. Or do you need more?"

I don't answer. When it comes to the security of my employees, I need to know that nothing is being spared.

"Do you want an escort for them to and from their residences?" he presses.

I'm too scared to say yes, but I can't even quantify how much that will put all of our minds at ease.

He doesn't wait for an answer, just nods as he says, "Done. I'll add that to the contract."

"Kylian, that's tens of thousands of dollars a year."

He smirks. "Much, much more. We hire and train our own security here. It's not cheap. And that's the only way I know that you'll all be taken care of. Do you trust my security?"

I can feel his eyes on me while I think, and before I can speak again, he pulls a device out of his pocket and presses a button on it.

Less than five seconds later, there's a knock on the door, then it opens before Kylian can answer, and a man-beast with a neck the size of a Sequoia tree trunk comes in, eyes sharp, assessing the situation.

He sees Kylian and freezes, as if waiting to be addressed.

"Oh, hello, Frank. This is Kiara Yin. She and her employees will be working here when we open. As prop players."

Frank nods and makes a noise like a pig digging for truffles.

Kylian doesn't seem too perturbed by the Man-Beast's behavior. He must be used to it. "You'll be in charge of coming up with a schedule for them, the total package please. I will send you the details when I have them."

He snuffles again, but his eyes don't seem to miss a thing.

"Thank you, Frank, that'll be all," Kylian dismisses him, and Man-Beast shuffles out the door, slamming it closed behind him.

I open my mouth to say thank you when Kylian presses his index finger to his mouth, shushing me, and then bangs on the side of the door, yelling, "Did you really doubt I could take care of you, bitch!"

I'm so stunned my breath freezes in my throat.

Kylian winks at me and takes a step back just in time for the door to come flying open, and the Man-Beast barrels into the room, eyes wide and raging, hands on his weapon.

Again, he stops in his tracks when he sees Kylian standing back and me perfectly safe on the couch.

Kylian grins at him. "Hello, again, Frank. What can we do for you?"

Man-Beast grunts again and then finally speaks for the first time. "I thought..."

"You thought I was hurting Miss Yin," Kylian finishes.

I expect him to show some embarrassment, but he doesn't. His balled-up fists just fall to the sides, but his head holds high.

Kylian continues, "I'm sorry to have scared you, Frank, but I just wanted to make it blatantly clear to Miss Kiara that she and her employees will be safe, even if it's from me endangering them. Please always react that way again if you get even the tiniest inkling that something might be wrong."

Frank takes another breath, giving me a once over and backs out.

"Oh my god! You could've given me some warning!" I yell, jumping to my feet and whacking Kylian's arm.

"Ow! Careful, Frank might hear you and come crashing in here to save me."

I shake my head in disbelief. "Nuh-uh. You said to protect me from you, not the other way around."

He lowers his voice until it's almost inaudible and I have to lean in to hear him. "That's because you don't need protection from me."

The words slice into me, and I spring back to avoid getting hurt, clearing my throat before I say, "That leads me to the last and most important condition."

He looks amused. It makes me want to slap him again. "Lay it on me."

I take a deep breath and hope to get through it in one breath before my courage gives out. "We agree that under no circumstances are we going to have a physical relationship. No kissing, no sex. No what happened yesterday. This is a purely professional relationship."

Kylian bridges the gap between us with one step, his hand coming up to cradle my head and he leans in, his mouth by my ear. Even before he speaks, my whole body is vibrating. Just the touch of his hand grazing the back of my neck sends reminders of what it felt like to be touched by him. "Do you really want me to promise that I'm never going to stand this close to you again?" he whispers.

My mouth opens, but no sound comes out.

He continues, "No. Deal. I am not signing anything that tells me that I have to keep my hands off you. Don't you know that I'd sign away my life to finally get to kiss you for the first time? Don't you know how much I want to do that?"

I force the question out of my mouth, "Are... you planning to... kiss me?"

He exhales; it whistles past my ear. "I'm saying I'm not making any deal that requires me to stay away from you. I'm a man of my word, and I promise you, I will not be able to keep myself away from you. What happened yesterday was just a prelude." He takes a deep breath, like he's breathing me in, and then pulls away with a sigh. "So it's up to you. But please don't make me sign something that will make me miserable for the rest of my life."

Sixteen
Kylian

I DRIVE KIARA BACK to her apartment after we end the discussion and I finish giving her a tour of the casino. In the car she sits with her arms folded, face scrunched in thought, no doubt thinking about what I'd said earlier, and, maybe, whether or not she should believe me.

But I know that every word had been the truth.

The minute I saw her at Amber, I knew I was done with the phase of my life where I try to push back my feelings for her. And those feelings were just exacerbated when I saw her face when she heard the explanation for the layout for the main game room. I knew that she understood what this project was all about. What it meant to me and how much of myself I had poured into it. This wasn't just any other tech acquisition whose sole purpose was to raise Baxter's portfolio, this was about doing something that fueled the soul as well.

Jade Bay and Watch have been the two ventures in the last five years that have meant the most to me.

And she gets it.

I glance over at her. She's still staring straight ahead and has a row of goosebumps traveling up her arm. I turn the air conditioning down, and she gives me a look of gratitude.

"You can turn it down yourself, you know. You don't have to wait for me," I say.

She shrugs. "But I don't want you to be hot."

"And I don't want you to be cold, Kiki."

I pull up outside her apartment building, then get out of the car to open the door for her. Once she gathers up her things, I take her hand and drop my car key and a security key tag into it.

Her face is a picture of confusion when she looks up at me. "Wha...?"

"You need a car. I have a lot of them. You can keep this, one or you can just use it until you find another one or they find your old one. Maybe Ananya could use it or one of your other employees. Either way, it's yours."

"Kylian. This car probably cost you $180,000. This could be sold and buy ten more cars."

"Then you can do that, too." I laugh, but she doesn't appreciate it. "Look. You need a car. You're busy. You don't have time to go get one. So take this one. Like I said, you don't have to keep it, but I'm sure that you're going to need a car in the coming days. After that, if you want to return it, that's fine. Just call my office, and someone will come pick it up. Or you can keep it and do whatever you like with it. It's yours."

She thinks about it and then nods, squeezing her hand around the keychain. "And this?" She hold up the security key card.

"You'll figure it out." And before she can go inside, I touch her forearm. "And one more thing. I want you to know something. I didn't make the deal about you and me for a good reason. This is going to happen. This thing between you and me. It's going to happen. You know that, right? Everything that gets in the way? We're going to figure it out. I know I hurt you five years ago. And I'm so sorry. You don't know how sorry I am. You don't know how much of my life has been about wanting to make it up to you. So now I will. Make it up to you. I'm going to show you that I know I made a mistake. And that everything I do... is going to be about showing you that I am in your life to stay."

I don't know how Kiara reacts after I tell her what I feel; I don't hang around to see if it's a look of disgust, rejection, or agreement on her face. I spin around and walk away as fast as I can without seeming like I'm fleeing, until I turn the corner onto the main road and let out the breath almost bursting in my lungs.

Part of me wants to run back and take back every word.

Part of me wants to run back and force her to tell me, right now, whether or not I've imagined everything I feel between us.

Part of me wants to run back to her and beg her to run away with me, away from everything that's clouding the inevitable, that we're supposed to be together.

And every single part of me wants to run back to her just because when I'm with her, everything is better.

Somehow in the last few days, I've become addicted to the only thing I've ever forced out of my life. I flag down a cab and sink into the worn leather, letting the cool air dry the sweat on my face.

The buzz in my pocket has me whipping out the phone, hoping to see her name on the screen and then remember that I don't even have her cell number. The name that does appear dumps a figurative bucket of ice water over my head.

"Gerald" flashes as I watch the call ring out and go to voicemail. Uncle Gerry. My father's younger brother, my grandfather's only other child, and the interim CEO for another year until my brother Kingsley turns forty-two years old and the board keeps their promise to my grandfather and votes him in as the CEO. The deal had been brokered by my grandfather who had raised Kingsley to take his reins after my father decided that he no longer wanted to work for the family company. Gerry's interim term was to appease the board who were afraid that Kingsley would be too young to take over. The idea was that he would mature into the role under the tutelage of Uncle Gerry, or so that was the plan. Instead, what we've been doing for the last few years is fending off attack after attack by Uncle Gerry to undermine Kingsley's and the rest of our leadership in our respective regions.

Just a few months ago, Gerald had colluded with Clarissa Masters, the only daughter of Terry Masters, the director of the board, to blackmail Damien. She tried to force him to take her back after he broke up their relationship of convenience under the threat that if Damien didn't marry her, she'd convince her father to throw his support behind Uncle Gerry. Instead, Damien, with the help of My-Linh, proved that he was an asset to Baxter Enterprises all on his own. And Terry, hardly the family man, disowned his own daughter in a show of support for the Baxter brothers.

That was the last we'd heard of Uncle Gerry's scheming for a while, but there had been rumblings that he was back to his old ways. Our father is an honest, hardworking man whose life had been derailed by his own marriage of convenience, but he only had good intentions at heart. Uncle Gerry, on the other hand, is sneaky, sleazy, a slimebag in every respect, and that is both in and out of the boardroom. How our grandfather had any part in his conception and raising completely eludes us. But what Gerry lacks in business acumen and actual work, he makes up for with knowing people's weaknesses and how to drive a sledgehammer right through the heart of them. Most of our interactions are isolated to weekly company briefings and official board meetings. And that is more than enough. I don't know why he's calling, and frankly in this case, I feel like ignorance is definitely bliss.

The phone buzzes, he's calling again. I have to give it to him that he's tenacious. What he doesn't know is that my brothers and I will die before we leave grandfather's company under his leadership.

I grit my teeth and press the accept button, already bracing for the sound of his grating voice.

"Yeah?" I answer with the most civility that I can summon.

"Kylian, my boy. You're a hard man to catch!"

I blanch at the cliché. "Maybe you need to work out more. I'm actually very slow on my feet."

He pauses, trying to come up with a response. "Heh. Well, I guess I could try to hit the company gym more than once a year."

He's so dumb he doesn't even know that I'm mocking him. "What do you want, Gerald?"

"Gerald! Remember when you used to call me Uncle Gerry?"

"I'd rather not. Look, I'm about to start a meet—"

"You can't take a minute to talk to your boss?" he interrupts.

My teeth gnash so loudly I'm sure he can hear me. *Your boss.* That's the phrase he likes to throw around when he's feeling like we've got the upper hand, whether it's because he can't understand what we're trying to explain about a business report or when he thinks someone else in the conversation prefers us to him.

"What would *my boss* like to talk to me about?" I say, dripping with condescension.

"Well, I was just wondering, last week you mentioned that you were working on making a deal with Yin Tech about Watch. Any update on that?"

I curse my past self for having brought it up before something was set in stone. "When I have one to give you, you'll get it."

He clicks his tongue. "Yin Tech is an ally of Baxter. It shouldn't be too hard, right?"

"I'm more than aware of Yin Tech's relationship to Baxter. It's my relationship. I am the Baxter with whom Nathan Yin has the relationship."

"Yes, well, it's more than just your little friendship with Nathan Yin. We have other networks with them. Like the one that tells me that Yin Tech is more than willing to sell Watch. So if you can't make this happen, whose fault is that going to be? Not one that the board is going to take too well, I think."

It's good he's on the other side of the world or else I'd lodge my phone right up his ass. "Is that a threat?" I hiss. I know without an ounce of doubt that it is, but there's something about making it clear to him that we always know what he's doing.

"Not at all," he says with a voice thick with sarcasm. "It's just a little friendly reminder from your dear ol' uncle."

I've never wished more that Dad was an only child.

"Well, I think you can imagine what I'm going to do with that unsolicited reminder, Uncle," I add, matching him for sarcasm. I'm the youngest Baxter brother, and if he thinks he should be aiming for me to be the weak link, then he doesn't know a damn thing about us. I'm the one who doesn't give a fuck what anyone thinks, in or out of the business. And the one who will defend his brothers with his last breath because I know they would all do the same for me.

"Okay, well, that's all I wanted to say. What meeting are you having now?"

"Read your fucking memos for once," I snap and hang up the phone, fumes threatening to waft out of my ears

The conversation was worse than I had expected. I don't know who his source is at Yin Tech, and I am going to have to do some digging, but he was obviously angling to swoop in and rip the acquisition right out of my hands.

Over my dead, fucking, rotting, stinking body.

Watch is my baby, and the only reason I want to bring it under the Baxter umbrella is because I need the capital to take it to the stratosphere. But it will still be under my control. And if the board doesn't agree to that, then I will sell every organ I have to keep it for myself.

The cab stops outside my apartment building, and I tuck a wad of cash into the driver's hand and jump out of the cab. Despite the heat prickling my skin, I shiver, the lingering effects of my conversation with Gerry still trickling through my veins like liquid hydrogen. He's a piece of work.

We are going to have to keep an eye on him.

Just another thing to worry about.

Seventeen

Kiara

I DON'T KNOW HOW long I've been standing outside my apartment holding Kylian's car key in my hand after he turns the corner and I can no longer see him. His words, however, echo in my brain over and over like a broken record, singing my favorite song ever.

I had never thought that him sharing our inexplicable attraction that night in London had been anything but physical and that what had happened yesterday had been anything but him wrapping up unfinished business or a boost to his male ego, or a little combination of both. I had never thought that he'd wanted anything more to do with me than some bragging rights. But to say what he just did... everything has changed. Every cell in my body had screamed to grab his hand to stop him from leaving.

And now he's gone.

What the fuck am I doing?

Hadn't he shown how much he had changed since London?

Hadn't everything he'd done in the last few days shown that he was no longer that smug son of a bitch? That maybe, just maybe, now when he said something, he meant it.

I squeeze my hand, and the end of the key digs into my palm, painfully pulling me out of my day dream.

"Fuck," I murmur under my breath.

I have spent so much time trying to pretend that every single breath I take isn't lined with the whisper of his name. And now... I turn the key card over in my hand. It says "Baxter Tower" on it. A key card to his apartment building. To him.

"Fuck!" This time, I yell the word as my body moves into action. I jump into his car and don't even bother putting on my seatbelt and turn into traffic.

"What the fuck am I doing?" I say and then instantly push the thought out of my brain. No thinking. My whole life is spent thinking and overthinking every single decision I make. Maybe there's some sort of poetic beauty about the one time I'm going to be spontaneous is going to change the entire trajectory of my life.

It takes a few minutes of sitting in traffic for me to realize that I hadn't needed to adjust my seat or mirrors when I'd gotten in Kylian's car. A feeling of something warm but also sharp lodges itself in my ribcage as understanding looms, that Kylian had adjusted the seat according to my body. He'd gotten it almost right, it takes only the slightest adjustment of my passenger side mirror before it feels like I'm sitting in my own car.

No one in my life had ever shown me such thoughtfulness before. Not even my own family. My foot presses on the gas pedal a little harder, and the car lurches forward.

I've always known his address, of course, Nathan passed along invited to me to all of Kylian's parties. I had never considered ever attending a single one.

And yet now I'm going there of my own accord. What I'm going to say once I get there, I don't know. I guess I just need to look into his face one more time to see if he really means what he says when he promises not to hurt me this time.

I arrive at his apartment sooner than I expect before the right words have formed in my head. The car screeches to a stop in front the valet station and I throw the keys at the attendant.

"Miss!" he yells after me, stopping me from barging into the building's lobby. "Isn't this Mr. Baxter's car?"

"Yup!" I call over my shoulder. "But it's mine now. Park it somewhere close please. I might not be here long."

I run inside where I'm stopped by a short, stocky doorman. "Hello, Miss, can I help you?"

I try to sidestep him, but he blocks me. "Yes, I'm going up to Kylian's apartment," I say, short-breathed.

Something about the way I refer to him by his first name makes the doorman's eyes widen. "Oh, well, please... see the woman at the reception, and she will call up to see if he is taking any visitors."

I wave the security card in his face. Rudely. On purpose. I've always found that people tend to be more amenable if they're caught off guard.

"Kylian gave me this, so I can go up to his apartment any time I want. Would you like to call up and tell him that you stopped me from going up there?" The doorman looked so scared I was almost afraid for him. I don't mean to cause him any problems, but I need to get there now. So I change tacks. "Okay, look, if you must, get someone to come up with me, but I'm not going to linger here and wait for you to call him. If you have problems with that, you can call the police and tell them Kiara Yin of Yin Tech is here."

His face instantly pales. "Oh. Um, Miss Kiara..." He sighs and waves the security guard over. "Please take Miss Kiara up to Mr. Baxter's apartment please. Just make sure she gets there okay."

I grin. This man is both smart and tactful. "You are wasted working here. Call my brother, Nathan Yin, if you're looking for another job. Tell him Kiara sent you."

"Really? I thought you were bringing me more employees, not trying to steal mine," a male voice jokes.

I whip around, and he's there.

"What are you doing here, Kiara?" he asks, his face neutral but his eyes dancing with curiosity.

My voice sticks in my throat, and all I can do is hold up the security key card he pressed into my hand before he left.

"You left this at my place. I thought you might need it."

The corners of his mouth twitch as the lobby around us goes quiet.

I lean in and whisper. "Can we... go somewhere quiet to talk?"

He bites back and smiles. "Er, actually, no. I can't. I don't have my key card. Someone had to let me into my own apartment before. I'm just down here to get another printed out."

Embarrassed, I stretch out my arm, holding his card out to him.

He looks at it and then back up at me before he shakes his head and turns to the desk. "Miss Lu, do you have a new card for me?" The woman at the reception desk hands it to him wordlessly, and he flashes his smile at her in thanks. "You keep that one," he says to me. And then without another word, he grabs my wrist and leads me over to an elevator.

Once it arrives, he gently presses his hand against my back and guides me inside. It feels like I'm watching everything from out of my body. Everything feels surreal and yet hyperreal all at once. His hand feels feather-light against me, but then like it's searing into my skin at the same time.

He presses the highest floor's button and scans his card against the panel. We don't say a word until the elevator comes to a smooth stop thirty-three floors later.

The door opens into a small foyer area that leads into a spacious living room

"Kiki. Come in," he says once he realizes that I'm not following him into his apartment.

I follow him at half speed down into a sunken living area that is surrounded by floor-to-ceiling windows that open up into a panoramic view of the city below from up here in Victoria Peak. If I looked hard enough, I could probably see my own apartment from here.

He could see me. If he wanted to.

"Kylian," I say because that's the only word in my brain. *Kylian.*

"Yes, Kiki?" His insistence on using my nickname isn't helping the neurons in my brain fire. He pours himself a drink and lifts the bottle to me, offering me some.

"No, thank you." I couldn't swallow right now if I wanted to,

He finishes his drink and walks back to me. For the first time since I arrived at his apartment building, I notice what he's wearing.

Dressed only in a pair of gray sweatpants and a white undershirt, every single line of his body is accentuated, from the toned muscle of his thighs to the angled curve of his oblique. His blond hair is wet and slicked back so that for once his eyes aren't partially covered by his fringe, and I can see every microexpression in his face. There is the slightest hint of a five o'clock shadow over his jaw, and I wonder what it would feel like rubbing against my face.

"What are you doing here, Kiara?" he asks again, his voice light, but the twitch in his jaw and the way he shoves his hands into his track pants pockets betray his fake nonchalance. He takes a step forward, and I take one back. "Did you want to tell me something?" he prompts.

I open my mouth, hoping that it will kick-start my tongue to start moving, but it's dry, stuck to the roof of my mouth.

He takes another step forward, and again, I step back and up against a wall behind me.

And another step. There's nowhere for me to go now.

He's so close now I can smell the faint fragrance of his soap. It's soft, clean, probably something as simple as Dove.

"I-Is th-that D-Dove?" I stutter, completely surprising the both of us.

A frown. "Dove?"

"Your soap?"

He laughs.

Throws his head back, grabs his chest, and laughs. It fills the room and everything in it, including me

"Why are you laughing?" I growl, confused about the response. I've never been one to take a joke about myself well. "She takes herself too seriously," is what everyone always said about me.

"I'm laughing because you came all the way over here to ask me what soap I use?"

"It's not that far," I sulkily reply.

But somehow it's broken the ice between us. He looks more relaxed, even if his eyes have darkened, deep like there's a secret he knows that he's waiting for me to find out.

"You came here to ask about what I told you before I left."

My mouth doesn't answer, but my head does in a nod.

"What do you want to tell me, Kiki? I can't say it for you."

No going back now. "Did you mean everything you said?"

He nods. Twice. "Every single word. We should be together. We should've been together all this time. I didn't know it that day at Bottle. But I knew it the moment you walked away. And every moment since."

He says it like it's not a bombshell. As if it's something we both should've known all along. The laissez-faire way he says it makes me doubt him. He can't be this sure about us. "I don't believe you."

He smiles. It has the effect of turning my insides to molten lava. "Yes, you do. You're just scared to."

The claws of the past dig into me, warning me. "No, Kylian. You hurt me."

The smile falls, and his eyes now flood with regret. "I know. God, I know. I'm so sorry. I was so confused. I didn't know what to do. And the only thing I could think of doing was hurt you in a way that you'd never want to see me again. That night outside of the night club, I thought it was just an anomaly. We were drunk, the music, the atmosphere. And I didn't want to fuck things up with my best friend over a one-night stand, no matter how amazing it would've been."

An image of my brother's face appears in the space between us: angry, disappointed, hurt.

"And how do you feel now?"

Kylian shrugs. "I love your brother. He is my best friend and one of the best men I've ever known. And my life would fucking suck without his friendship. But this thing between us... it's real, Kiki. And we deserve the chance to see what it's about. Don't you agree?"

Nathan's face disappears, and I'm so close, I'm so close to believing. But then the memory of that night when he told me to meet him... and then he was there with someone else. The pain comes rushing back, everything hurts. I shove him, stepping away from the wall, gasping for breath. What am I doing? How can I even be considering this?

"No!" I yell. "I can't... I can't be hurt by you again." I run toward the elevator.

"Kiara!" He chases after me, grabbing me around the waist and pulling me against him. "Dammit, Kiara, please!" he begs, spinning me around to face him. His fingers grip my chin hard, forcing me to look up at him. "Look at me! Will you look at me? Can't you see that I regret hurting you more than anything I've ever done in my life?"

His voice, husky with desperation, moves me. The same way his eyes are begging me, pleading with me, to believe him. He looks almost... hurt. Suddenly, all those years I wished to witness him feel just a tiny bit of the hurt he caused me vanishes.

At this moment, there's no past, just us and now.

"I believe you, Kylian." I exhale. "I believe you."

The words hang between us like a balloon, and then, in slow motion, it pops, and everything held within, the secrets, the longing, the pain, explodes.

His breath is ragged as he stares at me, taking in what I've said.

And then, finally, he kisses me.

Kisses me like our lives depend on it; hard, passionate, his lips press against mine as my hands come around to grip his biceps, digging my nails deep into his muscle fibers as he kisses me.

"God, Kiara..." he murmurs against my lips as he drags a breath into his lungs. "Sweet Kiki, I've wanted to do this for so long."

I want to admit that it's the same for me, but I don't want to pull my lips from his.

I could lose myself in this moment forever, his hand sliding down from my chin to grasp around my neck, feeling my pulse against his palm.

He suddenly pulls away, and he stares, not into my eyes, but down at my mouth. Like he just realized we've finally kissed for the first time.

He runs the pad of his thumb over my already swollen bottom lip and then lifts it to his mouth, sucking in the aftermath of our kiss.

"You drive me fucking crazy, sweet angel. Do you have any idea?"

With his hand still gripping the base of my neck, he leans in, his mouth brushing the side of my ear as he growls, "I'm going to make you mine. Do you hear me? Nothing, no one that came before is ever going to matter. And when you think about anyone touching you, it's going to be my mouth, my hands, my cock in you."

Everything I ever thought I knew about Kylian dies in that moment.

All that chattiness, the golden halo floating above his head, the so-called golden retriever energy dissolves into the burning ether of the man in front of me now. The way his hand is bruising a ring around my neck, his words imprinting on me, the way his eyes dare me to fight him, is who he is to me.

"Nod if you understand, Kiara."

But he doesn't even give me a chance to before his mouth is on mine again, nipping at my bottom lip still hot from the touch of his thumb before.

His hand not around my throat drops down to slide under the hem of my dress. "Are you going to be wet for me, angel?"

The way he says "wet for me" makes me want to push his head down and make him recreate the last orgasm he gave me when we were in this situation. But he changes the script, and without warning, slides two fingers deep inside me making me scream.

My back bows from the sensation of him inside me. "Fuck! Kylian!"

He hums his approval. "Hmmm, that's right, Kiara. You just keep screaming my name and remembering who this body belongs to now."

My legs instinctively widen, making room for him. He knew I'd be dripping wet for him or else there's no way his two fingers would've fit inside me without any preparation.

He gently slides his fingers in and out of me, slowly, methodically. A soft whimper escapes my lips, partly of arousal, partly frustration.

"I know, baby, trust me, we need to do this. I don't want to hurt you when I fuck you for the first time, okay?" His thumb moves to press against my clit, and I struggle to hold back a moan. "Move your hips, baby, rub your clit against my finger. Show me how you move."

My core lowers as I feel my hips move in a circle up and down as I rub myself on him. With each rotation, he pumps his fingers in and then out of me again. The rhythm builds, and each time I draw a circle with my hips, I think I'm going to fall over the edge. My first orgasm always comes easily, but it's not always as intense. I already know, though, that I might not ever recover from this one.

The last time he was making me come, it was about an urgent need that had been building inside me for so long. This time, it's about a conscious choice that we've both made. To fall together.

He kisses my cheek as he presses his fingers deeper into me. A chaste action that feels so fucking dirty. "That's it, baby. You feel so good moving against me. Is this how you're going to move with my cock inside you? Are you going to ride me like you're doing now? Use me to come all over my cock?"

My head threatens to tilt back, but his hand gripping my throat holds me in place. Instead, I force my eyes open and look up at him.

His chest rumbles as he watches me. "Don't stop moving. If you stop, I'll stop. Is that what you want?" he growls so low I can barely hear him.

"No."

He nods his approval, and something inside me aches to please him.

I concentrate on pressing my clit harder against his hand, and the whites of his eyes become almost invisible as his pupils dilate watching me.

"I'm going to come," I say in a strained moan.

His eyes darken. "Did I say you could come?"

The question alone steals the little breath I have left from my lungs, but then he squeezes the hand at my neck.

I shake my head.

He relaxes his hand. "That's right. No, I didn't. But you will come soon, angel, don't worry. You're going to come so fucking hard, but it's going to be with my cock deep inside you, not my fingers. Understand?"

I nod, eyes wide. My hips frozen in place.

I don't want to know what's going to happen if I stop because I can't go back from here.

"Kylian?"

"Yes, angel?"

"Make me yours."

Something shifts in the air as soon as I say it, and he kisses me, crushing my lips hard as he pushes his track pants down his legs and steps out of them. I catch a glimpse of his cock as he pulls his hand away from my neck, and I let out a desperate whimper, missing his touch already.

"I'll put it right back, I just have to do this." There's the sound of a foil wrapper tearing.

And then, just like he promised, he's right back against me, his hand tighter on my neck than it was before.

"I didn't know my angel was such a kinky girl," he whispers.

"I didn't know I was until your hand was around my neck."

His eyes close, then suddenly his fingers are inside me again, pushing deeper, stretching me. "Ready?"

I don't have an answer. Physically, I don't know. Emotionally, fuck yes.

Not that it matters. He rips his fingers out of me, and when he rams back into me, it's his cock. Hard. Thick. Inside me.

He throws his head back and lets out a roar. "'Fuuuuuccck."

I'd do the same except I can't think of anything besides that Kylian is inside me.

Through gritted teeth, he growls, "If you need me to go slow, you're going to need to tell me. Because I don't think I can otherwise."

I touch his cheek. "Take me. Hard."

And he does.

Eyes locked on mine, his cock hammers into me. There's not a hint of grace in what he's doing, but I couldn't want for anything else. I don't want grace, or tenderness, or consideration, or mercy. I want him so aroused, so primal, so needy for me that all he cares about is fucking me until we both come, screaming, gasping, exhausted.

I rock my hips to meet his, and everything burns, sometimes a little less and then a lot more. Every time he pulls back, my pussy feels like it's gasping for breath, only to choke on the exhale when he slams back in. It pushes me back to the brink of coming. But all I hear in my head is him saying, "Did I say you could come?"

My eyes squeeze shut as I try to hold back, clenching to stop the flow, but it just emphasizes the thickness of his cock drilling in and out of me. And every time I clench, he lets out a groan telling me that he feels it, too.

Finally, when I think I can't take another second, he slides inside me, then stops. One hand squeezes just enough to not cut off all my breath as he braces his other hand against the wall behind me, his eyes locked on mine.

My mouth turns desert dry as my orgasm claws from my core outward through every vein, every capillary, only the fear of disappointing him stopping me, begging to be let free.

His forehead glistens from the effort of fucking me as my pussy cleaves to his cock, pulsing and gripping him from the inside.

"Say it. Beg me to let you come."

There's not more time for niceties and stubbornness. I stare back at him through glazed eyes. "Please?" I choke out.

The hand around my neck tightens in answer.

His voice whirls in my head as he asks, "And who do your orgasms belong to?"

He pushes away from the wall and reaches down between us and pinches my clit. "I said, who owns your orgasms, angel?"

It's all I need to tumble over the cliff and into the climax that feels like it's been building forever.

"Oh fuck, Kylian. They're yours. My orgasms are yours. My body is yours."

Through the haze, I see him watching me, his face flushed, teeth gritted as he bears down with his own orgasm. His hand clamps dangerously tight around my throat, making everything all the more intense.

"Oh fuck..." I murmur over and over, the pleasure rocking through me, even as he pins me against the wall as he resumes grinding his cock in and out of me.

"Fuck," he groans. "Kiara, you look so fucking hot, angel, coming so hard on my cock," he murmurs.

My shaking hand reaches up to his cheek again, this time to say, "Come for me, Kylian. Come for me. It's my turn to watch you come for me."

The words flick a switch in his brain, and he rams into me, two, three, four more times, and then he lets go of my throat and pulls me into his arms as his entire body stiffens like a frozen moment in time and then jerks as he grunts out his orgasm.

"Fuck. Kiara. My sweet angel. God..." his words come out shaky, interspersed between heavy breaths.

I breathe with him as his climax fades, and his whole body shivers in my arms

My hand strokes the back of his head, damp from the shower he had before I arrived and the sweat from fucking me.

"Shhh," I mumble, although what I really want to say is that I've become addicted to the way he calls my name when he comes.

We stand there, leaning against the wall for how many minutes, I don't know. But finally, when he does pull his head up, the trademark Kylian smirk isn't on his lips.

"Hey... what's wrong?" I ask, the orgasm cloud already dissipating and reality sinking in.

"Not a damn thing. But..." He runs a gentle finger along the redness of my neck. "Did I hurt you?"

I'm smiling for the first time. "Didn't you promise that you'd never hurt me again?'

"Yup. And I meant it."

"I'm older now. If you broke a promise to me only minutes after declaring it, do you really think that I would let you get away with it?" I end it with a small wink that seems to drain the worry from him.

"Well," he clears his throat and straightens up, "I am incredibly good in bed. I can see why you'd give up your morals to get a little bit of this." He runs his hands over his still-covered chest while sticking his tongue out and giving me an exaggerated wink.

The relief seeps into my body. This is the Kylian I know. I guess I don't mind if he's a little intense during sex, but he wouldn't be him if he wasn't annoying me with stupid jokes.

"What are you thinking?" he says as he pulls up his track pants and smooths my dress down, picking up my panties from the floor and tucking them into his pocket.

"Um, those are mine." I point to the lacy hem still poking out of his pocket. "Why did you put them in your pocket?"

He waves my question away and instead replies with, "I asked you what you were thinking?"

"You ignored my question!"

"Er, excuse me, you ignored my question first!"

My face rearranges itself into a scowl. "Well, I've forgotten what your question was now. So, while I try to remember, why don't you answer my question first?"

"No problem. My question was 'what are you thinking?'"

"Okay, well, technically you just asked it again, and so my question now came before yours. You answer, and then I'll answer."

"Well," he pulls my panties out of his pocket and tucks it under his chin and adopts a thinker pose, "I can't say I remember what your question was about now. While I think about it, you should answer my question."

"Well, now I've forgotten agai—" I can't even finish the sentence because we both lose our battle with laughter and let out loud hoots and snorts.

As soon as Kylian manages to take a breath, he yells, "Kiki, you are so fucking stubborn!"

I gasp, both for breath and in indignation. "Me? Your middle name is Stubborn!"

His mouth drops in shock. "Excuuuuse me? I can't believe you don't know my middle name!"

My hands brace on my waist. "Excuuuuse me, I just told you what it is."

"No, my real, non-insulting middle name."

I hate to admit defeat, so I turn the tables on him. "What's my middle name, then?" And punctuate it with a tongue poke.

The second he smirks, I know I might be in trouble. "It's Cát Vy. Your father's college roommate was given the honor of giving you your middle name. He's Vietnamese, and he chose the name because it's alliterative. *K*iara, *C*át Vy... but it also means something very important. It means lucky. Or a child blessing their family with luck. Sometimes you use it when you don't want to go by Kiara, especially in London because you think it's harder for English speakers to pronounce and therefore they're less likely to use it because you don't like it when people call out to you. You think if they want to speak to you, they should approach you politely."

Now it's my turn for my mouth to drop open. "Did you just Google that?"

He laughs and takes my hand, turns it over, and drops a kiss on the inside of my wrist. "When are you going to realize, I meant it when I said that I remember everything."

Eighteen

Kylian

When Kiara was fifteen years old, I caught her cutting school, stumbling around downtown with a bottle of cheap bourbon in her hand, surrounded by a bunch of her deadbeat friends. I had gotten so mad, she had so much potential, could've done absolutely anything that she wanted. But she was always getting into some sort of trouble, at home and in school. Nathan blamed it on being the younger child, and as the youngest of four brothers, something about her behavior had resonated with me. But that being said, when I'd yelled out "Kiara" in front of her friends, she'd looked at me with such venom that later, when I'd driven her home, I asked her why she'd reacted like that. After a battle not unlike the one we just had about answering a damn question, she'd admitted that at school, everyone called her "Cát Vy" and, she liked it because she felt she could pretend to be someone else while she was there, away from the shadows of being Nathan Yin's little sister.

We'd stopped for a coffee and a sandwich to help her sober up, and she'd pointed me to the park next to an elementary school. Black, no sugar, she'd asked for. And then after one sip, she'd stolen my sugar and cream packed before I even noticed. We'd sat drinking the coffee in silence, watching the kids being let out of school and all the parents waving their children from their cars.

"I love this place. It reminds me of when Dad or Nathan would come to see me at lunch sometimes and other times after school to pick me up. Sometimes they'd let me stay a little longer after school while I played with my friends, but they were never too far away, usually waiting with a drink or snack for when I was tired out from climbing the monkey bars. It was so nice to know that there was someone waiting."

Later when I'd dropped her off, she'd made me promise I wouldn't tell Nathan about cutting school or else she would tell him that I was the one who'd given her the alcohol. To this day, I don't know if it was an empty threat or not, but the look on her face surely hadn't looked like she was kidding.

The thought brings me back to the moment, both of us in varying states of disarray, her panties in my hand, standing in the entrance to my living room, having had sex. I tuck the undergarment back into my pocket and gently take her hand.

"Come on. I'll take you for a tour of the rest of my apartment. You haven't seen it, have you?"

She shakes her head. "And I hear that I'm one of only a handful of people in Hong Kong who can actually say that," she says, her tone bone dry.

"Hey, whose fault is that? I asked Nathan to extend an invitation to you every time."

"Yup. He did."

And as has happened every time her brother's name has been mentioned, the air becomes a little heavier, making it a little harder to breathe. We'll have to talk about this at some point. But not now.

She squeezes my hand as we take the two steps down into my living area that is sparsely furnished with three large, gray couches positioned around a round wooden coffee table that has followed me to every place I've ever lived. It used to sit as a small game table in the salon of my family home in London. We would sit there playing cards or board games long after we should've gone to sleep. It's the single object in my apartment that reminds me of my mother. On the day she'd gone to the small designer's studio to pick it out, she'd taken me. She didn't often play the games with us; her favorite game was to choose which child she was going to shower her affections on while neglecting the others. I was only three years old that day, but I remember it like it was yesterday. So when I graduated high school and moved to the United States, I took the table with me, although she had long left us to fend for ourselves. I'd taken it into the college maintenance department's workshop and begged them to cut it down to a coffee table height. On the rare occasion it stirs up old feelings of bitterness and resentment, I just remind myself that, in the end, it's just a beautiful table.

"That table is exquisite," Kiara says, walking over and running her fingertip along the beveled edge. "Where did you get it?"

I blink, making sure my face carries a neutral expression before I answer. "My mom bought it for our game room when I was little."

"Oh, Nathan said your mother... isn't around? Is she still alive?"

"Oh, yes, very alive and well and causing problems for her four sons and however many former and current step children she has, too, no doubt. She was never one not to call in any favor anyone owed her."

Kiara's eyes widen. "Wow."

I wince. I hadn't meant to share so much. "I'm sorry, I don't usually talk about her, and when I do... it's usually with the level of vitriol you just heard."

Kiara just waves her hand as if saying don't worry about it. "Trust me. I get mommy issues."

That surprises me. Nathan and Kiara's mother was generally accepted as a pleasant lady with no obvious personality flaws that made her stand out in the community. Rich, liked to throw her money around, but not in an obnoxious way. Generous. And incredibly loved by her family. And she was always very kind to me, commiserating when my mother swung in and out of my life, usually between husbands, demanding attention, or money, or both.

"Want to talk about it?" I ask as I walk over to her, pressing my hand against the small of her back and leading her over to the bar. My hand fits perfectly there in that curve, snug like her body was molded to fit my hand.

"Not even a little bit." Then she leans back so slightly I can only sense it in the way her back presses against my hand. An involuntary action of comfort at my touch.

So I do the thing that I think will bring me comfort; I bury my face in her hair, inhaling deeply. Her hair has always been her most standout feature. Long with a rare kink pattern in it that makes it flow down her back in a black, wavy cascade. And it smells like it looks: soft, feminine, beautiful.

A small "mmmmmm" rumbles out of my chest.

She pulls away and smiles up at me. "What are you doing?"

"What I've wanted to do for a really fucking long time?" I laugh. "Your hair is just stunning, Kiki."

I'm awarded with a beaming, proud smile. "Thank you. I grew it myself."

Now it's my turn to reward her with a laugh that fills my whole body. "I'm the one who's supposed to make the jokes around here, thank you very much!"

"Well, you weren't doing your job, so I was taking up some of the slack."

"Oh. Ouch." I clutch at my chest and feign a mortal injury, falling to my knees onto the rug.

She just stands there and looks down at me, completely unmoved. "If you die, can I have your couch?"

"No." I playfully pout, not-so-surreptitiously trying to look up her dress. "I'm going to be buried with it."

"Fine, that one, then." She points to one of the other identical couches.

"Sorry, taking that one, too. What if I want to choose when I'm stuck down there?"

Her face scrunches up. "You're very needy for a dead person."

She doesn't get another word in before I reach up and grab her hand and pull her down onto my lap, cradling her head with my hand. "Only for you, Kiki. Needy only for you." Then I lean in and kiss her, and it's just as thrilling as it was the first time.

"Hmm," she murmurs against my lips.

"Everything okay?" I whisper against her cheek.

"Yes. You... are delicious." The words come out small and shy.

I kiss her again, pulling her up so that she's kneeling, allowing me to lift her dress over her head. I can't believe I've already been inside her without even seeing her completely naked.

The dress now gone, I see she's not wearing a bra and her breasts are small and tipped with light pink nipples that stand out against her pale, opaque skin. The pad of my thumb aches to touch it, but instead, I lean in and flick the very tip of my tongue across the very tip of her nipple instead.

Her breath stills in her throat, and her hands are instantly in my hair.

I reach out to lick her nipple again, this time with a long, slow, decadent lick, imprinting the shape of her nipple into my memory. It hardens into a pebble under my tongue, and her arousal at my touch stokes my own need.

She moves so that she leans back, bracing her hands on her ankles, offering herself up to me.

And, leaning over her, I accept. Hungrily, needily, burying my face in her skin, inhaling her scent, her sweat, drawing my oxygen from her cells. My mouth finds her breast, sucking on her nipple, savoring the way it hardens even more with each flick of my tongue. Her soft moans tornado around my head, and I'm lost.

I force myself away from her nipple to kiss my way down her body.

Her skin is taut under my lips, slightly salty from the sweat of our last fuck.

Knowing what is coming, she leans back even more, holding herself up by bracing her elbows on the floor, her knees sliding wider apart, her pussy lips slightly agape, already glistening.

My tongue traces the gap between her pussy lips without dipping too far, making her shiver at my touch.

"Your pussy is fucking pretty, angel. I could sit here and do this all day. And one day I will. Lick you until you pass out from coming on my face."

And then my tongue slides deep past her pussy lips and against her clit. I'm careful not to spread her with my fingers. I want the only thing she comes from this time to be my tongue on her clit, showing her that's all I need to make her come harder than she ever has in her life.

My face buries against her as I press my tongue flat against her clit. Soft moans envelope me as she grinds on me, just like she did before, circling her hips, mashing her pubis against my face as my tongue laps at her.

"That's good, angel. Just like that. Fuck my face."

I don't know if she can hear my muffled words, but the way her movements quicken tells me that she does. I settle onto my stomach on the floor for traction with both of my hands reaching around to cup her ass, lifting her hips up so that my mouth can push harder against her.

"Uhhhh. Kylian. Fuck..." The words come out barely intelligible. "I want to... I need to come."

I want to draw this out, but I can't. My cock is aching in my pants, and I need to fuck her, but not before she comes. Not before she screams my name while my mouth is on her clit.

"Come, baby... Come for me. Scream my name, angel."

With that, I grind my tongue against her, shaking my head side to side, catching her clit on all sides, her body vibrating around me as her ass trembles under my hands, urging her to her orgasm. "Fucckkkkk k.... Kylian. Oh god, I'm coming, oh fuck!"

I don't stop.

I can't.

Nothing can physically stop me from touching her.

My tongue dips down to collect the cum in my mouth, and I drink her, parched. Then two fingers ram into her.

"Ahhh!" she screams as I curl them up, pressing against her G spot as I push up onto my knees, my fingers still buried into her. With the other hand, I slip my pants down past my waist, and then in one movement, I pull her up so her back is against my chest, and she's perched over me.

"Fucking hell, Kiara. Your fucking pussy is so perfect for my cock."

Sitting like this with her knees on either side of me sitting flush on my lap, my cock deep inside her, her pussy is vice-tight around me,

She reaches back, bracing her hand on my thighs as she lifts up and down, my hands coming around to cup her breasts. Her movements are fluid, sensual, a fucking siren calling me to ravage her.

She squeezes around me, milking me as I suck on the back of her neck.

I might fucking faint.

"Ride me, baby," I growl into her ear. "Show me how much you love my cock in your tight little pussy."

My words spur her on, and her head leans back on my shoulder as I ram my hips up, meeting her with my thrusts, my cock pounding into her, her warm wetness driving me fucking insane.

"Kylian..." she moans, her breath hot against my face.

"Open your eyes, angel. I want to watch you as you come." Every word takes almost inhuman strength.

She obeys, eyes lidded with arousal. "I'm so close. Your cock is so thick inside me."

The way she says "your cock" almost completely tears my restraint to pieces. "I'm close, too, but I can't come inside you."

She looks up at me. "But I want you to. I'm on the pill."

I grit my teeth as I confess, "I haven't been with anyone for a long time."

"Me either. Over a year," she adds.

The irrational thought that she's been with other men rips through me, injecting an acidic venom into my veins, and I drive it out of my mind by pistoning myself into her in a punishing rhythm.

"You're such a little slut for me, aren't you, angel?" My teeth dig into her shoulder, marking her as mine. Fucking mine. "Come for me, baby."

As if she can sense my jealousy in the way I take her, she whispers, "And only you, Kylian."

I pick up speed to finish us off, my fingers finding her clit, pinching it as I try to quench my need for her by making her come.

"Oh god!" she screams, almost deafening me as she climaxes. I wrap my arms around her stomach, holding her to me as we lose all sense of rhyme and reason.

"Fuck. Kiara. Baby..." I grunt, feeling her pussy ripple around me, and I come with her, my hips jerking as I empty myself inside her. "Baby... baby... my angel." My body hums with the pleasure of fucking her.

I fall to the side, exhausted, and take her with me, keeping us connected, my hardness taking its time to soften.

She curls up next to me on the rug, her breaths slowly subsiding.

"Your pussy is perfect for me, angel."

She purrs as I stroke her hair. Then sometime later in the haze of the aftermath, we fall asleep.

**

The moon is staring at us through my window when I feel her stir later as she tries to free herself of my arms. That doesn't work for me, so I pull her closer.

"No. Don't go," I murmur against her shoulder.

A little giggle vibrates through her body and against my chest. "I have to use the bathroom."

"No, you don't. Hold it."

She wriggles a bit, and I stop it by squeezing her more tightly, which elicits a little adorable yelp. "Kylian! I have been holding it. Trust me, any longer and you're not going to want to be buried with this rug."

"Fuck the rug, I'll get another one. Just don't leave."

"Kylian!" She finally manages to wriggle free and gets up after slapping me gently on the chest. "Where is your bathroom?" She jumps up and down.

I shrug. "Don't have one. Might as well stay here."

"This is not funny, Kylian!" She runs into another room.

"That... is not the bathroom."

She comes back. "After I pee, I'm going to find out why you need a room that is full of Korean movie posters."

"I can tell you now... it's because I like—"

"Kylian!"

"Sweet angel of mine, you're going to have to stop making my name sound so sexy when you yell it or else I'm going to have to ravage you again right now."

She opens her mouth, probably to yell my name again, but thinks better of it and runs into the other side of the apartment. Luckily for her, that is where the downstairs bathroom is. I jump up and wander into the kitchen situated next to the living room; when I return with two glasses of orange juice, she's not back yet.

In the distance, I can hear the shower running, so I follow her to the bathroom. She's standing with her back to me, naked under the shower, her hair in a thick wet rope down her back. I step out of my pants, open the shower door, and step in behind her, grabbing the body wash from the shelf and squeezing some onto my hand.

She turns and gives me a look and then faces the shower again saying nothing but a little "oh" when I rub my hands, building up a lather, and rub it all over her back, shoulders, and arms.

A sigh hums through her, and she takes one step back until she's against my chest, so I can run my soapy hands over her front, taking a moment to cup her breasts, remembering the way she responded when I touched them before. Then my hand travels further down, my head resting on her shoulder as I reach down, my hands gently washing between her legs. I can't help but wonder if she's sore. We've fucked twice, and both times without too much preparation. And I was anything but gentle.

She lets out a small hiss when I dip my fingers between her pussy lips.

The sound makes me wince. "I'm sorry. Did I hurt you?"

"Are you going to keep asking that after we have sex? Because I have to tell you, it's not very sexy."

"I just want to make sure you're okay... so that next time I can fuck you harder," I mumble into her shoulder.

"Promises, promises."

I lower myself behind her to wash her legs, enjoying the feel of the softness of her thighs under my fingertips.

When I'm done, she takes her time washing me, my chest, my back, my semi-hard cock in her hands as she runs her fist up and down my shaft.

"Careful."

She just grins and then moves on.

When we're both clean, I reach over to turn the water off, then lift her into my arms and carry her out of the bathroom.

"Kylian! I'm dripping wet!"

"Oh... I know. I've tasted." I tease her. And I'm going to again. But not right now. Right now, I want to go back to falling asleep with her in my arms.

I lay her down on the couch and run back to the bathroom to grab a towel.

Her eyes bore into me as I gently rub the towel up her legs, gently patting her skin all the way up her body, and then wrap her wet hair in the towel.

Then, after I dry myself, I sit back on the couch, and I pull her onto my lap.

"Get some sleep, angel."

"So it's 'angel' now?" She giggles and wraps her arms around my neck, her nose tickling right under my ear.

"You're Kiara, Kiki, Angel... everything."

This time there's no giggle, she just closes her eyes and lies against me.

And sleeps.

Nineteen
Kiara

I have no idea where I am.

There's a bed under me, but it's not my bed.

There are crisp white sheets, also not mine. Mine are dark blue.

And it's bright.

Definitely not my bedroom. Mine is perpetually dark. Blinds closed so I can get some sleep during the day after working all night.

And... finally, there's a smell of something cooking, warm and comforting.

Then I remember.

Fuck.

I shoot right up, jumping out of the bed, taking the sheet with me.

I'm at Kylian's home... and we had sex... multiple times last night.

I wait for the dread to fill me, but it doesn't. It feels right. I sink back onto the bed, dizzy from jumping up so quickly, and grab my head.

"Hey! Are you okay?" Suddenly, he's sitting right there next to me, dressed in just a pair of black track pants, a ladle in his hand.

"I'm fine," I say but lean against him, needing confirmation that he's real and not something I've conjured up.

"Morning, Kiki," he coos comfortingly and hugs me to him with the non-ladle-holding hand.

"What's that for?" I point at his hand.

"This?" He waves the ladle in the air.

I nod.

"It's a ladle. It's for ladling things"

"Like?"

"Things that need ladling. But also good for spanking." He holds it over his head menacingly but with a smile on his face, and I duck away. "I'm making you some chicken congee for breakfast."

I look at him through narrowed eyes. "You made congee."

"Yup. Chicken."

"*You*. Made. It?"

He throws me an exasperated look. "Yes! I didn't have any coriander or green onions, though, so we'll have to pretend they're in there."

"But what you're saying is, you made it."

He lowers the ladle and peers at it. "I'm starting to think that this ladle really is for spanking."

"I didn't know you could cook!"

"I'm a great cook. That's what happens when you live to eat." He kisses the top of my head. "There's a toothbrush in there and one of my college T-shirts; it's long enough to cover you down to your knees." He points to a door to the left of the bed. "When you're dressed, or not, it's up to you, come downstairs and eat the delicious congee I made for you."

"What do you mean, downstairs?"

He looks confused at my question. Which is fine, considering I'm confused about what he means by downstairs.

"Well, we're upstairs in my bedroom."

"How did I get upstairs?"

"I carried you. Now, hurry up. I don't want to overcook the congee."

I roll my eyes and gather the sheet around me as I walk over to the bathroom. "You can't overcook congee."

"Ohhh, so now everyone's a cook."

I guffaw as he leaves. Honestly, I could overcook boiling water, but I have no intention of telling him that.

When I go downstairs, he's nowhere to be seen. There's a pot simmering on the stove, and the kitchen bench is laid out for two.

I find my purse on the coffee table; he must've retrieved it from the floor in front of the elevator where I'd dropped it. He's so fucking thoughtful.

The elevator dings. He must've ducked out to grab some ingredients, which is good because I have no intention of giving him an easy review on his cooking.

"Did you doubt my ability to imagine little specks of scallions in my congee?" I say at the same time as someone else says, "Hi, honey. I'm home. Where the fuck were you last night? I must've called you a hundred times. And the apartment switchboard said that you had set yourself as 'do not disturb.' I came to pick up the shirt I left in your bedroom yesterday morning since you were too lazy to bring it to me last night."

The person attached to the voice turns into the kitchen and stares at me standing at the stove.

It's a woman, a blonde woman, a blonde woman I've seen before. A face I can never forget that haunts my dreams.

"Oh. Hi. Who the hell are you?" she says in a way that is both combative but confident. Like she knows she'll win whatever fight I want to get in.

"Um... nobody," I mumble.

"Is Kylian here?"

"Um, yes, somewhere. I think." Where is he?

I stumble over to where I left my purse and pick it up with my shaking hands.

"Well, where is he, then?" she snaps.

"I don't know."

"Should you still be here, then? Isn't he done with you?" Not a lot of women can intimidate me. But she is all venom.

"I-I guess," I stammer. I have never met any woman who is so blatantly rude and confrontational, and it knocks me off guard.

"Then you should leave." She dumps her bag on the counter and stares me down.

"I'm going. Tell Kylian..." The words fade into nothing.

I take a breath, swallow, and pull myself together. I haven't done anything wrong, and I shouldn't act like it. I set my jaw and stare at her back. "Look, I just came to return this." I slam the key card Kylian gave me into her hand.

She looks at it and then up at me. "Why do you have his key card?"

I push past her as I make my way to the elevator, hissing with more courage than I actually have, "I could ask you the same question."

Then I flee.

Luckily, the elevator is still there, so I'm zooming down the inside of the Baxter apartment building and then out into the road in less than a minute.

And I run.

Where?

Anywhere but here.

Twenty

Kylian

"Hey, I found something that my assistant left here the other day. Maybe it's a little more decent than my Wharton T-shirt. I'm sure she won't mind."

I step into the kitchen to see a blonde standing in the space where I'd expected to see Kiara.

"Um, hi, honey, I'm home," she says in a sarcastic tone.

"Yeah, hi, honey," I respond, rolling my eyes as I do every time she's said it for the last ten years, with the sole intention of annoying me. "What are you doing here? Didn't I say you had to call before stopping over?"

"I came to pick up your dry cleaning that I left here yesterday. And what the fuck do you mean 'my assistant won't mind' if you give away my dress?" She reaches over and snatches it out of my hands. "I can tell you now, I most certainly would mind if you gave this dress away. That's a Stella McCartney."

"Yeah, I know, Odette. I'm the one who made the mistake of taking you to the fashion show where you saw it and demanded I get it for you or else you'd quit. And it had been almost a whole week since the last time you'd threatened to quit, so I almost took you seriously." I push past her and walk over to the stove, checking on my food.

"Hey, it's not my fault that you don't pay me enough to buy one myself."

That deserves the loud huff that I give it. "Odette, you're literally the highest paid executive assistant that exists on this earth. Some of the VPs are envious of what you get paid."

She giggles. "I know."

"Bitch."

"Fucker."

I grab the ladle and give the congee a stir, making sure it's not clumping and sticking to the bottom. "Where's Kiara? I heard her voice out here. I thought she was talking to me."

Odette's face blanches. "Wait. What? Shit. That woman was Kiara?"

Something is wrong. "You saw her?"

My executive assistant squirms, and that's never a good sign. Usually she takes no shits and is unapologetic in everything she does. Unless she's fucked something up that she knows I'm going to be pissed about. "Er... yeah. I thought she was like... some floozy you picked up."

Worry sparks in my stomach. "Okay... and what did you say to her?"

Odette bites her lip. Something I see her do once every leap year. "Yeah. It's not what I said... so much as how I said it."

I slam the ladle down and glare at him. "Did you tell her you're my assistant?"

"She didn't ask! Anyway she... she left. Like two minutes ago."

"Odette!"

"What? I was protecting you."

Fucking hell. "From what, exactly?"

"Floozies!" She throws her hands up into the air. "Duh!"

"Fucking hell! When have I ever brought a 'floozy' home?"

She shakes a finger in my face. "Hey! You used to bring them over all the time. And I'd have to kick them out after you went to work. Granted, you haven't done that in ages. Like five years since you've been brooding over..." her voice trails off as she realizes what she's done.

"Yeah... exactly."

"Oops?"

"You're fired."

I dash out of my kitchen without my keys, wallet, shoes. Nothing but the fear weighing like an anchor in the pit of my stomach.

The lobby is empty when I get there.

She couldn't have gone far.

I frantically flag down the doorman. "Did you see Miss Kiara, the woman from yesterday, leaving? She was driving my Jag."

"Yes, sir. But she didn't take your car, she jumped into a taxi a few minutes ago."

"Get my car!" I yell as I run out into the street with nothing on but my track pants.

"Which one, sir?"

"Any car! Just hurry!" I shout, the desperation in my voice shocking even to me.

She's not there at the end of the road when I get there. No Kiara, no taxi, nothing that tells me where she's gone.

"Kiara!" I yell.

But there's no answer.

And for the second time in my life, I wonder if I've lost her forever.

I drive like a mad man to her apartment, hoping that I'll find her there. If not, I'll tear this fucking country to pieces to find her. A taxi is just pulling away when I get there, and hope springs in my chest. I slam my car to a stop in front of her apartment building, and I jump out. She's not in the lobby, but she can't be far.

I take the stairs two at a time up to her floor.

The oxygen empties from my lungs when I turn into the hallway and she's there.

But she doesn't see me.

She's just standing outside her apartment, staring at the door handle.

"Kiara!"

She looks up to see me, and the look on her face freezes the blood in my veins.

Twenty-One
Kiara

The door to my apartment is open.

The door to my apartment is only supposed to be open when I open it to come come home and when I leave.

There is absolutely no other time when it should be open.

My apartment is the only thing I accepted financial help with from my father when I moved back to Hong Kong, to have a place that was safe enough that I would not have to worry about this.

Again.

And now, the door of my apartment is open.

And I'm not the one who left it open.

"Kiara!"

I turn to the sound of the voice.

It's Kylian.

I'm glad to see him, but I shouldn't be. I should tell him to just go away, but I can't do this alone, and I can't call the only two other people I trust in this moment.

"Kiara, what's wrong?" he asks as he runs up to me. "You look like you've seen a ghost."

I point at the door, still slightly ajar.

He frowns, not quite comprehending.

And then he does.

"When's the last time you were home?"

I shake my head. I don't know. Sometime before last night. I think. Everything's a blur.

"Did you come up here after I left you on the curb yesterday?" he asks.

"I don't think so. No."

He nods. "Okay, good. So it was probably before that. And you definitely locked your door before you left?"

"I would never, ever, ever not lock my door." Some things you can just be absolutely sure of.

He looks around the hallway, probably trying to see if there is any clue that could tell him what happened here. "Stand here and I'm going to go inside, okay?" He reaches for the door.

"No!" I grab his hand. "It's not safe."

"Kiara, whoever broke in probably did it hours ago. Maybe even yesterday morning after I took you to the casino. I don't think they'd still be in there."

I look at him with what I imagine to be wild eyes, shaking my head. "No, no, no, no, no."

He steps away from the door. "Okay, I'm not going in if that makes you feel better, we'll just call the police, okay?"

"A-and you won't go in?"

"Not if you don't want me to."

I should want him to.

I should want to send him into a war-zone and blown to fucking smithereens, but I don't. The only thing that would make this morning worse is if he wasn't in this world at all.

"Do you have your phone?" he asks.

"Um… yeah. In my purse."

The handbag on my shoulder is gently removed and I see him digging through it.

"What's the password?" he prompts.

"Nathan's birthday," I hear myself say.

The phone clicks as Kylian taps in six numbers on my iPhone, presses a few more buttons, then holds it up to his ear.

A few minutes later, he hangs up and tucks the phone into his pocket. That's when I realize that he's dressed in nothing but a pair of black track pants.

"Where are your clothes?"

"At home," he answers and shrugs. "The police will be here in a moment." Then, after looking at me, he says, "Do you need a drink or something? I can go inside—"

"No!"

I feel my body wrapped up in his arms, my face against his chest. "Okay, okay. I won't go inside. Can I ask one of the neighbors for a glass of water?"

My head shakes against him. "I'm fine. Just... please stay with me until the police get here."

He grips my shoulder, pushes me forward, and crouches so that his eyes are on mine. "I'm not leaving, do you hear me? Not now. Not ever."

And then I'm in his arms again. And just for now, I let myself take comfort in Kylian Baxter.

Once the police have come and gone, I'm more or less back in my right mind. The apartment was completely trashed, but I knew it was going to be. It's not the first time I've come home to a door purposely left open; it's done to strike fear in my heart from the moment I see it. The trashed apartment is just the icing on the cake.

As far as I can tell from a cursory glance around the rooms, nothing is gone. Robbing me is not the point. Driving me insane is. And I'm not going to let him do it to me again.

I shouldn't have let Kylian call the police, but he'd caught me off guard. And in his presence, I'd completely crumbled, which is not like me at all. *Kiara could withstand the zombie apocalypse,* everyone used to say. *She'd be running rival gangs behind the scenes after a few days.*

And yet now, at the sight of a broken-into apartment, I'd completely and utterly lost my shit.

What was wrong with me?

Has one night with Kylian fucked so hard with my brain that I can't even function any more?

Kylian gave me the space I needed when the police came and took my statement, but I could still always feel him there, listening to every word, ready to jump in if I ever needed anything. The moment they'd stepped away, he was right there by my side with a bottle of water in his hand. Without me asking, he'd said, "It's sealed, I found a case under your bed."

I don't know whether to be touched that he'd made such an effort to look so hard for a drink that I could take with peace of mind or that he now knew I had a secret stash of water and food in my bedroom, just in case I'm ever stuck there after an earthquake. I'm not much of a doomsdayer, but dying of thirst before rescuers can find me is a way I'd rather not leave this world.

And now it's just the two of us, standing in a trashed apartment.

"I'm just going to go grab something to throw over my sexy chest," he jokes and leaves the room.

I wait until he's gone before I check one of my secret money hiding spots. All my money is there, and I let out an exhale of relief. I'll check the potted plant in the bedroom once Kylian comes back out. It's not the money, it's the knowing my hiding spots have not been found.

After a few minutes, he comes ambling out. "Well, no luck. I never thought that I'd be mad that everything you wear is tight. But I'm not really in the mood to go out there wearing a dress that looks like a crop top on me."

Absentmindedly, I run my sweaty palms down the front of the T-shirt I'm wearing. He drops his eyes to my torso and winks. "Looks a million times better on you than it does on me."

It takes me a moment to remember that I'm wearing his T-shirt. Immediately, my fingers tug at the hem, wondering if I should take it off and offer it to him, even though it's the last thing I want to do right now. I didn't realize how much it was a source of comfort until now.

He waves his hand. "No. Keep it. Your neighbors will just get an eyeful of me when we go down to the car."

What's he saying? "To the car?"

"Yes, you're not staying here. It's not safe."

"It's fine. I'm sure he won't be back." Lies.

"Who?"

I bite the inside my lip. I shouldn't have sounded like I knew who it would be. "I'm just saying, whoever it was probably got whatever they came here to get."

"Oh? I thought you said that it didn't look like much was missing."

Fuck, he was observant. Maybe him listening and hovering wasn't such a good thing after all.

"Well, I haven't looked closely. I did also say that."

"Yes, you did." He wants to say something else but doesn't.

I force myself to straighten up. "I'm not going with you, Kylian."

"I'm not giving you a choice, *Kiara*."

I bite back a hiss. I don't take kindly to anyone telling me what to do, let alone him. "I wouldn't go with you if you begged me." I say the *dickhead* part in my head.

"Good, because I have absolutely no fucking intention of doing so." He lifts a bag; it looks full of my clothes and toiletries from the bathroom. He wasn't looking for a shirt. He was packing me a fucking bag.

"Put. That. Back." The numbness and shakiness from coming home to see my door open is gone, and all that is left is fury. Fury at the violation of my home, and fury at Kylian acting like he has any say in my life. That right flew out the window two hours ago when a woman walked into his apartment like she belonged there and treated me like I didn't.

His jaw twitches as he stares me down. "You're going to need it when you move in with me. Or you can come without it, and we can go buy whatever you need."

"That's hardly a choice," I scoff.

"It's all the choice you're going to get." His tone dares me to challenge him. Unfortunately for him, I'm up to a challenge right now.

"When did you become such a motherfucking bossy fuckwit?" I yell, the anger spewing from me in words that I've never used before.

He glares at me, his fist white-knuckled around the handle of the bag. "I get that you're angry right now. But there's no point in taking it out on me. I'm on your side. I'm here for you. And I'm not leaving without you, so the sooner you get with the program, the better it's going to be for the both of us. Let's. Fucking. Go."

He has some nerve. Is this the kind of bullshit other women he's been involved with tolerate? "I'm not moving in with you, and I'm not your girlfriend! Who the fuck do you think I am? Like I'm not embarrassed enough about what happened last night. I'd rather stay here and get killed than go back there with you!" His back stiffens along with the twitch in his jaw. But it's not my problem if he doesn't like what I'm saying. How does he think it feels experiencing it? So much for his promises. "How could you do this to me, Kylian? Again! Do you have any idea what it was like to feel like I was just some convenient fuck you'd brought home?"

He flings the bag to the ground and clears the almost ten feet between us in two steps, grabbing my wrist and pushing me up against the wall, knocking down the picture frame I've hung there. It crashes to the ground at our feet, not that either of us are looking at it because he holds both of my hands over my head with one hand, and the other is gripping around my throat.

His eyes, as I've come to know, change from icy cold to raging hot within a matter of seconds and lock on mine, reflecting glaciers. "You're a little bratty today. Do you honestly think that I'm going to let anyone hurt you?"

"*You* hurt me. Again," I hiss, struggling against his hand that feels like a cable tie around my wrists.

"No, Kiara. You hurt yourself. Who do you think was at my apartment this morning? Who do you think that was?" The way his voice remains calm while I'm feeling like every emotion races around my mind as though they're trying to come in first place makes me so angry.

"I don't care, Kylian. Who fucking cares who she was?"

He studies me, his eyes scanning my face and the way my body is trying to fight him. "You do care, that's why you ran out of there without telling me. You do care, Kiara. Do you think I'm with her?"

"Are you even listening? I said, *I don't fucking care!*" I scream, my throat raw with pain.

His answer is infuriatingly calm in comparison. "Oh, sweet angel, I think you care so much you don't know what to do with yourself."

He catches my mouth with his before I can move. His lips cool against mine, a contrast to the feverish way he's kissing me. Like he has a raging inferno inside him, driving each kiss deeper as if he wants that same fire to consume me, too, and suddenly I'm melting into him. Gasping for breath against his mouth as it ravages me, his hand still strong against my neck. That only cripples me with the knowledge that somewhere, inside, I trust him. I wouldn't let him control my breath if I didn't. Or maybe it's just because I want him. I want him so much. The memory of him inside me last night draws a moan from me.

"Kylian..."

"Shhhh," he murmurs against my lips and then, with just his hand around my neck, yanks me away from the wall. He kisses me again so roughly my lips feel like they're on fire. "I'm going to show you, right now, that there's no other cunt I want to be in but yours."

"Please..." the plea trips over my lips before I can stop it.

His hands grasp my hips and wrench me toward him, his hands sliding down my back and over my ass as he devours my mouth. Somewhere in there, he lifts the T-shirt up over my ass, grabbing at my flesh, moaning his arousal.

Then I'm spun around, pushed against the wall as he cups my ass again, then without warning, his hand comes down to slap across my right ass cheek.

I gasp and exhale at once, my brain short-circuiting from what's happening. One thing stands out, though, my ass is fucking stinging. And I want more.

"You have been such a little brat today, haven't you?" he growls, as he grips my smarting ass so hard I can't think about anything but his hands on me.

I don't answer, just let him push my legs apart with his bare foot as his hand comes down again across my ass cheek.

"Ohhh..." I moan as it stings, heightening every single sensation I'm experiencing.

"I said, you've been such a brat today, haven't you, angel? Answer me or else I'm going to spank you again."

I brace against the wall, resting my head against my forearms as I feel two fingers ram inside me. "Oh god..."

"I think you like those spankings, why else would you be so wet, angel?"

"Fuck you, Kylian," I hiss.

"Oh, no, my sweet angel, no, I'm the one who is going to be doing the fucking. Ram my cock into you until every single last doubt about you and me is fucking right out of your head." His hand comes down over my ass, making me feel things I never imagined I would. "You didn't answer me. Haven't you been such a little brat?"

I shake my head. Less because I don't think I have and almost wholly because I want him to spank me again. I'm already addicted to the way it hurts, making me more aware of my body than ever before.

More.

I want more.

More of the spanks, more of his fingers inside me, more of him.

All.

I want all of him. Everything he has. The sweet, thoughtful, golden boy who washes my hair and adjusts my car seat and this dominant, demanding, controlling fucker who angers me and then soothes that fury with the way he touches me. I want it all. Every facet of him. Dark, light, and shadow.

"Maybe I've been a brat because you've made me," I finally say.

There's a little rumble from his chest, and then his large hand lands two hard slaps right after each other across my ass cheek.

"Ohhh. Fuck."

His fingers spread inside me, stretching me, getting me ready for his thickness. I push back, waiting for him to punish me with his cock, but out of nowhere, he pulls his fingers out, and then there's nothing.

No more spanks, no more fingers inside my pussy, no feeling of him pressing up against me.

Nothing.

"Turn around." His voice is hard. Restrained.

When I do, he's standing three feet away, arms folded, his eyes dark, fury swirling inside them. I've never seen him like this.

And it scares me. I wonder that I might've done something wrong.

"Tell me, why did you run out of my apartment?" he asks, giving nothing away. "I want to hear you say it."

My top row of teeth bites down on my lip until I can taste the tang of blood. "That woman..." Is he really going to make me say it?

"What about her?"

"She... is..."

"The same woman you saw me with in London," he finishes for me.

My face falls; hearing it out loud makes it so much more real. My hands tug down on the T-shirt, trying to cover more of myself even though I can feel the wetness he drew from me drenching my inner thighs. "Yes."

"And?"

"And..."

His look in unwavering, veins in his arms popping as he's tensing every single muscle in his body to refrain from letting loose. I can't help but squirm under his gaze like a kid in the principal's office. Except that never scared me. This does. Disappointing him scares me.

"And I thought you were still with her."

He shifts his balance and drags in a breath. "I was *never* with her."

"You're lying."

He shakes his head. "Not now. Not then. Not ever."

"But I…"

He uncrosses his arms and tucks them into his pockets, flexing onto his toes, making him look even taller. "I made it look that way. I wanted you to hate me enough to forget about the idea of us ever being together. She's my executive assistant. She runs my life, is annoying as fuck, and is around a lot, but there's never been anything between us. And there never will be. And do you know why?"

I'm too afraid to entertain the thought. "You don't fuck employees?"

The left corner of his mouth twitches, the only thing to crack his serious demeanor. "You're my employee. And we've fucked."

"Kylian…"

"And we're about to fuck again. Face the wall and pull the T-shirt up over your ass."

I can't even pretend that's not what I want, but the new information has me reeling.

"I'm not going to wait all day, Kiara."

I snap out of my thought and obey, lifting my arms up to brace myself against the wall.

"Arms behind your back," he growls.

"But…"

"Arms behind your back. Face against the wall. I'm not going to tell you again."

The timbre of his voice, firm, no nonsense, travels right down to my core where I'm throbbing so hard I wonder if he can sense it. I stand one foot from the wall, my ass curved up in the air, and I pull the T-shirt, so it exposes my ass, then lean forward, left cheek against the wall.

It's so quiet in the room. I can hear the blood thump in my veins.

"You are so fucking gorgeous, angel. Do you have any idea what you do to me?" His words tug at my legs, and I widen my stance, trying to imagine the view that he has and what I can do to make him want me more. The leg spreading seems to do it because there's a low growl that tickles the damp skin of my bare back.

"That's a good girl, stand there just like that. It makes me so hard to see you standing there, waiting for me."

There's nothing but the sound of my breath for a minute.

Two minutes.

Three.

It's torture and heavenly both at once.

Then his voice is in my ear, "I should have you sculptured in this position. You look perfect, Kiara. Standing there like an angelic little slut waiting to be fucked."

And then his cock is inside me.

In one movement, he pulls my hips back as he pummels his hardness into me,

"Ohhhh, fuck," I moan, my insides feeling so full I might explode. "Kylian!"

"I love when you say my name, god, I love it," he growls into my ear as he pulls all the way out and then slams back in, the tip of his cock driving the sides of my pussy apart, stretching me, making my clit ache.

"Kylian. Fuck me like you promised."

"Baby, you have nothing to worry about." He thrusts his hips forward, pushing himself even deeper inside me. With each slam, my face presses harder against the wall, my hands locked in the small of my back, leaving me completely vulnerable to him.

The room is filled with the sounds of my moans and his growls. Each one louder than the last.

He controls his rhythm with his hands gripped around my hips, pulling me back onto him until for one glorious moment, we're as connected as any two people can be.

"Dammit, Kiki, I can't get enough of your perfect little cunt. It's like it was made for me."

"It was," I moan. And I know it was.

"Sweet. Little. Kiara." He pulls me back to take his cock with each word, as if he wants to remind himself who he's fucking.

I don't know how my legs are still holding me up other than sheer will,

"This is my cunt. Say it."

"It's your cunt, Kylian." The vulgarity of the wording makes me squeeze on him.

"And I take care of what's mine. And baby, this cock," he pulls all the way out and slams all the way in until it feels like it's choking me, "every inch is yours, never forget that. Nothing is going to happen between me and any other woman because my cock belongs to you."

"Promise?"

Suddenly, he fists my hair and yanks it back, my back bowed as he ravages my mouth while he pumps into me.

"I promise. And I never break my promises." He finds my throbbing clit and pinches so hard it feels like he might twist it right off, but it's exactly what I need to come. My whole body squeezes so tightly I almost pass out. Stars explode in my vision as I come.

He roars as he joins me. Grunting as his body squeezes with pain and pleasure. Dizzy, I still press my hips back against him, wanting every single drop of his cum inside me.

"Mine," we both murmur as our breath mixes in the aftermath.

At some point, we collapse onto the floor for a few minutes before he gets up and comes back with a towel, gently patting between my legs and making me jump when he grazes my pussy.

"Oops, sorry. I was trying to be gentle."

"Definitely not gentle."

He grants me a gentle laugh. "I didn't mean when we were fucking, you little brat." It's said with so much affection in his voice it almost hurts to hear.

He throws the towel over his shoulder and then pulls me back into his arms.

"Hey! You're making a mess," I protest.

"How can you tell?" he says, nuzzling into my neck.

I pout, embarrassed that this is how he's seeing the place I live in. "This isn't my fault. It was spotless before it was ransacked."

"I believe you," he chuckles.

"I can't stay here."

"Okay," he agrees.

"I... can't stay here knowing that someone has gone through everything I own, touching everything."

"Okay."

"I'm going to have to get rid of everything and buy new things."

He nods. "Okay."

"Is that all you have to say?" I poke him in the chest.

"Yes. I already said everything before you decided to be a brat and fight me."

"Come on, you know what that was really about."

He props himself up onto his elbows and looks down at me. "About you not trusting me?"

"You haven't exactly been a beacon of trust."

"I know. But I've explained everything now. You know as well as I do that... if something had happened back then, we'd have been in a tornado of shit. And that shit would be called Nathan."

"That tornado of shi—I mean, Nathan still exists. It's not like he's gone anywhere."

He collapses down onto his back and pulls my head to his bare chest. "Yes, but me pining for you for five years before I made a move has got to buy me some points rather than jumping his drunk sister who was in a club in the wrong side of town."

"You were pining for me?"

He closes his eyes and shakes his head. "Really? That's what you're focusing on?"

I giggle. If he pined for even a day, I want every single detail. It's nice to know I wasn't the only one. "Come on, tell me how you pined for lil ol' Kiki."

He opens his eyes and looks at me, propped up on his chest. "I thought you hate when I call you that?"

"I like it now," I admit. "But no one else is allowed to call me that name."

"They better fucking not. I'll snip their balls off with a pair of nail clippers. But since you like it, I'm going to have to find a different nickname now."

"I like angel, too."

"Me, too." His hand is against my cheek, gentle, tender.

"Wait... you didn't answer the question!" I shout once I realize.

"I don't remember what the question is," he jokes.

I slap his shoulder; he catches my hand and brings it to his lips and pulls me closer.

"Yes, I pined. I pined like that most pathetic motherfucker who's had his heart broken by a woman that you've ever seen. I was fucking useless for the longest time. So much so that everyone around me had no idea what to do with me. I was told to go away for a few months and sort my shit out because I was alienating everyone."

I absorb all of his words and gather them to hoard in a pocket next to my heart.

He continues, "Anyway, I went away for a month, and I came back still miserable but kept the pining to myself."

I ask something else I've been wondering, "Why didn't we ever see each other until now? You've been living here for three years, and I've been here for a year."

"You know why."

"The tornado of shit."

He laughs and crosses his arms behind his head. "I'm glad that you're on board with my nicknames for both of the Yin siblings."

I scrunch up my face. "I'm not sure he's going to feel the same way."

"I don't know. I'm pretty sure I've called him a tornado of shit to his face many times."

"I meant the angel part!"

This time, it's his turn to scrunch his face up. "Right. That might take some more work." He rubs his hand over his face, but the worry remains. "Come on." He jumps up and reaches for my hand. "Let's get you out of here."

"Where are we going?" I let him pull me to my feet and into his arms.

"Where we were going to go all along. My place. Unless you want another spanking."

The look I give him has him laughing before he pulls me into his arms for a kiss.

Twenty-Two

Kylian

Odette is gone from the apartment by the time we come back. I didn't have my phone with me to text her to get her ass out of my home, but apparently she figured out all on her own that she should make herself scarce.

After Kiara let me borrow back my Wharton T-Shirt so I didn't have to be traipsing up to my apartment half nude, we made our way back, her packed bag in the trunk. The anxiety that I'd tried to fuck out of her seemed to be seeping back in, but whenever I asked how she was doing, all I got was a shrug and an "I'm fine."

She enters the apartment hiding behind me, obviously afraid that the fire breathing Odette is still there. I'd seen my executive assistant's work firsthand, and I can only imagine what she said to Kiara; we will have to talk about that later, but right now, I'm focused on making Kiara as comfortable as possible.

"Where's the guest room?"

"Um, I don't have one," I say, carrying her bags upstairs.

"Kylian. Didn't you say that your brothers stay here when they come to Hong Kong?"

"I meant the building. We have a family apartment on the floor below,"

I'm not lying. Technically, we do have that apartment, but that is more for friends or other family members who might want to visit. When my brothers or father are here, they stay here in the guest room that I'm pretending doesn't exist. I'm just glad she hasn't had a chance to go exploring around the apartment and that I didn't have a chance to give her the whole tour before we were distracted.

"Kylian," she says in a tone I imagine she thinks is a warning.

I find it cute. And I say so as I climb the rest of the stairs to my bedroom. "Are you coming or not? I warn you, if the answer is not, I'm going to hang up your stuff in a way you don't like."

She waves a hand and walks over to the windows, unlocking the door that opens onto the balcony. "Just leave them on the bed."

With her permission, I throw her bags onto my bed and go down to the kitchen.

Odette at least had the presence of mind to turn the stove off. I see a dress hanging on the back of one of the breakfast bar stools. It's the Stella McCartney dress. She wouldn't have left that here unless she'd meant to on purpose. This was her way of extending an apology, an olive branch. I just can't tell if it was to me for her scaring off the woman she knows I've been obsessed with for five year, or to Kiara for saying whatever she did that had Kiara running out into traffic with nothing but a T-shirt on.

I turn the stove back on as well as the kettle for some tea. The jasmine tea canister sits in the cupboard directly above the kettle. I open it and am immediately reminded of My-Linh. She brought me this tin of Jasmine tea the last time they came here a few weeks ago. I wish that trip had been delayed now, and My-Linh could've had a chance to meet Kiara. And vice versa. It might be nice for Kiara to know that my family isn't filled with just a set of rowdy and grumpy suits.

I stop.

Had I just thought about Kiara joining my family? Throughout all the years of pining, I never, not once, thought about how far I would want to take the relationship if it actually came into being. Yet somehow, over the course of the last few days, I can no longer imagine a family that she's not a part of.

I spend a moment watching her on the balcony, watching her lean as far as her short frame will let her over the rail, her hair whipping around her face. She must see me because she waves and then comes back inside.

"Wow, it's windy out there! But so refreshing. Was it okay that I went out there?" she asks, a little note of uncertainty in her voice.

"Kiki, this is your home right now. You do whatever you like."

That earns me a big smile, and she skips over and plants herself on a stool, watching me stir the congee and make a pot of tea.

"Something smells good. What is it?"

"Me, of course."

Her eye roll is the reward I need. I jog up the stairs to get dressed for work.

"Holy fuck!" she shouts when she sees me descend the stairs into the living room; she's moved to a couch and had been staring out the window.

I'm dressed in a tailored single-breasted two-button jacket from Sartoria Dei Duchi that fits me as well as any suit can. Prussian blue with a Prada Baltic Blue tie and a pair of my favorite black Berluti Infini leather dress shoes.

"Fuck, you're hot," she says in a way that no one has said straight to my face before.

"Aww, thank you, angel." I give her a big smile, my heart fluttering in my chest as I pinch my shirt cuffs together with the handmade cufflinks that were made for my great-great-grandfather, the original Baxter who started it all. He had almost fifty different sets, enough for all of us to get some passed down to us.

I tug on the shirt cuff, and Kiara pretends to slide off her stool and faint to the ground before she sits back up again, looking up at me. "Your eyes look like they're going to jump right out of your head."

That comment makes me laugh as I tuck my phone and wallet into my pants pocket. "That is the strangest but absolutely the best compliment I have ever received, Kiki."

"I didn't say it was a compliment," she says as she jumps to her feet and comes over, straightening my tie that doesn't need straightening.

I stand completely still to let her because I don't want to make a single movement or sound that will make her stop and move away from me.

"All good?" I ask after she finishes adjusting my tie and runs her hands down the front of my jacket.

"Perfect."

"I thought so, too, when I looked in the mirror."

She snorts and starts to move away, so I grab her wrists and pull her in to me, kissing her long and slowly.

"I have to go to work. I'm sorry, Kiara, I have two meetings this morning, and I can't miss them. But I can come home right after, if you don't want to be alone." I hate the thought of leaving her here alone after what happened with her apartment.

"Actually"— she shrugs— "alone sounds pretty good."

I pretend to be offended, but I understand. For all the extroversion pumping through my body, I do have the occasional need to be totally alone.

She kisses me gently on the cheek. "Thank you for looking out for me. I'm just going to try to sleep and if the last day has been anything to go by, sleep and Kylian Baxter do not meld well."

I pout. "I'm a great snuggle buddy."

"Go to work, then come home and snuggle with me. I'll be okay. I'll call you if I need you." She rises up on her tiptoes and presses a kiss to my lips. "Have a good day, baby."

Butterflies swarm in my ribcage at how she calls me baby, and my face breaks out into a grin before I can stop it. I must look like a complete idiot. "There's some congee warming up on the stove. Eat a little before getting some sleep, okay? And if you want to go anywhere, the Jag is still here. Just call down, and they'll bring it around for you."

She nods, and I grant myself one last look before I blow her a kiss and leave wanting nothing more than to join her in bed for some sleep with her body warm against me.

"Hey. Wicked Witch of the East," I say, poking my head into Odette's office the moment I arrive at Baxter's Hong Kong headquarters. "My office. Now."

As my executive assistant, Odette has an office right next to mine. She handles just as many confidential calls and documents as I do, and I was not kidding when I said that she is definitely the highest paid executive assistant in the world. That's because she could go on to do anything else she wanted. But most days, I'm sure she's the secret to my success and, therefore, worth every dime as well as every second of my time that she needs.

"Can't we just meet in here?" she whines, not even bothering to look up from the files on her desk.

"No! This is a boss-employee talk. I, the boss, need to sit in my boss chair and lecture you, the employee. Hurry up and take off those bunny slippers you have on under the desk, and be in my office in thirty seconds."

While she does indeed arrive within thirty seconds, she has made no effort to change out of those ridiculous slippers. I sink into my chair, more tired than I realize. That's what happens when my nighttime routine gets messed around. In this instance, though, considering what happened last night and this morning, I'm more than happy to deal with a little fatigue.

"I told you to take off those fucking bunny slippers."

Odette stays standing in the middle of the room, lifting one of her feet to show off her fluffy footwear. "Firstly, they are not bunnies. They are koalas. And secondly, who died and made you boss."

"My grandfather."

She makes a face. "Oh, yeah. Well, that's just because he didn't know how good I was yet. One more year of knowing The Odette and you'd be my executive assistant. Except that you'd be utterly shit at it, and I'd have to fire you and make you my pool boy or something so you could have a job and not starve to death."

"Hush! Do you ever stop talking?" The irony of me saying this to someone else isn't lost on me.

"Fine, I'm hushing. Geez, no need to yell. I'm like standing right here, like if someone measured how far that yell would go, it would probably be way—"

I cut her off. I have to if I ever want to get a word in edgewise. "Oh. My. God. Is this what it's like when other people are trying to talk to me?"

"No." She stomps her foot once to emphases her point. "Talking to me is pleasant. Anyway, why am I here? I'm trying to finish summarizing the notes for your Charlton meeting in half an hour since you won't read anyone else's notes."

"No one else draws pictures for me or writes mean notes in the margins, designed to motivate me to keep going."

She shakes her head. "How much did you make last year? And I don't mean the value of your stocks."

"Anyway, I called you here because we have to talk about what happened at the apartment this morning."

Her expression doesn't change. I can't tell if she doesn't realize how royally she fucked up or doesn't care. "You mean you running off and almost letting your apartment burn down? No thanks for turning your stove off, I see." She adds in a mutter under her breath, "Ingrate."

"Yeah, thanks, whatever. No, I mean what happened before that."

She pretends to think about it for a moment. "You giving my designer clothes away?"

"Before that." I'm starting to get a very specific type of headache. We even have a name for it. An Odette, as a loving tribute to the person who causes me to get weekly deliveries of Tylenol.

"Ohhh." She snaps her fingers. "I got it. You mean when your little girlfriend ran away."

Finally. "That. What did you say to her?"

"Wait." She walks up to my desk and slams her hands down on it. "You didn't deny her being your girlfriend."

"She's not, but I'm working on it. Now what did you say to her?"

She lets out a low whistle. "But she's so pretty. Way too good for you. Have you ever thought that when she ran away after you made me pretend to be in looove with you in London, it's because she thought 'thank god, now I don't even have to let him down easy.'"

My head is thumping again. "Odette. For the love of wine, shut the fuck up, and tell me what you said to her!"

"Well, which is it? Shut up, or tell you what I said?"

"I'm going to push you out that window and then jump after you." And I mean it.

"Ohhh, so romantic, like Romeo and Juliet?"

"Odette!"

"Sheeeeesh, fine. I didn't say anything. I just came in, and she was there, and I asked her what she was doing there, and then she ran off."

"Yeah, I know your mouth. What exact words did you use, and how did you say it?"

She shrugs and plays with the notepad on my desk, avoiding my eyes. "Um. Probably super nicely."

"Odette."

"Ugh, fine!" She sinks into one of the guest chairs. "Look, I let myself in, and I didn't know she was there, and I said, 'Hi, honey, I'm home!' like we always do, and then... I may have... been... a little ... acerbic in my questioning."

My eyes narrow at my assistant, not for the first time wondering how hard it would be to find a replacement. "And you didn't think to clarify?"

"Why would I clarify? I thought you were hoping I'd come in and shoo her off."

"Did you not recognize her from London?"

She rolls her eyes. "You mean from five years ago at Bottle when your big nose was in my way? No. I didn't."

"Okay, fine." I point to my office door. "Go away. Go finish the notes. I want them in ten minutes."

She stands, one hand twirling small circles in the air. It's her tell for when she's formulating a thought in her mind and wants to get it right.

"Spill."

"Look, I'm sorry. I know how much you've been a pining puppy dog for her even before you fucked it up. Do you want me to talk to her?"

I shake my head as hard and fast and as long as I can considering my brain feels like it's been put in a vice. "Fuck, no."

She looks offended, and that's okay with me. "What? I'm a hoot. Five minutes after meeting me, she'll forget that I pretty much accused her of being a hooker."

"What!"

This time, she does look scared. "Er, shit. Sorry, gotta go earn my money. Bye!"

She runs out of the office before I can stop her.

Now that I know what happened between Odette and Kiara, I have a better idea on how to make sure it doesn't happen again. The thought of Kiara releases a tickle in my ribcage that I have been holding in since I left the apartment, and I have to bite down a smile so that I get some work done.

***

Two meetings crawl by at the speed of a sloth after an aromatherapy massage and heavy turkey dinner. It's almost midday by the time I emerge from our conference room where I'm immediately flagged down by my administrative assistant, Julie.

"Mr. Yin is on the phone, sir. He said you weren't answering your cell."

I shake my head at her. "Thank you, Julie. You'd think the man would know what it was like to run a company. Put him through to my office, please."

I throw the portfolios from the last meeting on the desk and sink into my chair, glad to be in a quiet room, and press the flicking light on the phone panel when Julie transfers my best friend through.

"Nathan, what's up, man? You know if I don't answer my phone, it's usually because I'm busy, right?"

"What would you be busy doing? Aren't you done for the day by noon on a Friday anyway?" my best friend shoots back. It's noisy in the background, he's calling from a car.

"It's called skillful time management."

He laughs. "It's called lazy. Anyway, I'm in the area, wanna grab a drink?"

I perk up. That actually sounds like a good way to start the afternoon, seeing him. He always is good for sharpening my brain. "Who's paying?"

"Me, the one who actually works."

I check my calendar and grimace. "Actually, I've got another meeting at 1:30. Can you just drop by here? I've got a bottle of 1989 Macallan."

He lets out a slow whistle. "Sold. See you in a bit. And, hey, this time actually buzz me up, alright? I'm still not living it down that Nathan Yin was escorted out of the Baxter Building by security last month."

He hangs up before he can hear me almost choke on my own laughter.

Ten minutes later, he's strolling through my office carrying a bottle of 1972 Clynelish whisky under his arm. "Hey."

I meet him halfway and give him a tight hug. "Nice to see you, man."

He hands me the bottle. "Here. I'm leaving this here so that the next time I drop by, I have something decent to drink."

I push him good naturedly, and he pretends to almost drop the bottle before setting it down on my desk. We wander over to the couch and sit down where I've already poured two glasses.

"Fine. No Macallan for you. More for me," I sigh.

"Give me that glass before I knock you over the head with this bottle."

We clink our glasses and sit back, just enjoying being in each other's company. Some weeks we see each other once or twice, and sometimes we'll go months without being able to get our shit together. These spontaneous drop-ins are really what keep us updated on each other's lives.

"So how are things going with Kiara?" he asks as I reach over to fill up his drink.

I'm careful not to drop the bottle, even though I'm surprised he's asking without any other small talk. He must really be concerned with what's going on with her. "Wow. No, how are you doing, Kylian? How's that bruise you got the last time we played racquetball?"

"Um, you got the bruise because you cheated and purposely blocked me from getting to the ball. Anyway, I know how you are. Everything you do is plastered all over the papers. I can't read a business section without that ugly ass mug on the front page. Half the time it's not even about business, it's something like, *'Kylian Baxter was spotted going to Magnus and Novus, what could he be needing a new suit for?'*"

I grin and poke him with my elbow. "Hey, get some plastic surgery to fix that thing on your neck, and maybe you'll end up in the papers, too."

"What thing on my neck?" he asks, just as I'd hoped he would.

"Your face, you dickhead!" I tease him, knowing full well that anywhere there are eligible single women, there's talk of Nathan Yin, Hong Kong's most eligible bachelor.

He growls and then takes another sip before he asks again, "So Kiara?"

Guess the stalling only lasted so long. "Um, well, we've talked like I told you the other day. But after I showed her the casino, I think she's on board. She seemed really impressed with The Light Room."

He frowns. "So she'll work at the new casino? Doing what?"

I eye him. There are two people I won't play poker with, my cousin who cheats and is a bad loser and Nathan who, for as far as I can see, has no discernible tell. That isn't normal. Never play with someone like that. They will rip your heart out and feed it to you.

I wonder how much he knows about her business, so I put the ball in his court. "Well, how do you think she'd best fit in at the casino?"

He snickers. "Other than as someone who goes around picking everyone's pockets... I don't know, a hustler?"

I laugh. I know that's not exactly what prop players do, but some believe it is. Still, in poker you can't blame someone for being better at reading you than you are at reading them. "I don't know how she'd take to being called that."

"I do. She'd be proud and say thank you. I say that from firsthand experience." He shakes his head at the apparent memory of this run-in with his baby sister.

"Okay, so, um, do you know what else she does?" I suddenly feel a sense of protectiveness over her. If she doesn't want her brother and father to know about her work, then they're not going to hear it from me.

His eyes narrow. He knows me too well. "You know, don't you?"

"Know what?"

"Kylian. Left finger tapping on the thigh."

I grin. He must know that I don't intend on playing poker with him ever again if he's telling me he thinks he knows what my tell us.

"So"—he leans back into the couch—"what do you know?"

I shrug. "I know what she wants me to know, and I'm guessing *you* know what she wants you to know."

He doesn't like that answer and leans forward again, serious. "Kylian. If she's doing anything she shouldn't..."

"Shouldn't? Come on, man. She's an adult. Don't you think she should be able to make decisions for herself?"

He takes a sip from his glass, watching me drink mine from the over the rim of his glass.

I try to ignore it by pouring some more whiskey into my glass. "What?"

"You're drinking her Kool Aid."

"What in the fuck does that mean?"

He cocks his eyebrow. "I mean, she's given you some spiel about how hard life is as a Yin and she just wants to be her own person."

"You'd might be surprised to hear that I have heard no such speech. I have heard the one where I'm an asshole who always goes running back to Nathan with everything and that if we're to work together, then that's not acceptable. So what do you want me to do, tell your Dad that I can't offer her a job because Nathan wants me to report back to him everything that she's doing?"

"That's not what I mean. I just want to make sure she's doing okay."

I hold my palms out. "Then you're going to have to find that out from her."

"Find *what* out from *who*?" Kiara says, stepping into my office with a big smile on her face and a basket on her arm. Her face immediately freezes when she sees her brother sitting there and then looks at me, a panicked expression on her face.

He stands up. "Kiara, what are you doing here? Are you here to see me? I told my assistant that if you or Dad looked for me, I'd be here for lunch."

She walks over to him and lets him give her a hug while still trying to sneak a look at me. "Erm, yes! I had to come and talk to Kylian about... something... um, oh, work, and then I called to see if you wanted to have lunch and was told you'd be here, so two birds. Hey, um, look, I brought some sushi and miso soup. Come on, guys. I'm sure you're both hungry. You probably didn't think to get anything to eat with those drinks."

Nathan and I shoot each other a look and laugh as Kiara kneels down at the table in front of the couch and lays out the food, her hands visibly shaking. Nathan seems too interested in the spread to see his sister throw me worried glances every few seconds.

I try to look as reassuring to her as I can. There's a legitimate reason for her to be here, and if she relaxes, there's no reason for her brother to suspect anything.

"Wow, this looks delicious, thanks, Kiara. It's a good thing Nathan came here for a drink."

"Did he at least bring his own for once?"

Nathan jumps up and grabs the bottle on my desk. "Actually, I did, thank you very much. And you shush. Kylian and I go way back. What's a little drink between friends?"

He says it as a joke, but it strikes a nerve with both Kiara and I as we settle on opposite ends of the coffee table as far away from each other as possible.

"You didn't buy any of the ones that I like!" Nathan complains.

"Just shut up and eat," she says, handing her brother a pair of chopsticks. "Ignore him. He can get a bit funny around people because he's so fucking ugly. He has no idea how to conduct himself in public."

I glance over at my friend who might as well have been a model with chiseled cheekbones and pink heart-shaped lips. "Yeah, I see what you mean."

We fall into a silence as we eat with only the occasional request to pass a dish. The food is almost gone before we all put our chopsticks down and speak again.

"That was good, Keeks, thanks. Even if you didn't buy the sushi that I like. I ate it just to be polite," Nathan teases his sister.

She holds her hand out. "Give it back, then!"

Nathan responds by miming sticking his finger down his throat, and Kiara squeals and jumps up. "You're so gross! Do you know you're like thirty years old now? And run a billion dollar company?"

"Excuse me, it's a hundred billion dollar company. Don't devalue me, right, Kylian?"

I hold my hands up in defense. "Yeah, I'm going to stay out of this little sibling squabble; having three brothers has taught me that at least any two of us will be fighting at any given time, and the worst thing you can do is get in the middle of it."

Kiara turns to me and scowls. "What's there to get in the middle of? He's an immature ass, and you know it! You've been friends since you were like thirteen."

"Well, maybe that's just it. He's the same as he's always been. I can't tell the difference." I grin at my friend.

Nathan beams. "Aw, thanks, man."

Kiara rolls her eyes. "I do not think that was meant to be a compliment."

"Of course, it was. Kylian is my biggest fan."

"So he blows smoke up your ass is what you're saying."

Nathan turns to me and adopts a shocked look. "Kylian? Is this true? You worship my ass?"

I try not to laugh, but it's almost impossible. "Pretty sure that's not what she said. You need your hearing checked, you're getting old."

"Well, you guys ought to make up your mind. Am I immature or an old man?"

This time, Kiara and I respond at the same time yelling, "BOTH!"

Nathan pushes himself to his feet, huffing. "Well, I can see that my presence here isn't appreciated. I'm going back to the office where everyone is paid to appreciate my presence."

We get to our feet, and I reach over to give my best friend a hug, affection swelling in my chest for him. There aren't a lot of people who can keep up with my banter, but he does a good job. "Thanks for dropping in, man."

"Well, you seem so lonely. When have you ever even had any company that isn't a Baxter or a Yin?" He's joking of course, it's been a few months, but my parties prove that I could have plenty company if I wanted it.

"Who else is worthy?"

"Seriously though, man, I can't even remember the last time you dated anyone."

Out of the corner of my eye, Kiara pretends she's not listening to every single word of the conversation. And I can only hope that she remembers everything I said to her this morning at her apartment.

Shit, was that really just this morning?

Time seems to have no concept to me since Tuesday when I ran into Kiara at her dad's bar.

"Maybe you're just not looking closely enough," I offer.

He turns to his sister who is making a big show of collecting up the food containers.

"Hey, Keeks, do you have any single friends you can introduce to this ugly ass here? She doesn't have to be pretty or rich or good looking or anything. Just breathing."

Kiara clears her throat and turns to look at her brother, clearly avoiding my eyes. "I don't know what his type is."

"I just told you. Breathing. But who am I kidding? You're more of a romance avoidant than him. Ever since..." his voice fades out, and his mouth clamps shut.

"Hmmm?" I prompt, not able to help myself. If it has to do with Kiara, I want to know about it.

"Er, nothing, ever since she moved back to Hong Kong," Nathan says nonchalantly but fooling no one.

"I've been busy," she hisses through her teeth, trying to keep her voice light, but the balled-up fists by her side tell me otherwise.

"Whatever. I've got to go back to the office. Keeks, you want a ride?"

She shakes her head. "I drove here. And anyways, I haven't talked to Kylian about my contract yet."

"Okay, well, have our legal department look it over. Can't trust these Baxters." He grins at me and then turns back to his sister. "Can you come out here for a moment? I want to talk to you about something."

"Er, yeah, sure."

I wave them off as I sit back down on the couch, pulling my phone out of my pocket. "Take your time, Kiki. I haven't done today's Wordle yet."

"It's 'drink.' You're welcome!" Nathan yells out as his sister pushes him out of my office.

"Asshole!" I yell back.

"That's not five letters. Fuck, you're as stupid as you are ugly!"

In the distance, I can hear Kiara shush her brother, and it makes me laugh.

And it takes everything in me not to move closer to the door to eavesdrop. But if I'm going to ask her to trust me, then I'm going to have to trust her right back.

Twenty-Three
Kiara

"What do you want?" I ask my brother, sounding more impatient than I mean to. The truth is, I'm not mad at him, I'm just ready for the most anxiety-inducing lunch in my life to end.

"Hey," Nathan says, voice lowered. "I heard your car got stolen the other night."

"And where did you hear this from?"

He looks at me like I've asked the world's stupidest question. "I have my sources."

"Spying on me again?"

"No. So what happened?"

If I had an answer, I wouldn't have driven here in Kylian's Jag. "I honestly don't know. I had the car one moment and the next, I didn't"

"But you said you drove here."

I pause for a second, making sure I have my story straight. "I borrowed one."

"You should've just told me. I can send one of the company cars over."

I wave his offer away. "I have it sorted, Nathan."

He doesn't say anything for a moment, knowing that tone in my voice. "Okay. Well, let me know."

"I will. Thank you."

"Are you really thinking of working for at the new Baxter casino?"

"Yes."

He's more surprised than I thought he would be. I thought he'd be happy. "Wow. Okay, but why Baxter and not Yin Tech?"

"Well, when you build a casino, maybe I will."

"You know you just have to say the word. Dad will lay the first brick himself."

"Yeah, it's the rest of the bricks I'm worried about," I joke trying to lighten the mood.

"You're a brat."

"That... may have been mentioned before." My cheeks blaze, remembering the last time I'd been a bit bratty to the man behind the door.

He leans in, lowering his voice. "Okay, I love Kylian like a brother, but look out, okay? They're not Baxter Enterprises because they're a pushover in business."

I squeeze his arm gratefully. "I will."

"Also, I wasn't joking about being careful around him and his wandering hands. He wasn't known as Lady Killer Kylian in college because he stayed away from women."

This time he gets an eye roll. "Yes, Nathan." I give my brother a hug and then walk back into the office only to find him following me in.

"Sorry about that, man," he says to Kylian who's still sitting on the couch. "Just some big brother little sister stuff. Anyway, I forgot to say that Dad wanted to have a cookout next Tuesday." He points at me. "You are expected." Then he points at Kylian. "But you are invited. He said he's sorry he didn't hang around to talk the other day at Amber, he was a little tired from staying up to read."

Kylian flicks his eyes at me. "Are you okay with me coming?"

Nathan interjects before I can answer. "Why are you asking her? He specifically asked me to invite you."

"I'm asking her to be a gentleman, fuckface! Maybe she wanted to spend some time just with you guys," Kylian answers, looking at me.

This time I nod. Unless he's out of the country, I know my Dad would not take Kylian refusing an invitation lightly. In addition, it would be likely to stir up more suspicion than us being there together.

"Okay, then, of course. Sounds great. Tell your Dad thanks. And I'm bringing him something my brother's fiancée brought over to me from Australia."

When Nathan finally leaves after a few more false goodbyes, we stand in place for what feels like a good five minutes before taking a breath, making sure he's gone.

Finally, Kylian gets up from the couch and pushes his office door closed and then walks over to me, taking my hands in his. "It's so good to see you. I could barely think all morning."

I can't help being touched by the way he just says what he's feeling. "I missed you, too. That's probably why I showed up here in the middle of your work day with food. I almost died when I saw Nathan in here! Your assistant said I could come in."

Kylian blushes, his cheeks blaring red, and in that moment, he looks utterly adorable. "That may have been my fault. I said to Julie that unless I was in with King Charles, you were to be put through no matter what."

I giggle, thrilled by the special attention. "Kylian. You shouldn't have done that. Nothing is that urgent."

He pulls me in and hugs me in the way that I'm becoming addicted to, squeezing me as tightly and as closely as he can. "I felt so bad about leaving this morning. I shouldn't have left you alone after what happened. I should've just called in to my meetings. How was your morning?"

"Okay. I got a little bit of sleep... but it felt a little weird without you there." As if on cue, I let out a big yawn.

"You still tired, Kiki?"

"A little," I admit. "I have to work tonight. I have to take a few new trainees out into the field and observe them."

His hand tickles the back of my neck. "I'll come with you."

I shake my head against his chest. "No, that's okay. I have a driver for tonight, and the club will have security."

"Yeah, me. I'll come, and I won't get in the way. Think of it as me coming to see how your employees work and if they'll be a good fit for Baxter's casino."

I nod, my eyes closing, feeling so safe right here in his arms.

"Sweet angel," he murmurs, kissing me gently on the forehead and rubbing his hands up and down my back.

I feel like I'm in a daze, exhausted from the last few days. Even so, I hadn't been able to fall asleep in his bed without him.

My body is lifted and then lain down on the couch.

"I'll be right back," he whispers. "I'm just turning the light off."

Soon everything is dark. I hear the murmur of him saying something to someone else, then he's right there, lifting my head onto his lap, his hands stroking the hair out of my face.

"Sleep, sweet Kiki."

"Youhaveameeting... Ihavetogo," I slur two seconds from sleep.

"Shhh. I'm right here. You just get some sleep."

And then I fall, and my dreams are filled with tender whispers and cornflower blue eyes.

Twenty-Four
Kiara

For most people, night time in Hong Kong is almost cool enough to be outside without breaking into a sweat within seconds. Not that it's a problem for me. I was the only child wearing their sweater in the middle of summer when we lived in England. Now in Hong Kong, I could permanently live outdoors and feel like I'm finally warm enough.

Even thirty floors up outside on Kylian's balcony, the wind was warm, washing up against my skin, bringing with it the smells of sky and city.

It's almost 10 p.m. now, and after an impromptu two hour nap in Kylian's office, I drove to check on my employees in the other apartments where some of the more experienced of my players live. I was taking six players out and pairing them up for some training. Usually we'll train the new girls in house for a period of intensive playing to teach them the mechanics of the game and different types of bets and players. But after about two weeks, we noticed that those with an affinity for the game had quickly picked up their fellow roommates' tells, ticks, and tricks, and we needed to branch out to a new pool of players for them to be exposed to all sorts. The club we are playing at tonight lets me bring my trainees without having to pay a cover charge.

After briefing them on the game plan for tonight, I drove back to Kylian's apartment and let myself in. A long bath had massaged out the soreness of a few days with little sleep, and then I'd spent an hour meditating on Kylian's yoga mat, somehow feeling so close to him like I was communing with him through our spirits alone. I'd borrowed a dress from one of the other women, not wanting to go back to my apartment alone, and I hadn't wanted to take up more of Kylian's day than I already had. He must've missed at least one meeting to sit with me as I slept.

But I needed it, and those two hours refreshed me more than a whole week's sleep does sometimes.

Kylian was having a dinner with a business partner and promised to be home by 10 p.m. to go with me to the poker club. Dashing around the apartment, using what little makeup I could borrow from the girls and random household items to help me do my hair, I wanted to be ready when he got home so we could leave as soon as possible. When my hair and makeup was finally done, I slipped into the tight black dress, slightly worried that I might not cover enough to be decent. A quick check in the mirror showed me that the hem hung barely half an inch below the curve of my ass and each step showed the slightest hint of the lace hem of my panties.

Something about Kylian coming home to see me dressed like this alights parts of my body that I didn't know I had.

And now I stand here on his balcony, waiting for him to come home. Something about it feels so domestic, so intimate, and not like two people who have really only spent one night together.

"Are you trying to kill me in that dress, Kiki?"

I spin around, and he's standing at the door, his suit jacket slung over his shoulder.

His back is to the light streaming from his living room, but the moon bathes his face in a soft glow.

Every time I'm away from him, I forget how staggeringly, devastatingly handsome he is. Perfectly symmetrical sharp angles everywhere, cheekbones that seem like they don't stop until they hit his temple, which should make him look aloof, unfriendly, but the purity in his blue eyes paint the whole effect in an almost angelic glow. He calls me angel, but he looks like Gabriel the Archangel himself.

"Hi," I say, my voice thick with missing and wanting.

His left eyebrow twitches, conveying his approval in what he's seeing. "Hey." He doesn't move any closer as if he's afraid of what might happen if he does.

"Did... um, did you have a good day at work?"

"Some of it was better than the rest. Dinner was boring as hell. I couldn't tell you one thing that anyone said. Maybe I was focused on something... someone else." By the way he's looking at me, scanning his eyes up and down my body, taking in every detail, there's no question who that someone he was thinking about is. "Did you have anything to eat yet? I brought you a pecan and arugula salad. It's on the coffee table."

So thoughtful. Above all else, he's just so thoughtful.

Not that that's what I'm thinking about right now.

I lean back against the balcony, hooking my arms around the top rail, legs taking the smallest of steps apart but enough for me to know he can see what lies between them.

"Angel..."

My eyes lock on him. I tug at my dress, pulling it higher and higher up my thigh all the way up to my hips. "Kylian. I've missed your mouth on me all day."

That's all he needs to hear to tear down that invisible barrier between us. I don't know why I feel so comfortable with him, considering this is all so new, but maybe all those years before count.

He throws his jacket down and walks to me, unhooking my arms from the rail, then pulls them up to wrap around his neck, and he kisses me. Roughly. Hungrily.

"We're going to be late," he whispers against my lips before he ravages my mouth again.

I reach down and pull down his zipper, sliding my hand in past his briefs and wrap my fist around his already hard cock. "Then you better fuck me fast."

He groans, gasping as I fist him, squeezing the head of his cock as I jack him off. He exacts his revenge by reaching down and tearing what there is of my lace thong off me and plunges two fingers into my pussy. I know I'm already drenched for him, and he moans his approval as he pumps his fingers into me.

"One day, I want you to fuck me without fingering me first," I confess. "Don't you want to feel if my tight little pussy can take your thick cock?"

"Uhhh, you're fucking killing me, angel," he says, ramming his fingers deeper and harder into me. "Are you ready for me?"

"More than ready."

He kisses me one last time and grabs my hips and lifts my legs up around his waist and drives himself into me.

"Oh fuck, Kylian..." My core is aching, and only his cock can ease it. My hips grind against him almost obscenely as his fingers dip into the flesh of my ass.

"You feel so good, angel, always so fucking wet for me."

"I missed your cock, Kylian. I'm so addicted to you fucking me."

"Good because I honestly don't think I can ever stop."

He buries his head in my neck as we lose ourselves to the feeling of his cock boring deeper and deeper inside me, connected in the most primal way. With each thrust, he grazes my clit, pushing me closer and closer to the edge.

"Kylian... oh, baby. No one's ever fucked me like you do."

"And no one ever will. Who's pussy is this?" he growls, biting down hard on my earlobe.

"Yours." I get light-headed just from saying it. "Yours and only yours."

He presses me harder against the rail and looks down at me. "Come for me, angel. I want to watch you come on my cock." He drives into me, the concentration of him trying not to come himself etched in sweat on his face.

"Oh, Kylian, I'm coming, baby!" My orgasm hits like someone is slamming into my chest, knocking the wind from me, and I gasp as the pleasure bursts like stars all over my body.

He lets go right then, his lips grazing my forehead as he grabs my hips and pulls me in harder against him, burying his cock as deeply as he can just before he lets out a groan that echoes around me, making me drunk on the sound of him coming.

His head drops down to my shoulder for a moment, and then my hips still around his waist. He carries me back inside and gently lays me down on the couch, falling on top of me.

"You're an insatiable little angel. You can ask me for anything, and I'd happily give you everything I have, Kiara Yin." He rests on me for a moment and then pulls away. "I'm going to jump in the shower, and then we can go, okay?"

"No." I grab his wrist, causing him to fall back down onto me. "Don't shower. I'm going to suck your cock later, and I want to taste me on you."

"Ohhhhh," he moans against my neck, tickling me with vibrations. "Angel, I'm serious. You're going to kill me."

I bat my eyelashes at him. "I could stop."

He laughs and then drops a gentle kiss on my forehead. "Don't you dare. I want you to tell me everything you want. And I will do everything in my power to give it to you."

"Well, you could buy me a new G-string. You ruined that pair."

I get a scrunched-up face for that suggestion. "No, let's agree that there should be nothing stopping me from your pussy whenever I want it."

"To be fair, you disposed of it pretty quickly."

He thumps his chest. "Me Hulk. Hulk smash and tear panties with a single rip."

"That's one hell of a mish mash of movie references, there, Mr. Hulk."

He does a little mini-roar, jumps off the couch, and runs upstairs to change out of his ruined suit, yelling over his shoulder. "I would wear this, but every man will be drooling over me at the scent of your cum. I'll be right back, baby."

I take the opportunity to smooth my dress out. I think about replacing my underwear, but the thought of him sliding his hand between my legs and finding me bare pushes the idea right out of my head. A quick refresh of my smeared makeup in the bathroom later, I meet him at the elevator. He's wearing a pair of white tailored pants and a navy blue Isaia shirt, the top two buttons open, and changed out his Rolex for an understated Longines watch with a sun blue dial and distressed blue, leather band. As always, he looks perfectly put together, not at all like he just had a quickie, and I'm jealous. I have "freshly fucked" all over me, but I don't mind when he pulls me to his side, whispering, "You're making it very hard for me not to tell you to fuck work and stay home and fuck me instead."

The elevator dings just in time, and I push him into it. "Come on, Lady Killer Kylian, save your charm for the poker club, and help me make some money tonight."

"Will do, sweet angel." And then he kisses me all the way down to the first floor.

The car is waiting downstairs when we get there. He waves the driver back into the car and opens the door for me, closing it when he's made sure that I'm safe, then runs to the other side to slide in next to me.

"Ready?"

I nod and then lean back against the seat, eyes closed, taking a moment to get myself into work mode. The soft scent of his cologne is slightly distracting, and soon I'm just staring at him as he sits back with his own eyes closed. "I can feel you looking at me."

"Sorry."

He reaches over and takes my hand and lays it against his chest. "I like it. I miss it when we're not together."

I sigh, glad that I'm not the only one feeling this way. "I miss your eyes on me, too. It makes me feel very special." I tickle his chest.

A little chuckle escapes his lips. "I could take a picture of my eyeballs ogling you, and you can use it as your phone background."

"Okay, deal, as long as you use a picture of me naked on your phone."

"That might be hard to explain at the cookout with your dad next Tuesday."

I scoff. "I'll deal with that later. Tonight I'm mostly concerned with the amount of women who will be throwing themselves at you dressed like that."

His eyes flutter open, but he doesn't deny it. How can he? I used to have my own friends call and ask if he was over visiting Nathan so they could come over and perve on him.

Instead, he says, "And you're going to see each and every one of them walk away having no doubt in their minds that I'm for one person and one person only. Okay?"

"Okay."

"Good. Now sit back and relax, we'll be there soon."

I sit back and watch the world zoom by while feeling everything I could want is already sitting next to me in the car.

⟫⟫⟫ ⟶ ♥ ⟵ ⟪⟪⟪

An hour later, we're standing at a bar table. Kylian's cradling a cognac, I'm drinking water in a wine glass. We're standing between two tables, each with seven players, two of them being one of my experienced players and one trainee. The experienced player, the mentor, is actually working so is just there for support and to give her shadow some discreet hints, but I prefer them not to communicate or socialize when they're in a club. We're there to provide a service to the poker club and to give their patrons a good night at the poker tables. Part of that is to maintain the image that everyone at that table is there just to blow off some steam. Somehow, when you know someone is doing something for money, it takes the allure out of it.

"She's doing well," Kylian says, gesturing to the table to our left.

This is only the second time the trainee has been playing in public, but she has a keen eye and is bold. Bets like a demon, takes care to mix them up, keeping everyone on guard. She plays like she has nothing to lose, and that's one of the hardest players to read.

"Gotta get her to work on that that flick of her tongue on the left side of her mouth," Kylian adds. "She's done it the last three times she got a double pair or higher. Maybe get her to chew some gum. That always helped a guy I played with in college," Kylian suggests, keeping his voice low.

Something about the way he not only embraces my work but also is interested enough to give me feedback and suggestions makes me want to kiss him right here and now. I restrain myself, though, since I'm sure that somewhere in this room is someone who has a direct line to my brother's ear, and I'd rather we weren't ambushed at my dad's house about why I was kissing his best friend in public.

I jot the note down on my phone as I've been doing for the last thirty minutes. It's not always as easy for the experienced players she's paired with to notice everything going on in the game when she's worrying about her own game. But with that trainee already tripling her chip count for the night, we can probably concentrate on the other trainee, Annie, who is not doing as well. Her chip pile is down to almost half, and the worry on her face is broadcasting clearly to everyone at that table that she is playing it safe.

"She's nervous, it's her first time," I whisper to Kylian, and he nods.

"Is she out anything if she loses?"

I shake my head. "No. We cover them for $1000 a night. They lose that, night's over. And I make it clear that I don't expect the trainees to be bringing anything back for a few weeks. Playing here is not the same as in your bedroom with your friends."

"I'm not sure she believes you. She's clutching those chips like they're her children."

"She knows. All the girls talk. They know how this works. I have never pulled a girl for doing badly, only when she decided it wasn't for her, and then I've always found her work somewhere else."

He considers my words for a few moments. "Let me know if I can help. We are always looking for good workers."

Before I can answer, we hear a shout at one of the tables, and we look over to see one of the players stand up and slam his hand onto the table. Security is immediately behind him, the dealer says something to them, and he's escorted out of the club.

Mai-Li, the mentor on that table, stands up and walks over to me.

"Sorry, boss, he was really rude to Annie, making inappropriate comments about her dress. I told him to leave her alone, and he got really mad and threatened me."

It's obvious that the incident has rattled her; even under her makeup, she's pale, and her hands shake. I take her hands and look her in the eyes, trying to ground her. "Hey, it's okay. Why don't you tell the dealer that I'm going to sit in for a few rounds because you need a break, okay?"

"No, I'm okay..."

I squeeze her wrist. "You're not. Night's still young. Take a break." I give her a reassuring smile. A lot of these women got out of their strip clubs and brothels to get away from this kind of disgusting male behavior. Most of the time, the attention wasn't too bad, but now and then a sore loser channels his misogyny toward the women and shows the whole world the kind of man he really is. *Booze and cards,* as my father always says, *will show you a person's true character.*

The poker room has gotten considerably busier as I watch Mai-Li talk to the dealer to explain the situation. She gestures to me, and the dealer nods.

"I'll be back," I tell Kylian as he's focused on a hand going on at another table.

"Hmm? Oh, I'll come with you. I can fill the jerk's seat."

I eye him, seeing how he reacts when I say, "You really want to play with me?"

"I mean, I won't if you're scared," he taunts me.

"Oh, Kylian Baxter, I hope you brought your wallet."

He pulls it out of his pocket and waves it with a grin, then follows me to the table and hands the dealer his credit card. She pushes $5000 in chips and his card back him; he pulls them toward him and winks at me from across the table.

This goes against every single one of my rules about staying focused and objective while working, but there isn't anything I can do about it now. Still, the distraction is immediately evident when the dealer has to remind me to bet.

"Ma'am. You're the big blind," the dealer politely prompts me.

Embarrassed, I slide my bet across into the pot.

Immediately, the memories come flooding back.

A year ago, I sat in this poker club two tables away, alone, stacking my night's winnings, when a woman sat down. She looked a little older, late thirties maybe, holding a deck of cards. Without a word, she dropped $1000 onto the table and dealt each of us five cards.

I didn't know what she was doing, but I matched her stack of chips and fanned the cards in my hand. Two cards were pulled from my hand and slid face down across the table to her. She dealt me two cards and then dealt one for herself.

"Well?" she said, gesturing at my sack of chips.

"$500." I threw the chips into the middle.

"Raise, $1000," she countered

"Check and raise, $1000."

She grinned at me. "We could do this all night, or are you going to put your money where your mouth is?" She threw a $50,000 chip into the pile.

I eyed her. I only had about $39,000, but I was going to be damned if I didn't see this through. "All in."

"That's more like it."

She spread her cards out.

Three sevens.

I nodded. "Nice, but not as nice as a flush." I turned mine over. "Diamonds are so pretty, don't you think?"

She grinned and stood up, handing me a business card. "Call me. I have a proposition for you."

On the card was a name, Ananya, and a phone number.

The next day, sitting in my new, completely empty apartment that I'd bought with money I'd had to ask my dad for, I called the number, and my life has never been the same.

Ten rounds later, I have a grudging respect for Kylian that I didn't expect to have. He's daring, sharp, and restrained in equal measure, already doubling his investment and all the while seemingly keeping his eyes trained on me the entire time.

Annie is seated next to me, and that seems to have given her some confidence as her game picks up and she even manages to win two rounds with, no doubt, a small concession by Kylian when he folds during one round when it's the only two of them left. She gives him the biggest smile of relief as she drags $2500 worth of chips into her pile. He winks at me while she audibly sighs. It doesn't help with my training her, but it helps with her confidence which can be just as important.

The beautiful, older woman sitting next to him has also been trying to draw him into conversation the whole time, despite me throwing her daggers every time she reaches out and touches him on the hand or the shoulder. He brushes her off each time, politely and one time even gestures across the table to me, as if informing her that he's taken.

But it is just as I'd predicted, women throwing themselves at him, left, right, and dead center.

There must be something in my expression because during one shuffle, he gets up out of chair, hands in his pocket, strolling over to me. Then, pulling me to my feet, he kisses me. Sweetly at first, then with his whole body, wrapping his arms around me with one hand tangled in my hair. I'm not sure how long the kiss lasts, but when he finally pulls away, everyone at that table and some at the surrounding ones are staring.

Thi"I think that should do it, don't you?" he whispers into my ear before helping me back down to my seat and then returning to his with a big, lusty wink when he gets there.

Blondie huffs and pulls away from him, sulky as she picks up her cards with a scowl. The next few rounds go by uneventfully until the man wearing a novelty cowboy hat, sitting on the other side of Kylian, and I get stuck in a betting war after everyone else has folded.

"Big bet for a little lady," Cowboy growls when I raise again. "Your pretty boyfriend here give you some pocket money after you let him do dirty things to you?"

Kylian puts his hands on the table and is about to jump out of his chair, but I stare him down. *Sit down*, I mouth.

He grits his teeth but stays perched on the edge of his seat in case he's not happy with what else the man is about to say.

I make a show of checking my hand again as I say, "You know, most men would treat a 'little lady' with a little respect. But I guess you're not a man. How about a side bet to make things a little more interesting? If I can guess what you're holding, you give me whatever's in your left pocket."

Cowboy downs the rest of his beer and snarls at the idea but is too drunk to be able to refuse. "Fine. But if I guess what's right, I get a little of what you're giving Pretty Boy here."

Kylian stares at me across the table, his anger palpable. I have to ignore him and focus if I want this to turn out the way I hope it does.

I shrug, pretending I'm not totally disgusted at the idea of him touching me. "Deal. Everybody here is a witness."

He licks his lips like he's already imagining the things he wants to do to me. *Enjoy it while you can, sleazebag.* "You've got a full house."

I feign a look of shock. "Wow, what a good guess. My guess for you is two pair. One face cards, one not."

He growls and throws his cards onto the table. A pair of fives and a pair of queens.

I lay mine out. A two, a seven, an eight, a ten, and a king. Different suits.

There's a gasp around the table.

I lean back, locking my fingers in front of me. "So looks like you won the pot."

"Damn right I did..." he grunts and reaches out to drag them all toward him.

I wait for him to finish before I say, "But lost the side bet. Pay up, please."

He growls, salivating at the pile of chips in front of him. "That's ridiculous."

Blondie yells out, "Booo! You would've made her pay up. We all saw you take the bet. Pay up."

"You shut up, bitch!" he spits.

This time there's no stopping Kylian as he stands up and towers over the sleazebag. "Apologize to both ladies for speaking to them like a stinking, fucking ogre. And pay up. Then you can take your measly pot and get the fuck out of here." The tone in his voice is glacial, but his eyes rage.

The asshole loses a little of his bravado. "But... she played me, man."

"How? Did she cheat? No. I don't think so. You've been bleeding chips to everyone at this table. It's not her fault you suck at playing poker as much as you suck at being a man. Now apologize. To the two ladies. And then to everyone at this table for wasting their time with your bullshit."

He avoids eye contact with Kylian by staring down at the table. "But I..."

Kylian takes one step closer and breathes down his sweaty neck. "Now."

"Sorry," he mumbles under his breath.

"Louder."

"Sorry! For fuck's sake!"

Kylian steps back. "Good. Now empty your pockets."

Cowboy tucks his hand into his right pocket.

"I'm sorry, I do believe you bet your left pocket. Or do you need a lesson about left and right as well as wrong and right?"

He looks up at Kylian, shoulders dropping in defeat. "Come on, man, it was just some good-natured fun. I didn't mean to be rude to your girl. I can apologize."

Kylian returns his look with one of steely indifference, but everyone at the table knows that crossing him now will not be in their self-interest.

Cowboy finally slides his hand into his left pocket, pulls out his bulging wallet, and throws it onto the table. "Take that, bitch."

And those are the last words he speaks before Kylian's fist slams his cheek, making a sickening crack before he falls to the ground. Out.

We all watch as Kylian nudges him with his foot as the dealer calls security over. "Well, I'm sorry for that unpleasantness, everybody. And I think these might belong to you, Miss," he says, throwing the wallet at me.

I grin, catching it with one hand before laying it on top of the pile of chips in front of me.

Kylian pushes all of his chips to the dealer as an incredibly generous tip and then walks over to me.

I take his hand and stand up. "Well, I think that's enough of us for now. Thank you everyone, I'll be returning this seat to a person who has less of a penchant for drama. Wishing you all a lucky evening."

Mai-Li arrives to reclaim her seat and play resumes.

"Did you really have to punch him?" I say under my breath, trying to stifle a giggle.

"One of us was going to, and he might have a chance for survival if it was me," he replies, pulling me against his side.

My fingers come up to tickle the side of his neck. "Well, then you owe me a drink. I left my water back at the table."

"Should we go back to the bar?"

"No, Mister Baxter. You're on my turf now. And I have something to show you."

His mouth nibbles on my bare shoulder, as always, alighting something hot and urgent in the pit of my stomach. "Lead the way."

Twenty-Five

Kylian

I wasn't sure how Kiara was going to react to how I acted during the incident at the poker table, and that makes me uneasy as she leads me through the poker club. Most of the time, I'm one of the most level-headed of my brothers. Words over fist is usually my motto. I'm not really sure where the macho Kylian came from, but it's not the first time that has happened this week. And it's easy to guess that the reason is the beautiful woman in the world's miniest of minidresses leading me into an elevator right now.

She grabs a bottle of champagne from the kitchen's fridge, waving hello to the cooks in there as she leads me into a back hallway and into the service elevator. She assures me that the owner is okay with her being back here, and to be honest, even if they weren't, I wouldn't have been able to tell her no anyway.

"Come on, Lady Killer," she teases me, taking my hand and dragging me out to an open rooftop that overlooks the neighborhood. LED lights drape over the railing that runs along the perimeter. Other than those, it's completely empty except for us and a tarp folded up in the corner.

"Wow, this place is incredible," I sigh, enjoying the twinkling lights.

"Well, it's not the view from Baxter Tower, but it's pretty."

I smile at her. "The view is most definitely better."

She blushes and tries to hide it by handing me the bottle of Cristal. "Didn't you say you owed me a drink?"

"I did. Wait here." I feel her eyes on me as I pick up the tarp and unfold it, laying it out on the middle of the roof. I'd meant it when

I said I liked her eyes on me. It makes me feel stronger, bolder. She walks over to me, a swing in her hips that I hope I put there, and lowers herself down onto it gracefully, ladylike. You wouldn't have known that two hours ago she was begging me for my cock inside her.

A gentle, cooling breeze washes over us, and everything feels so peaceful. "This place is beautiful, how did you know about it?"

A cheeky grin spreads itself over her face. "Um, I may have spent some time here."

"Yeah?" I tear off the foil and unwind the muselet keeping the cork in place. The champagne pops open, and I hand the bottle back to her. She tips it into her mouth, taking a thirsty sip, a single drop leaking out of the corner of her mouth and over her jaw. I lean over, dragging my tongue along the length of her neck, collecting the drop of champagne on my tongue, and then continue to her lips.

She returns the kiss, pressing her mouth gently against mine.

When I pull away, she hands the bottle to me, and I take my own drink, preferring the single drop I'd licked off her neck.

"So my whole operation? It started here."

"No kidding. How did that all come about?" Finding out more about her thrills me almost as much as her body against mine. I want everything about her. Her past, her future.

"Yeah, when I came back to Hong Kong, I'll be honest, I didn't really know what I was going to do. I came here to be close to my mom."

I'd done the same when grandfather was taking a turn for the worse. We all dropped everything and congregated back in London so we could be with him. Nothing else mattered during that time. And when he took his last breath, the four of us and our father were there, holding his hands and sending him into the afterlife with us telling him how much we loved him and appreciated all the things he'd done for us. If everything else turns to shit in my life, I will be glad that I was there for that moment. To pay tribute to the great man that he was.

"I remember I was glad to hear that you made it back in time. You only got to spend a few weeks with her, is that right?"

"Yes." Her voice is sad, and it makes me want to hold her and take it all away. "But she was okay during that time. In a lot of pain but still happy to see me and eat all her favorite foods."

"You didn't cook for her, did you?" I nudge her playfully. "She actually liked my congee."

Kiara looks wistful. "I bet she did. She loved all sort of Asian cuisines. They were her favorites. We used to tease her about that being the reason she married Dad."

"Hey, I don't blame her. I'm sure it's one of the reasons Damien is marrying My-Linh. How have you been since she's been gone?"

The wire cage from the bottle twists in her hand. "I... don't know. Um... she and I didn't have a perfect relationship. It wasn't bad, but... well, mothers and daughters. Isn't there some saying about that?"

"I wouldn't know. My mother only had sons, and none of us speak to her now."

She frowns and scrutinizes me to see if I'm being flippant, probably. But I'm not. It's one of the aspects of my life I've made peace with. It would be hell if I hadn't.

"Should I be sad about that? No matter what happened with me and my mom, we could still always talk."

"I'm pretty sure that, considering most of us have a drinking problem because of her, it's better for our livers that we don't talk to her too often. Kingsley definitely has an unhealthy relationship with his drinks cart. Matthias's unhealthy relationship is with his dick. But Damien is probably the worst. I thought he was going to die from alcohol poisoning when Mom decided to grace him with her presence a few months ago."

Kiara gasps. "Oh, that's terrible. Why did she come back?"

"She was about to get married to her fourth husband. She needed someone to walk her down the aisle. And Damien was always her favorite. He looks just like her. Beautiful in a sad kind of way, although his sadness is probably from the way she's always fucked with his head."

Her head shakes as the reality of how truly shitty my mother was dawns. "Well, my problem with my mother is nothing I can do anything about. And I can't really talk to anyone else about it."

I gently touch her cheek. "What about to me? Despite appearances, I'm actually a good listener as well as a good talker."

She takes another drink, catching the last of the drops on her tongue.

"If there was anyone I would talk to about it, it would be you. I promise. And maybe one day. Just... not today."

Her skin is covered in goosebumps, and so I try to envelope her with my arms and legs, my face burying in her neck, breathing her in.

"You smell like everything... everything..."

"Everything... what?"

I take another deep breath. "Just fucking everything."

She lets out the tiniest little laugh. "You have quite the silver tongue." She pauses like she's not sure if she should say the next thing. "Is it because you've had a lot of practice?" she teases but not without a tinge of wonder.

I grimace. "There is no way to answer that without you hating me. But what if I told you I haven't had that much practice in the last five years?"

She looks skeptical.

"You really need to believe what I mean when I say I pined. Okay, sure, I flirted, had a few flings, and when I mean a few, I mean... very few compared to what I was like before. They were purely physical. I couldn't even tell you their names or pick them out of a lineup." My face screws up thinking about what a fucking asshole that makes me sound like. But it's the truth. All I wanted in a woman that whole time... was her.

"I didn't see you at the funeral," she says, changing the subject. "Were you there?"

"Yes. Of course. I came a bit early and made sure your dad and Nathan saw me. Then I hung around the back. It was a very crowded service; it wouldn't have been hard to miss me. Especially when I was trying hard to not be seen by you."

"You didn't have to do that."

"Yes, I did. The last person you needed to see when farewelling your mother was the face of, and I quote based on what Nathan told me, 'The dumbest man to ever taint English soil who embodies every stereotype you've ever heard about the British and their teeth.'" I can barely get through it all before I'm laughing so hard it shakes us both.

She doesn't react... like she's frozen, and then her whole body shakes with a laugh that feels like a cold beer on a hot summer day. "You deserved it! I don't have any idea why I had a crush on you for so long."

"You mean since London."

Her eyes shift side to side, and then she nods. It's not entirely convincing.

"Well, well, well, little Kiki Yin, did you have a crush on me before that?"

She shoves me so hard I almost tip over completely onto my side. "What? No! You were just my stinky brother's friend. Ugh, shut up."

"Oh, Kiara. You liked me from before London," I tease her. Her face pales, but she doesn't respond, probably waiting for me to talk myself into a hole. "Your family wasn't even living there anymore," I continue, "and you were studying in the U.S. Why were you even in England?" I stare at her. "Kiara, were you in London to see me?"

This time she holds her gaze, facing straight ahead, a twitch in her jaw. I've touched a nerve.

"Hey," I say softly and hug her around the shoulders, kissing her neck. "Did you really come to London to see me?"

"I... I missed London. And my friends. So I didn't *not* come to London for you."

"That's too many negatives for me. Clarify for the dumbest man to ever taint British soil."

Her chest fills, and then she turns her head, meeting my gaze, the look on her face tearing my heart in two. "Yes. I came to London hoping to see you. I was... I wanted to see you without my family around. And maybe, if it felt right, I might see if there was anything between us."

Something twists, agonizing, in my chest. "Oh, Kiara."

She sniffs and tries to move away from me. "It's fine."

"It... is the furthest thing from fine." I jump to my feet, replaying that night outside the club in my mind, how I'd felt, what we'd said to each other, how we'd almost kissed. How my insides had churned all night wondering what had happened and where these feelings had come from. And then trying to drown them in alcohol. And the worst memory, the look on her face when she'd seen me and Odette at my bar.

"Oh my god. I can't believe I was such a fucking asshole," I murmur, stumbling to the rail running along the roof, trying to drag air into my lungs and still my spinning head. "What the fuck did I do?" I say, trying to process it. I've already been struggling with how long it's taken us to get together. Three days in, I already can't imagine a moment of my life without her in it. And it turns out all this time that it was my fault. I thought that it had been just a passing fancy for her, that I had just been another body at the club that night, and the music, the dancing, the drinks are what had made her notice me for the first time. The thought that she came to England specifically to see me and I had hurt her in the worst way makes me want to shred my skin from my body.

A hand on my back surprises me, and I spin around.

She looks back at me, hand still outstretched, eyes shining.

"When's the last time you went back to England? When's the last time you went dancing?" I ask, afraid to know the answer.

She thinks about not answering, I can feel it. But the last thing I want is for her to spare my feelings. I beg her with a look for the answers.

"That was the last time."

"Last time you've been back to England or dancing?"

"Both. I don't go to London or night clubs just for fun anymore." Her eyes glance away after the confession.

"Kiara. Oh, god, Kiara. I am so sorry."

"You've already said sorry." Her smile reflects a sadness I put there.

"I didn't know. I had no idea. I thought it was just... it was just a coincidence that night, us meeting like that."

"I hadn't planned to see you that night. That was a surprise even for me, and when I realized it was you, I thought"—she lets out a wry laugh—"I thought the universe was meddling in the best way. I guess I was wrong."

"It was me. I was so fucking stupid. I didn't realize until it was much too late that the feelings I felt that night were real. By then, I had already done a pretty good job at making you hate me forever."

She smiles, and I press my hand harder against my cheek. "Unfortunately, not quite that long. But I never ever thought we'd get to where we are right now."

"And where is that?"

"I don't know. I'm almost too scared to think about it or look at it directly. Like if I breathe on it a little too hard, it's going to just disappear into the wind."

She pulls on my wrist and rests her head against my chest. "But whatever happens, I'm going to remember these last few days forever."

"I'm not going anywhere. And if you go somewhere, I'll follow you. To the ends of the earth and back. So don't even try it. Because I'm a pretty fast runner."

She snorts, and it breaks the tension. "Please. I've run away twice from you now."

I throw her an exasperated glare. "Those don't count. You caught me off guard both times! One time you even slapped me."

She giggles, and the sound vibrates through my ribcage and permeates my whole body, healing the cuts her confession sliced into my soul.

The tension broken, we stand there for a minute, enjoying the view and the company.

After a moment, she pulls away from me and looks up. "Can I ask you something?"

"Anything. Except what my tell is."

"Oh, please, you tap with your left finger. You try to hide it by moving your hand down under the table, but that just makes it all the more obvious."

"Rude. Ask away."

She clears her throat. "Have you always been so... er, bossy during sex? I didn't expect that from you."

My mouth drops open. "Excuse me! Bossy?"

She lets out a nervous laugh. "Yeah... I mean, I like it. I just haven't ever been with anyone like that."

Every time she mentions the men before me, I want to commit bloody murder. "I'm going to want every single one of those names, by the way, and a gun."

"Oh, shush... answer the question."

"So I guess the answer is yes, I like to be in charge during sex. And get you into the best position for you to come as hard as you can. I know what you want, even if you don't." I kiss the curve of her neck. "I can make you come harder than you ever have, you just have to give into me."

She doesn't say anything, but there's a sharp intake of breath. She knows it's true. "And what about you?" she whispers.

"Angel, I'm not worried about my orgasm. I know how to get my orgasm from you."

She looks out over the balcony and then says so softly I almost don't hear her, "Show me. Show me how you'd use me to make you come right now."

I feel my eyes dilate in that instant. Every dirty thought that I've been trying to push out of my head so that I can function as a non-sex-crazed human when I'm with her comes crashing to the fore, emptying my brain with anything but the thought of her.

But she's about to see what my thoughts would be like if I let them run rampant.

I take my jacket off and lay it down on my feet, then I touch her cheek, and I say, "Get on your knees."

She takes a moment as if she hadn't actually expected me to respond. But she's underestimating me if she thinks I'm not going to take what I want, what I need from her on this rooftop right now.

"Now," I add, in case she's having any thought of not obeying.

Her knees bend, and she lowers herself to her knees, face level with my crotch.

"Take my cock out."

Her breath slows as she reaches for my zipper, my hardness begging to be set free. As her shaking hand pulls the zipper down its track, her tongue pokes out to run along her lower lip, and my arousal explodes off the scale at the thought of my cum dripping over her perfect little mouth.

"Fuck." The curse slides out of me when her hand brushes against my hard cock as she reaches in to pull it out. I'd not changed into another pair of underwear at the slight chance that she actually was going to follow through with her comment about wanting to taste her pussy on my cock.

It had been almost impossible to concentrate during the poker games while the head of my cock tented the crotch of pants because I'd had an image of my cock ramming against the back of her throat playing on a loop.

I look down, and she's staring at my cock like she doesn't know what to do with it.

But I know she does.

She's so fucking sexy, her entire being is saturated with sensuality, and I know she's going to give my cock the care it deserves.

But something about her question before makes me wonder if she wants to lean into the fantasy of me taking what I want from her. "Do you need me to tell you what to do, or are you going to be a good girl and suck my cock better than it's ever been sucked?

"I want to show you how much I've thought about doing this."

I lean back against the rail and brush my fingers down her cheek. "Show me, sweet angel. Taste your cum on my cock. Just like you've always wanted to."

Her fingers, tentative, nervous, grab my cock at the base, and her tongue, warm, wet, flicks out against my cockhead.

Don't moan, Kylian. Not yet. Make her work for it.

I watch as she purses her lips and drops them around the tip of my cock and spreads them over the head, catching on the ridge.

Fuck.

With my cockhead trapped inside her lips, she presses her tongue flat against the underside seam, licking up and down.

"Hell..."

She pulls off and looks up at me, eyes wide, innocent. "Did I do something wrong?"

"No, baby. You're doing just fine. Keep going."

"Okay." Her voice comes out small and shy.

It thrills me. She doesn't know yet, but I'm going to throat fuck that shyness right out of her.

She grips my cock at the base, and then, just as I'm waiting for her to start slow and easy, she slides her mouth over my cock, taking me halfway. It's not all the way down, but I had not expected that she could do that. My cock isn't extraordinarily long, but it's thick and definitely more than she can take without any preparation.

"Yes, baby. Take me into your mouth. Show me how much you want my cock."

She tries to murmur something, but it's nothing but a humming on my cockhead.

Her tongue presses against my underside as she pulls off and then back down again, taking a little more of me.

"Oh, angel. That's good. Keep going. I want you to get used to it for a bit first."

Her mouth drags up, hitting all the right places. "First?"

"Yes. Don't stop."

"Before what?"

"If you keep talking, I'm not going to give you the opportunity to get ready. Is that what you want? Be very careful how you answer right now."

She looks up at me and moves her hands to lock behind her back. She already knows how much I like that. "Show me."

There's no going back. I lean down and kiss the top of her head. It takes the last ounce of tenderness I have in me, and then I press down on her chin until her mouth is wide open.

Then I push my cock into her needy little mouth, slowly but deeply, until I'm pressed against her tensed throat.

She instantly gags, and I pull back.

"Breathe, angel."

She takes a deep breath, her lips trembling. The effect is so fucking beautiful. Even without touching me, she's notching my need up to unbearable levels.

"Don't take your eyes off me. Not once. Not until I cum into your pretty little mouth, understand?"

She nods.

I wait until she takes another breath and opens her mouth wide, and I slide into her, faster this time. She knows now that she's going to choke on my thick cock.

But it is going to get easier. She just has to give in, completely.

And then she's going to become addicted to taking me down her throat.

I slide in and out, each time a little deeper, pulling out a little every time she gags, waiting for her to recover and then thrusting in again.

"A little more, baby, relax your throat, make my cock wet with your spit."

She looks down at the cock ravaging her mouth, and I grip her chin.

"Eyes locked on me."

She immediately flicks her eyes up; they're watery, just like I want them.

She's ready.

I grab the back of her head, fingers tangling in her hair, and ram my cock into her.

She doesn't gag this time and swallows as I pull out, just in time to drive into her throat again. My cock stretches her red lips, and damn, she looks so fucking hot, earrings swinging by the side of her flushed face as she struggles to take my thick cock down her throat.

"God, baby. Fuck, you're taking my cock so good, angel. Just like I knew you would. I wish you knew how many times I've jacked off to the idea of you sucking my cock like this."

She makes a noise, and something in her eyes flash. Something deeper than I can comprehend right now as I fuck her mouth.

"Oh fuck, oh fuck, oh fuck." My moans cascade out of me with each thrust into her.

It's hot and so wet and slippery but also so tight as her lips stretch around the base of my cock and then around the rim of my cockhead.

"My perfect little slut, I'm going to cum so hard in your mouth. I want you to swallow every drop."

She nods as well as she can with my cock choking her.

I'm close.

I need this.

I want this.

I grab the back of her head, holding it still as I pound into her, bruising her throat until I'm almost bursting, then I pull out with just the head in her mouth.

"Open, angel," I grunt and jack my cock until my balls explode and my cock erupts into her mouth, dripping out of the corner of her lipstick-smudged lips

My climax screeches down my back, full of stingy, burning, hot pleasure.

I drop to my knees and pull her to me, kissing her hard as we pass my cum between us until she finally swallows, her hands reaching down to stroke my softening dick.

"Fuck," I whisper again. "You are everything in this world that I have ever wanted. And more."

She holds my face in her hands and answers me with a kiss.

Twenty-Six
Kiara

We sleep late into the morning the next day. I heard him leave a voicemail for his assistant to cancel any plans that he had for the day. I questioned what meetings he would have on a Saturday, but he just brushed them off and undressed me before we climbed into his bed and fell asleep wrapped up in each other's exhausted bodies.

When I wake up around 11 a.m., he's still out, still facing me, his face completely relaxed in sleep. I watch him for minutes, hours, how long exactly I don't know. I watch to remind myself this is real. That I'm sleeping in this beautiful man's bad and... he wants me as much as I want him.

I hope.

I think.

The doubt remains there right in the back of my brain, but after everything that has happened, I feel like I owe it to me, more than to him, to give it a try.

If nothing else, we will have had these last few days.

And if it doesn't work out, my mind and body will never be the same.

The memory of the way he looked while he was fucking my mouth last night refuses to let go of the chokehold it has on me. I should feel embarrassed that I basically begged him to let me suck him off. But I feel nothing but the need to do it again. The idea of waking him up with my mouth on him almost takes over my want for him to sleep.

He can sleep after.

Kiara, you have lost your fucking mind.

"I can feel you looking at me," he murmurs, eyes still closed.

I was so busy thinking about the taste of my own pussy on his cock that I didn't even notice the change in his breathing.

"Sorry, I'll let you get back to sleep."

Before I can slide out of the bed, he's reached over and grabbed me around the waist and pulled me against his warm, sleepy body. Eyes still closed, he fluffs the sheet back over the both of us, burying his face into my shoulder.

"Don't leave."

"I was just going to let you sleep some more. And maybe make us some breakfast."

"I said, don't leave. Ever."

"Okay, I won't. Sleep, baby. I'll be here."

That seems to placate him, and soon his breathing is soft and regular again.

The feel of his body against mine, his breath against my neck, his arm around me brings me more comfort than I've ever thought I needed.

And I fall.

To sleep.

And other things that I should know better than to fall into.

We sleep for another hour and wake up to the sun overheating our bodies through the window.

Kylian kicks the sheet off of us and points the remote to turn the ceiling fan up. "Good morning, Kiki."

"I think it's closer to lunchtime."

"Good morning, lunchtime, afternoon, evening, and night!" he shouts, obviously refreshed from his sleep.

"That's a lot of gooding."

He chuckles. "Have you always been this dry?"

"Poor Kylian, you really think that Nathan is the most sarcastic one in the family? You obviously weren't around my mother that much."

"Enough to know she was no shrinking violet either. You're definitely her daughter, though. Nathan is your father's son."

My face freezes, refusing to react. He hadn't meant anything by it. It's true. "He is Dad's clone, through and through. I wonder if he'll meet someone who will knock him off his feet and love the playboy right out of him."

"You mean like you did to me?"

I feel the blush spread and hide it in a pillow.

He climbs under the sheet with me, kissing me in a way that's different to every kiss between us that's come before.

I fall into it, ready to lose myself in him.

And then a rumble permeates the sound of the bedroom.

"Um." He pulls away and stares down at my stomach. "Was that you?"

I force the blood rising up my cheeks to go back down. "Was what me?"

"That sound! It came from you!"

"I'm pretty sure that I have absolutely no idea what you're talking about."

He grins and reaches over and pokes me in the belly. "I think it's time that I put something in there."

My jaw drops open, knowing full well what he had meant but feeling like he deserves to be teased. "You want me to have your baby? Kylian! Yes! I will be your baby mama!"

But instead of reacting like I'd hoped, turning pale, spluttering, running out of the room and leaving me forever, his eyes darken, and his face is more serious than I've ever seen it. "Okay," he says.

"What?" I yell, jumping out of the bed. "I was just kidding!"

"Oh, well, I wasn't."

"Kylian! Have you lost your ever-loving mind? We have"—I wave in the space between us—"only been doing this for one day! We cannot be talking about this. Oh my god!"

He shrugs, dripping with nonchalance. "Why not?"

"Because... I don't even know your middle name!"

"It's Francis. Let's make a baby."

The words sound warbled and crystal clear all at once. And now, instead of scaring him, I've scared myself. I run out of the room and into the bathroom, jumping into the shower. Thoughts swirl around my head about what the hell he and I are doing.

And then I notice... he hasn't chased me. He normally would've run after me.

Wait.

I storm out of the shower, not even bothering to turn it off, and storm back into the bedroom. He's sitting back, hands clasped behind the back of his head, waiting with a fucking shit-eating grin over his face.

"Wow, you're naked and wet," he exclaims, waggling his eyebrows at me.

I ignore him, shake my finger at him, glaring. "You're teasing me about the baby thing, aren't you?"

He grins and shrugs.

"Kylian!" I launch myself onto the bed, straddling his legs while I hit him with a pillow as he tries to defend himself with his elbows. "I thought you were fucking serious! I was thinking about all the ways I had to let you down about having your baby right now without hurting your feelings. I'd thought you'd been possessed by some baby hungry guy."

He tries to protect himself. "Ow. Help! Kiki's attacking me!"

"Who are you talking to?"

"The baby hungry dude who's possessing me. He says you came in here naked and wet; you must be onboard with the idea!"

"Shut up!" I pull back for some momentum and swing the pillow at him.

But he's too fast. He ducks out of the way and then grabs me, pinning me to the bed, his body weighing deliciously heavily against me.

"I was teasing you. But that doesn't mean that I wouldn't do it in a second. You and me, Kiara Yin. This is it for me. This, right here. You and me. This is it. Get used to it." He brushes the hair from my face. "Tell me you don't feel the same."

And I can't.

>>> →♥← <<<

He punishes me for the pillow fight by taking me to the edge of coming for almost an hour. When he finally feels like I've had enough torture, he takes me on my back, legs wrapped around his waist as he slides in and out of me at a frustratingly slow pace that builds to an orgasm that almost has me passing out and falling asleep again. At some point, I jolt awake remembering that the shower is still running, and we take turns cleaning each other.

My stomach continues to protest the state of its emptiness, and finally Kylian takes pity on me. He tells me to go pick a bottle of wine from his specially built vault while he ducks out to grab some supplies. When he comes back, he banishes me from the kitchen while he "gets ready." I hide in the bedroom, making the bed and lying back down on it, grabbing the shirt I ripped off him when we got home from the poker club and burying my face in it. Can you get drunk on a smell? It smells just like him, a combination of his soap, aftershave, and something unidentifiable. But it's the scent that floats around me every time he pulls me in close to him, desperate and urgent like he can't bear for me to not be touching him at all times.

This is not at all what I had imagined being with him would be like.

All the thoughts, the wishing, the fantasies, I guess they had never gone much further than the first kiss... and maybe the first time we'd be together. I didn't think that I'd be instilled with an inebriating giddiness around him. Last night, I had barely been able to concentrate knowing he was sitting across the poker table watching my every move. That's something I have never ever experienced. At the poker table, I normally have laser focus. Every move, every breath, every word that's happening around me, my brain filters out the important information, finding patterns, identifying the difference between the authentic, involuntary reactions, and the disingenuous movements aimed at manipulating and controlling the game.

But last night, the only moves, breaths, words that I cared about were his.

I am lost in him.

I don't know my way out.

And I don't know if I want to.

"Ready?" His voice startles me, and I jump up. "Do you need to borrow a shirt, Kiki? That's my dirty one from last night."

"Oh, is it?" I fling it away as if I wasn't sniffing it like a coke addict

The smirk on his face suggests that he knows exactly what I was doing.

"Ready?" he says again.

"Ready for what?"

His hand stretches out, and I take it. "Come and see."

I'm not sure what I'd expected, but when I look out the living room window, there's a blanket, some cushions, and a picnic set up on the balcony.

My stomach rumbles again in approval.

"Come on. There's a little bit of everything. I don't really know what you like to eat."

He leads me out onto the balcony, and the air is still out here today.

The spread really had a little of everything. Cheese and crackers, little skewers of BBQ'd meat, har gow and shumai dumplings, a fruit salad, little bowls of the congee he made yesterday...

"Is there anything here you like to eat?" His voice carries the tiniest timbre of doubt at my silence.

I reach for a shumai to pop into my mouth. "It's perfect. And I'm telling you now, fuck Asian etiquette. If you take the last har gow, I will stab you with a chopstick. Right through the heart."

He laughs, and it whips in the air around us, filling me with happiness.

Twenty-Seven
Kylian

After our picnic lunch, the wind picks up enough that we move inside and lie down on the couch, languishing in the aftereffects of the morning and the meal. We dip in and out of sleep, and it's her voice that pulls me out of a two-minute nap.

"Who's your favorite brother?"

The question comes out of nowhere, and it makes me wonder what she's been thinking about.

"Groucho. No, Harpo," I joke.

"I'm serious!"

I tickle the back of her neck, making her sigh. "Um, I don't know if I have a favorite."

"*I* have a favorite brother," she says as if that's valid.

"You only have one. That makes it easier."

"Er, you haven't lived with him. His bathroom habits alone should make him ineligible to be a favorite anything."

I splutter. "Excuse me! I have as well! We lived together when we were at Wharton together."

"Oh yeah, 'bromancing.' I'm not entirely sure that you're not just using me to get to him."

I chuckle. "Oh please, he couldn't get me. He can't cook."

"I can't either!"

"Baby girl, you do other things that make up for that. I don't know and I don't want to know what Nathan is like in bed.'" I scrunch up my face. "I lied."

"You do want to know?"

He gives me a look. "Absolutely not. No, I mean, I do know. That apartment we had in Philly had very thin walls. He's a grunter."

"Ewwwwww." She covers her ears with two cushions.

"You're telling me."

"Are you avoiding the question about your favorite brother?"

I'm not. I just don't have an answer. "I... like each of them for different reasons. Damien understands me better than the others. He's closest to me in age, but he's a totally different animal. He's careful and measured, cares so much but pretends he doesn't. So sometimes he alienates people with his intensity."

"Maybe his fiancée will change that?"

I think about that for a moment and then nod. "I think what she does is help him translate that intensity into actions and communications that people can understand. For example, he used to glare at people when they came onto the elevator because he felt like it was wasting his time to stop at each floor. My-Linh helped him see that they're wasting just as much time waiting for another elevator, and who the fuck is he that his time is worth ten of his employees' time."

She giggles. "That's funny. How did she do that?"

"She literally said it straight to his face."

"I like her! Okay, what about Matthias?"

I shudder. "Matthias and I have to live on different continents for the good of mankind."

She sits up, her face alive with curiosity "Oh, why?"

"We're the same person, but he's like ten times worse. You think I talk a lot. I'm basically a mute when I'm with him. And he has no concept of propriety or fear. He will wake up one day and decide that he wants to jump out a plane and will do it himself. And he is a shit stirrer. When you meet him, do not let him bait you into saying anything you don't want to say. He will use it against you with no mercy."

She sees right through what I'm saying. "You sound proud of him."

"I want to be him when I grow up."

"And your eldest brother? You said he is going to be the CEO of Baxter Enterprises when he turns forty-two?"

"Yeah, that's the plan."

She frowns. "Is there a reason why that might not happen?"

"Based on Kingsley's track record, absolutely not. He is, hands down, the absolute best person to head our company into the next decade, for sure. But not everyone is worried about that; they're just worried about their own self-interest. The thing that Kingsley worries about is Baxter, and that means alllll of Baxter, from the janitors to the middle managers to the workers in the cafeterias and the lunchroom in our headquarters. He lives, breathes, and bleeds Baxter Enterprises. He is more intense than the rest of us put together."

"I guess that's what happens when you were always raised to be the heir."

I get up and grab two bottles of water from the fridge. "After our father left when he was sixteen, Kingsley has known what his future is."

"Is he talkative like you?"

I loosen the lid of her water bottle and hand it to her. "You will be lucky to get a word out of him if you're not Damien, Matthias, or me. He does not trust anyone but cares about everyone, if that makes any sense."

She smiles like she does get it. "It does. Did your grandfather have a favorite?" She takes a sip of the water.

"Maybe, but not that we would know. He could work a roomful of strangers, and every single one of them would leave thinking that they were now a part of his family. He's the one who took the company to where it is today."

She gets up and wriggles, shaking her legs out before she climbs back on the couch, tucking her legs under her. "So you talk about Kingsley and your other brothers and their work with Baxter, but you haven't told me much about your work. You probably know more about my work than I do about yours, and I don't think there is another person on this earth that I can say that about."

Her confession feels good. I'm not going to lie, there's something special about someone trusting you enough to share their deepest secrets. I owe her the same. "Does your family know about what you do? I didn't want to out you to Nathan when he came to see me yesterday."

I also don't want to tell her that her father knows about her apartment where some of the woman she rescued are staying. I don't know what else he knows, and I don't want to say anything unless that's all it is.

"Um, they know-ish. I'm not embarrassed about it or anything like that. It's more like the more they know, the more they're going to want to meddle. They're not good with letting me do what I want. Little Keeks always getting herself in trouble, that kind of thinking. So they know that I provide prop players to some of the poker clubs in Hong Kong and some of the casinos in Macau. But... they, er, they don't about the other part of it. The rescuing part."

I don't know if that's true or not, but I'm not ready to get in the middle of the Yin family issues. Especially since I think that Kiara is more than capable of handling the men in her life.

"Well, I think if they knew the whole story, they'd be incredibly proud of you. But that is for you to tell them if and when you're ever ready. They won't be hearing about it from me first." I pretend to pull a zipper across my lips as I sit back down on the couch next to her.

"Good. Now, stop skirting the question!"

"I didn't mean to that time!" I protest, and she laughs and cuddles back against me.

"Okay, I'll give you a pass for that one. So you told me some of the things that you're working on, but what's the one you're most excited about?"

Only one thing pop ups in my mind. Not because I'm not excited about others, I love my work, but right now, I'm focused on one project above all else.

"Watch," I say. "It's the streaming service that I started with Nathan under the umbrella of Yin Tech."

"Of course, Nathan's told me about it. He said he doesn't really have much to do with it, though, that you're co-founders and he put up half of the capital but it's really your brain child."

Nathan having told her that means so much to me. My friend is a not a credit hog, and that's not something you can say about everything. "It's my heart child, really. The story of Netflix completely disrupting the entertainment industry is one of my favorite stories. And while Watch isn't an innovator, I think it can become a really important part of the movie and TV streaming landscape in Asia."

"Don't tell me you watch K Dramas!"

"K Dramas, C Dramas, all the old TVB stuff, all the stuff coming out of Taiwan, Thailand, Vietnam. If one has been made, I've probably watched it."

Her mouth drops open. "Kylian Francis Baxter! You never cease to amaze me. I would never have pegged you as a soap opera fan."

I dig my fingers into her sides as punishment for teasing me. "Hey! Not like the crappy stuff my gran grew up on. I mean, sure they're interesting to watch to learn about how to pull a story out into a year and a half of content. But for true drama, comedy, suspense? Asian dramas are the real masterclass. Sure they get their money's worth out of a good amnesia storyline or missing twin, but hey, I've seen that on *The Young and the Restless* more times than Victor Newman returned to Nikki."

She looks at me with a combination of horror and wonder. "Who *are* you?"

"You don't watch them?"

"Not really. I watched a little with my mom while she was... er, while she was in bed. But I've never really turned one on to watch myself."

I look at her stunned, then shake my head in sheer disappointment. "Wow. Kiara, I'm so sorry your life has been so empty."

She punches my shoulder. "Just tell me more about your company!"

"Well, we have to move fast. Already you can see that Netflix is buying up the licenses for a bunch of Korean and Chinese dramas and short series. But they're only the biggest ones and mostly for an English-speaking audience. And those TV shows' producers are getting seriously ripped off!" I jump onto my feet and wave my hands over my head. "Okay, so you haven't watched K Dramas... or so you say, but did you watch the first season of *Squid Game* when it came out?"

"Of course. It was amazing."

"Yeah, it was one of the all-time most successful shows on the platform. In fact, based on Netflix's data, *Squid Game* ranks as the show that got the most hours viewed in its first month of release. Do you have any idea how insane that is! It made over $900 million dollars and only cost $21 million to make. And do you know why? Not paying the people who made this gem for you what they're worth! I would never treat the Asian dramas and producers so badly. The more money you pour into the industry, the more you're helping it grow. I want there to continue to be new amazing shows for me to watch! Why would I want to stifle the industry?"

I don't even realize I'm yelling until Kiara presses her finger to her lips, trying to shush me, but laughter shakes her shoulders instead.

I can't help but laugh along. "What? Do you think I'm being silly?"

Her laugh fades to a bright smile. "Not at all. I'm just... I'm blown away by your passion for this project."

"You have passion for your work, I have passion for mine, too."

"I can see that, Kylian. And it's amazing to see." There's a respect in her eyes that I haven't seen until now. Granted, a few days ago she was looking at me with pure hatred, so this is a big step between us that I should reasonably expect. "So what specific plans do you have for Watch?"

Not everyone understands my nerdy rants about my work, so she's really opening the floodgates by asking. "Well, I'm in talks to buy into a film studio here. And a production company."

"That's so cool. But can I ask, why don't you start one? You can build it from the ground up."

Her question makes me feel like she's really listening and not just humoring me. "Well, to be honest, these companies that I'm in talks with have amazing track records; they've produced quality films before, but cash flow has become a problem. I honestly don't think I could do any better than what they've done and are doing. I just happen to have caught them during a time when they need money and I have money. They also share a lot of my vision for the film industry in this area of the world. I don't have any plans to overhaul their operations, but I do have some idea on how to use my resources to capitalize on their potential to turn into a self-sustaining organization. And I don't know if having in house production companies is the way to produce some of the shows I'd like to invest in for Watch, but we'll see."

"You... know what you're talking about."

That makes me laugh. "You sound surprised. And interested."

Her grin is followed by a sheepish shrug. "I am interested! It's just that in our household, business talk usually revolves around software this and hardware that and bits and bots, so hearing about something that is real life based is really interesting to me."

"You want to come work for Watch? You can be our marketing guinea pig; you can tell us if the way we're targeting our service to people who don't watch dramas is working."

"Would I be on Yin Tech's payroll or Baxter's?" she jokes with a wink.

I laugh, a little nervously. If things go my way, Watch will soon be a subsidiary of Baxter Enterprises. So if I was actually prudent, I wouldn't be talking about these ideas with her. It's hard to expect her loyalties to lie with me, considering Yin blood is coursing through her veins. And business is business.

I take advantage of the pause in the conversation to turn it back on her. "So do you have any plans for the long-term future? Will your passion project be something other than what you're doing?"

A sly look in her eyes tells me that what she's thinking of has nothing to do with work. Her finger crooks at me, and she pats the couch. "Come here, I'll show you that I can have more than one passion project at the same time."

It doesn't take anything more than that to convince me.

I grab the bowl of strawberries and whipped cream from the tray we'd brought in from the balcony picnic and sit down next to her. Her mouth opens as I feed one to her and feel myself hardening at the way she runs her tongue along her lips to lick off the cream.

She's right... this might be the best kind of passion project there is.

Twenty-Eight
Kiara

WE SPEND THE REST of the day lounging around on the couch, taking turns reminding each other how much we desire one another.

I would never have expected to want someone so much, but every time I look over at him, whether he's reading a book, watching TV, or looking back at me, I feel a pulse emanating from my core.

Every part of my body is sore... in the absolute best way. He suggested I remove my necklace because it was rubbing up against the raised red imprint of his hand around my neck, but there was no way I was going to do that. Every time I twist my neck, the chain drags against the tender skin and I remember the way he gripped my neck with one hand as he made my body his.

Again, on Sunday morning, I wake entwined with him. His arms, legs, body fold around me so that I can't tell where he starts and I end. If I even try to move, he pulls me closer, grumbling in his sleep.

I've never been the best sleeper, but with him, sleep comes so easily.

Deeply.

And unbroken.

When I wake and his breath gently blows against the nape of my neck, I wonder if there's any other place I've been happier in my whole life.

"You're awake," he murmurs, rolling over unto his back and taking me with him, so I can rest my head on his rising and falling chest.

"I've slept more in the last two nights that I have in the last month."

He tries to stifle a yawn unsuccessfully and rubs the top of his tousled head. "Me, too. I didn't even meditate last night. I'm usually tossing and turning if I don't spend at least half an hour meditating."

"Ohhhm," I say, feeling the sound vibrating inside my chest and onto his.

"Ohhhm," he copies and then giggles, rubbing his hand over his face and finally opening his eyes.

I'm looking up at him when he does, addicted to the color of his irises. "Good morning."

He lifts his head off the pillow and purses his lips. "Where's my good morning kiss?"

My hands hold him at arm's length. "You'll get it after I've had my good morning teeth brushing."

"Fuck the teeth brushing, come up here and kiss me like I've just come back from the war and I've been sending you dirty letters for the last few years."

I snicker. "Is that the plot of one of your new shows?"

The way he laughs must echo throughout the entire apartment building, making everyone wonder what the hell is going on up in the penthouse. His eyes are squeezed shut as he laughs, so I reach over and tickle his chest with my fingertips, which makes him yell and roll over, trapping me under him. My legs are under his as he straddles me, digging his fingers into my sides, making me squeal.

"Help! I'm being attacked! By a soap opera watching billionaire who gets mad if you tell him that watching people fall in love in the rain isn't really your cup of tea!"

"Shhhh," he says, cupping his hand over my mouth. "You don't really want to be rescued, do you?" His eyes are as bright as the cloudless sky that we woke up to, blue almost glass-like as if there's no end to them. I always hear about things being bottomless, but Kylian's eyes look like they open up into the heavens, and there is no limit to the heights ones can reach staring into them.

His head drops to press a kiss to my lips, pushing the thoughts about his eyes away, and my arms wrap around his neck so he can't pull away.

"If someone came to rescue me from you, I'd call the police on them," I whisper, my heart skipping a beat at my own confession.

His left eyebrow crooks, and I wonder what romantic notion he's about to say that will out-romance me. "Angel, that sounds like it should be the opening narration for a true crime documentary."

"What? Take that back! It was incredibly romantic. Not my fault you have no appreciation for poetry." I reach down and slap the back of his thigh, and he whines, feigning pain. "Might have to call an ambulance instead," I giggle.

"Sweetheart, I'd never let them take me away from you, even if I was bleeding from you breaking my heart."

"Damn."

"What?"

"That got me in the feels."

"I was actually aiming for getting you somewhere else."

The phone on his nightstand buzzes. "You should get that," I say.

"Not a chance in hell," he says.

It buzzes again, and something about the thudding of the vibrating phone feels like our sanctity is being violated. I almost want him to answer it so that whoever is calling can go away and leave us alone.

"Please, you should answer it." I pat him gently on the chest. "I have to use the bathroom anyway."

He pouts and then says, "Whoever it is can wait."

I brace on the bed, leaning across it to give him a soft kiss.

"As someone who has waited for you, I feel for them. Answer the phone. I'm going to take a shower. Then I guess we should leave the apartment?"

His face reveals that he's not too hot for that suggestion. "Why? Why do we ever have to leave again? I can order food and groceries, we don't need clothes, we can declare this a clothes-free sovereign country. And there's a new season of my favorite Korean drama starting next week.

TV, food, sex, and sleep with you, I have everything I need here. But if you want to go, I'll take you anywhere you want to go on this planet."

His words touch a place inside me that has never been touched.

Between his body and his words, there are parts of me that might never have been discovered until now.

"What about work?" I ask, some part of me needing to sabotage every lovely thing he says. Still trying to hold on with my fingertips to the part that stopped me from falling completely into the hurricane that is Kylian.

"What about it?"

"Wouldn't you miss it? You were just telling me you love working."

"I do, but I..." His sentence fades into nothing, his eyes on mine. I wonder if he knows he's saying things with the way he looks at me that he can't say with his words.

"Answer the phone," I say and then walk down the stairs, blaming the exertion for my breathlessness when I arrive at the bottom.

What had he almost said?

I know what it was. Of course, I know.

It's too soon.

It's not a good sign.

It's too soon.

It's not real. Nothing that happens this fast can be real.

It can't be.

His voice drifts to me, and I run to the bathroom, away from the sound. Away from him.

It's too soon.

Twenty-Nine

Kylian

I watch as she runs down the stairs as if she can't get away fast enough.

"Fuck," I growl under my breath, reaching for the phone on the nightstand. What the hell was I thinking? I can't say that yet, not yet.

A glance down on the phone screen has me launching it over to the end of the bed. Dear ol' Uncle Gerry. What the fuck does he want now?

Whatever it is, he's going to have to wait until tomorrow. I've never been one to avoid work on the weekends; in fact, my presence at the office on a Saturday is usually expected. But today, just for once, I'm going to make a special exception, no work. And that means no Uncle Gerry.

Thank fuck.

I climb down from the bed and swipe on the screen so that his name doesn't ruin my day and see a text from Nathan. *Cook out, Tuesday evening at 6:30 p.m. Should still be able to catch some sunlight before we have to go inside.*

My best friend's name draws my teeth together in a stressed expression. It is impossible to avoid thinking about how Kiara and I are going to handle telling her family that we are together.

Is it too soon to be thinking about those things?

We've fallen into each other at such a velocity that the outside world has been like a hazy fog circling the fever dream of our affair.

But the reality is that we haven't really talked about what we're doing. We've just been too busy doing it.

Just doing what feels right.

And right now, what feels right is just being with her.

I do a quick ten-minute workout, kicking and punching the punching bag until I'm breathless, releasing my frustrations at not knowing where Kiara and I were going. I work up a sweat, blood pumping, and then take a quick shower, the whole time wishing she were in here with me. Something feels off after she ran off, and I have to fix it.

When I emerge, I pull on my favorite pair of Levi's and pad down to the living area, barefoot and bare chested.

"Kylian," Kiara says when she sees me, drying her hair with a towel on the couch. "You're going to need to put on more clothes than that."

I tuck my hands in my pockets and spin around. "You can't talk. Is that another one of my T-shirts?"

"Yes. Is that okay?"

I hate how she still feels like she has to ask. She can have anything and everything of mine that she wants. "If you're asking if it's okay for you to wear my clothes, absolutely, yes. Anything you see in the apartment, you can have. If you're asking me if it's okay for you to gallivant around my apartment with that T-shirt barely covering the tops of your thighs... then... absolutely, yes. Just don't be surprised when you put me in an early grave."

She covers her face with the towel and lets out a little giggle that is so fucking adorable it hurts to watch her.

"So where are we going today? Since you insist that the pleasure of my presence is not enough for you."

She skips over to me, humming a silly tune under her breath, and lifts her arms around my neck. She looks like a completely different person compared to the woman I ran into at Amber less than a week ago. Like a weight has been lifted. I wonder how, considering she'd had her car stolen and her apartment broken into in the space of a few days. But the smile on her face isn't the smile of someone dwelling on those incidents.

"I need some more clothes, for one."

"What's wrong with the ones I packed for you?"

She makes an exasperated noise. "You mean two evening dresses, a skirt that wouldn't fit on a Barbie doll, and two pairs of leggings?"

I blink. I hadn't really thought about what I was packing when I'd opened her closet and just shoved a bunch of things into the overnight bag. "I'm failing to see the problem. That sounds like an outfit I saw in the last photo spread in Vogue. It's not my fault you're just not avant-garde enough."

She runs back to the couch, then a cushion comes flying at my head, and I duck half a second too late, and my ear catches a zipper on the cushion corner.

"Ow. You're so violent. Maybe I am going to have to get Frank to protect me from you after all."

Her head tilts, and she studies me for a minute. "You know, I thought that I'd gotten used to how much you talk, but... I may have decided too soon."

I laugh and join her on the couch, and she settles on my lap. "Okay, so you want to go back to your apartment to grab something?"

"Yeah. But. Um... Can you..." she struggles to say what's on her mind.

"If you're asking me to come with you, I'd save my breath. There's not a chance I'd let you go alone."

"Thank you," she murmurs against my neck. Maybe she hasn't been taking this as well as I thought.

"Go put something on, and I'll take you over there now."

"The evening dress or the Barbie skirt?" she says as her voice is filled with giggles.

I get to my feet and help her to hers. "Something that won't be make me want to ravage you. I've missed about ten meetings since you've come into my life."

I say it with a laugh in my voice, but her expression instantly sobers. "Kylian. That's not good! Don't miss any more for me."

I gently cradle the back of her head and pull her up onto her tip toes so that her mouth is a breath from mine. "I'm not doing anything I don't want to. So don't worry about anything. When I'm with you, that's exactly where I want to be, and nothing and nobody could pull for me away."

"Maybe I should push you away."

I wrap my hands in her hair and gently tug her hair back, dragging my teeth against her throat. "Try it. Just try. I dare you."

A shiver ripples over her skin, but her eyes are defiant. "I could get my friends or family to hide me."

My lips nip against her pulse. "Then you'll have to explain to them why I'm burning their house down to find you."

And when I kiss her, it's all softness and submission. It's to brand the promises I've just made onto her lips. And I don't stop until I know she knows I mean every word.

"Now go. Before it'll be another day until we leave my apartment."

She sighs and pulls away. "But we'll come back here after?"

"Promise."

⟶ ♥ ⟵

She sings all the way to her apartment. It's off-key and again, so fucking adorable I don't know what to do with myself. I do make a point to not play my playlist with some of my favorite arias, though; I'm not sure my ears could recover from that noise.

There aren't any parking spots out the front of her building, so I drop her off and find a spot around the corner. I take the opportunity to take a quick look around. It's not a terrible area, but it's definitely not The Peak. I wonder how long it took for her to get Nathan and her father to agree to let her move here.

Since my workout this morning was so short, I take a chance to up my steps and jog up the stairs to her fifth floor apartment. She's placed a shoe in the door to stop it locking behind her. I let a little air hiss through my teeth when I step inside. I had forgotten what a mess it was. I wonder what her plans for this place is. I peek into her bedroom, and she has her back to the door, folding a pile of clothes. I step back out to the kitchen, giving her some space. It can't be easy being here. I feel violated on her behalf. It would take a stronger man than me to stay in a place knowing that all of my things have been touched by a stranger's hand.

Trying to return some sort of semblance of order, I try to pick up a bit. There's a cracked photo frame face down on the floor, and I remember what we did in this room just two days ago. My hand starts remembering the way I'd slapped it across her bare ass, leaving the imprint of my hand. Two chairs knocked onto their side get returned to their upright position and the pile of books stacked back on her shelf that was upended. I pick up some figurines that have fallen over and line them up along the little entertainment system where the TV sits.

It's strange that the TV is still here as well as her laptop that's still sitting on her coffee table.

Maybe they'd been in a hurry or had heard someone coming. The TV might've been too big to carry, but her MacBook would've sold for a few hundred dollars alone.

The living room looks infinitely better after even just a few minutes of picking up. I'm glad. The experience of being broken into is bad enough without the constant reminder that someone uninvited has come in here.

"Oh. Hi," Kiara says a minute later, stepping out of the bedroom with a small suitcase and two garment bags slung over her arm. "I didn't know that you'd come up. I thought you were going to wait in the car."

She seems... off.

"Are you okay? I wouldn't have left you up here on your own. I was just parking the car."

She nods but doesn't really seem connected to the movement.

"Have you got everything you need?"

"Er, yeah. Except for the potted plant. Do you mind grabbing it, please"

"Oh yeah, of course." I step toward her bedroom. "You're going to have to water it, though, I'm not good with plants. I have pink thumbs, or whatever it's called."

Her lips thin into what I think she imagines is a smile. But it doesn't reach her eyes.

I don't push, though; this isn't the place or time to be interrogating her. The potted plant is heavier than I expect, and I try to make her laugh again by making a big show of trying to pick it up. After a few seconds, it's clear that it doesn't really have the effect that I want, and she just says, "Please be careful."

Right. "Ready?"

She blinks and looks around her apartment. I'm sad for her that this isn't a place she feels safe in anymore because it's a nice little apartment, small but cozy. She's obviously taken the time to make this a place she wants to come home to.

She frowns at the bookshelf. "What did you do?"

"I just picked up some of the furniture and stuff that was knocked over from the shelf."

She nods. "Oh. Okay. Thank you."

Then, without saying another word she wanders out the door, not looking back. I follow, closing the door behind me, making sure it latches before going to stand as she waits for the elevator.

"Are you okay?" I ask, already knowing what she's going to answer.

"Yes."

It's a short, sharp, definitive answer, a galaxy away from her mood just a little while ago. But it's a clear signal that she's not going to be answering any more questions.

In the elevator, I take the bags from her. She doesn't meet my eyes the whole time, not even when we pack her things in the car and then make our way back to my apartment. We don't speak much on the drive. And about a mile from the turn back to my apartment, she reaches over and slides her hand into mine.

A quick glance over shows a pale white Kiara biting her bottom lip raw.

"Hey." I squeeze her hand, trying to reassure her. "Is this about being back at the apartment?"

"I don't want to talk about it. Please don't make me talk about it." She pulls her hand back.

"Okay, well, we don't have to go back. If you need anything else, I can take you to the mall, and we'll do a recreation of Julia Roberts's shopping spree in *Pretty Woman*. 'Big mistake!'" I quote the famous line from the movie.

"I've never seen Pretty Woman," she says distractedly, wringing her hands.

"What? What kind of heathen are you?"

She frowns. "I'm a heathen for not having seen a movie about a prostitute? You've got things twisted a little bit."

"I'm hurt. I'll have you know it's just a modern retelling of *Pygmalion* and a saucier version of *My Fair Lady* without the singing."

The conversation distracted her a bit from whatever is going on in her head, but when I look over, she's biting her nails, something I haven't seen her do once.

I turn into the valet bay and reach over and take her hands in mine. "Hey. Whatever is going on with you, and I know something is, you don't have to go through it alone. I'm here, and when you're ready, I want you to tell me, okay? Nod if you understand."

A swallow and nod, but it's clear she's not ready to get out of the car yet.

So I wait. I wait until she is ready and not a minute sooner.

Eventually, she takes a deep, deep breath and pushes the air out in a long, slow exhale.

"Ready?"

She nods. "Ready."

I jump out of the car and jog over to her side, opening the door for her. She climbs out in her leggings and my T-shirt. Her hair is pulled back in a ponytail, no makeup. She looks five years younger, smaller; I wonder if it's fear that's shrinking her, and my heart aches for the way she looks so lost.

How could there have been such a big difference in the last thirty minutes that I barely recognize her. She stands by the curb as I grab her things and drop them at the feet of the doorman. "Could you organize for someone to bring these things up for Miss Kiara, please?"

"Of course, sir," he says, glancing at her, concern painting itself on his face.

"Thank you, she's just not feeling too well."

I take her hand and lead her into the elevator. She follows, eyes trained at a spot somewhere on the floor but not really looking at it.

It takes everything I have in me not to shake her, demanding to know what's going on with her, why she looks so lost that if I asked her name, she wouldn't know what it was.

"Come in, Kiki, we're here," I prompt her when the elevator doors open and she doesn't follow me out even though I'm gently tugging on her arm.

She blinks and then looks in my direction, but right through me, before her feet shuffle out.

The living room is bathed in a harsh midday light, but it's still the best place for her, so I lead her to the couch as I feel her slipping away a little more with every step.

"Come here, sit down, I'll get you a blanket." I move to drop her hand, but she grips it, grabbing onto my forearm with her other one.

"No, please," she says, her voice drenched in fear, and it cuts me like a scythe right through the heart. "Don't go. Please!"

My knees bend, dropping down on the floor in front of her, gripping her hands in mine. "Hey. Hey... it's okay. I'm not going anywhere, okay?" I bracket her chin, forcing her panicked face to look right at me. "I'm right here, angel. I'm right here."

Like a deer in headlights, her eyes widen, and she freezes.

Then, almost in slow motion, every inch of her face starts to fall, crumbling right in front of me. And tears come. One after the other. Streaming like two waterfalls over her cheeks and down her jaw, darkening the T-shirt when they fall.

But it's not the tears that worry me.

It's the way she's completely silent.

No sobs, no whimpers, no screams, as if sound has died in her throat.

"Kiara, angel, Kiara, I'm here. I'm here."

Her head bumps up against my chest as I pull her into me, one arm around her front, the other wrapped around her back, squeezing her tight, grounding her to me.

She cries for what feels like hours. Until the sun is a falling fireball on the horizon bathing us in a burnt orange light.

After some time, she stops shaking, collapsing in a dead sleep against me. But when I try to lay her back down to get up to get something to cover her, her eyes fly open and she grabs my arm.

"I'm here. I'm here. Go back to sleep, sweetheart," I say, easing back down next to her.

She closes her eyes as I gently stroke her hair, whispering promises that I'm never ever leaving her as every possible scenario of what might have happened races through my brain. And what I'm going to do to the person who did this to her.

I jolt awake sometime later, and she's gone.

"Kiara?" I yell, the panic threading through my vocal cords and seeping into my words.

The apartment is dark except for the moonlight filtering through the windows and the lights under the kitchen cabinets.

"Kiara! Where are you?"

I race up to the bedroom. The sheets are messed up on the bed from the morning. She's not in the en suite. I jump down the stairs two at a time, feeling like my heartbeats are visible against the skin of my ribcage.

Not in the kitchen.

Not in the bathroom.

Not in the guest room that she found when she explored the apartment last night.

Not in the office, nor the movie room.

"God, no," I mutter as I run to the elevator, going where, I don't know.

But I don't have to go far.

She's standing in the foyer, her belongings at her feet, holding a book in her hands.

"Oh my god! Kiara! Didn't you hear me call after you? I thought you'd left me again. I was scared fucking senseless!" I yell from the adrenaline.

And then I notice the tears streaking her cheeks, new ones over her face, so pale she almost looks translucent, like if I blow, she'd dissipate like the ectoplasm of our time together.

"What's wrong? You have to tell me what's going."

She doesn't say a word and just holds the notebook out to me, open.

And when I look down, I feel like I'm going to fade into the wind with her. And then, like a firestorm, I'm put together, wild and furious as I pull her against me a little too roughly, trying to squeeze the pain out of her.

Thirty

Kiara

Kylian's apartment is so far up from the ground I feel like it's the only place I've ever heard silence since moving back to Hong Kong. At my dad's house, he leaves all the doors and windows open, trying to soak in as much of the city as he can, making up for the decades he lived in England.

But up here, except for the gentle hum of his appliance and his soft, regular breath in my ear, it's like... there's nothing and no one else in the world.

Oh, how I wish that were true.

My tongue, plastered on the roof of my mouth, peels away almost painfully, and there's no question why. I'm so dehydrated, having had nothing to drink for the last six or seven hours. What moisture I did have in my body was squeezed out of my eyeballs.

Kylian stirs a little in his sleep, and I take the opportunity to roll off the couch as gently as I can.

I drink two glasses of water, feeling my cells thirstily suck in every drop, plumping up, happy. I don't want to go back to the couch in case I wake him up. And he needs his rest. He's probably exhausted from having to deal with a mad woman.

I wander around the dark apartment, taking in the few pieces of artwork on the walls. No Picassos, no Monets, no Hirsts, just beautiful paintings and sketches from names I've never heard of. Not surprising. For all his style, there's so much substance in that man. A surge of affection washes through me, and I feel an urge to climb back onto the couch and crawl into the safe space of his arms. But the last thing he needs is for me to wake him up and demand more attention. I can't imagine what he's been feeling. But I couldn't have talked about it if I'd tried.

In the back of my mind, I remember that Kylian had brought my potted plant with me, and I search for it in the apartment. Finally, I remember that he'd asked his doorman to have my stuff brought up.

There's a pile of my things on the bench in the hallway outside the elevator, and I'm happy to be reunited with the plant. I gently run my finger along one of the dark green leaves, feeling a little piece of home with me. But it doesn't last long; I catch a sight of a dark red corner poking out of my bag.

A slight panic runs through me, but I crush it down. I know what it is already, it's not where I saw it the first time.

This time, I'm here. Safe. I'm safe here.

Gingerly, almost like I'm trying to diffuse a bomb, I pull the notebook out of the bag.

In my hands, it falls open where a stack of photos was crammed in.

Photos of me... in my apartment, in various forms of undress, completely naked climbing into my bathtub. Based on what I'm wearing, photos taken over a period of months.

Photos showing me bent at the waist, bracing against the wall as Kylian fucks me from behind. Of Kylian standing, arms folded, watching me as I stand there, waiting for him, obeying him. Of Kylian and me, collapsed on the floor, him looking at me like... like there is no one else in the world.

My most private moments photographed and printed out, grainy and pixelated, poisoning all the memories with an acid-tipped dart.

If Kylian is anything like Nathan, this is going to destroy him. His daily business is shared with the world, so he fiercely protects his privacy.

And now... someone has pictures of him slapping his hand across my bare ass. His hand gripping my throat as we fuck.

"Oh my god! Kiara! Didn't you hear me call after you? I thought you'd left me again. I was scared fucking senseless!" he yells, his words an outward expression of everything I'm feeling inside.

I don't know if there's any way to hide this from him any longer, and I shouldn't. This affects him as well.

Wordlessly, I hold the photos out for him to see, the picture of us together on the top.

He stares at them for a moment, and then, eyes wild, he knocks the notebook out of my hands and pulls me in hard against me.

"Why didn't you tell me about this before? I would've—"

"Would've what?" I shout. "What would you have done? It's too late now. Look!" I point to the scatted photos on the ground, picture after picture after picture of me in my most private moments. "Look! He's been watching me this whole time! I thought I was safe, but I wasn't. He was watching the whole time!" My head falls into my hands, tears pouring down my face again. I'm drenched in humiliation. How could I have not known this was happening? "He's been watching me, he's been watching this whole time, Kylian!"

He watches me, horrified. I can't even imagine what he's thinking about me. The only source of relief is that he's the only man I've been with in my apartment. At least he doesn't have to see pictures of me with someone else.

"I... I have to go." I don't want to. I want to crawl into bed with him and pretend that my sense of safety hasn't been ripped from me forever.

"Kiara!" He grabs my shoulder and gives me a little shake. "You are not going anywhere. Do you hear me? You are not going anywhere; I will not let you go anywhere. This is where you live now, and I will protect you. Nothing has ever mattered more to me than protecting you."

His hands dig into me, painting my skin with bruises, but I'm grateful for it. It roots me in reality.

"I... I don't want to go, but... I didn't know if you'd want me to stay."

His jaw drops. "Don't tell me you really thought that. Tell me you didn't think that, Kiara! Tell me!"

I rip myself out of his arms and run toward the living room. He's half a second behind me, reaching for the hem of my T-shirt and wrenching me into his arms. I beat my hands against his chest. Confusion, frustration, humiliation, fear, all mashing together to create an emotional storm inside me that is tearing all sense of reason apart.

"You're not going anywhere, okay? And if you did, remember what I told you? I would follow you. To the ends of the universe and back." He whispers it over and over and over and over until the words all melt into one and wrap around me like a shawl.

"I'm sorry," I whisper once I regain my voice.

"What for? Making me almost rip my own T-shirt?"

"No. The pictures."

"Oh, those. Yeah, and I look hot, don't I? A little grainy, I look better in 4K, but still hot."

His jokes comfort me in a way I didn't expect them to. He can't be too mad at me if he's joking. But his face sobers, and I know the question is coming, the question I thought I could avoid until now.

"You keep saying 'he' like you know who did this. Do you? Do you know, Kiara?"

And I know I owe him the truth. "Yes. At least, I think I do... he, um, he's done this before. Not the pictures, but the breaking in. He... he's done this before." I stop when my voice cracks and take a breath before I speak again. "I just didn't think that he'd find me here. Why is he here?"

"Oh, angel. I wish you'd told me. I could've been out looking this whole time. And I don't know why he's here, Kiki. But we're going to find out, okay?" He blinks like he's running a question over in his head, trying to ask it in a sensitive way.

That's not fair on him, always having to ask the questions when I know what he wants, deserves to know. So I tell him what I probably should've told him from the beginning. "He... is my ex-boyfriend. I... dated him for almost four years in New York."

"Four years?" His eyes swing back and forth, doing the math.

"Yeah."

"So, um, after London?"

"Yes. We met in college; he had been asking me out for awhile. So when I got back, I agreed to go out with him."

He looks at me like I betrayed us when we both know that he betrayed us first.

"What happened?"

"How it always happens. It was okay until it wasn't. And I couldn't even tell you how and when it happened." I swallow. I've never talked about this. Never. "And then one day, it went from bad to unbearable, so I left. He didn't like that. So I went into hiding. I was moving from place to place. I didn't want to go home and bring all this with me. My mother didn't need it in her last days."

"How did you finally... end it?"

"Nathan came one day. I hadn't answered his calls in a few days. He flew over from Hong Kong and tracked me down at a hotel. Whisked me back to Hong Kong and never spoke about it again."

"He never told me."

"Good." It's the only good thing that's come out of all this. Even if Kylian has to know about it now, at least it's coming from me. And I can give him the whole story.

"You said he used to break into your house?"

"Yes. When we started dating, he was thoughtful and sweet. But, just like it happens all the time, he just slowly chipped away at me. I didn't have a lot of friends in New York, not close ones anyway."

He winces. "I wish I'd known. Matthias would've taken care of him. Did he hurt you?"

"In a word, yes." Then I brace for impact.

Kylian's nostrils flare, jaw flexes, hands ball into white knuckled fists. Then he takes a deep breath, visibly shoving the anger down, so I continue.

"Once. But... it was bad. That's when I left. He apologized over and over. But I never believed him."

Kylian nods. A small gesture of approval at my decision to leave, and it helps.

"So then he started stalking me. Little things at first, showing up at the coffee place when I was there, acting like it was a coincidence. But then he would wait outside my apartment in the mornings and be there at night under the pretense that he was watching out for me. And when I'd get to my apartment, it would be trashed." I shiver at the memory of seeing him every time I left my apartment, wondering if he'd follow me inside and that would be the last anyone would hear of me.

"Did your family know about any of this?"

"I think they suspected after a while. They only met him once. When they came over to visit me. They didn't like him." I let out a hollow laugh. "I was a stupid girl. Always trying to rebel for no reason. I did it all to myself. I should've known better." The admittance is deathly bitter, and I smack my lips, trying to get rid of the sensation drying out my mouth. "But... it was all for nothing. He's been watching me for who knows how long. I had no idea. I thought I was safe here in Hong Kong."

He squeezes my hand. "You're safe now. I won't let him get to you again."

"It doesn't matter. He's ruined everything. Again." Shivering, my arms come up to wrap around my body, not to warm myself... but to cover up. I feel dirty. Violated.

"Hey, hey," Kylian whispers. "What are you doing?"

"I just feel him everywhere. Everywhere he touched, everything that's he's seen."

Kylian's brushes the hair off my face and gently presses a kiss to my lips. "Come with me."

"Where?"

"We're going to take it all back. Take every piece he took of you back."

I don't know what he means, but I don't want to be alone, so when he leads me to the bathroom, I follow.

Without ever letting go of my hand, he turns the shower on, making sure it's warm enough.

"Can I take your T-shirt off?" he asks quietly. I nod. He pulls it over my head and throws it to the side. "I'm going to take your leggings off, okay?"

I swallow and nod.

He gives me a smile as he hooks his fingers into the elastic of my pants and slowly drags them down my legs. He stands back up and takes my hand, helping me to step out of them.

I wait for him to ask to take my underwear off, but he doesn't.

"I'm going to take my clothes off, too, is that alright? I can keep them on in you want."

This time it's a shake of my head.

He keeps his eyes on me as he slowly strips, never making a sudden movement and keeping his briefs on as well.

Then, picking my hand up again, he holds the shower door open and leads me in.

The shower is about the size of my entire bathroom when I lived in New York, with a bench running along one side and four showerheads so that no matter where you're standing in the shower, you're getting a full spray.

He stands me in the middle of the shower, letting the water cascade over the both us. He doesn't bother with the water washing over his eyes, but he reaches over, brushing the drops that make their way between my eyelashes and wetting my already wet eyes.

"I'm going to wash you, okay?" he says and waits until I show that I've heard and agree before he reaches for the loofah he'd left out for me and pumps some bodywash on it, rubbing it with his hand to lather it up.

He stands in front of me but reaches around, starting on my shoulder blades. Slow, gentle concentric circles, getting me used to his touch. Then he leans in, whispering into my ear, "We're going to wash every last trace of him. Every place he touched you, every place he ever laid his eyes on, we're going to wash it all away. He's not ever going to have any claim over you again. You hear me?" The last few words are spoken with a firmness I didn't expect, and it makes me believe him.

He gently maneuvers me around, so he can reach further down my back and over the curve of my ass, running the loofah over every inch of my skin. Down my legs, over the back of my thighs and my calves, all the way to my ankles. His touch is featherlight, but when I close my eyes, I can feel him stripping, scrubbing, sanding away the parts I'm ashamed of. When he's standing up again, he's facing me, a gentle smile on his lips. "Is it okay? What I'm doing?"

I reach out and touch him gently on the chest as a thank you.

"I'm going to wash your front now, okay? Tell me if you want to stop."

He starts slow, pressing the loofah to my collarbone. The pressure on my skin almost makes me jump, and he stops, giving me a moment. Then the circles start again, covering my body with soap suds and letting the water wash it away, taking my ex's fingerprints away.

Over my breasts, he lingers for just a moment, and then he washes my nipples, making sure whatever memory I have left of him touching me there is sucked down the drain and gone forever.

As he lowers himself, washing from my inner thighs down to the instep of my foot, inch by inch, my shame begins to fade.

But the job isn't done. And we both know it.

I take his hand and place it on the elastic of my panties.

"Are you sure?"

"Yes. Please," I say for the first time since we entered the bathroom. "Please."

The water is warm against me as he peels off the last of my clothing and then eases my legs apart so he can wash the most intimate part of me.

And when he's done, he stands up and lightly kisses me.

The water's turned off, and he reaches for a towel, gently patting us dry.

"Come on."

"Where now?"

"We've washed his touch from you. Now I'm going to reclaim every part of you he ever laid his eyes on. And when you think about anyone watching you, it's going to be me."

My breath empties from my lungs, and I don't know what he has in mind, but my body already buzzes in anticipation.

He leads me into his walk-in closet, and I look around in amazement. My father was never fashion conscious, but Nathan is about as vain as he is smart. However, even his closet would be dwarfed by this room.

Rows and rows of suits and jackets and shirts line the walls of the plush carpet floor. Floor-to-ceiling mirrors sit between each row of clothes. Down the middle of the closet runs a twenty-foot-long cushioned bench.

I follow him into the middle of the room where he sits me down on the bench and takes a step back.

He's still wearing a drenched pair of boxers, but he's focused on me.

"Kiara, do you have any idea how beautiful you are?" He presses his face against my stomach and takes in a deep breath. "Do you know that you're the most beautiful woman I've ever seen in my life? That everything you do is the epitome of grace and elegance. That I am utterly mesmerized by you and everything you say and do. And if for a second you think that a slimebag excuse for a man was worthy of you, then I hope what's about to happen is going to remind you that no one is good enough for you. Nobody. And especially not me. But my life's goal is to show you that I will do anything to make myself worthy of being with you."

With that, he reaches for the back of my neck and pulls me to him, his lips grazing against mine, bruising both of our mouths.

Despite the anticipation of the moment building over the last ten minutes, it catches me off-guard, and his mouth presses against my open mouth as I let out a gasp.

He instantly recoils. "Are you okay?"

"Don't stop."

A smile tugs at his lips as he takes me by the shoulder and spins me around so that I'm facing the mirror dead on. I watch as his lips catch on the side of my neck, nuzzling as his hands come up to hold me around the waist.

"Tell me... in those photos, what parts of your body do you remember seeing?"

The panic from before clutches at my mind, and my body clenches in anxiety.

His voice calms me, speaking directly into my soul when he whispers, "Kiara. Stay with me. I'm here. Me."

I breathe through the urge to flee. "Um. I was naked in one, climbing into the bath. You could see my breasts."

He nods, eyes locking on mine in the mirror as he moves both of his hands up to cup my breasts.

"He can't see you now. I'm taking back each part of you that he violated, angel."

My nipples peak at his voice, husky against my ear, as his fingers find them, rolling them, drawing a soft exhale from me as I watch him in the mirror.

"Where else, baby?"

"In the photo of us, when you... you spanked me... you could see my ass."

His hands travel to my ass, his hands kneading the flesh. "It's my hands on you now. It's my eyes on you. We're going to watch you together."

My hips involuntarily push back against his hands.

A soft rumble in his chest grows to a low growl against my neck. "Remember when we did this on the dance floor in London, baby? Do you have any idea how much I wanted you that night? Do you know I went home that night and jacked off all night imagining myself coming all over your perfect little ass. But most importantly, I touched you here before he did. I was here first. He touched what's mine, and I'm taking you back"

The memory anchors in my lungs, remembering how that night I thought I was dancing with that stranger, the whole time thinking maybe I could finally kick my Kylian addiction. And it was him the whole time.

My body knew before my mind did.

He wraps his hands around me, grinding against me, his briefs damp from the shower pressing into my ass. He's hard. I wonder how he's holding back from fucking me right now.

And I hope he stops holding back soon.

"Where now, angel?"

"He saw your hands on my pussy."

He hisses. "Well, that's going to be his last time he's going to see it." There's not a sliver of doubt in his voice. "Do you hear me? And do you know why?"

I shiver as his hands travels down over my bare stomach and edges my legs apart. I watch as two fingers break into a V as he slides them over my outer folds.

"I asked you," he says, his voice thick with need for me, "do you know he's never going to see this pussy again?"

I can't.

I need him to say it.

I need him to reassure me.

"Why?" I ask, my voice shaking.

"Don't pretend you don't know, angel. Tell me you know why. Tell me you've known since that first time in my office with my tongue inside you why no one else will ever see, touch, lick, and fuck your pussy again?"

One finger teases me, dipping inward a little more, my clit cleaving toward it. Aching. Needing.

"Kylian, please..."

"Kylian, please, what?"

His finger nudges the side of my clit, and I forget my own name for moment. "More, Kylian, please..."

"You know what I want. Say it, and I'll give you everything you need and more, angel."

"Fuck." My hips chase his fingers, but he pulls back each time. I whimper with disappointment.

"Kiara. Say it. Whose pussy is this? Whose clit is this?"

I bite down as he grinds his cock against me, promising me more. "You're a fucker."

His chuckle is dark and husky, so fucking sexy. "I will be once you stop being so stubborn and say what we both want you to say." He bites down on my shoulder, sending my senses into overload, and the words spill out of my lips.

"Fuck! Kylian... my pussy is yours"

"Was that so hard? And what else?" he says, grazing my clit with a single swipe.

"Oh god, please stop teasing."

"I will, angel, I promise to stop. Once you give me what I want."

My gasps do nothing to provide oxygen to my body, and I'm dizzy as I shout, "No one's ever going to see, touch, lick, and fuck my pussy again because my pussy's yours. I'm yours," I add without realizing it.

"Good girl."

The words hang in the air as he clamps his fingers around the sides my clit and rubs back and forth in a fast, hard rhythm that pushes me to the cliff of my orgasm.

"Oh fuck."

"Soon, baby girl. Watch you writhing with my fingers on your clit."

It should look vulgar, my legs spread as I cup my own breasts while he circles his fingers over my clit, driving me so fucking crazy I can barely breathe.

"Kylian... oh god. I've never..." My breathing hitches as he changes his rhythm, grinding the palm over my clit hood.

"Never what, baby," he whispers, his voice so thick with need I want to scoop it up and pour it down my throat. I want him inside me in every way. "Brace against the mirror, angel."

He places my hands against the mirror and spreads my legs.

I hold my breath as he drops to his knees and crawls between my open legs and flicks his tongue against my clit.

"Oh fuck... Kylian... oh my god."

"Come for me, sweet angel. Come... and watch yourself as my tongue catches every drop of your cum."

His hands grip my hips and push me down on his face until I know I must be hurting him.

"Kylian! No," I say, trying to move off him. "You can't breathe."

"Shut up and ride my face. I'll have everything I fucking need to live."

With that, he flicks my clit again, and my knees buckle under me, and I lean onto him, his hands digging bruises into my hips as I grind against his tongue, knowing nothing but him as I inch closer to my orgasm.

I catch a glimpse in the mirror and remember his order to watch myself as I come on his face.

His tongue presses flat against my clit. Hard. And I'm gone.

The wave of my climax breaks, and I watch through my eyes, lidded but open, my body heaving and writhing as every muscle squeezes in the most exquisite way. It hurts in a way that is addictive. Kylian making me come is addictive.

Before I can recover, he pulls me down, onto his lap and impaled on his cock.

We both roar at the same time.

My pussy screams, still pulsing from my orgasm, stretched more than I've ever been stretched. It's primal in the best way; I feel him stretching every part of me. Infiltrating me. Making me his in a way that there's no going back.

"You wanted me to fuck you without preparing yourself. Well, your wish is my command. But you might regret it, angel. Because right now, I can't imagine fucking you any other way. You're so fucking tight on my cock." Every word sounds like a strain as he lifts me almost all the way off his rock.

"Ready?"

I'm not, but that's the best part about this.

Every time I think about being fucked from now on, this is what I'm going to remember.

I drop myself down on him before he can do it himself, and he responds by thrusting up into me, pushing even deeper than before.

My pussy weeps, screaming with an intoxicating burn.

"Kiara," he chokes out, brushing the hair out of my face as he pulls my face down to kiss me.

He kisses me like he's starving and I'm everything he's ever wanted to devour in his life.

"Baby, baby, baby, I'm so addicted to fucking you."

"I'm addicted to you fucking me. Your cock feels so good inside me."

"Whose pussy, angel?"

"Yours, yours, yours. No one has ever touched me before now, and no one will again."

Something about my words push him past the point of restraint, and he pulls out and arranges me on my side. He spreads out behind me, bending my leg up as he slides into me from behind.

"Watch me fuck you. Watch me claim your pussy as mine and fuck every memory of everyone else who's ever fucked you out of your head forever. He didn't deserve it, and he no longer has a single part of you, angel. Not a damn fucking piece."

I watch. Watch mesmerized as he pulls out and then rams back in again, my pussy whimpering every time he's out until he's back again.

I reach down and play with my clit, knowing he's got to be close.

"Come with me, Kylian," I say to his reflection.

"I will, I can't take much more. You're the most delicious fucking torture."

One hand on my hip holds me as he pummels into me as I flick my clit like he had before. The image of us making love burns indelibly into my brain.

And then... I come. I come so hard I can't keep my eyes on our reflection as he pulls me against him and explodes against me, grunting over and over as his desire fills up my aching pussy.

"Kiara, my sweet angel."

He collapses behind me, pulling me on top of him.

"Kylian?"

"Hmmm?"

"Thank you."

His eyes open just enough for me to see the emotions in his eyes. "There's nothing to thank me for."

"I may have been spiraling."

His hand presses gently around my neck. It makes me feel safer than I've ever felt. "Then I'm glad I was here to catch you."

I lie back, ears pressed against his rib cage, listening to his heart thud against it.

"Kylian?"

"Hmmm?" It's sleepier this time.

"Thank you." This time his eyes open wider, confused. "This feels like déjà vu. What are you thanking me for this time?"

"For reminding me who I belong to."

His Adam's apple bobs up and down as he swallows as if he's biting back something, and then he rolls me over and straddles over me.

"Well, my sweet, I think I better remind you again... just so you don't forget."

And this time, when he takes me, he doesn't have to ask me who my pussy belongs to. There's only the two of us in that room, and every single ghost of the past is banished to hell.

Thirty-One
Kylian

"You're making a mess on my pristine bed," I say as she takes a bite of her toast.

The snort that escapes her lips is just about the least lady-like noise that's ever come out of her that I've heard, and also just about the cutest thing I've ever heard. However, it also makes her spit out a mouthful of crumbs over my bed.

"Hey! What did I just say?" I make a show of brushing the crumbs off the sheet and onto the floor. "If we get carried away by ants during the night, I'm blaming it on you."

"Well, I blame you for making a funny joke."

"What joke?" I say, reaching over and picking up her piece of toast to take a bite.

"About the pristineness level of your bed. I bet this bed gets more use than an escort on a Friday night in Amsterdam."

"Wrong! I haven't ever had anybody up here that wasn't a Baxter." She makes a sickened face. "Ewwww."

I laugh, appreciating the quickness of her mind. "That's not what I meant, and you know it. I'm telling my brothers you pick on me. They're going to be sooo mad at you for being mean to their poor defenseless baby brother." I punish her by eating the rest of the toast on her plate. She's not worried; there's a whole tray of food in the middle of the bed that she can choose to eat instead, and after a second of considering, she chooses a small glass jar of yogurt.

The way she tears the lid off, licks the yogurt stuck on the lid, and then folds the foil into perfectly equal fourths before putting it on the edge of the tray thrills me. Just as every little thing she does. It doesn't have to be sexual, just mundane, everyday things. I could just sit and watch her doing them all day.

I grab a spoon and hold it out to her, but just as she reaches for it, I dip it into the yogurt and then deliver it straight to my mouth while she squeals.

"Hey! That was mine. Food stealer! Who would've thought that 'Blond Billionaire Bachelor Kylian Baxter' would steal a poor starving woman's food?" She says 'Blond Billionaire Bachelor Kylian Baxter' like she's reading a headline off a newspaper, which is where she saw it in the first place. She hasn't let me live it down yet.

"I suddenly don't feel so bad about stealing your food. Anyway, I can't help it, you make it look so delicious." I wink, and she blushes as she giggles like a school girl. I try not to think about how she was just a school girl when I first met her. That and my best friend's sister. It's better to not think about that right now.

The jar clatters on the tray once she finishes it, and she grabs the basket of strawberries and moves up the bed so that she's leaning back against me between my legs.

"Hmm, yum. Thank you," I mumble as she reaches back and feeds a strawberry into my mouth.

Another strawberry gets closely examined and then popped into her mouth.

"That's one lucky strawberry," I say, the words muffled as I nuzzle against her neck.

She smells like... Kiara. I don't know how else to describe it. Fresh and natural. Like the air after a summer rain.

"Want another one?" she asks, turning and dropping a kiss to my cheek.

"I'm good. I already ate some toast and yogurt."

She splutters and shoves another strawberry into my mouth as punishment. Too bad, I'm still chewing the last strawberry, and I almost choke.

"Kiki! You almost killed me. Can you imagine the headlines if my body was found sprawled out on my bed by my cleaner?"

"Yes. 'Blond Billionaire Bachelor Kylian Baxter Found Dead Wearing a Pair of Lacy Underwear.'"

"Wow." I force myself to sound hurt, but I don't think she's falling for it. "Is that the thanks I get for making this delicious spread for you?"

"That you ate!"

I grin. "It was delicious." My lips brush her ear as she protests. "As are you, my sweet angel."

I reach over and grab the tray off the bed and put it on the floor nearby as she wriggles against me, getting comfortable with room now to spread her legs.

She grabs my arms, pulls them tightly around her, and closes her eyes.

"Kiara sleepy," she says, her voice already fading.

"Kiara should sleep, she's had a long day." The tiniest little frown flashes around her forehead and I want to kick myself for bringing it up. Luckily, she doesn't ponder it too long and soon, her face completely relaxes and her breath slows.

"My sweet, beautiful Kiki," I murmur, running my fingers up and down the length of her upper thigh as she falls asleep. My heart wants to burst from my chest, and the word that's too soon to say tickles my lips.

Once I'm sure she's sleeping, I grab my phone, ignoring another message from Gerald, and text Frank, the head of my security detail, telling him to meet me at my office tomorrow.

There are some things I'm going to need him to help me with.

And they're things I don't want Kiara to hear being discussed.

>>>———→♥←———<<<

Monday at the office feels like it's the day before the end of the school year; outside the weather is warm, the sun is shining, and I'm stuck inside.

My morning meeting with Frank went just as I'd expected. I assigned him to taking care of Kiara's security detail. Someone to watch her when she's not with me and to teach the dipshit who's had free rein to harass Kiara a lesson once and for all. I'd showed him some of the pictures, not the most graphic, and he agreed that they were taken from angles that could not have been from someone outside the building. It was from cameras inside her apartment, I was sure about it. And there was no way I was going to let her go back there, for any reason, until I was sure that no one was watching her. I'd taken her security card from her bag before I left for work this morning. It will give Frank a chance to have a thorough look and see if he can find anything that could tell him where he might be hiding out.

She hadn't told me any details about the guy, just the name, but a cursory look had proven empty. He had stayed in the country illegally and was hiding to not be found.

I'm going to find him and make sure he never causes Kiara another minute of pain and worry again. Whatever it takes.

The look on her face when she'd told me that she'd felt dirty, violated by him, that everything he'd touched was tainted, had torn at my heart like a rusty wire brush.

Overnight as I held her, making sure that even if she had nightmares with me, her reality was safer than it has ever been, I was inundated with thoughts about all the painful, torturous, life ending ways I could deal with this lowlife.

I'm glad she was asleep because I'm sure that she would've been able to read the thoughts from my face, and I'm not proud of any of the scenarios in my head. But that doesn't mean that if I ever get my hands on him, I'm not going to do each and every thing I'm imagining... and enjoy it.

"Hey. Do you, like, even work here?" Odette skips into my office after a manager has left, telling me about some problems in the office. "I feel like I haven't seen or talked to you in days."

"That's because we haven't. Everyone deserves a day or two away from you." I don't even bother to look up at her. I can tell from her voice that she isn't in my office to talk about work.

"Aw, absence makes the heart grow fonder, you must, like, be pining for me."

I frown. "Hey, don't joke about that anymore."

"Huh? Why not? Ohhhh, Ki-ahhhh-ra." She rolls her eyes but stops when she sees the expression on my face "Wow, lighten up."

I stare at her, unblinking. "If you want to have to find a new job, this is the way to do it."

Her mouth drops open. "You're kidding me, right? We've always joked like this. What's the big deal?"

"The big deal is that, out of respect for the woman I'm with, let's not do that anymore. You can understand why she wouldn't take it well."

"Sounds like she doesn't trust you. That's no way to have a relationship," she sulks.

I try not to sound as pissed as I am at her. Not really sure why she feels qualified to give me relationship advice. "I've given her every reason not to trust me. And with you, I might add. So let's cool it a bit, okay? It's not personal."

"It feels fucking personal. This is so stupid, Kylian. This is how we communicate. We've been friends for a fucking decade, and now you get some—"

I put my pen down, humming with anger. "I'd be really fucking careful about what you're about to say. I mean it. I can replace you. I can't replace her."

Her eyes narrow into thin slits, and she storms out of my office. Good, give her time to calm down a bit. I'm sorry that she thinks our relationship is changing just because I don't want her making jokes about us having a relationship, but I have one priority. Making Kiara feel safe. And if Odette has a problem, that's going to be her problem and hers alone.

There's static on my intercom. "Mr. Baxter, you have a call from Mr. Gerald Baxter. And... he, er, he sounds quite unhappy."

Fuck. I guess he'd gotten sick of my ignoring his calls and texts. I had meant to call him once I'd gotten to this office in the morning, but I'd forgotten amongst all the issues with Kiara.

"Put him through." There's no reason to put her under fire. He was the CEO... interim CEO, but he's known to cause problems for anyone who does anything he doesn't like.

"Uncle," I say as civilly as I can.

"You fucking idiot! Can't you do even the simplest thing? I thought you were supposed to be the smartest out of the whole fucking lot of you incompetent dicks, but I've yet to see any evidence of that."

The barrage of insults catches me off guard. Uncle Gerald is an asshole of the biggest order, but he is a snake. Everything he does is behind closed doors, going behind people's back and creating toxic allies that he then betrays. This front-on attack is new. Something is monumentally wrong.

"I'm going need you to be a little clearer about why you're calling. If not, maybe you should wait until you've cooled down a bit and can talk in a civilized manner," I hiss through my teeth.

"Fuck you, you little shit. I can talk to you any way I want, and you better fucking get used to it. Especially if you're going to fuck up deals because you can't be bothered to answer a text message."

"What are you talking about, what deal?"

"The Heracles chip. Lim Tech sold to the Chen Group."

Fuck. No. "What? They were taking offers until the end of month. We still had two weeks."

"Well, maybe if you'd picked up your fucking phone, you'd have heard me tell you to get in contact with them and put in your offer. The merger's been announced. We just lost a 300-million-dollar deal that would've added value to 40% of our Asia portfolio. What the fuck is wrong with you?"

Fuck. Fuck. FUCK! The Heracles chip was a pivotal part of our strategy for our tech companies going into the next few years. This was a huge fuck up. And it was by me. I had been cocky and thought of it as a lock. Something had changed last minute, and I had not kept up with it. Suicide in this business.

"Look, I'll have a talk to Jason Lim. There must be some sort of misunderstanding here."

"The Financial Times doesn't post misunderstandings. You're going to pay for this fuck up, you stupid little shit."

The phone hangs up, and I'm still reeling from the acidity of his words. This is a new low for him. We lose out on accounts all the time, not as many as other organizations, maybe, but enough that we've all had bitter losses. Especially when it's to our competitors, it burns.

A quick Google search tells me Gerry wasn't lying, which I wasn't entirely convinced of. There, on the fucking first page of the Hong Kong Economic Times says, "Chen Group puts in winning bid on the patent for the Heracles chip set to revolutionize the RISC-V code."

"Get Henry on the phone now," I yell to my admin assistant. As my acquisitions VP, he dropped the ball as much as I did. I'll take the hit, but he's going to have to explain how he didn't pick up on it either.

"He's in Singap—"

"I don't care if he's on the fucking moon with his dick up a space cactus cunt, get him on the phone now."

My phone dings, and I know without looking it's one or all of my brothers to simultaneously rub it in and commiserate, but I ignore it. I want this conversation done so I can go home and be with Kiara, my only true source of comfort right now.

Thirty-Two

Kiara

You're late, the text message says at 6:31p.m.

"Is that Nathan?" Kylian asks from the driver's seat when he sees me roll my eyes.

"Yeah. I was waiting for it. Like he's never late. He probably had it all typed out, ready, just hoping I'd be late."

"Sorry, traffic was brutal," Kylian apologizes, patting the hand I have on his thigh.

I can't stop touching him. He doesn't seem to mind, but I wonder if one day he will.

"It's okay, I should've gotten a ride there, would've saved you having to come home and get me." Something I say makes him smile so wide I can't see his eyes hidden by sunglasses, but I can feel the warmth emanating from them. "What?"

"I like when you call my apartment 'home.'"

"Oh. I meant *your* home," I tease him, and he pretends to clutch his chest.

"Why are you so intent on hurting me?"

I'm surprised I don't have to bite back the response that used to linger on my lips, 'you hurt me first.' I don't feel that way anymore.

"I'm just kidding. But you know that I'm going to have to find another apartment."

"Um, why do I need to know that? That's not something I think I need to know, and it's a thing I think you should try to forget."

"Kylian, I can't stay at your apartment"

"Um, why?"

"Well, we're not..."

"Not?"

"Living together."

"But we are. Do you feel comfortable there? I know we haven't had a chance to personalize it for you, but we can. We'll do it ASAP."

"Um. No."

"I'm going to need an actual reason."

"I think... I don't even know what we are."

"We are Kiara and Kylian. And I am going to throw the biggest tantrum you have ever seen if you move out of my apartment."

"Kylian!" I poke him in the arm, trying to get out my frustration for him being so difficult.

"Kiara! Look, you can't go back to your apartment for obvious reasons. And you haven't found another apartment... right?"

"Right. But I should start looking."

He shrugs. "So then... just stay."

"It's not as easy as that. We have been doing whatever this is for like a week. That's too soon for me to move in."

"Yeah, but why?"

"Because... everyone knows that!" I yell, frustrated at his obtuseness.

He shrugs. "I don't know that."

"That's because you're so dumb!"

That makes us both burst out laughing

We spend the rest of the drive arguing, but when my family's home looms in front of us, the sight instantly sobers us. We both agreed not to mention anything about us other than the work. It's too soon, and unlike with the apartment, he seems to agree with this.

He taps on the steering wheel, pulling his sunglasses on top of his head, and says, "I wish I had kissed you one last time before we got here."

"You could. But you're not dressed for the shit storm that will come after."

"You never know, your dad might be glad you're with me. He likes me."

"Yeah, my dad isn't who I'm worried about." That goes without saying, and we both know it.

Nathan's reaction to things can be hard to guess sometimes, but his best friend having sex with his little sister was not one of those things.

"We're here," I yell out as we walk into the house.

Kylian follows a few feet behind. He better get that worried look off his face or else Nathan is going to definitely know something is going on.

"Kiara! My girl!" My father shuffles in from the garden to greet us. "I missed you for lunch today. But I didn't want to make you have to come meet me twice this week."

"I would've been happy to, Dad," I say and lean over and kiss his soft, wrinkled cheek. He looks like he needs to get more sun, and I tell him so. "Get the gardener to set up a little bench for you near Mom's rose garden."

"He's too busy."

"He works you for you, Dad; he's busy with doing what you tell him to do."

"Ahh." He waves away my words. "I have this patio set here. That is plenty for me. I came from humble beginnings."

"Dad. You inherited 600 million pounds."

"Yes. Very sad, poor childhood," he grins, eyes still sparkling as ever.

"Good afternoon, sir," Kylian says, coming up to us, and stretches his hand out to shake my dad's hand.

"Oh, Kylian, you're here. I would've made dinner a little later, but sunset is coming earlier now, and I didn't want to waste the daylight."

Kylian hands him a wooden wine box. "It's a bottle of 1976 Penfold's Grange Hermitage."

Dad looks up at Kylian with a wistful expression that tugs at my heart. "Oh my. Kylian, what a special gift." He runs his hand over the writing on the box like it's precious and rare.

"My brother, Damien, has a small boutique winery in Barossa Valley in South Australia. And his fiancée's second cousin has a winery there, too, Simpatico Winery, and they got together to win an auction with fifteen bottles of the Penfold's Grange Hermitage. I helped him with his fiancée once, so he gave me this as a thank you. I thought you would enjoy it much more than I would."

Kylian helps him pull the lid off, and Dad's hand runs over the simple paper label, lost in his thoughts. This is a special bottle, and I don't know how Kylian knows, but I guess I shouldn't be surprised.

"We drank this on our... My wife and I drank this on our..." Dad's voice cracks, and he stops.

"Honeymoon trip to Australia," Kylian finishes with a kind smile.

Dad beams and hugs the box to his chest. "Kylian, this is just... I don't know what to say."

"How about 'Kylian, I've opened a bottle of that Argentinian wine you like so much that I brought back from my last trip'?"

Dad laughs and carefully hands me the wooden box so I can put it on the table, and he hooks his hands through Kylian's arm. "Kylian, my dear boy, I've opened a bottle of that Argentinian wine you like so much."

Kylian pats my dad's hand. "Wow, sir. That sounds absolutely perfect." He turns around and gives me a sneaky wink as they make their way out to the grill area.

"Charming fucker," I whisper under my breath. If he can charm Dennis Yin, then I had no chance. My dad was one of the fussiest people on the planet. If you did one thing he didn't like, he would secretly hold it against you forever.

"Speak of the devil and the devil appears!" Nathan says, coming in from the garden, clicking a pair of tongs in his hand.

"What were you saying about me?"

"I didn't say anything. You said 'charming fucker', and voila, here I am!"

He comes over and gives me a hug, and I resist the urge to flip him onto his back, only because if he breaks a bone, I'd be the one expected to pick up the slack in his life, and that was a 'no deal' for me.

"You're late," he says after we pull away from the hug.

"Nice to see you, too."

He waves the BBQ tongs in the air like they're a sword and he's fighting a dragon for ancient scrolls. He flips in the air and lands with a flourish, raising his eyebrows at me, as if I should be impressed. I'm not. I've seen him flip, tumble, jump off a roof, and break his wrist enough times to not be impressed by his tong Muay Thai. "How did you get here?" he asks when he sees he's not going to get applause from me.

"Um, Kylian gave me a ride." I try to keep my voice as light as I can, which isn't easy when it comes to talking about Kylian.

Nathan eyebrows flick upwards.

"What?" I snap defensively. "We were talking about work, and then he said he might as well give me a ride."

He flicks his eyes to my torso and then back at me. "Whose jacket is that?"

We both know exactly whose it is. It's the jacket that Kylian covered me with that first night in the car when I was cold. I have been wearing it since the day, and the only indication that he even noticed was the other morning. He'd raised his eyebrow when he saw me pull it off the back of the chair and take it with me.

"Kiara..."

"Nathan..."

"Be careful."

"And what am I supposed to be careful about?"

He comes closer, lowering his voice. "You know what they call him, right?"

"You mean the Blond Billionaire Bachelor?" I say, letting out a little snort.

"Yeah, you don't just get that name."

Despite him having a point, it still irks me that Kylian's own best friend has this impression of him, and I feel instantly protective of him. "Come on, he's a rich, not ugly, blond Englishman who lives in Hong Kong who speaks Cantonese, or at least tries to. He's always going to get way more attention than ugly Jason Lim."

Nathan rolls his eyes. "He's a dog. He could have any woman he wants."

"So you're asking why he would want me?" If that's what he really means, then that hurts.

"Come on, Keeks, you know that's not what I meant. But while we're on the topic, you're not his type."

I wave my hand at him. "Go away, Nathan. You're an asshole."

"I'm just saying to be careful!"

"And I'm telling you, there's no reason to be giving me that warning. Unless you just can't help but interfere in my life."

"Fine. Don't listen to me, but I hope you don't get in a situation that you can't get out of again." As soon as he says it, he clamps his mouth shut. "Sorry. I didn't mean that."

But it's gone too far. He's acting like a fucking idiot, and it's been made clear even to me how he's going to react when he finds out about Kylian and me.

I take a breath and try not to let the rage take over. "I'm not the only one who needs to know when to take myself out of a dangerous situation. For example, I suggest you quickly extract yourself from this situation where I want to kick you in the fucking balls." For dramatic effect, I do a flip that's just as high as his.

His breath hisses, but he doesn't respond, just turns and storms up the stairs.

"Hey, your dad wanted me to come in and see what was taking Nathan so long with the meat," Kylian calls out to me as he comes back into the kitchen.

The anger is still building inside me, but if I'm honest, it's because somehow there's this tiny edge of doubt, something I thought I'd managed to get rid of.

"Um, he went upstairs to get something. The meat's probably in the butler's pantry fridge." I busy myself with straightening up flowers on the table.

"Everything okay?"

I give him the brightest smile I can summon. "Everything. I'm just trying to forget that this family loves you more than me."

"What can I say, I'm a charming fucker." He grins.

"You heard me?"

"Heard what?"

I throw a cushion, and it hits him on the ass as he runs toward the kitchen.

The dinner turns out to be delicious, relaxed, and fun.

Kylian is, annoyingly, a perfect addition to my family, equal parts intelligent, funny, and sarcastic. Nathan, once he stops sulking, joins us, and the two of them shoot off insults back and forth like a tennis rally.

Dad mostly sits back, watching with a smile on his face. I make it a point not to attract any attention because each time they remember I'm there, they gang up on me.

"Kylian, I heard the Chen Group won the Heracles chip deal," my father says when Nathan goes inside to take a call.

Kylian's jaw tenses; it'd probably be imperceptible to everyone except anyone who's favorite hobby is watching him. He hasn't said anything to me about it, so it's news to me.

"Ah, well, yes. I guess there was something about their deal that they preferred to ours." His voice is even, a sure sign that he's trying to control it.

Dad doesn't say anything for awhile, just stares at him. "I heard that they might not have actually received an offer from you. Did Jason Lim go under the table again? I wouldn't be surprised. Dirty business man.

It's a pity his R&D is second to none." He doesn't actually spit, but I feel like he did.

"What happened?" I lean over and ask Kylian. The tension in his jaw is still there, and its traveled up to his eyes. He just shakes his head, forcing a smile on his lips, not looking at me.

"Dad? What do you mean by that?" If he's not going to tell me, I'll ask someone who will.

"Lim Tech has been known to close its offer window without much notice. It's some sort of power play. Sometimes he'll give you an hour to send in any offer. You have to be prepared. He thinks it gets people to send in big offers and fast. This time, he did it only two days into the offer window being open. As far as I know, only Chen Group was prepared."

"They planned it that way. Gathering hype for the sale," Kylian adds, sounding no more impressed than my dad is about it all.

"You didn't get a chance to put in an offer?" I ask Kylian. His shoulders square as he answers. "No. I didn't get a notification that he was closing the window. I was... busy."

"When was it?"

He flicks his eyes up to look at me and then away.

"On Sunday."

Me.

He was busy with me.

Guilt streaks through my body.

Was it those phone calls and text messages he ignored?

I should've made him answer them. I should've grabbed the phone, pushed it into his hand, and forced him to read the message.

"I'm sorry."

"It's okay. Overpriced little chip. There will be others," he says. "Another day, another chip, right, sir?" he says and raises his glass to my dad who responds in kind.

"You talking about the Heracles chip deal? I hear Chen Group and Lim Tech did it on purpose."

Kylian doesn't say anything, just takes another sip from his drink. The conversation is bothering him, and there's nothing that I can do to help him.

"Anyone up for tea? It's getting a little cool out here." I jump up, watching his discomfort hurting me.

Nathan looks at me like I'm crazy. "Keeks, it's like seventy-five degrees with 70% humidity. Do you have ice water dripping through your veins?" I ignore him and run over to the pool house. It has tinted window panes so that you can look out into the garden, but unless it's dark, people outside can't see inside.

The drink bar is fully stocked with cold drinks, but I have to rummage in the cupboard to find the kettle.

"I have some tea you might like to try," Kylian says, joining me in the pool house, holding up a small pouch. "It's a concoction of white jasmine, green tea, and orange peel."

"Oh, hey, that's sounds great." I reach out to grab it, but as soon as my fingers close around it, he pulls it back, and I fall against him.

"Careful, angel," he whispers against my ear and sends a shiver all through my body.

"I'm kind of sick of people saying that to me today," I growl as I steady myself and snatch the tea bag out of his hands.

"Who else said that to you?" He leans casually against the bench, back toward the garden where my family sits.

"It doesn't matter. You should go back out there; you don't want them to see us here."

He watches for a moment, and even though I'm facing away from him, I can feel his eyes on me. "We're just talking, Kiki."

"Yeah, well, apparently Nathan doesn't even want us to do that." I fill the kettle with water, then turn it on.

"Ah, so it was Nathan. What happened? Did he tell you I was a filthy manwhore and you should be careful in case I ravage you one day when we're supposed to be working?" The lighthearted tone of his voice doesn't hide that he wonders if I believe what Nathan said.

"Something like that."

"He's just being protective. I mean, I fully intend on ravaging you, but the other thing, I haven't been that for a long time. He's just holding onto an old image of me."

"It's not like that. You and me. I hate him talking about it like it's some casual fling."

"Hey." He grabs my hands, and I nervously look to make sure they can't see us from where they're sitting in the garden. "I know it's not like that. It's not some dirty, casual fling. And maybe if he knew that, he'd be okay with us."

After how he reacted just knowing Kylian drove me here, I highly doubt it. "I just... I don't know how to tell him."

He kisses my hand. "We'll figure it out. Now, how can I help you with the tea?"

"No. I've got it."

He stands up, jaw set. Something in the air has instantly shifted. "I asked you, how can I help?" His voice lowers, firm, daring disobedience. I don't know how he can joke about squirrel testicles one moment and then speak to me in a way that makes my knees buckle under me.

But my stubbornness stops me.

"I said I've got it."

"I'm going to ask you one last time, Kiara. What can I do?" There's flicker of something dark in his eyes, and I don't know what comes over me, but I want to push him to see that flicker burst into life.

"Nothing. Geez. I can do it myself." Even as I say it, my core turns to liquid, anticipating what's coming.

"Don't say I didn't warn you." He moves so that's he's behind me, then presses me so that my front is bent over the kitchen island. I gasp as he wrenches my skirt up so that it's bunched up over my ass.

"Oh my god! Kylian, what are you doing?" I hiss.

His hands drag up my inner thighs. "I'm reminding you what happens to stubborn brats."

"I—" I start to pretend to protest, but the sound of him unzipping his pants dries my mouth. And I lick my lips before saying, "Kylian... they're going to see."

He fists my hair and yanks my head until my back resembles a bow, buzzing with the potential energy, that's going to explode when he lets me go. "So let them see. Then they can see for themselves just how serious it is between us," he snarls, pressing his face into the nape of my neck. "Now we know what a loud girl you are. So if you don't want me to stop right now, you're going to have to be quiet, okay?"

His hand still grips my hair, so I can't nod. Instead, I let out a choked moan.

"Good girl, now press that gorgeous ass back against me, feel how hard you've been making me all night."

He's rough as he lifts one leg up, so my knee is resting on the bench, and then he slides deep inside me.

"Fuck." He takes the word right out of my mouth.

He's deep inside me as he presses down on my back, getting traction before he starts to fuck me.

Brutal. Savage. Needing. Claiming.

"Take it, angel."

"Ohhh." His cockhead hits so deep inside me I see stars. Constellations in the shape of all the orgasms he's given me. Messy, bright, brilliant balls of fire, consuming everything in their wake.

"Quiet, angel. Do you want them coming in here?"

I can't answer. I can't even really understand what he's saying as he fucks me with such viciousness that I haven't seen.

He's pissed about Nathan, too. And now he's reminding me that what we have is real.

"Kylian... fuck!"

The hand on my back slides around to cover my mouth.

"I said, quiet. Because if they come in right now, they're going to see me balls deep in you. Is that what you want? Because nothing's going to stop me coming inside you right now. In my perfect little slut's cunt."

He marks each word with brutal thrusts.

His hands drop from my mouth to press at the base of my throat as he thrust into me, slow, short thrusts that feel more sensual than when he's fucking me with abandon.

Our bodies rub against each other as his other hand reaches down and rubs my clit.

"Oh god... Kylian..." I moan.

"I just wanted to remind you that my cock is yours. And whatever anyone else says, that's the way it's always going to be. Forget what your brother said. Can you feel me fucking you, sweetheart? My cock deep inside you at your dad's house, even while we're supposed to be hiding our affair?"

I nod, eyes glazed, not closed, only occasionally open to make sure that they can't see us. But the sun is setting, and the glare will be gone, and they'll be able to see Kylian, my dad's surrogate son and Nathan's best friend, with his cock buried inside me.

And it shouldn't, but it thrills me.

He moves faster in and out of me; he's close.

One more thrust and we come together, muffled grunts, his against my back, mine against the edge bench, deliciously sharp and cool against my skin. The pleasure hardens every part of our bodies and then wrecks them in the fall.

"Oh fuck," he mutters, his head against my back for a moment before he pulls out and zips up. "Step out of them, angel," he says as he pulls my panties down my legs.

"I need those," I gasp, still coming down from the orgasm.

He ignores me, lifting my feet up one by one and then tucks the panties into his pocket. "Shhhh. You don't need them. I need to know you can feel my cum dripping over your pussy lips and down your inner thighs."

I shut my mouth.

I want that, too.

"Hey! How long does it take to make some tea? The kettle's been whistling for like five minutes," Nathan says, making us both jump. "Kylian, did you take your call?"

Kylian clears his throat next to me, ignoring me looking at him. "Er, yeah, it was just a voicemail from Matthias."

"Oh, yeah? What did he want?"

"Um, he's coming here next week. Was just sending me the details so I could pick him up."

"Cool! We'll meet for a drink, okay?"

"Sure thing. Anyway, I was just helping Kiara with the tea. My-Linh brought some with her when they were here a few weeks ago."

Nathan gives me a rare, genuine smile. "I love her."

Kylian makes a cross with his fingers, fending off a demon. "Yeah, don't let Damien hear you say that. He will rip your throat out of your ass, make it into ass tartare, and feed it back to you."

"She's too good for him."

"No kidding."

I'd be jealous, but Kylian has talked about his future sister-in-law in a way that I think that I'd probably love her, too.

"You'll probably get to meet her at the casino opening, Keeks," Nathan says.

"I hope so. Hopefully she'll like me."

"How can she not? You're a Yin," Kylian teases me.

Nathan eyes us as he pours himself a cup of tea. "Anyway, Dad is going to go lie down for a bit; he didn't sleep too well last night. You guys want to continue this in the library?"

"Of course. I'll just help bring in some of the food," Kylian says and jogs outside, leaving me with my brother.

"You okay?"

"Never better." And I mean it.

Thirty-Three
Kylian

Nathan, Kiara, and I stay up well into the night talking and playing games. I rule poker out—I'm still stinging from the lost Heracles deal—I have no intention of losing my wallet to the Yin siblings, one who keeps her cool at the poker table better than anyone I've seen and the other with a tell that only his sister knows.

We play a range of words games and board games, and the night ends after an angry game of gin rummy has Nathan demanding a recount.

"There's nothing to count, Nathan! You lost. You have to put all the games away now. Those are the rules," his sister taunts him.

Countless glasses of cognac, Japanese whiskey, and then a dicey bottle of homemade wine had us talking with few inhibitions and zero volume control on our voices.

It reminds me of the games nights we used to have before my mother decided she wanted to beat Elizabeth Taylor's record for number of husbands and my dad moved to Australia to get away from the memories of their disastrous marriage of convenience. Nights filled with laughter, trash talk, and taking turns splitting into teams to beat the others. It's the reason I kept the games table, because it carries with it the echoes of unadulterated joy before the divorce.

"You two play games like your lives depend on winning," I tease them, as even now, they're bickering about who really won the most games.

They both turn to me, offended. "Um, that's because our lives so depend on winning. I thought you had brothers!"

Memories of similar fights and Matthias being sent to bed sulking, while Damien and I wrestled for the title of Game Night Winner makes me laugh out loud. "Oh, trust me, I do. But you two fight dirty. I'm pretty sure I have a dent on my forehead from when Kiara threw that Scrabble tile holder at my head."

"I was just handing you the best one. You're welcome!" she says through laughs.

The best thing about the night is how relaxed Kiara is. She's shown in many different ways that she's comfortable at my place, but this is her family home. Whenever I go back to our home in London, it feels like I never left. All night she has been the most animated I've ever seen her, the same excited woman playing games with Nathan like she is at my apartment talking about her work.

I bite back the urge to say "I already gave you your thanks this morning in the shower," but instead just shrug and give her a wink when Nathan has his back turned.

"You two have had too much to drink. Kylian, I've hidden your car keys, man," Nathan says, patting me on the back. "And I did it back before we drank the sludge that is Dad's homemade wine, so I couldn't tell you where they are even if you asked. I've had the housekeeper set up the guest room next to mine for you."

I'm not sure why he feels like he has to tell me where the room is, that's basically been my bedroom since the Yins moved here. "Thanks, man. You're such a good host."

He stumbles out the door, and Kiara and I wait, holding our breaths. After a minute, she skips over and closes the door to the library and then jumps into my lap, wrapping her arms around my neck and kissing me.

"I've been waiting to do that to you all night. We haven't been alone even once since before."

"Before was very nice. I like all the befores with you. And I cannot wait to have all the afters with you," I mutter, pulling her head down to kiss me.

There's a noise outside the room, and she jumps to her feet. We stare at the door, but no one comes through it.

Kiara wipes her forehead. "Okay, too close. Stop being too handsome, winking at me and making me want to kiss you."

"You can't talk! You think I don't know you picked to sit in that seat all night so I look up your dress?"

The way she giggles tugs at my heart, a reminder of all the laughs we had tonight. With my best friend and his sister.

"I'm going up to bed. Do you need anything?" she asks.

"I'm good, Kiki. Sweet dreams, I'll see you in the morning."

The sweet smile she gives me ensures that all my dreams are of her.

We all emerge from our rooms around 7:30 in the morning, freshly showered and no longer slurring or stumbling around.

The smell of food greets us in the hallway, and I race Nathan downstairs to the kitchen.

There's a full spread with three types of juice, cereals, fruit and our own personal chef in the form of Dennis Yin in an apron standing at the grill with a bowl of eggs in front of him.

"Wow. How come we don't have breakfast like this every day?" Nathan asks, popping a grape into his mouth.

"You do. It's just at the restaurant," Dennis shoots back and whacks his son across the back of his head with the spatula.

"Ow."

"What would you like, Kylian?" Dennis asks.

"Some fried eggs, sunny-side up, please." I say, downing a glass of apple juice, thirsty from all the alcohol we drank last night."

"Kiara?"

"None for me, Dad. I'm going to have some avocado toast."

"Nathan?" he finally gets to his son.

"Why am I last?"

"Because you're the host. Kylian and Kiara don't live here."

"How is that my fault? A plain omelet, please."

He serves us in short order, and we eat in silence for a few minutes.

"Dad? You're not eating anything?" Kiara asks after taking a sip of her coffee.

"Oh, um, no. Actually, I ate already, dear. That's what happens when you fall asleep at 8 p.m.," he laughs. "Well, it was a lovely night. Thank you for coming home, my children." He makes a point to look at me when he says it, and if I wasn't shoving an egg into my mouth, I might have been a little more emotional. "Kiara? I'll see you next week?

"Of course, Dad. I might even drop by this weekend."

He waves her offer away. "Oh, no. That's okay. I know you're busy on the weekends."

Nathan snorts.

"What? Are you suggesting I'm not?"

His sister's confrontational manner is not a good match for Nathan's short temper. "It's not a real job, Keeks. How many times are we going to have this conversation?" Nathan says, his voice full of derision. This isn't the man I know. Why is he treating his sister with so much less grace than he does other people?

"It is a real job." Kiara looks at me, her eyes hurt. "Don't say that in front of Kylian, who's hiring me.

"It is," I say before I can stop myself. Before coming here yesterday, I'd made a pact to myself that I was not going to get involved in any familial spats, but... I can't let him talk to her like this. "Have you two even seen her work? Do you have any idea about her operation? She is so good. She knows what she's doing. She's strong and resourceful but kind and thoughtful all at the same time." I swallow, knowing that I should stop talking. That this conversation shouldn't have a part for me in it. But I can't let them talk to her like that, not knowing the amazing things she's doing. "She's in the trenches. We always talk about how much good we're doing because we're throwing money at the people who are out there, day in day out, doing the hard things. It's easy sitting in our ivory tower, but she's out there, on the ground. Don't judge it unless you've seen her firsthand. Please. And Kiara, you don't have to worry about me taking in what Nathan is saying. I wouldn't hire you and your agency if I didn't think you could do the job."

This time, Nathan's annoyed look is aimed at me. "Oh, what a surprise, Kylian being on Kiara's side." The way he says it makes me want to punch the smugness right off his face. "It's not a stable job, so don't pretend it is, man. And it's dangerous. You mess with people's money and they want to make sure you know they're not okay with it! She's going to get into trouble."

"Come on, man. Really? Every single day, we play with people's money. And not a few thousand in poker chips. Hundreds, thousands, millions of dollars. You don't think that's dangerous? You don't think some middle manager out there who's put all of his savings into one of our businesses only to have a drop right when he's about to retire doesn't want to shoot our fucking brains out? If you don't want her to do this because you can't control her, just fucking say that! Don't pretend it's something it isn't. "

His anger blasts across the breakfast bench area and burns a mark in my skin. Sure, we've fought, but it's never been over a disagreement like this. "What the fuck are you suggesting? I'm genuinely afraid that she is going to get hurt."

I stand up, face to face with him, looking at him dead in the eyes. "I'm not going to let that happen. Ever. I trust her to do her job well. And you should trust me to make sure that Kiara and her employees are safe at Baxter."

He hisses, and it takes everything I have not to flinch when he raises his hand, but then he turns and storms out of the room.

The three of us glance around, reeling in the aftermath of the argument, until Kiara breaks the silence. "You'll have to excuse him, Kylian. He's been making dramatic exits often lately. Must be some sort of business strategy he's trying out."

I grimace as I address their father, my heart sinking at the prospect that he's disappointed with me for arguing with his son. "I apologize, sir. I just feel very strongly that Kiara isn't getting enough credit for the work she's doing."

He doesn't say anything immediately, thinking over my words before he gives me a small nod. "Me, too. But Nathan is just looking out for her. We care about our girl. And, personally, I am more than happy that she's joining your company." He nods, a secret gesture to me about the deal he offered.

And I wish I could tell him that I didn't offer Kiara a job because of our deal and that I already had what I wanted most in the world.

⇢♥⇠

The next few days flash by in a blur. I try to catch up with work, alternating between going into the office and working from home if I don't have in-person meetings.

Odette shows up one day at the apartment with a bunch of flowers and a sushi platter as a peace offering, and by the time I finally kick her out three hours later so that the both of us can get some work done, she and Kiara are best friends.

"She's sassy," Kiara says after Odette shouts a goodbye through the closing elevator doors.

My head hurts from the effort of making sure my assistant didn't say anything to confuse Kiara again. That and the sheer amount of words she'd spoken while here. "No kidding. I hope you don't mean that as a compliment; it's not easy to work when you have a deadline."

"She does give you a run for your money when it comes to talking, doesn't she?" Kiara laughs, slapping the cushion next to her.

My look is deadpan. I don't like being out talked and have no qualms about making that known.

Gratitude fills me, though, as I remember how Odette had sat, hands in her lap, explaining to Kiara in clear terms that what Kiara saw in London between Odette and I was all for show and nothing actually happened. And that it was actually her idea when I had come to her confused and didn't know what to do. Kiara had listened and then reached over to give Odette a hug.

"Why didn't anything ever happen between you two? She seems like she'd be just your type? Beautiful, smart as a whip, funny," she'd says later in bed.

I nuzzle her neck from behind as we'd lie in bed. "My type is you."

She giggles and burrows back against me, and I feel like the Odette issue, for now, has been resolved.

It's surprising to me how I don't need to meditate once for sleep, but I'm feeling more rested than ever with her in my bed.

As for Kiara, she spends the next few days looking for apartments, all of which I inform her are absolutely not acceptable, and catching up on her work. I listen from another room as she negotiates with a poker club the rates to retain her players. He ends up giving her everything she wanted.

Her partner, Ananya, seems to be holding down the fort just fine. The three of us drive around for an afternoon, visiting all three of the apartments where the girls live. Ananya proves to be my Odette to Kiara. After talking to her for ten minutes, I leave feeling both secure in the knowledge that as long as Kiara and she work together, they'd both have a trustworthy friend and sounding board. I also get a healthy dose of ego bashing.

"He's too blond," she says to Kiara in Cantonese the second she lays on eyes on me, probably unaware that I understand the language.

"She's too opinionated," I shoot back in Cantonese, which makes her double over with laughter and grab my wrist and yank me into the apartment.

They talk to me about their plans, needing larger and more secure premises and better security. Over the last week while Kiara had been staying at my apartment, they spent hours over Zoom discussing locations and formerly rescued women, now back on their feet, who could help them expand. It's impressive.

As far as I know, Kiara has not spent a second in a business classroom and has absolutely nothing to do with her family's business other than to attend a ribbon cutting or two when they're in Hong Kong, but she was blessed with natural acumen. The plan, though not a formal business plan, is thorough and well-thought-out, ticking all the boxes for an unofficial SWOT test with data-based future projections.

It also thrills me to see that Baxter's casino, Jade Bay, plays a part in their plan.

And I silently vow to do everything thing I can to help.

My suggestions for grant applications or a business sponsorship are shot down with offended glares, and it isn't until we are in the car driving home do I understand it's because I was trying too hard to legitimize their operation. Kiara's agency is registered, and she taught all the girls how to declare their incomes and pay taxes, but that is as far as she wanted anyone to know about her operations.

And seeing how even Kiara's family had reacted, I don't blame her for wanting to retain their privacy as much as possible.

On Friday morning, Julie buzzes Frank into my office.

"Hey. Thanks for coming. I think it's easier to talk about this in person."

He doesn't say anything, just opens up the bag in his hand and empties it onto my desk. The contents scatter all over, some rolling right off the edge of my desk. Bending over to pick it up, I already know what it is before I've touched it.

"It's a camera." Disgust gurgles in the pit of my stomach like a thick tar sludge. This camera was in Kiara's apartment, watching her.

In true Frank form, he doesn't say anything, barely nods. In Franklish, this is a resounding yes.

"And what are those?" I point to one of the small metal disks in the pile.

"Audio bug."

"There's five of them. And"—I do a quick count—"eight cameras?"

This time he doesn't even bother to nod; instead, he drops a stack of 8.5 x 11 inch enlarged photographs on my desk. They're pictures of Kiara's apartment with red crosses marking where the camera and bugs were placed. They were everywhere. The sick fucking bastard was thorough. I wonder if he did this all at once or if he did it over time. Was he angry that he was missing the show in a place he didn't have a camera?

"Fuck!" I shout this time, sweeping my hand over my desk, knocking everything, the picture, the surveillance equipment, all over the ground. "He had every inch of that place covered. I want to kill him!" I hiss, fuming. "Find. Him."

"The signal was already disconnected when we got there and retrieved these. I had someone posted outside her apartment right after we talked on Monday, so he didn't have a chance to come back and get them. He must've turned them off after she found the photos. It would be stupid otherwise. We could trace it."

"No. He's sick. He wants her to know he was watching; that's what the photos are about."

"Any leads on where the signal went?"

"No. But we're looking into it."

The not knowing is driving me insane. I want him gone so that she can get on with her life. As much as I love her living with me, I want her there because she wants to be, not because she's forced. "Look harder. You know who to call if you need more tech help."

It's back to the nods.

"Okay, thanks. As soon as you learn anything, let me know, whatever time of day it is, wherever I am. Also, tonight, I'm going with Kiara to a poker club in Wan Chai. I want extra cover. Make it two guys, alright? Inconspicuous ones. She doesn't need to be worried about being babysat while she's working."

"Sir."

"Thanks for all you're doing. I want everything that can possibly be done to find this guy. Do not spare any cost, a single person... And when you do find him, tell me and only me."

There's a small grunt, and he gathers up the cameras and bugs, and leaves. It takes two drinks for me to feel like I can leave my office without inadvertently punching or yelling at an innocent person because of my anger.

By the time I arrive home to get ready to go with Kiara on another mentoring evening, all the frustration of the day fades the moment I step out of the elevator and she's standing there in a floor-length, black velvet dress that drapes so low in the back that if I wasn't focused on her beautiful face, I'd probably catch the tiniest glimpse of the dip of her ass.

"Wow. Angel... you look breathtaking." I take her hand and twirl her around slowly, taking in the full effect of her dress and the way she moves in it.

"Can you help me with the top of the zipper? I can't quite bend that way."

She swings her hair over her left shoulder and lifts her right arm to show me the zipper running down her side. I pull on the zipper, leaning down to press a kiss on her bare shoulder. Her freshly showered skin smells like my soap

"Zip me up, Kylian," she says firmly.

"In a minute."

My hands slide under the dress and onto her silky soft skin, taking in a moment that shows how perfect she is. And then I sigh as I pull the zipper up all the way.

"I'll get changed and be right down, Kiki."

Her hands tickle the back of my head as she give me a sweet kiss. "I hope you don't mind; I chose a suit for you."

It's hard to not feel like my soul just took flight, the idea of her going through my wardrobe and picking something she thinks would look good on me. "Of course not. Which one is it?

"It's the silk, midnight blue one. Wear a plain, white T-shirt underneath."

"Anything for you, milady." I bow low, kissing her hand.

And when I come back down, the look of approval in her eyes touches parts of me I thought had died when I'd hurt her.

In the car, she lays her hand on my thigh as she's wont to do every time now. The skin under my pant fabric is hers. The thought of anyone else touching me there is physically repugnant. It's hers. As is every other part of me. I long for a red light, trying to time my driving so that I can lift her hand to my mouth and kiss her palm.

"The universe granted me something so that we could be together. Some grace and a lot of—"

"Luck," she finishes and gives me a bright smile.

I tickle her palm that's been returned to my thigh. "Poker players shouldn't be talking about luck."

Her face screws up like a bunny. "That's BS. Sure, playing the player is the game. But imagine how much easier it would be if you were dealt a royal flush every hand."

"You'd be escorted out by security for cheating, even if you weren't. So maybe a non-attention getting amount of luck?"

"Perfect," she laughs, indulging my stupid ideas.

"Yes, you are."

"Oh, Kylian..." She lowers her face to her hand.

"Yes, my sweet angel?"

"That was fucking lame."

I laugh and laugh until we reach the poker club. I park in front of the valet station, and I'm about to get out when Kiara pulls her cell phone out of her pocket and quickly scans the message.

"We have to go, Ananya texted, there's a girl."

I turn the ignition without needing another word from her. "Where?"

She hesitates for a moment before answering. "Illumination."

I wince internally. Illumination is a nightclub on the very outskirts of Wan Chai, notorious for providing a more full-service experience for patrons than most other clubs will publicly admit to. If a girl is in trouble there, we need to get there as soon as possible.

"Ananya has a friend there who helped a girl getting attacked, and they're hiding in the bathrooms right now. If we don't get her out soon, the owner is going to find her."

I press my foot on the gas, hoping that the car that's been discreetly tailing us is following us now, the one with Frank's henchman. I have an uneasy feeling that we're going to need them.

When we get there, men and women stumble around outside, some watching us through glazed eyes as I stop the car in the alley next to the club.

She gets out of the car, and I follow, body tense. In the corner of my eye, I see the black sedan park on the other side of the road, and it provides a little relief.

"Can you help me? I need to rip this dress so it's shorter. I can't go in there looking like I've just come off the Titanic." There's a tinge of sadness in her voice. "I really liked how you looked at me when you saw me in this dress."

I cup her cheek, and she leans into it for just a split second. "Angel, I look at you like that no matter what you're wearing, and usually when you're not wearing anything at all. In fact, this stupid thing is covering too much of you. The less of it the better"

I reach down and find a seam and then rip it, tearing it all the way around so that the dress now hangs a few inched above her thigh. "There, much better."

She lets out a small, grateful laugh. But I can see she still mourns her gown.

"I will buy a hundred thousand more, I promise."

The smile fades, but her eyes shine with emotion. "That's a lot of dresses for someone who doesn't want to see me wear any clothes? Were you bullshitting me just then, Mr. Baxter?"

A text message interrupts our moment, and she frowns.

"We have to go in, Ananya's friend is freaking out. You need to wait here."

"You've got to be fucking kidding! I'm not letting you go in there on your own. Especially doing what you're going to do. It's a mad house in there. If I lose sight of you for one second, I might never find you again. I know it's important to you so go. But I'm coming with you."

Her eyes turn fiery red. "You're going to draw attention to us. Dressed like that, looking like that! You might as well go in there with a neon sign pointing to your head."

I rip my suit coat off and throw it into the car, then tousle my hair, so it looks like I just woke up from a hundred year nap. "Is that better?"

"No! You need to stay out here and get the car ready to go. Do you really want to leave your Mercedes out here for even five minutes?" Her voice lowers right at the end of the sentence, but the anger is no less pronounced.

"Are you shitting me right now? Do I look like I care what the fuck happens to the car? I left the Jaguar that I'd just gotten a week ago in the middle of the road to chase after you, just in case you've forgotten."

"Can we not do this now? I have to go in there."

"Fine, go. But I'm coming in with you. I'll just hang back, and no one will know we're together."

She looks like she wants to argue but checks her phone, huffs, and storms to the entrance. Not surprisingly she's let in right away without even having to pay. I'm not as lucky. I hand her a hundred Hong Kong dollar bill and run in after Kiara.

I lean in, touching her on the arm just so she knows I'm there. She reacts by shoving me away.

"Hey, asshole, I said no! Go hit on someone else already. If you come close again, I'm going to make it so you need to pee out of a bag."

I hold my hands up, playing the role, and let her walk away, "Geez, sorry. I was trying to be nice."

She's about ten feet away, but in this club, it may as well be a hundred. The club is basically one big dance floor, and it is teeming with bodies. Hot, sticky, writhing, drunken bodies. And there is no way to move anywhere quickly.

My extra few inches come in handy so that I can watch her make her way through the crowd toward the bathrooms in the back. Out of the corner of my eye, I see two men enter, and I give them a nod. Frank's men. I'm glad to see them. Although, if something were to happen where either Kiara or I am standing, I'm not really sure how they're going to be able help. Let's just hope that Frank chose his two best men.

Ahead someone shouts, and the crowd lurches, moving to the right in a big uncontrollable wave. Fear burns as I lose sight of her. The problem with a crowd like this is it's not that easy to fall over, because you're all squished in like sardines. But if you do, it's game over. In the dark, I pick out her head again; she's moved another few feet toward the back.

I elbow a guy breathing his beer-drenched air on me and follow her.

She surveys the club, turning her head to take in the space, calm but tense. I catch her eye and wave, but as soon as I lift my arm, she looks away. I'm not sure if I should feel proud that she's trying to do this the best way she knows or fucking frustrated that she won't let me help. I'll have to ponder that in a moment when I'm not in a pit of living, breathing, five hundred headed drunk, human monsters.

She's almost reached the back where there's a line for the bathroom. I watch as she pushes through and stumbles past the door. I can't see her, but I'm hoping that it's safer in there than it is out here.

Another crowd surge pushes me too far to the right, and I have to fight against the current to regain the progress I'd made to get to the bathroom.

I'm almost there when she appears again, pushing her way past the crowd waiting for the bathroom and onto the dance floor, as well as keeping a scared young woman by her side. The girl's eyes are wide, wet, and I'm worried that if she enters the crowd, she's going to be crushed.

"Kiara!" I shout, and she looks at me as I gesture for her to take the woman around the edge of the wall. It's a dangerous option in most cases; getting crushed against the wall is a sure-fire way to an injury. But timed well and with a little bit of luck, the crowd might move in the opposite direction, and there's a short period of time to run. As if the universe is listening, the crowd yells, and everyone gets pushed to the left, making a rare pocket along the wall where Kiara can go.

"Go!"

And for once, she listens. She grabs her friend's hand, and they run, the lights washing over them, letting me watch their progress as I make my way over to them.

"Oof!" Someone steps on my foot, and I know there's going to be a bruise there tomorrow. I shove him; I don't have time for politeness. He scowls, but then, as if the beer in his hands flips a switch in his brain, he lifts his hands in the air and starts singing along, forgetting that I'm there.

On any other occasion, I'd probably become friends with him, but tonight, I only have one goal. Getting Kiara out alive.

They're almost to the entrance when there's a loud angry shout. I look over to see a smaller man with two security guards behind him appear from a side door, pointing at Kiara. They spot her and make a beeline for her.

"Fuck."

Adrenaline pumping, I create a path for me to push through. I don't know how many feet I step on, how many faces I accidentally elbow, how many drinks I knock out of hands, and I don't fucking care. My hands wave in the air, trying to get my body guards' attention. They see me, and I frantically point to Kiara and the guys trying to get to her.

She's ignoring everything around her and just trying to make it to the door.

It's a race between the club's guards, me, and my two bodyguards to get to Kiara. My heart beats painfully in my chest, feeding oxygen to my legs.

"Go, go!" I shout, not daring to hope that she may just make it once she gets to the door.

And then I watch in slow motion as one of the club's security men gets to her. My heart comes to a complete stop as I watch him grab her hair, yank her back, and throw her over his shoulder like she's a ragdoll.

In the struggle, her friend manages to break free and run to the door. I can only hope that she can get to it safety and that she and Kiara have discussed a contingency plan in case something like this happened.

"Get her!" I yell as I meet up with the security guards as we break free from the crowd and into the lobby. They carry her down a dark hallway, and we chase after her, legs burning to catch up with her.

I run, run until my heart almost bursts. Run until she's within inches, and I reach out and grab her leg, dragging her to the ground.

"Kiara! I've got you!"

She falls at my feet as the club's security guard turns around and grunts.

"Run, Kiara. Fucking run!"

She doesn't listen; instead, she jumps to her feet and tries to grab my hand. "Come on! Let's go!"

I barely hear her as the guy who sent the security guards after her steps out of a room and eyes me.

"Are you the owner here?" I shout, all reason lost.

"Who fucking wants to know?"

"The person who is going to beat your ass for trying to grab my girlfriend here." I lunge at him, and he takes a step back.

"Your girlfriend needs to be taught a lesson. She shouldn't be trying to kidnap my employees. And now I've lost a worker, and I need a replacement. Your girlfriend looks like she's going to do very well; I hope she likes it rough."

The blood thudding through my ears sends a surge of adrenaline to my muscles, and I charge at him again.

Someone else grabs my arm and swings me against the wall, and I bounce off it, winded.

My bodyguard charges forward with his shoulder, ramming at the one who attacked me. I run to catch up with the club owner disappearing back into his office; I get there just in time and shove the door open.

"I don't like it when men exploit women. And I especially don't like it when men rough up my girlfriend." My voice sounds foreign to my ears. And then I jump over the table he's hiding behind like a little bitch and wrap my arm around his neck, throwing him to the ground.

There's a ferocious banging outside and a loud yell, but I can't focus on that right now. My anger blurs my vision but not enough to stop me slamming my fist into the club owner's face over and over. My knuckles feel like they're cauterizing, layers of skin ripping off each time I smash his face. Through the red haze, I can hear him splutter, spitting blood. I roar as I lay into him, my height an advantage as I twist his arm and shove him to the ground, pressing my knee into the back of his neck while I twist his leg until there's a sickening crunch.

He screams, and it thrills me.

"Don't ever fucking look at my girlfriend again, or I will break every fucking bone in your body."

"Just fucking try. She's never going to set foot into a single club in Hong Kong again," he screams just as Kiara shows up at the door, a scratch on her face stoking the rage in me again.

I slam my foot down on his hand, feeling his fingers break under my shoe.

She listens to him scream and then runs in to grab my hand, pulling me out the door. "Come on, let's go!"

I look back just once to see him cradling his hand, crumpled on the ground in a bloody mess.

Behind us, my bodyguards follow, barely touched.

When we reach the entrance, I yell, "Go, I've got this," and I watch them jump into their cars but don't leave, following orders to make sure that we're okay.

Frank has trained them well.

Kiara and I run until we reach the car, but before I can open the door for her, she swings her arm, her hand connecting with my face in a stinging slap.

"What the fuck was that about?" she shouts at me, her face a confused mess of emotions.

"What? You were in trouble! I was helping!" I yell out of surprise from being attacked when I was just trying to help her.

"I had it under control!"

She's got to be kidding. Did she hit her head and just forget what happened? "Kiara, they had grabbed you!"

"It's not the first time! They take me back to their offices and rough me up a bit, but I always make it out. Always!"

The realization that this is not the first time that some sleazy club owner has had his goonie lay his hands on her makes all the anger from before coming flooding back to the fore.

"Kiara! That is not acceptable! Getting roughed up on a regular basis is not fucking normal!"

She storms off three steps and then comes back, a dark, furious cloud swirling around her head. "When have I ever told you that I want something normal? This is the job!" She points to the building and yells, "Now that bridge has been burned! I'm never going to be let in here again!"

"Good!"

She shakes her head, disappointment leeching into her darkened pupils. "You don't even see your privilege. I thought you were better than that, Kylian. But you're really no better than Nathan. You talk about understanding all this, but the second it becomes a little bit hard, you bail."

"Hang on, wait a minute. I didn't say you couldn't do it anymore."

Her eyes narrow. "Just try it, go on. Just try telling me I can't do this."

I take a step back, hoping that putting some space between us will help calm her down. "I just meant you have to be more careful. We were underprepared today. I don't know what would've happened if we didn't have my bodyguards."

The bombshell drops, and she stares at me. "Why did you have bodyguards here?"

"I asked Frank to have some guards follow us tonight. I thought you might need some help. And you did."

"And when were you going to tell me this?"

"When you needed to know."

She wraps her arms around herself, rubbing her palms up and down her bare arms. "I can't believe you. You are all the fucking same, thinking that I can't make any decisions for myself. I built this agency on my own, without any of your help. With these two hands." She waves her hands in the air. "You have no idea what it was like when we started nor the contingencies I've put in place to get us to where we are now. You think you can just swoop in and take those decisions out of my hands? You don't trust me to run my own business. How would you feel if somebody did that to you?"

Everything about her in this moment makes me remember why I fell for her that first night when her car was stolen. So much strength, so much compassion, so much conviction in her work, no matter the cost. I had to respect it, hell, I had to admire it. And she's right, I'd taken all that away from her. I hadn't come to help her if she needed it, I had come to force her to do things my way.

"Kiara. I'm sorry, that's not what—"

She doesn't even wait to hear what else I have to say. "At least my family doesn't pretend that they trust me and go behind my back."

She's right. Fuck, she's right. I had sat in her family's kitchen, telling them to trust her, to give her a chance, and I'd gone around and done the exact opposite. Yes, she was in trouble, yes, but we should've had a game plan before I went in guns blazing.

But she's not done yelling at me. "You and I... we don't get to choose who needs helping and who doesn't. Don't you see that the girls in the worst places are the one who need the most help?"

I nod. "I do now. I'm sorry. I... just thought I was doing the right thing; I almost threw up when I saw them taking you away. I... I just wanted to get you back safe."

"The best way you can do that is involving me with your plans. Just talk to me, don't treat me like a child."

Now seems like as good a time as any to tell her what else I know. I pull an envelope out of my inside jacket pocket and hand it to her.

There's a moment of confusion on her face as she takes the folded piece of paper out of the envelope and scans the text.

And then comprehension hits, and she covers her mouth as her skin turns deathly white.

"This is..."

"It's a summary report of what Frank found at your apartment. All the recording equipment and where they were found. They're trying to find out more. But this is what we know. He's here illegally, and he's doing a good job of hiding his tracks. But we'll find him. He'll make a mistake, and we'll get him."

Her chest heaves, like she's about to be sick, but then her eyes read over the page again as she shakes her head. "I don't want to deal with this right now. I'm trying to forget him."

"I know. And you don't have to deal with it. I'm dealing with it, okay? I'm dealing with it, Frank, the walking tank, and his team are dealing with it, and we're going to find him. and then you're not going to have to be scared any more. But this is why I have the bodyguards for you."

Her chin wavers. "For me?"

"Angel, I'm not the one who needs protection right now."

The truth stings, but it's better to know.

"Can I hold you?" I ask, needing to reassure both her and myself that she's going to be okay.

"I... don't know." Her eyes beg for me, though.

I take her hand and gently pull her into my embrace, stroking the side of her face as I apologize. "I'm sorry. I... I will talk to you more. I know what this means to you. I'm sorry I affected your way, please, forgive me.

Tears wet my hands as the back of my hand caresses her cheeks.

"There's nothing to forgive. I just need you to understand what I'm telling you. I know you worry about my safety, but I feel that for every one of these girls who are trying to get out. I chose to do this. You have to let me do it my way. This is not going to work between us otherwise."

Her words slice me open, and I'm bleeding. I hate knowing that there is something in the world that could keep us from being together. It scares me. And I don't want to be scared with her. I reach down and run my thumb over the cut on her cheek.

Instead of pushing me away, she lets me kiss her, softly, gently, as an apology.

There's a flash of the headlights on a car driving past that remind us where we are, and I open the car door for her. "Where to?"

"There's a laundromat around the corner; that's where I told Peta to go if something happened. Let's go get her."

"Anything for you."

Thirty-Four
Kiara

When I moved back to Hong Kong, I was both hiding and seeking. Hiding from the last four years of my life and seeking a new reality. But the death of my mother tempered my new resolve to take the time to really understand myself, and soon I was throwing myself at my work, letting it lead me rather than the other way around.

It was unlike me. I tease Nathan about being wound so tightly, but truly, I'm no different. It just manifests in different ways. My lifestyle and occupation choice are my way of retaining control.

And now, I feel like my future has been thrown into the air, the broken particles of my resolve floating around without any centering mass to draw the pieces together, no gravity to make sense of the debris of my life to give myself direction.

After we left the club, we found Peta huddling in the corner of a nearby empty laundromat, but she was so scared she didn't even recognize me at first. I guess the prospect of being dragged away in a car driven by a blond Englishman didn't settle her fears as much as it should've. We spent almost an hour trying to get her to come with us, and finally, Ananya managed to get in contact with her friend who met us at the laundromat and then followed us in her car with Peta in it to the apartment.

It showed me how I was flying by the seat of my pants and could've put her in even worse danger than she already was. Something I could not forgive myself for.

By the time I crawled into bed with all my clothes still on and lulled to sleep by the sound of Kylian taking a shower in the en suite, I didn't know up from down. Left from right. Right from wrong.

So when I wake up, I do the only thing to do in those moments: I go see my dad.

"More rice?" he says, holding his hand out to dish out some more to me.

I wave a no as I finish chewing the last mouthful.

It's a simple meal, steamed rice, top tier soy sauce, and some pickled mustard greens. It's the meal I eat when I want nothing else in the world, when I want to remember my childhood, when my soul needs healing.

"This is good, ha?" my dad asks, pointing to the jar of his pickles.

"Much better than your home-made wine, Dad," I tease. "Nathan, Kylian, and I almost didn't even wake up the next morning. You shouldn't be able to cut the wine with a spoon!" His laugher fixes everything, and after a few more minutes of teasing him, I feel whole again.

"It was such a nice surprise to see you here, my dear."

"Well, I didn't think we got a lot of chance to talk the other day with those two chatterboxes around."

Dad chuckles but in a way that feel infused with love. "They are quite the talkers, aren't they? That's how Nathan takes after your mother. And you take after me."

I force a smile.

It's the first time he's ever said anything like that, mentioning ways that I might resemble him. And before I stop myself, I say, "I thought only Nathan was the one who takes after you."

"Well, you are your mother's child. Through and through. Beautiful, intelligent, kind of... grumpy," he adds, with a sly smile.

"Dad!"

"But you are also tenacious, very good at reading people." He laughs, seeing me make a face. "When your head isn't preoccupied thinking of other things, that is. And you see opportunity in places no one else does. In that way you're more my child than Nathan. He's hot tempered, vain, and doesn't think all people are worth his time."

The resemblance is uncanny. "Mom."

"She was flawed, yes. But she was wonderful in so many other ways."

Flawed. So, so flawed.

"I miss her."

The sadness that hasn't left his eyes since Mom died spreads over his whole face. "Me, too. But I'm lucky. When I miss her, I look at you."

I don't know what to make of that. It's a compliment I don't deserve, but I don't want him to take it back. "I want to make her proud."

He frowns and then holds his hand out for my hand. Instead of telling me that she is proud, he surprises me by saying, "That's no way to live. You be proud of you first. Are you?"

"I... don't know, Dad. Sometimes I feel like I can't do anything right. Especially the things that I do to make me happy. They might not make everyone else happy."

"But your happiness is the first place to start, my dear. You can't know what everyone else is feeling, but you can know what is going on in your heart."

I lean back, his words hitting hard.

"Have you been seeing anyone recently?"

"What do you mean?" I know exactly what he means. And he knows I know.

"It's been a year now. Since you came back. You've had time to heal."

I want to tell him about Kylian, I want to tell him so much. But tell him what exactly?

That we fuck like rabbits and after only ten days we're practically living together?

That he approves of my work in theory, but I'm not sure he approves of how it fits into his life? That someone who is ready to lay his life down at any given minute isn't ideal?

That the reason we can't tell anyone is because we're afraid of how my brother will react? And that no matter how much we feel about each other, I'm not sure either of us is ready to lose Nathan's presence in our lives? And that's something we've never actually talked about. So all I say is, "If there's a man in this world who fits into my life, then he's in for a wild ride."

The joke doesn't land how I hope, and he frowns, muttering frustrated, "Kiara. You're not a child anymore."

"Exactly. So please don't treat me like one." If anyone else had said that, I would be long gone.

But he looks determined to say what's on his mind. "It's time you start making decisions for the future."

"I am, Dad. But they're just that. My decisions."

He scratches the back of his head, agitated. "You can do anything you want at Yin. You can do whatever you were—"

"Please, Dad. I don't want that. I don't want to work at your company."

"Tell me why!"

"It's just not what I want."

"You think Nathan doesn't want to be the CEO of Yin Tech sometimes? Of course, he does. We all do. But we do it because of the responsibility. You talk about helping people, but you can't be bothered to help your own family. Nathan understands that family comes first. You two are just so different. He takes after me. Not like you." And this time, it doesn't sound like a good thing. It sounds saturated with disappointment and disapproval.

Before he can see me cry, I push myself off the chair. "I'll see you later, Dad."

He looks up, blinking like he forgot I was there, instantly regretful. "Oh, Kiara. No, please don't go. We were having such a lovely time."

"But it stopped being pleasant when you remembered that you only have one golden child."

I force myself to walk over to his side and press a kiss to his cheek before I flee out of there to the car waiting for me outside my family's complex. Kylian and I had agreed that, for now, if I want to go somewhere, he could either have a car take me, or if I absolutely wanted to drive, then he would have a bodyguard follow me in another car. It was a concession he didn't want to make, but it was the only compromise.

Relief comes when I remember that I had chosen to be driven. I don't think I'm really in any condition to drive.

And when I'm escorted back up to Kylian's apartment, I sit in the dark, thinking about what my dad had said and if he really understood what it means. And why me choosing not to work at Yin Tech is the best decision for all of us, even if Nathan and he don't know why.

Thirty-Five
Kylian

Kiara and I spend a perfect week together. Idyllic, as we pretend to be a normal couple instead of one of us being a billionaire, the other a daughter of a billionaire, and runs an agency with prop players for poker game rooms.

She and I spend more time talking than anything else, and every day, I feel like I understand her a little more.

And she understands me almost completely.

Sometimes she comes with me to the office to get out of the house while she is still safe. I set up a desk for her in my office, and sometimes all I do for minutes at a time is sit and watch her.

Then we go home together, stopping by a grocery store to make dinner at home, after which we fall asleep together.

It all happens and fits so naturally together that for a moment, I forget that we're on borrowed time. And when all the secrets that we've kept come back to haunt us, no one is more surprised than us.

I wake up late on Monday morning, jumping in the shower and pressing the in-shower screen to find that I have over forty-three texts and twelve voice mails. Someone was really trying to get in touch with me. I ignore them; I'll check when I'm out of my shower. Instead, I press on the news screen and pump some shampoo into my hand as the speakers crackle before audio streams out of them.

"Blond billionaire bachelor Kylian Baxter was seen outside a strip club in Wan Chai with a prostitute. Based on these pictures, it's hard to see if he was just hiring her for the night or if he's in a relationship with her."

What?

Mid lather, I stare at the screen to see pictures of Kiara and I standing outside the club the other night. She's wearing the torn dress with her back almost entirely exposed.

One picture shows me handing her the envelope with Frank's report in it. Another shows me hugging her and then holding her face in my hands and kissing her. She's hugging me back, her arms tight around my back. There's no doubt who the people in the picture are.

What the fuck.

I'm listening to the rest of the news report when my phone rings. I answer it, dread curdling in the bottom of my stomach, making me sick.

"I thought you were fucking dead!" Matthias yells at me.

"Let me guess, you've seen the news."

My brother lets out a low whistle. "Yeah, everyone has seen it. When did you hear about it?"

"Fifteen seconds ago." I say, still in shock.

The scalding hot water feels like ice against my skin as I rinse the shampoo out of my hair. I need to get out of this damn shower and figure out what the fuck is going on.

And tell Kiara.

Fuck.

I have to tell Kiara.

She has to hear about it from me.

"Wait, are you in the shower?" my brother interrupts my thoughts with the inanest question ever.

"Shut up. What do you know about this?"

I turn the water off and quickly dry off, trying to work out a script in my head of how I'm going to tell Kiara about this. I have no answers for her; I don't even have them for myself.

"Nothing. We're all asking around. It popped up first in the Hong Kong newspapers, but it's been picked up everywhere. As far as I can tell, there are four pictures. They're all of you guys in front of or next to that club. In one, you look like you're arguing. In another, I have to admit, it looks like you're paying her. It's Kiara, right?"

"Yes, it's Kiara! What the fuck?"

"Hey, I've never met her, I was just making sure. Maybe it wasn't actually a—"

"A hooker? No. I'm with Kiara."

"Really? That's great!" He sounds genuinely happy for me.

I pull on a pair of boxers and grab my phone. "I don't know if she's going to feel it's so great right now. I have to go talk to her. She's... this is not going to go down well."

"Which part, the being called a prostitute or the being linked with you?"

"Nathan." How did my best friend's name become a taboo word for me.

"Well, you'll sort that out. And let's not pretend you're not going to hear about this from the board."

"Fuck them. I'll explain. It's not like none of them have been caught with their hand down someone else's pants."

"Go. Call me when you're on your way to work, and we'll talk about what to do about this."

Kiara's all curled up in a little blanket cocoon when I come out to the bedroom. For a split second. I wonder if there is any way to hide this from her. But snippets of our conversation the other night reminds me that I have promised to treat her like an adult. Like a person who has a right to know the things going on in her life.

My weight sinks the mattress when I sit back down on it, and I pull her into my arms,

"Morning, angel."

"I sleep."

"Yeah, um, you can get more sleep later. I need to tell you something."

One eye peeks open. "You've showered? I thought we agreed you'd wake me so I could join you."

I brush the hair out of her face, and she pulls the sheet right up to her chin, closing her eyes again.

My heart feels like it's tearing itself to pieces knowing I have to tell her that, once again, her privacy had been violated. And that a shit storm is about to be upon us.

"Kiki, we need to talk about something. Can you open your eyes, please?"

This time she opens both eyes, the tone of my voice telling her something bad is coming.

"What is it? Is it everyone okay? Someone hurt?"

"No. No, it's nothing like that."

Her shoulders relax, and I wish I could just leave it like that.

It's now or never. "Um, do you remember the other night outside the club? We talked for a little while before leaving?"

"Sure."

"So, er, someone must've seen us and took some photos. Those... those photos are being reported on the news."

Her forehead resembles a page of sheet music, furrowed lines, confused. "What do you mean?"

I pull up the news story on my phone and hand it over to her. Headline and all. Ice shards pierce my veins as she clasps her hand over her mouth and looks up at me, her eyes filled with horror.

"Kylian! This is... this is us." She holds up the phone, the picture of us embracing plastered on the internet for everyone to see. Everyone. "Oh my god."

Realization dawns.

Her body leaps into the air. "Oh my god!" She looks down at the phone again, as if she's hoping that it's all a bad dream. "No, no, no, no. This can't be happening."

"Kiara. Sit down, please. You're scaring me"

She flings the phone at the headboard, and it crashes on the ground, the case breaking and skidding across the floor.

"They know, Kylian. They know. And... the way they describe me! Oh my god." Tears spring into her eyes. "Why would someone do this? Who took this picture?"

The question doesn't have an answer that I know yet. "I don't know. I'm trying to find out."

"Okay." She sits back down on the bed, biting her nails as she rocks back and forth. "I'm going to have to talk to them. Explain. About us." I nod. "Now. We have to do it now. What's the chance they haven't read the paper?" She laughs, but the hollow sound stings. "Okay. Let's go. We have to go."

I take her hand. "Kiara. Remember, whatever happens, this is real, okay? You know that. What we're doing here, it's real. We did this for our own happiness."

"That's just it. When did our own happiness mean more than my family's? When Nathan came to pick me up from New York after... after everything happened, do you know what he said to me about it?" She picks at her fingernails. "Nothing. He didn't say anything. He didn't scold me, he didn't lecture me, he never held it over my head. He just told me that if I ever needed his help again, all I had to do was call. And that it didn't matter what he is doing, he will drop it to make sure I am safe. Do you know what else he said? He said that other than my parents, he only feels that way about one other person."

I know who that person is. Because he said the same thing to me once, too.

"And now, those two people have been having sex behind his back and lying to him," she says, twisting the knife. "And now he's found out at the same time as the rest of the world."

I drive her to her family's complex during which the guilt grows like a balloon, cutting off the air in the car.

When I reach for my car door, she lays her hand on my leg. "No. I... have to do this alone."

"No, you don't. This involves the both of us."

"But this is my family. Not yours."

The words sting, but I know what she's trying to say.

"I'll wait out here."

She squeezes my leg. "No. This... this can't be good for you either. I didn't even think about that. Go to work. Find out who did this. I have to do this on my own."

She absentmindedly pats my hands and then leaves.

And I watch until her body disappears through the gate and doesn't look back.

Five minutes tick by before I finally drive away, just hoping her face will appear and tell me that everything is okay.

With them and with us.

"Call brothers," I command the system and drive away from the one person I want to be with right now.

Thirty-Six
Kiara

The house is empty when I open the front door. And silent.

Nathan's car is still in driveway, and I'm not sure if I wish he was at work or not. Maybe dealing with them one at a time would be easier.

Or maybe it's better just to tear the Band-Aid off in one skin-tearing rip

"Kiara." My dad's voice calls to me from his seat on the patio.

"Dad." I walk over like I'm five years old and he's caught me playing marbles on his mahogany table. All the words I thought I had in my head fleeing. "Where's Nathan?"

"He's on the phone talking to Lionel."

On with the family lawyer. They are calling in the big guns. Unless they're talking about a different matter, but something tells me that's wishful thinking.

The chair next to my father is empty, but I choose to sit in the one facing him instead.

He's looking tired, pallid, bags under his eyes. I wonder when he found out about the pictures.

"How long?" That's all. That's the most important thing to him about all this. How long have I been lying to him.

"It's new. Just... since the other day at Amber."

"Two weeks ago."

Had it only been that long? It feels like I can't remember a time when I wasn't waking up with him next to me.

"And what were you doing outside that club?"

"I was working, Dad."

"With him?" He frowns, trying to make sense of what I'm saying.

"Well, he comes with me sometimes, to keep me safe."

"He should hire bodyguards," he says, as if he thinks Kylian wouldn't have thought of that. And it grates. Kylian is the only one who actually knows what I need.

"He does. But he wouldn't be able to see with his own eyes that I'm okay.

"Kiara!" Nathan's angry voice booms through the house.

I stand up, arms immediately crossing, defiant. Against my brother my whole life.

"What the fuck are you and Kylian doing? How long have you been"— he waves angrily in the air, trying to conjure the right word—"fucking?"

I flinch. Then I get angry. "Don't you dare talk to me like that. Don't you fucking dare."

He storms at me like he's not going to stop and intends to barrel me right over.

"Nathan," Dad says once he's only a step away, and he stops.

Instead, he reaches over and grabs my shoulders and shakes me. "I told you to be careful. Didn't I tell you to be fucking careful? Didn't I warn you something like this would happen?"

I shove him away. "Something like what? What do you think is happening, Nathan? You haven't asked me a single question. You have no idea what is going on between Kylian and me."

His best friend's name breaks whatever it is that's restraining him, and he yells, "Don't you ever say that name in my presence again. He is fucking dead to me. And you..."

"What? I'm dead to you, too? Why don't you think about that for a little bit. Are you mad because Kylian has hurt me in some way? Which, by the way, he hasn't. He has been nothing but kind and supporting and... loving."

Nathan spits on the ground and wipes his mouth on the back of his hand, eyes raging. "He's never loved a woman in his life. He just fucks them and uses them."

"There's a first for everything. Or are you mad because we hid it from you? While we were still trying to figure everything out for ourselves, without you, because we were afraid you were going to act like you are now."

His eyes are marble hard. "I'm trying to protect you. He is going to hurt you."

"Then let me let him."

He snickers, no humor in the sound. "I guess that's your way, isn't it? Finding men who are going to hurt you. Some kind of kink? Am I going to have to pull you out of a closet while you're hiding from him?"

I recoil, my hand up against my cheek like he's physically slapped me. "Why were you two going out there anyway? Role playing being a slut and him hiring you?"

"Nathan, that's enough." Our father stands up, bracing against the arm of the chair, a little shaky on his feet from standing up too fast.

But I'm too focused on the argument with my brother to notice. "You're going to regret saying some of the things you're saying out of anger right now. And when you sober the fuck up, you're going to see that the two people who you supposedly love the most in the world are happy together... without you."

I don't know why I say what I say, but he hurt me. And when I'm hurt, I lash out.

"You're fucking deluded. You act like you're going to change him. He is... *was* my best friend. You think I don't know who he is? I know everything there is to know about him."

Cocky Nathan is my absolute least favorite of the versions of my brother. Time to show him he's not the fucking god of the world. That things happen in this world without his knowledge or approval. "So you know that five years ago I practically begged him to sleep with me, but he rejected me? Because of you? Do you know that I ran away to

New York because I couldn't bear to be around you because that meant that he would be around? That he purposely hurt me because he was afraid of how you would react? Do you know that?'

Nathan's mouth drops open, staring at me.

"I didn't think so. So much for the boy genius, Nathan Yin."

Dad's voice is closer now as he comes over to us, shaking with anger. "You two, I said that is enough. Emotions are running high right now. Let's calm down and talk later."

But Nathan doesn't listen. "All you care about is yourself. It's always been that way. While I'm trying to hold this family together, you just run around doing whatever makes you happy."

"Why does that make you so mad? Shouldn't you want me to be happy? Or does that make it harder for you to control me like you try to control every other facet of your life?"

"It makes me mad because we worry about you every moment of every day! Dad hasn't been able to sleep for months because he's worried about you. Don't you care about your own father?"

And then I yell the thing I had vowed never to say. "He's not my father!"

Everything around us stills as my declaration hangs in the air.

"Kiara," Dad says, pain etched on his face.

And I'm instantly sorry, my head flooding with all the things I should say to apologize, that I'm not the heartless brat I sound like right now.

But there's no time.

He clutches his head, letting out a pained moan that steals the breath from my lungs.

And then he falls to the ground.

Everybody hates hospitals.

It should go without saying, but that doesn't stop us.

Nevertheless, hospitals are the perfect example of how our brains are geared to always have sadness trump happiness in the most devastating way.

All the lives brought into the world here, forgotten in the hours spent on the backbreaking plastic chairs, gripping the mud-tasting coffee in our hands, looking up with hope every time a doctor turns into the hallway only to watch them deliver life changing news to a different family.

Parallel experiences with complete strangers.

But isn't that what life is about? A series of events that just keep replaying, happening to billions of people before and after you, and each response is different.

"No update?" Nathan says when he comes back from taking a phone call, even though he's only been gone no more than three minutes.

"No."

"What's taking so long?"

"They're doing their best. Sometimes these things take a while." I take a drink from the already-cold coffee cup in my hand. "He looked tired when I got there."

"He hasn't been sleeping."

I hiss at him under my breath. "Are you blaming me right now? Is that really the road you're choosing to take?" Nathan turns away from me, ignoring my question. "If anything, it was both of us going at it. He doesn't like seeing us fight. He's always said that. We shouldn't have done it in front of him. I'm never going to forgive myself."

"Stop talking like he's gone, Kiara."

"I wasn't, I was just saying, I'll regret it."

"Regrets are useless," he snaps.

"You say that like you have done everything perfectly in your life, like you've never done anything wrong."

"Guys."

We look up to see Kylian standing there, face almost as pale as the white walls around him.

"What the fuck is he doing here?" Nathan shouts at me.

"I texted him. He cares about Dad, too."

He scoffs and moves to another chair in the far corner of the waiting room

"Hey," I say, giving him a weak smile.

"Hey," he says, starting to lean in to kiss me and then glances up at Nathan, who is trying to pretend he's not watching us, and pulls back. "Have you heard anything?"

"No. They said his vitals were all over place on the ride here. They took him into surgery, and we haven't heard anything yet."

"Okay, well, hopefully you'll hear soon. Has he been sick?"

"We don't need you here," Nathan says from his seat, still not looking at Kylian.

Kylian squeezes my hand and takes a step toward Nathan.

"Er, hey, man, I'm sorry your dad's not doing too well. I hope we get news soon."

Nathan doesn't respond, just stares over at me.

"Come out here for a moment." Kylian touches my elbow and guides me to an empty spot in hallway.

"Are you okay?" he asks, his voice low but strained.

"Oh, I don't know. I need to know what's happening."

"What happened at the house?"

I swallow. "Um, Nathan and I were fighting, and then Dad stood up, and now that I think back, he looked a little unsteady. But then he grabbed his head, and he was just... down."

A cold frost consumes me as I remember the way he'd turned a pale green and his face scrunched in pain as he'd passed out.

"So I guess the conversation didn't go well."

"It went worse than anything we could've imagined. And... Dad heard it all. We said some really horrible things. I said some really horrible things, Kylian. Oh my god." I drop my face into my hands, remembering the last thing I said to him. "I think I'm going to be sick."

Kylian springs into action and grabs a sick bag from the medical cart, holding it in front of me, rubbing my back as I lean over it.

The nausea passes, but the bitter taste in my mouth doesn't.

Nathan comes around the corner, looking older than he has ever looked to me. "Hey. The doctor is here. It doesn't look good. Come on. Let's go talk to him."

My brother grabs my wrist and yanks me toward him, and I wince as his hand bruises me.

Kylian pushes Nathan back, freeing my hand and says, "Hey. She gets it, you don't have to hurt her."

Nathan gets in his face, spitting, "I'm going to need you to mind your own fucking business when it comes to my relationship with my sister."

Kylian ignores him and asks me, "Do you need me to come?"

"No. She doesn't," Nathan interjects. "This is for family. Just... go!" Nathan yells at him.

I rub my hand over my face. "Nathan, would you please keep your voice down! We're not the only people in the waiting room, and they don't need to have to deal with our family drama." I look up at Kylian and lay a hand on his chest. "I'm okay. I'll come out and tell you what's happening, okay?"

"Of course, don't worry about me." His hand cups my cheeks, and for a moment, in this hurricane of resentment and hurt, it's just the two of us.

"Come on, Kiara. The doctor is waiting. He has other patients. He can't wait for the two of you to make googly eyes at each other."

I follow him, sensing Kylian's eyes on me. I can't help feeling how he must hurt right now wanting to be there, not only for me, but Nathan as well.

The nurse leads us into a conference room where the doctor is waiting.

"Doctor, this is my sister, Kiara."

He nods to me, his eyes already answering the only important question.

"He's... not going to make it, is he?"

The doctor shakes his head sadly. "I'm sorry, but no, I don't think he's going to wake up. He's on a ventilator right now, and... we're not seeing any brain activity."

All the air leaves my body, and I stagger to the closest chair. Nathan follows, putting his hand comfortingly on my shoulder.

The doctor opens up a file. "Did either of you know he had a brain tumor?

"What?" I shout, my shock totally evident.

"Um, yes, his medical records show that about ten months ago he was diagnosed with a glioblastoma."

Ten months ago. When he called me to say that he wanted weekly lunches with me.

Ten months ago. All this time, he knew. He was saying goodbye to us and not giving us the chance to do the same.

"What happened today was that his tumor hemorrhaged, and so there was no oxygen to his brain, and his brain cells are dying. He is not going to wake up."

"How long?" I instantly feel the irony in asking the question when he asked it of me only a few hours ago. But that was about a beginning, and now we were counting down the time until his end.

"Any time. He's on life support now, but that's just keeping his body alive. I'm so sorry, but essentially, he's gone."

I try to swallow, but I can't, and the nausea is back.

And all I want to do is run to my dad and hold onto him forever. Nathan's not doing much better when I finally have the presence of mind to look over at him.

The doctor continues giving us information. "He will be on life support until you decide what you want to do. We are taking him to a room now. A nurse will show you there when you are ready. I am so sorry to give you this news."

"Thank you, Doctor." Nathan stands and shakes his hand, but it must be just muscle memory, he looks like a ghost standing next to me.

"Nathan..." I gasp, grabbing his hand. "Is this really happening?"

He just shakes his head, his eyes looking right through me.

"Oh my god. What are we going to do?"

"I don't know, Kiara. I just... I don't know."

A shiver feels like it's about to pass me, but it lodges in my heart instead.

The last words I said to him play over and over in my head, the look on his face, the way he'd clutched his head.

"Oh my god." Every single part of my body feels like it's suffocating. "Oh, god, Dad!" I shout. "No! Don't leave me!"

"Kiara," I hear someone say. And then someone screams again. I think. I don't know. Maybe it's me. It's definitely me. My throat feels raw as my chest tries to force air into my lungs.

"Noooooooooooooo!" I scream again. This time, it feels like I'm inside the scream. Every decibel swirling around me in an audible drawing of my loss.

Tears cake my eyes, painting everything in a watery, dreamlike landscape.

Maybe it is a dream.

Maybe this is all a dream.

"Kiara," Nathan says, and he reaches out to touch me. His hand on my shoulder. It feels like he's pressing a banding iron into my skin.

"Dad!" I yell, pushing him away as I run out of the room, calling for Dad. "Dad! Where are you?" Maybe if I call him, he'll come back. Maybe he just needs a reason to come back.

"Miss."

I spin around; through my tears, I can see a face, kind, sad. "Come with me, he's over here."

She takes me by the hand and leads me into a private room.

He's lying there, sleeping, oxygen mask covering his face, arms by his side.

"Dad?" I say, picking at his sleeve as if he'll lift up his arms and say boo! But he doesn't move. "Dad? It's me. Your little Kirabella. Your little rainbow. Your bossy britches." The nicknames he gave me chokes me as I realize I'm never going to hear him call me those names again. Although, I used to hate each and every one. "It's me, your little strawbaby. Remember how you called me that after you took me strawberry picking in London and I kept calling everyone a 'strawbaby' for the longest time?"

I slide my hand into his. It's warm. He can't be gone. His hand is still warm. "Daddy? Are you just sleeping? Do you need me to let you keep sleeping?" I run a finger along his face. He didn't shave this morning. Why didn't he shave?

It's because he woke up to the news that I've been lying to him.

I shake my head. That's not why. He was sick. He was sick, that's all. Not because I lied to him.

But somehow that thought makes it worse.

"Why didn't you tell me were sick, Dad? We could've spent so much more time with you. So much more time. We could've done all the things we talked about. We could've made more batches of the worst wine I've ever tasted. And I would have something to remind me of you when you left. Why didn't you tell us? Why did you suffer alone? We could've helped you. I... I could've had a chance to make you proud of me. You robbed me! You robbed me of a chance to tell you all the things I wanted to tell you! You robbed me of the chance to ask you why... ask you if you knew."

"You knew what?" Nathan says.

I hadn't seen him come into the room. "None of your business. Go away. I'm talking to Dad."

"I want to talk to him, too."

"Go away! Please! Just please, leave me alone with him for a few more minutes.

He backs out, and I drop my head on my dad's arm, sobbing, feeling my heart break a little more with each second. I lift his hand and put it on my head, pushing it back and forth like he used to when I needed him to stroke my hair to get me to sleep.

"Who's going to help me sleep now, Dad? Why didn't you tell me? Didn't you trust me to keep your secret? Is it because I didn't share my secret with you? I'm sorry, Daddy... I'm so sorry."

I whisper the same words over and over until I have no more energy left to keep my eyelids open.

When I wake, I'm leaning back in a chair by the bed, a jacket covering me. Nathan is standing on the other side, tears on his face as he looks at our dad's face.

"We have to... we have to let him go, Kiara," he says when he sees me awake.

"No."

"Kiara."

"He's still here, Nathan. Feel him, he's warm. He's still here."

"He's not. He's gone. This is just his body." His voice cracks.

"It's still something. Please don't make me say goodbye," I said.

"It's kinder to let him go. He's suffered long enough. Alone."

His words start the tears again, and I reach over and take my father's limp hand in mine. And then it occurs to me to ask Nathan a question.

"Did he tell you?"

He just keeps staring at our dad's face.

"Nathan. Tell me, did you know?" When he refuses to answer, I feel betrayed all over again. "You knew."

"I guessed. He didn't want to tell me either."

"And how did you feel when you found out?" I ask, my voice shaking.

"It was his choice, Kiara. I had to let him feel like he at least had control of this one part of his life. And death."

I angrily wipe away the tears. "I wouldn't have said anything."

"Kiara. You are, hands down, the best poker player I've ever met in my life, but when it comes to your life, you are a terrible liar. You would've started coming to visit more, changing your behavior, and that's not what he wanted. I had to stop myself doing those things all the time."

"I could've done it this time. I could've been there for him."

"He didn't want that."

And we stay there, thinking all the things we never said to him in the silence of the room, knowing he'll never hear them and wondering if the pain will ever subside.

We decide to turn off the life support two days later after we've gotten a second neurologist's opinion. And some advice from Dad's family doctor.

Throughout it all, Kylian has never left my side. Not once. Only standing back when Nathan is there, respecting his best friend's feelings. But when he's not there's, he sits beside me, his hand squeezing mine. Forcing me to drink some water when it's been hours since I drank some. Pulls little pieces off a protein bar to feed me so that I have something, anything in my stomach, while I have to make the hardest decision I've ever been faced with.

Finally, when I come back from the bathroom on the second day, Nathan meets me in the hallway and says the words I need to hear.

"It's time to let him rest, Kiara. It's time. This is what he would've wanted. For you to show the kindness he always showed you."

I've never liked being told what to do, but in that moment, I wished my father would wake up and tell me that this was the right decision.

It's only Nathan and I in the room when the doctor turns the oxygen off, gently removing the mask from his face. And everything but the EKG machine is switched off, drawing the last of his moment on earth with an eerie green spike on a screen.

"I love you, Dad. You were the best father I could've asked for. No one else could've loved or done more for me. I want you to know that.

And I want you to know that I know. That there was never any other father for me. I love you. I love you so much."

Nathan leans in and whispers his own farewell into Dad's ear, stroking the hair from his head, his tear falling on Dad's cheek as he says goodbye to the person he idolized his entire life.

Dad's heart takes its last beat only minutes later.

And then everything is still.

And we sit in the knowledge that our lives will never be the same again.

Thirty-Seven

Kylian

Nathan and Kiara go into their father's room and come out an hour later, both looking like they will never recover from this moment. And I wish I could take them both in my arms and hug them and tell them that what they're feeling is real. And don't let anyone give them empty platitudes and that the ache might never ever go away. You just learn to live with it. And that's okay. Life is peppered with moments like these amongst others that make life worth living.

Nathan glances at me and then storms down the hallway to the nurse's station while Kiara comes and stands next to me.

She runs her thumb over my face, wiping the tear dripping down my chin.

Dennis Yin had been there for all my most important moments in my teen years. Endless memories of my life have him standing in the photos, smiling proudly.

I will miss him every time I see a bottle of wine, or hear someone mercilessly roast their children, or negotiate a business deal that would take anyone's breath away

"He's gone," she says. Simple. Matter of fact.

"I'm so sorry, Kiki. I don't know what to say."

"I think that not saying anything is what is going to help me most right now."

"You got it."

She lays her head against my chest, and I pull her against me a little too tightly, somehow hoping her pain can transfer onto me,

"We need to talk." Nathan suddenly appears next to us, scowling.

Kiara looks at him, stricken. "No! I can't right now."

"What did you mean at the house when you said that he wasn't your father? And what was that whole speech about how he was the best father you could've had?"

She glances at me, then back at him. "I said not now."

"She said not now, Nathan. Can you give her a little time?" I say, knowing what pain he must be going through but also needing to protect Kiara.

He looks at me like he wants to step on me and squish him with his shoe. "Can you go away? I'm trying to talk to my sister, and your constant presence is really intrusive."

Kiara grabs my hand and roots me in place. "He doesn't have to go. You're the one ambushing me. So if you want to talk, then talk."

There's an internal struggle, and then he asks, "Do you know something I don't?"

"You mean like how you kept the secret about Dad being sick?" Her voice, unlike her words, is soft... sad.

"This is not the same thing. I'm your brother; if you know something, tell me."

"Don't worry, Nathan, we're only half-siblings."

He staggers back. "What?"

"Dad is not my biological father. Mom had an affair. I'm that guy's kid." I can't believe what I'm hearing, but I push it down. This moment is about her.

Nathan shakes his head. "No."

Kiara nods. "Yes. Mom told me when I was in high school. She was drunk, and I'd annoyed her somehow. And she said that I wouldn't have been so rebellious if I were Dad's child."

He shakes his head again. "She was lying."

"Blood tests don't lie, Nathan."

The blood drains from his face as he processes the bombshell. "Did Dad know?"

"I don't know."

"Who's the father?"

"I don't know that either."

"It doesn't matter," he says dismissively.

Kiara looks at me, her eyes filled with a sadness that I've never seen. "You don't get it, do you, Nathan? It does matter! When we were growing up, all Dad used to talk about was how much I took after Mom and how much you inherited from him. How he loved that the business was staying in the family. Because that stuff mattered to him! Can you imagine what it must've been for him to think that part of his fortune and business was going to go to some other man's child?"

"But he loved you."

"Yes. He loved me so much. And I felt that love even after I knew the truth. That doesn't stop me knowing that he took me in and had to live with the knowledge that I was not his biological child. Bloodlines mattered a lot to him. You know they did."

Nathan stares at his sister, unable to process what he's just heard. At the worst time to hear it. "People change. Maybe after you came along. He was always trying to get you to work at Yin."

Kiara shrugs. "Not Dad. He didn't change. And he wanted me to work there to watch over me. He didn't want me owning it. Those are two very different things. And if you don't understand that, then we can't have this conversation."

"You're wrong."

"Then you didn't know our father as well as you think you did. I don't blame him. He loved me, he provided for me, but family is different to business. And he wanted his business to go to one person. You. So you might think it doesn't matter. It mattered to me because I knew that it mattered to him, even if he didn't say it. I didn't want him to have to hurt like that."

Nathan sighs, conceding. "But, Kiara. It's... it's not his company anymore. You can work there now. We'll find something, we'll create something together that you can be proud of."

She lets out a slow sight, shoulders dropping. "Death doesn't change a thing. You think I would disrespect him in death when I wouldn't in life?"

"You'll change your mind."

I watch as she transforms in front of me, from sad but calm to hardened eyes, and she balls up her fists, rising up on her tiptoes, ready to unload on her brother.

"Stop it! Stop telling me what I should and shouldn't feel and what I should and shouldn't do! Just let me live my life! You don't get to tell me how to feel about something you have no idea about. Look, I do not resent him even one iota. He gave me the best childhood I could have asked for. Just let me manage my relationship with him. And you worry about yours. And ours."

A hard mask slides over Nathan's face, one I've seen when he's shutting down, what's happening in reality getting to be too much for him. "Kiara, can we talk about this later?'

She lets of a disbelieving snort. "Oh, so now you want to talk about it later. Is it because I'm not doing what you want?"

Nathan grabs her shoulder. "You're purposely twisting everything I'm saying."

"Hey. Don't do that," I say and push Nathan's hand off her. I don't think he would hurt her, but I want to make it clear that even touching her roughly will not be tolerated.

He grabs my hand and throws it back at me. "Don't fucking touch me. You're not a part of this."

I stand my ground, taking a step in front of her. "Kiara's a part of it, and that makes me a part of it."

He sniggers, his face an ugly mask I've never seen before. "Wow, when did you become such a knight in shining armor? I remember the way you fucked though half of our college class."

Reminding myself that he just lost his father and is not in his right mind, I don't react. "You know that's not true, so stop pretending it is. But I know you're hurting, so if you need to lash out, I'd prefer you did it to me and not your sister."

His spits at my feet. "You make me sick. Who do you think you are? You think this is going to make it okay that you're fucking my sister behind my back? Who do you think is going to have to pick up the pieces after you've had enough to cast her aside?"

Behind me, Kiara whimpers. Enduring more injuries from the only other person who understands what she's going through today. And I hate him for that. Hate him with a searing fury. Fuck him. She doesn't need him.

"I'll be the one picking up the pieces after you've broken her heart worse than I ever could. So much for being the big brother. You're a fucking child. Look at what you're doing to her."

I step back, so he can see Kiara's face crumpled in pain. So he can see what his selfishness is doing.

"You're supposed to be comforting her, not being the reason she's crying. I admit I was wrong. I should've come and talked to you about my feelings for her. But what you're doing is worse. Your dad would be fucking disappointed. So much for being his legacy."

I can't duck out of the way when Nathan charges at me, his shoulder slamming into my solar plexus.

"Uhhh," I grunt, winded as he straddles me, landing punches on my face one after the other. "Go on, hit me. Take it out on me. I can take it."

I don't know if he hears me through the haze, but he keeps punching.

"Put your hands up!" he yells. "Fight like a fucking man!"

"No," I say through my cut lip. "Go on, hit me again. Did Kiara tell you that we almost got together five years ago when she came to London just to see me? How does that make you feel?"

Nathan gets to his feet, drags me up, and shoves me against the medical supplies cart, spilling everything on the floor. "Shut up. Stop talking."

He grabs for my neck and squeezes.

"Nathan! Stop!" Kiara shouts, but this doesn't involve her anymore.

He squeezes as I stare into his eyes. His hand's not big enough to cause any real damage, but I struggle anyway, and as I stare at him, I watch as the tears that must be prickling the back of his eyes flood over his cheeks.

"Stop it! Both of you, just stop it!" Kiara shouts again. "Dad just died! And this what you're doing?"

Nathan growls and then reluctantly lets go.

"I know you're hurting man. And if you need to, come find me," I say. As angry as I am at him, I'm so sad about the pain he's going through. He wouldn't be acting like this otherwise.

He grits his teeth, grabs my shoulders, and roars as he shoves me back against the wall, "Don't ever talk to me again." Then he lets me go.

My head rings as I try to clear my vision just in time to see Kiara running down the hallway and around the corner.

"Kiara!" I shout after her.

"Leave her alone," Nathan spits and steps back.

Behind him, I can see staff and visitors start to mill around.

I get to my feet. "I have to go after her."

"No, she needs her big brother."

I summon what strength I have left and shove him into a chair. "No, she needs to be with the one man who loves her more than you love her."

When I follow her steps, they lead me outside into the blazing heat, but she's not there.

She's not down another hallway or in the cafeteria.

She's not at the coffee machine where we'd trekked a worn path in the last few days.

She's not at my apartment or hers. Or at any of the three apartments where her employees live. She isn't at their family home.

She's nowhere.

No one knows where she is. Not just the people who should know, every single person I know that might know anything about her.

Ten hours after she runs out of the hospital, I get a two-word text from my former best friend.

Found her?, Nathan's text says. And in those two words, I can sense the total fear and panic in his body. It is a clone of the fear and panic running through mine.

It's not just his father he lost today; part of the reason I want to find her is to put Nathan's mind at ease so that he can concentrate on his grief.

But after looking all night with no luck, I wonder if she was ever anything more than just a figment of my imagination.

Sometime around 3 a.m. while I'm thinking of who else and where else I can look for her, I fall asleep. Face smooshed on the desk, pen stuck to my face, drool on the leather desk mat.

The events of the last few days, and frankly, since I ran into her three weeks ago, have wreaked utter havoc on the routines I've put in place so that I can maintain a functional adult human life.

And now that she's gone, I'm not sure if I can, or even want to, try to go back to the person I was before.

"Hey," a female voice says and touches me on the shoulder, yanking me out of sleep.

"Kiara?" I jump out of my desk chair, ready to pull her into my arms. But it's not her.

"Hey, it's us," My-Linh says, gesturing behind her where Damien is standing. He's almost a foot and a half taller than her, but right now, hunched over, face etched with concern, he looks so much smaller than he really is.

"Hey, guys," I say, genuinely shocked and happy to see them. They're not Kiara but definitely the next best thing. "What are you doing here?"

My-Linh reaches her arms up and gives me a tight hug. When I finally let her go, Damien takes her place. Our hug is a little rougher, not as long, but touches me just as much.

I'd been texting them regularly ever since the newspaper incident, and they'd been following with me through the whole time I was at the hospital and the last half day trying to find her.

"We came so you wouldn't have to be alone," My-Linh says as I sit back in my chair. Standing up, she's only almost as tall as me sitting down. To put her hand on my shoulder, she had to reach up. I sometimes forget how short she is until something like this happens.

I can't help but let out a little chuckle.

I must be delirious.

"What?" she says, looking confused. But my chuckle turns into a fit of giggles. Not funny in the slightest, but my body needs release, and this is what it's deciding to do.

My brother and his fiancée stand there watching me, My-Linh's hand still on my shoulder, me slapping the table in my incoherent laughter.

"He's lost it," Damien says in his trademark deadpan way.

"He's just tired. I think. What are you laughing at, Kylian?"

I look up, and her face peers at me, worried.

"You!" I blurt out between the giggles, still gasping for breath.

She snaps her hand back, and the look of worry is replaced with hurt. Damien touches her face gently and then nudges her to the side. Then, grabbing the desk chair, he spins it around so that I'm facing him dead on.

His voice has an undercurrent of danger that is hard to miss even in my mania when he says, "Hey. Pull up. You're hurting My-Linh's feelings."

And instantly, nothing is so funny anymore.

The words hang between us, the warning that doesn't need to be said: *Hurt her and I will decapitate you with a rusty butter knife.*

I look past Damien to see her watching us, eyes wide. "My-Linh! I'm sorry, I wasn't laughing at you, exactly, I just couldn't speak from the giggles. It was just so funny to see how much taller I am than you. I didn't mean anything."

Her eyes fill with relief, and she pushes past Damien to give me another hug. "It's fine. I was just worried about you. I didn't think laughing was what you'd feel like doing right now. Have you eaten or had anything to drink?"

I shake my head and walk out to the kitchen with them following behind me, whispering something to each other.

"Guys. I am so grateful for you guys being here, but I don't know if there's anything for you to do. I've looked for her everywhere. I'll get up in a few hours and do another round."

"What about her apartment?" Damien suggests.

"Well, the guard Frank still has posted there says she hasn't been back. And honestly, I think she'd rather sleep on the streets than go back there."

Damien nods; they know everything. He even gave me a few ideas on what my security team might be able to do to find her.

My-Linh turns the kettle on, pulls a packet out of her pocket, and pours it into the teapot.

"What's that?"

"It's chamomile, catnip, and valerian root. It's a new blend my mom just made, it's meant to help you relax. I brought you a whole tin as well."

"Can I overdose on that?"

"You could try, but it basically has a laxative effect if you drink more than four cups a day. So, if you want to be running to the bathroom every five minutes, go for it."

She brings the pot over and gracefully pours three cups. She picks one up and brings it over to me instead of just pushing it across the table. "Drink this. Please. I'm really worried about you."

I take it from her and lean over and give her a soft kiss on the cheek. She smells like cherry blossoms and older sister love, even though she's younger than I am.

"Thank you. And thank you for being here."

She goes back to sit next to Damien who picks up a cup of tea and hands it to her, and she grants him a smile as a thank you.

"You need some sleep. You look fucking rough," Damien adds in case I needed convincing.

"What I need is to find her, then I can sleep all the live long day."

My-Linh checks her watch. "Sleep until like 6 a.m., and then we'll all get together and make a game plan. Hong Kong isn't that big, and you know almost everyone."

"Everyone in our circles, maybe, but she… isn't a part of that world. Her best friend is a former card shark and hustler, for fuck's sake."

Ananya has been texting me intermittently to let me know she hasn't heard from Kiara either. She also gave me a list of places and numbers where she thought people might know where she is. With Kiara out, she's had to take up most of the slack in the training the girls.

"We just have to search this entire country until we find her."

"And if we don't?" my brother asks.

"Raze it to the ground."

I think the tea is doing things that My-Linh didn't tell me about as my eyelids droop and I start to fade in and out of the conversation.

"Kylian, get up." Someone gently nudges me some time later, but they were right, I needed sleep.

"Kylian!" This time, there's a kick to my leg, and I force one eye open.

"What? Make up your mind, do you want me to sleep or not?"

"It's Kiara's business partner," Damien says, ignoring me, and holds out a phone.

"Ananya?" I snatch the phone out of his hands. "Ananya! Do you know where she is?"

"I shouldn't be telling you."

"It's too fucking late for that now. If you know where she is, you need to tell me."

"She didn't say exactly," Ananya hesitates. It's a struggle between what she's been asked to do and what she thinks is best. And those two things often don't agree.

"Okay, well, what did she say to you? You talked to her?"

"She asked me to drop her passport off at the airport for her"

"The airport?" I jump to my feet. "Where is she going?"

"She didn't say. She just said she'd be gone for a little while, and she didn't know how long. She gave me some business instructions. And then she just said she was going somewhere where things made sense and where she felt safe. And then she hung up. She hasn't answered any of my calls or texts since."

"How long ago?"

"I left her about fifteen minutes ago. I didn't call sooner; it just felt like I might be betraying her. But she is doing very badly, and I don't think she should be alone."

A good friend. "That's okay. Thank you for telling me." I'm about to hang up when Ananya starts talking about Kiara.

"Kylian, she is feeling very lost right now. I have never seen her like this, and I've seen her in some incredibly difficult situations in the last year. She needs someone."

"I'm trying to be that person, Ananya."

I talk to her for a few more minutes, trying to reassure her that I will find her, and when I do, she'll be the first to know. After, I lie back down on the couch. If she has her passport, she could be absolutely anywhere.

"What did she say?"

I recall the phone conversation. "She said she's going where she feels safe."

"Any idea where that is?"

"We've only been together for a few weeks. I thought... I thought I knew everything about her, though."

"But do you know this?" Damien challenges me.

I go over every conversation I have had with her in my head. Every single one. From before and from now.

"Fuck." I know where she is.

"What?"

"Did you fly commercial here?"

"No, we took one of the company jets."

"Get your stuff, guys," I say, running up the stairs to my bedroom. "We're going to London."

Nobody sleeps on the flight to London.

Lunch is served, and all I can stomach is a bit of an apple that sits browning on my table after I take a single bite out of it.

My-Linh comes and sits by me for a while, not forcing me to talk, just sitting there, staring out the window.

"You wouldn't have liked me five years ago," I say finally.

"No? Why is that?"

"I was really selfish. Cocky. Unfeeling." It's not that hard to admit to because I think I've changed. How far I have to go is a different issue.

"Maybe. Maybe not. You're certainly not that way now."

"I don't know. But I don't really feel like I have any right to be cocky. Everything I'm touching lately turns to shit."

"Like what?" She moves in her seat so that she's facing me. Wanting me to know that I have her full attention.

"Like the Heracles chip deal. Like this thing with Kiara. Like my friendship with Nathan. And even with their father. He died thinking that I had betrayed him by going behind his back to be with her." A single tear falls down my cheek. "He's the one who taught me how to tie a tie, you know. We had a dance at school, and everyone was too busy to teach me. One day, Dennis overhead Nathan and I talking about how we should just get some of those elastic ties. The next day, he called us into his office, had a bunch of ties lying out, and he taught us how to tie all different types of knots for different occasions. Had us practice them for hours, just to make sure we never ever forget."

"And did you?"

"Never have, never will. It's a core memory at this point."

My-Linh sits, her hands in her lap, pondering over what I just said. "That was a lovely thing he did for you. It looks like he was a good father, not only for you."

"He loved his children so much."

She taps her fingers on the table in front of us, processing her thoughts. "I don't like cocky, selfish, unfeeling, lockpicks, or whatever the word is that you used. And you're not that. You've changed. So I'm proud of you."

I smile. Sometimes it's nice to see yourself through the lens of someone who likes you, it'll make you feel like superhuman like you can do all the things you never thought you could.

"I'm still selfish. I couldn't have pursued this thing with Kiara if I wasn't. But I couldn't stop myself. I could not physically stop myself from being with her. I want to be with her. I want it more than I've wanted anything in my whole life."

Instead of lecturing me, she just nods. "Life isn't black and white. It's gray and then green in some spots. There's a corner up the top where it's always kinda marble. And then weird spots that come and go. Sometimes it's not a question of either or. It's a question of changing the landscape. She feels the same way about you. You two wouldn't have put your relationships with Nathan in jeopardy if she didn't. So... maybe the relationship that has to change is the one that didn't allow you to be friends as well as his sister's partner. Maybe the relationship needs to mature. Maybe it's about giving him time to see that he wasn't betrayed. And that the two people he loves most just happen to love each other as well."

I nudge her with my elbow. "You're very wise."

She giggles. "I know, right? Infinitely wise for such a young, pretty lady."

"You are very young, practically a baby. And yes, incredibly pretty. Too pretty for... you-know-who." I crook my thumb to point at the seat behind us.

"Hey. Enough," Damien says, looking up from his laptop.

My-Linh and I share a secret look between us before I say, "Oh. Apparently, Damien doesn't think you're pretty. That's not very nice of him."

My-Linh pretends to wipe away a tear. "No, it's really not, is it? He must think I'm an ugly hag," she dramatically sighs, and I nod, playing along. "What should I do, Kylian?"

"Well, it all depends if you still want to stick with a Baxter or not. There are three other ones, and somehow you ended up with the ugliest one. Kingsley's even grumpier than Damien, if that's what you're looking for. Or if you want to catch an STI, Matthias is your man. I'm kind of taken right now, but if it doesn't work out..." I shrug. "Who's stopping us?"

She tilts her head, pretending to count off her fingers, measuring us up against each other, but then Damien appears, looming over us. "I said enough."

My-Linh bites her inner cheek to stop herself from laughing. I have no such intention of bending to my brother's will and laugh unashamedly.

"Oh, I thought you meant enough of the other serious talk. Not the hitting on your girlfriend thing."

"Fiancée, pencil dick." He grabs her wrist and drags her back to his seat and into his lap.

"Me Damien, You My-Linh," I say at my seat, but they're not listening. She's nuzzling against his neck, and the expression on his face is something I rarely saw when we were growing up. Happy.

The envy streaks through me, and I have to look away when it hurts too much.

I check the flight clock. Three more hours until we land and I can start looking for her. All I can hope is that I was listening to her properly this whole time.

Thirty-Eight

Kiara

I don't know how long I run when I push those hospital doors open and flee. I run until my legs want to give out, my lungs explode, and the day starts turning to night.

When I stop, I have no idea where I am.

Who I am.

I hurt everywhere, And I don't recognize my own face or body. I'm living in someone else's body, someone else's life. And I don't know how to get back to my own reality.

But I have to start somewhere, so I walk, walk back the way I came, but now everything looks different.

My phone has no charge when I think to call a cab, so I keep walking. Until my feet refuse to take another step, and I sit against a wall, watching the people get ready for their day.

And I wonder what it's like to have that sort of order to their lives, to wake up and know what the day is going to be like. It used to always sound so boring to me, but now I crave that normalcy, to know when I wake up, how the day will end. Instead of having to constantly worry about what's going to happen, where and how.

A cab drives by, and I jump to my numb feet and flag it down.

"Airport, please."

I buy a change of clothes at the airport. There had been one last first class seat from Hong Kong to London, and I paid with the stack of cash Ananya had brought for me along with my passport.

I'd given her one last hug before she'd left, not knowing when I was going to see her again.

And when the plane takes off, I say goodbye to the life I'd worked so hard to create and back to the one I'd left behind so long ago.

It's been five years since I came back to London. I had no reason to come back here, I had no desire to. But as the plane lands, I can't help feeling a stirring of curiosity at what life might look like now if I still lived here.

From the cab that takes me to a hotel, everything looks the same but different all at once.

A little like me.

After a shower, I head toward the place I came here to visit.

A school bell rings, and the kids swarm out of the doors for recess, chatting and laughing. There's a new playground set now in the park. Fancy, modern with new games, and the wood chips on the ground have been replaced by a rubber mulch, much easier on the knees.

Everything else looks the same.

But it doesn't feel that way anyway.

Because the one person who made this memory so beautiful isn't here anymore.

The one safe place I thought I'd feel him closest to me doesn't exist anymore. And it takes me until this moment, having traveled halfway around the world to realize, it was never about the place but the person. And when my mother in a drunken rant told me about my paternity, she ripped everything I had ever known away from me.

And in this moment, I have never hated her more.

Hate her for telling me.

Hate her for thinking that I could go on with my life, that nothing would change.

Hate her for driving the wedge between my father and I that would never really heal, no matter how much I loved him and he loved me. He did everything right by me, it was just impossible for me to handle knowing that I would never completely be what he wanted me to be.

Tears stream down my face as I mourn my dad, my mom, and the relationship I might never ever be able to heal with my brother.

Finally, the tears dry, and this place takes on a new meaning for me. A place of goodbyes.

I get to my feet, looking back one last time when I hear a voice.

"Hello, Kiara."

And he's here.

He found me, just when I felt like there was no one left who understood me.

He found me.

I run to him, and then I'm home.

**

"Where are we?" I ask when the cab stops outside a residence in Regent's Crescent.

"This is our family's city residence. Kingsley lives here mostly. We can stay here while we're in London."

My hands tug him back. "I'm not so sure."

He doesn't rush me, just takes my hand and gently explains. "Okay, so Kingsley is at work because he's Kingsley. Damien and My-Linh are here in London, but they won't be around right now. I asked them to make themselves scarce since you might not really be up so meeting people"

Always so, so thoughtful.

"Come on, we'll have a small wing in the back. There's a bedroom, bathroom, and sitting room. You won't have to see anyone if you don't want to. You don't even have to see me if you don't want to. I can stay in one of the other guest rooms, which, I would like to add, my grandfather did not even wait two seconds after I graduated and moved to college before he had a decorator in there tearing down all my playboy posters."

I giggle at that. And he takes that to mean I'm ready to go inside.

I'm no stranger to opulence, especially in real estate. My parents liked to buy beautiful homes for no reason other than to own them for a little while. My mother, with an eye for design, would play with the house until she was bored of it, then sell it off, never caring if she made a profit or loss. It was her hobby, and my dad indulged her every whim.

The thought of them hurts, so I push it back.

I'm not ready to go down that road again.

Kylian's family's house is pure luxury and class down to the little Edo Kiriko glass bowl on the bureau in the foyer for everyone to put their keys in.

"Wow. This house is incredible. How long has your family owed this?"

"My great-great-great-grandfather bought it back in 1950, I think. As a silver anniversary gift for his wife for sticking by him from when he was a lowly baker and all the way up to making his first million. He told her to go and point to whichever house she wanted, and he would make it hers. He probably shat himself when she went directly for the richest part of town."

We both laugh in appreciation, and Kiara says, "A woman who knows what she wants. I like her."

"I think you would've, she was wild. Took his money and ran with it, sometimes just standing at the market and handed out wads of cash to people on the way in, so they could go all out. There's actually a little stall in Smithfield markets called Esme's bench. Because that's where she could be found, eating a pie and having a cup of tea after a morning of giving away her husband's money."

"I knew it! I do love her."

He gives me a wink. "Yeah. She was a brat, too. "

"Wow, maybe I'm the reincarnation of her," I joke.

The horrified look he gives me makes me laugh so hard it hurts.

A good kind of hurt.

Something about this house makes me feel comfortable, or maybe it's the man standing next to me, who hasn't let go of my hand since he found me at the park. Not when he flagged down a cab, not when he paid the driver, not the entire time we've been here.

He didn't ask any questions, either, just made sure I was okay physically, then asked if I had a place to stay. I'd told him about the hotel but that the only things I had were already on my body.

"Come on, let's go get you settled," he says. "You're probably exhausted."

He leads me down a few hallways past a large living area with a piano and bar to a door that opens into a little private wing.

"The bedroom is back there, the bathroom is an en suite. And behind that cabinet, there's a coffee and tea station." He leaves to check something out. "There a robe in the bathroom. Do you want to write down some things you need, and I'll get someone to go pick them up? Kingsley's assistant will be here later to see if there's anything she can grab for us. If you need it urgently, maybe his valet can go out and grab it."

"Oh my god, we really are back in England, aren't we?"

He grins. "We are. I miss it here. I love Hong Kong, but I grew up here. It's my home. In a different way than Hong Kong is home."

Somehow, I know what he means. "Do you ever think you'll move back here?"

"No time soon. Okay, I'll be in the main house if you need me."

Panic rises. "Where... are you going?"

An apology jumps to his lips. "I just thought you'd want some time to yourself."

"Maybe from someone else, not from you."

He looks me over; I can't even imagine what I must look like. Although I had a shower at the hotel, there wasn't a hair brush or any makeup, so I'm wearing a pair of jeans, a plain white T-shirt, hair tied back in a bun, ballet flats. "Don't look at me. I'm a mess."

"Shush," he whispers and pulls me into him. "You look fucking angelic. Simple. Natural. All you."

"You look like a bloody GQ model," I shoot back, trying to hide how much his words affected me.

He strikes a pose, only serving to prove my point. Pure, physical perfection. Then he relaxes into just being Kylian again. "I missed you."

"I know. I'm sorry."

He pulls me into the bedroom and starts to take his clothes off, leaving on his briefs and undershirt, climbing into bed. "Get in. I'm tired. I haven't been able to sleep without you."

I pull my jeans off and slide in so that he's spooning me, his arm slung over my waist, keeping me close.

"Don't snore. I need some sleep," I speak. He retaliates by digging his fingers into my sides, making me squeal.

And just for a few hours, in this cocoon, everything is right.

**

"Kiara, this is my brother, Damien. And this is his much better half, My-Linh Tran," Kylian says, gesturing to a man who is definitely Kylian's brother with his blond hair and blue eyes.

But where Kylian is all friendliness and fun, Damien exudes icy danger. I wouldn't be sure he was a real human, if his arm wasn't pulling his fiancée close to his chest. He reaches out and offers me his hand. "Damien," is all that he offers.

But what Damien lacks in warmth, the perky woman next to him more than makes up for.

"Hi! I'm My-Linh!" Her Australian accent surprises me, considering she's Vietnamese. It's adorable, but I just wasn't expecting it.

"I've heard so much about you!" I say back, her sunshine contagious. She pulls out of Damien's hold and hugs me tight.

"I'm so glad to meet you. Isn't it cool we're in London at the same time? I thought I was going to have to wait until the opening of Jade Bay to meet you. But now we can talk and learn more about each other! What's your favorite type of food? Can you cook?"

"Kitten," Damien says and tugs on his fiancée's hand, pulling her back to him.

"Oh." She bites on her bottom lip and looks a little sheepish. "Sorry. I... get excited."

I smile, her warmth definitely catching. I'm not that great with meeting new people, which is sometimes a hindrance considering my job, trying to put the woman at ease, which is what Ananya is for, but I feel like I really could sit and talk to My-Linh all day long.

"I like most types of food, and no, I should not be allowed in the kitchen."

"That's okay, Kylian can cook for you. He's really good."

I nod. "I have had the pleasure of eating his congee. And the tea that he said you gave him. I may or may not have stolen some from him."

She beams and gives Kylian a wink. "Well, he is my second favorite Baxter brother."

"Told ya," Kylian preens.

I shrug. "I guess he's okay. Who's your favorite Baxter brother, then?"

Kylian and My-Linh roar with laughter, and even Damien shows a little glint in his eye.

"Oh! I almost forgot, here are some things you might be able to use," My-Linh says when we finally stop laughing.

She hands me a Harrod's bag. I look inside, and there are changes of clothes, toiletries, some other things she thought I might need. Now it's my turn to hug her. "Thank you so much."

Kylian winks, and we go back to our room, promising to have lunch with them tomorrow.

"I love her!" I squeal once we're alone.

"Told ya," he says for the second time in two minutes.

I dump the contents of the bag onto the bed, sorting everything into different piles. Clothes, hair products, lotion...

Kylian jumps on the bed, watching me, his legs crossed at the ankles. "Are you up for going out tonight? I have plans, if you feel like it."

I do. I need this distraction. "Where are we going?"

"No questions."

"No questions? That's what our entire relationship is built on."

"Then let's find something else for us to occupy our time," he suggests, eyes twinkling.

"But what am I going to wear?"

"I'll think of something."

Thirty-Nine

Kylian

At 11 p.m. on the dot, I wait at the front door for Kiara to meet me. She appears a few seconds later in a black dress that I ran out and bought for her that resembles the one we had to ruin for her to get into Illumination.

"Is it wrong to say I feel like a princess? Like a hot princess," she sighs, twirling to give me the full effect.

"Who would fight me if I agreed?"

"Nathan." She says it as a reflex, a joke. But neither of us are prepared for the casual mention of her brother's name.

In her sleep this afternoon, she'd cried, and even when I'd pulled her close, stroking her hair, she kept murmuring her brother's name in a way that tore my heart into a million pieces. I didn't know what was going to happen with him and I, but everything had to be done to repair his relationships with her.

I smile through the pain and hold my hand out to her. She takes it and gives it a little squeeze.

"Let's go," I say, trying to get past the moment.

"Have fun, guys!" My-Linh shouts, poking her head around the corner to see us off.

Kiara giggles as she gives her new bestie a wave as I walk her out to the car waiting at the curb.

"Ready," I say to the driver before I draw the partition shut.

"Where are we going?"

"You have a lot of questions for someone who said 'no questions.'"

"You said that."

"Oh, right. We should listen to me."

"No! Tell me."

"You'll see soon. Promise."

She snuggles up next to me as we watch the city zoom by. I wonder if she can hear my heart thumping in anticipation of where I'm taking her.

Twenty minutes later, we're a little way out of the epicenter of the city when the car turns into a dark alleyway and down a narrow street.

"Are you going to murder me and dump my body here? Is that your big surprise?"

"You don't recognize it?" I ask.

She frowns and turns back to the window. She stares for a few minutes before turning back to me. "Wait. No. It's not."

"It's not what?" Grinning. She knows.

"It's..."

"The club. Where we met."

"We didn't meet there," she argues, looking out the window again.

"But it's the place I really saw you for the first time."

The driver stops in front of the club, and we climb out.

"What are we doing here?"

"You'll see."

FORTY

KIARA

KYLIAN TAKES MY HAND and leads me to the entrance of the club. I didn't recognize it right away because it was completely dark, nobody coming in and out. The surrounding areas are dark and quiet, too.

There's a short siren, and two firetrucks join us, four firemen jumping out of them and coming over to shake Kylian's hand.

"Ready?"

They nod and give him a thumbs up.

"What is happening? What are you doing?"

"Doing what I should've done here five years ago." He takes my face between his hands. "Tell me again, what does this place represent to you?"

I hesitate. And then I decide that now, right now, is when I'll stop second guessing my feelings. "I hate it. This place is the start of a phase I'd rather not remember. It wasn't just you. It was everything; I had come here trying to hide from my life and put on a fantasy about you that wasn't fair. You hurt me. But I hurt me, too. That's what this place represents to me. A reminder I wish I can scald off the surface of the earth."

Purging my soul takes it out of me, and I feel light headed.

But he catches me, wrapping his arms around me, not letting me fall. "This is what I should've done that night."

And then he kisses me. Kisses me unlike any other time we've kissed. Kisses me like everything depends on this kiss, kisses me to erase all the lost time and all the unnecessary hurt and resentment between us.

Kisses me to say all the things we can't say right now because it's not the right time. But it's a promise of what's to come.

The heat from this kiss consumes any and every part of me that exists from that betrayal. And I'm drawn back to him, desperately pressing my lips up against his again.

"One more thing." Curiosity spirals around my body as I watch him pull out his lighter and hands it to me. "Burn it."

"What?"

He puts the lighter into my open hand. "I said, burn it. This... hellhole that has been the location of all my demons. All my regrets. All the things I should've just said yes to and taken the risk. A reminder of all the things that happened to you after that night. And you said it best, let's scald it off the face of this earth."

He's perfectly crazy. Crazy and perfect.

"Burn it, angel. Burn it to the fucking ground," he yells.

I only just notice the faint scent of gas. He prepared this, he planned this. This is a gift to me. An insane, perfect, personal, epic gift.

I click the lighter, but nothing happens, and I look to him for direction.

"Again, sometimes it sticks," he says.

A small flicker of doubt plays with the edges of my excitement. "Doesn't this club belong to someone?"

"It belongs to you. I bought it. In your name. To burn it down and rebuild."

This time, the lighter catches alight. I watch it flicker for a moment before I launch it towards the door of the club. We watch it, and everything moves in slow motion. The little flame burns, a tiny little flicker of yellow, and then it erupts into a giant fireball that bathes the entire building in flames.

And then it burns.

It rages blue and orange, consuming the inside and all the ghosts within.

It's exhilarating, the heat against my face, watching the past disintegrate into ashes.

I feel reborn.

"Thank you," I whisper.

"You're welcome."

We watch for a few more minutes, then one of the firefighters waves to Kylian, and he nods to them.

He touches the small of my back and leads me back to the car. "Let's go."

"Where?"

"Making up for lost time."

Forty-One
Kylian

It's funny how much of our time, how much of the progress of our relationship happens in the car. Something about it is so poetic, like we're always moving, never standing still. Always going somewhere, or leaving something behind.

The burning of the club healed something inside me, a cancer that kept threatening to mutate and take over my whole body. But now, like a chemo treatment, it was reduced to nothing but ashes. And I feel weight is lifting from me.

I take her dancing to make up for all the years she said she didn't want to dance. And it's fitting, we both feel so light on our feet, and each time I twirl her back into me, we fall into each other a little more. Until it feels like even a sliver of light would not be able to fit between her soul and mine.

I don't know where we're going from here, but now it feels like a clean slate.

I pull into the driveway of the property and lean over and meet her lips in a kiss.

"Thanks for a wonderful evening," she says to me. The oddly formal way she says it feels perfect for the night we've had.

"You mean grand arson?"

"Exactly, at least, I can say that no one else has ever burned down a building for me before."

"That makes me sound like not so much a nice guy. And technically, you're the one who burned it down."

"You're not a nice guy. But you're a kind and thoughtful guy."

She takes my arm, and we walk toward the house, talking about how she hopes My-Linh and Damien will be home since she would like to talk to them some more.

When a voice greets us out of the shadows, it startles us both.

"Kiara." Her brother.

"Nathan!" she yells in shock.

He walks into the light, and his face is gaunt, haggard. Dark circles round his eyes, his skin slack and green.

"It's time to come home, Kiara."

She shakes her head and backs away, like she's expecting him to reach for her.

"Kiara. Enough. Let's go."

"What are you even doing here, Nathan?" she shouts, moving to hide behind me.

"I came to get you. We have to go home. We have to... we have to plan Dad's funeral. And the business and..."

She shakes her head, wrapping her arms around herself, making herself smaller. "I can't. Nathan. I just can't. Just let me stay, please."

"You don't have a choice, Kiara. This is what adults do, we do things we don't want to do."

"Nathan." I barely get his name out before he holds his hand up to my face.

"Don't. Just don't, Kylian." He tries to push me away, but I hold strong, covering her.

"How did you even know I was here, Nathan?" she asks.

He looks at me and then back at her. "Someone texted me."

"Kylian? Did you text him?" The betrayal in her voice is stark

"No, no, I didn't. I left that up to you. It wasn't up to me to tell him where you were."

"Promise me!"

"I promise! I promise a hundred times!"

Behind us, Nathan snickers. "Do you really believe him when he makes you promises like that?"

Two thick lines dig themselves into her forehead. "What do you mean?"

"I mean, how well do you know him that you'd believe a single thing he says to you?"

"I believe him because... I know him." She doesn't sound as sure of herself as I'd hoped.

The laugh Nathan forces out is hollow, empty, sarcastic. "Really? You've known him for three weeks, and you think you're an expert on Kylian Baxter? So, tell me, do you know what his baby business project is?

"What is this about, Nathan?" I ask, foreboding starting to suffocate me.

"This is about showing my sister knew the truth about you. So it doesn't take her eighteen years to find out who you really are like it did me."

"Nathan, what are you saying?"

"What's his favorite little project, Kiara?"

She flicks her eyes to me. "It's Watch. It's the streaming service you guys started."

"Good. So at least you know that much. What you don't know is that all this niceness and wooing and getting you into bed, because you have had sex with him, haven't you? I mean, he wouldn't want anything to do with you if you hadn't."

"Nathan. That's not true, you don't know anything about us." I shout.

"You've met Odette, haven't you? His resident booty call? She's been hanging around him for almost ten years now. She's a little more than his executive assistant. She has the office next to his for a reason. Easy access."

"Oh my god," Kiara says.

"This is total bullshit. Don't believe him!" I beg her.

"Fine. But you didn't let me finish. I bet you didn't know that the reason he's paid so much attention to you was just to get Dad to sell Watch to him."

"What?" her voice comes out choked, disbelieving.

Nathan snickers, knowing he's making leeway into his sister's mind. "Yup, that day at Amber, Kylian was actually there to meet Dad. He made a deal with Kylian that if he offered you a job, made you nice and respectable, Dad would sell Watch to him. And surely you know how important the company is to him." He twists the knife.

"He loves Watch," she whispers, almost as a reminder to herself.

"But not as much as I love you!" I shout. The first time I said it wasn't meant to be in defense of myself. This is wrong, this is all wrong. I reach for her, but she's already stepping away from me.

"Don't. Don't say that. Tell me the truth right now. Did Dad make a deal with you?"

"No! There was no deal."

Nathan pulls his phone out of his pocket. "Don't take my word for it. Let the video speak for itself."

I watch, heart in my throat, as she presses a button on the phone. I can't see the picture, but audio from that day at Amber starts to play.

"My son tells me that you have a special interest in the joint venture you two share and that you might have your eye on buying him out."

"Watch?"

"Yes. It's doing well, yes?"

"If you can get Kiara settled somewhere at Baxter Enterprises in six months, Nathan will sell Watch to you."

When she finally looks up from the video, her face is steeped in the pain of betrayal.

"Kiara. No. It's not what it looks like. Keep watching. I said I didn't need it. That's not why I offered you a job, it's not."

Nathan jumps in between us, his back to me, his hands on his sister's shoulder. "Well, we'll never know what his intention was. But he did offer you a job, didn't he? So when the time came, he wouldn't say no.

You know he wouldn't. You wanted to know what Kylian Baxter is really like? This is him. In the flesh and blood."

I try to grab her shoulder, but she shakes me off, rewatching the video, her eyes blurring with tears.

"Kiara, angel, listen to me. It was never about the deal. Never. Ever! I promise. What can I do to prove it to you?"

"But you weren't honest about the job either. I thought..." When she finally speaks, her voice, her words, sticks in her throat. "I thought you offered me the job because you believed in what I was doing. You thought it was a good deal. I thought you wanted to be near me." The last one slashes right down the middle of my chest. Cutting me open. Bleeding out in front of her.

"Kiara. What happened between us, it wasn't about the job. Forget about the job! You and me, that's what matters. And you know that. You know this is real. I know you love me, too."

"Come on, Kiara," Nathan says, his voice now eerily calm. "Let's go home. With people who actually love you and not just for a business deal."

I turn around, spitting I'm so furious at him for interfering just because he's mad at us for going behind his back. "You are a fucking evil motherfucker. Tell her the truth, tell her that I would never have done anything to hurt her. That the deal was never important to me. You know I felt that way. I told you."

He just snorts sarcastically. "What's that thing you always say, Kylian? What a Baxter wants, a Baxter gets?"

"I would never do anything to hurt you, Kiki. Please believe me."

Her eyes are hollow when she looks at me, and it hurts more than anything that's ever happened. "Should've believed you when you hurt me last time. I shouldn't have let myself give you a second chance. I did this to myself."

The front door opens, and in the corner of my eye, I see My-Linh watching, her hand clasped over her mouth, and Damien, his face dark behind her.

"Kiara. Stay. Talk to me." I grab her hands, but she recoils, looking at me like she doesn't even recognize who I am. "I thought... I thought you understood me. But you did the one thing I have worked so hard not to do. Rely on my family for anything. You know that, and yet... you hurt me more than they ever could. At least they never lied to me." She looks at me like it's the last time she's going to see me. "Goodbye, Kylian."

And then she leaves.

She really leaves.

And takes everything that makes me *me* with her.

Two car doors close in the distance.

"I have to go after her!" I run down the driveway with the sound of Damien calling after me.

The car drives off before I can reach it, calling after her. I run into the middle of the street, watching the car's headlights fade into the dark.

"Kiara!" I shout until my throat is so raw I feel like it's bleeding.

Damien comes up to me. "She's gone, man. She's gone."

"She's not!" I push him away and run all the way down the road, but there's no trace of her left.

"She's gone, buddy." Damien says, breathless.

"She's not!" I scream, knowing in my bones that he's right. "She's... not gone. She'll be back."

I trip and fall to the ground, slamming my hand on the ground, fear, anger, and frustration condensing to stream down my face. "She'll be back."

He kneels down onto the ground next to me. "I hope so. I hope so, buddy."

"What did I do? What else could I have done? You heard the things that Nathan said; they were lies. They were all lies."

He doesn't say anything, but there's something unspoken in his eyes. "Say it."

"It wasn't all lies, man. There was some truth, the conversation you had with her dad. That was real. She saw the whole thing."

"It wasn't the whole truth. Yeah, he offered, but that's not why I... not why I tracked her down."

He sighs. "I know. Now you have to make her see that."

"Fuck! I can't believe I fucked this up! Fuck!" I scream with everything in my body. With every remnant of air and heart left in me.

"Come on, let's go home. We can figure it out together there."

I shake my head, the feeling of helplessness crippling me. "I don't know how."

"You'll figure it out. You're the Baxter Brain, remember?"

I feel myself dragged to my feet, and two arms wrap around me.

Damien's hugging me.

Damien who hates anyone touching him who isn't My-Linh.

"I've got you, buddy. I've got you." At almost two inches taller than him, I feel like I'm a child again and I'm crying after Mom left again. And even though his pain was always worse, he was always there for me, letting me sleep in his bed while he told me silly stories until I fell asleep and forgot about the pain... until next time.

But this time, there won't be a next time.

I pined for five years, not knowing what could've been.

Now I'm nothing but shell, she's taken it all. And I know I won't ever find anything like what I had with her again.

Forty-Two

Kiara

"Would you like a drink, Miss Kiara?"

I shake my head.

"She'll have some water and some orange juice, too, please."

"Of course, sir. And for you?"

"Scotch."

She lays the drinks on the table in front of me in the double residence suite that Nathan has on the plane.

"Drink your water," he says.

For the tenth time since we've gotten on the plane, he has tried to tell me what to do, and for the tenth time, I have no intention of listening to him. He got us booked on the first flight back to Hong Kong on a commercial line because he hadn't managed to get our own private jet flown to London to pick me up.

I pull the window shade down and pull an eye mask over my face, tucking the blanket under my chin as I try to block out the world.

But the dark only provides me a blank canvas on which to replay the last seventy-two hours over and over and over. Dad taking his last breath, telling Nathan the truth about my paternity, running away to London, Kylian finding me and giving an incredible symbolic gift, and then Nathan coming to swing a sledge hammer into it all as I stood and watched the house of cards tumble down around me.

When Nathan showed me the video, I thought I was going to be sick. The offer, the handshake, the passing of a phone number.

The realization that that's how he found me that night at Ananya's apartment. He'd been basically given the secret code on how to find me; it wasn't coincidence, it wasn't fate, it wasn't all these years of yearning manifesting a meeting. It was my family meddling in my life. And this time, not about money, not about business, my heart.

Nathan might've dropped a bombshell about Kylian, but he'd told on himself as well. How can I even be sure it wasn't Nathan's idea? He's Dennis Yin's son after all. He's every bit as ruthless as his father. And with bigger stakes. He's always felt like he had something to prove.

"Do you want something to eat? They're taking orders now." His voice interrupts my thoughts about him, and it does nothing but annoy me. I ignore him, pretending to be asleep.

"I know you're not sleeping. You used to do that all the time, and then I'd find you up watching TV in the library. You'd think you'd be better at it now that you're twenty-six years old."

I shut him out and resume my thoughts, wondering how I'm ever going to be able to recover from this. And how I'm ever going to discover who I really am without the interference of well-meaning but controlling men in my life.

I don't speak to him once on the whole trip.

What is there to say?

But he talks, he tells me his work plans, about some girl he went to school with who tracked him down, about a coffee shop opening on his apartment block. Talking just talk, when all I want is silence.

I go home with him. I don't want to go back there, but where else can I go? I can't move back in with Kylian, and I can't go back to my apartment.

There is only the place where my mother and father lived.

Lived.

"Do you have any plans for Dad's funeral yet?" I speak to him for the first time since we left London.

He blinks like he's not sure if he imagined me speaking or not and then clears his throat. "Um, just some preliminaries based on the plans he wrote up himself."

The thought of Dad sitting in his office, alone in the dark, as he flipped through funeral catalogs rips me heart right out of my chest, and I burst into tears again.

"He didn't tell me because I wasn't his child." I blurt out.

Nathan looks shocked that I would even think that, let alone say it. "What? No! Oh, sis, that's not it at all. I promise."

"You can't promise because you didn't know."

He reaches out to touch me, then thinking better of it, pulls his hand away. "There was nothing to know. He didn't even want me to know. I promise you he didn't. He fought it for days. But he heard me calling around to his doctors, and that was not the kind of rumor that we needed going around. So when he finally admitted it, he begged me to keep it a secret. He got down on his knees and begged me, Kiara." Nathan eyes shine with tears as he recalls it. And I don't know how not to believe him.

I don't know what to believe anymore.

"I just wanted to stop being the source of pain for him."

Nathan smiles at me through his tears. "That's just it. You never were."

When we get home, I don't go to bed, I avoid the patio where he sat, I try not to see the teacups left there from when he sat waiting for me just a few days ago to confront me about Kylian, and I go up to Mom's room.

Dad never moved a thing in her room in the entire year she was gone. The bed still has the indent from the last time she sat on it to pull on her shoes to go to the hospice from which she never came back.

I curl up in the armchair at the side of her bed where I sat listening to her sleep, my heart stopping every time her breath became too quiet for me to hear. And I'd get up and watch her chest rise and fall.

"Why did you tell me, Mom? What did you think it would achieve? Did you even imagine that it would derail my entire life and I would spend ten years trying to find myself?" My voice starts out quiet but then builds and builds until I'm standing there screaming at a bed that lost its owner a year ago.

"You made a mistake, Mother, when you had that affair. And then you made the second mistake of telling me. That was your burden to bear. I hope, if nothing else, you felt lighter for unloading it because it did nothing but weigh me down."

I slump at the foot of her bed until Nathan comes and carries me to my bed

"I'm sorry, Kiara. Your life was so much harder than mine ever was. I'm so sorry. I've done a shit job of protecting you."

"If you hadn't tried so hard, I might not have been so intent on running away. I understand why you did it. But it's time to let me go, Nathan. You have to let me make me own decisions based on what I think is wrong or right and what I think won't disappoint you. Please. We let Dad go, now you have to let me go, too."

He lies down next to me on the bed, and for just a while, we pretend we're kids again, that our parents are watching TV downstairs, and we're talking about all these things we're going to do when we grow up.

We plan the funeral for a week away on a Sunday, so there's time for all the people around the world who want to make it back. To say goodbye to a giant. My dad, Dennis Yin.

I busy myself with making plans, the wake, the service, the speakers. Nathan takes care of the invitation list. He has a mountain of other details to take care of on the business side.

But two nights after we come back from London, we meet in Dad's closet and find the outfit he'd asked to be buried in. It's the suit he wore on his wedding day. We pulled it out from the storage wardrobe of his suits that he didn't wear anymore, and took turns hugging it to ourselves, remember how every time he wore it, he would proudly tell everyone that Mom had picked it out for him.

Still, it doesn't matter how busy I am, I can't stop myself thinking about the man I'd left in London. About all the things we'd said and done together and trying to pick out which ones were lies and which ones were truth.

It's not until I sit down to write my eulogy do I realize that I left my laptop at Kylian's apartment the morning our pictures had been plastered all over the news. They are all gone now; most of the papers are focused on my father's passing of the flame to the new Yin leadership.

How fickle we all are.

I grab the car keys sitting on the bench and make my way out to the driveway. When I pull the door open, Kylian is standing there, his hand raised to press on the doorbell.

"Hi." His voice sounds like an echo in my ears. "How are you doing?"

"I'm fine. What are you doing here?"

"I brought you some of the things you left at my place."

"Oh. Thank you."

He clears his throat. "It's just your laptop, your phone charges, some clothes."

I've already said thank you. I don't know what else to say. I just stand there, holding the bag. "Goodbye, Kylian." I try to push the door closed, but he blocks it with his hand.

"Kiara. When you have time, can we sit down and talk, please? We need to talk about the things you heard the other day. Not everything... not all of it is the truth."

"Did you give me a job because my dad asked you to? And did he offer to sell Watch to you if you did? And did you conveniently forget to tell me?"

Pain splashes all over his face.

"I thought so. I don't think we need to talk. Come to the funeral, my father would want that. But, like you did at my mother's funeral, I'd appreciate it if you tried to avoid me as much as possible."

"Kiara. Did you not hear what I said to Nathan that night? I love you. Please. I love you."

"Love doesn't fix anything that's already broken, Kylian."

"Kiara," Nathan calls out to me from inside. "Close the door, and come inside."

Forty-Three

Kylian

It rains on the day of the funeral. But it doesn't matter. Almost five hundred of us stand there by the freshly dug grave as he's lowered into it. Sending with him all the love he'd blessed us with.

Both Nathan and Kiara eulogizes in ways that typify the people they are. Nathan's is equal parts funny and adoring, speaking about this businessman and philanthropist that his father was. Kiara speaks about the tender and kind man he was as tears stream down her face.

And I stand in the back the whole time, wishing that I could comfort my best friend and the woman who's stolen my heart.

Taking advantage of the crowd making their way toward the Yin's backyard, I break off from the pack and down the driveway to my car. The rain has let up, but the clouds still hang heavy and gray in the sky, a fitting reflection for my heart. I can still feel the smooth mahogany under my hand as I'd placed it on his coffin, wishing that I'd had a chance to say goodbye to him in person.

"Kylian?" Kiara stands in the door of the house, watching me as I walk away.

"Kiara."

She walks toward me, each step slow and measured until she's about three feet from me. "I just wanted to say, he really loved you. From the first day Nathan brought you home, he was very impressed by you. And every time you came around, for days after, he would talk about you." A soft, sad smile plays with her lips. "I would've been jealous if I hadn't understood why he was so taken with you. Anyway, thank you for coming today. No matter everything that's happened, it would've broken his heart if you hadn't been here. He... he wasn't mad about us. I don't think I ever told you that. He was hurt that we didn't tell him, But he wasn't sad. He loved you."

Something during her sweet speech makes the tears start to prick the back of my eyes, and when she finishes, the tears drip off my chin to join the raindrops on my suit coat.

"And I loved him. So much. I hope one day, if he's watching, he'll be proud of me like he was proud of you two. Because as much as he loved me, it was a drop in the ocean compared to how much he loved you both. I hope you never ever forget that. That there are people, living and gone, who love you beyond measure." I rush to say everything I want to, not wanting her to see me hurt.

She takes a step closer to me. "Kylian, I wan—"

"Kiara. Aunt Jenny wants to talk to you," Nathan says as he appears. Such a knack for timing.

"Oh, okay." She gives me a look and starts to walk toward the house.

But then Nathan speaks, stopping her in her tracks

"If you want to buy Watch, submit an offer by midnight Sunday five weeks from now. I might not have agreed with how you did it, but a deal is a deal. You gave Kiara a job. My father would've wanted me to go through with the deal. If I don't receive your offer by the deadline, at the following board meeting, I'll be putting it up for public sale. I have another buyer. And he's hungry."

Kiara turns to me. "Kylian, you should put in an offer. You want this. I know how much you love this company. Don't be stupid; put in an offer."

"I told you. This is not how I want it. Do what you need to do, Nathan. No hard feelings."

I call her every day, multiple times a day. In the morning when I get up, at lunch when I wait for everyone to come back to work and provide a distraction for me, in the evenings on my drive home, and before I go to bed. No matter how much I meditate, sleep eludes me. She was the only sleep therapy for me, and now I'm in withdrawal.

She never answers, and it goes straight to voicemail. Sometimes I leave a message, and sometimes there's nothing to say except the things I've said a hundred times. I don't know if she listens, but I talk anyway. Tell her about things going on with my family, about Damien and My-Linh's wedding plans, about running into my neighbors who always ask where the sweet but grumpy girl is, about silly things I've cooked and eaten and how they'd taste better with her. I start a new K-drama and give her a little summary after every episode. And after every message, I beg for her forgiveness, for not doing better, for being the cause for her hurt, and apologize for hurting her, when I'd promised that I never would. And how that will haunt me for the rest of my life.

On the Tuesday nine days after the funeral, I reach for the phone to call her at 12:30 p.m. only to see her name blinking on my screen. My heart flip flops as I answer. "Kiara?"

It's quiet for a moment, and I wonder if she'd dialed my number by accident.

"Kiara? Are you there?"

Her voice is almost inaudible when she finally speaks. "Can you come to Amber, please? It's... Tuesday..."

Nothing else matters in that moment.

I drive, heart in my throat, forgetting simple road rules in my quest to get there. When I rush in, she's sitting at her dad's private table at the back. She sees me but doesn't say anything, just picks up the tea cup in front of her, taking a sip.

"I'm here."

"Can you sit with me please? I can't do this alone. And I can't not be here on a Tuesday at lunch time."

"Of course." I pull a chair from a different table, not wanting to take her father's chair and sit with her. She doesn't say a word the whole time or even acknowledges me. Just stares into space, wiping away tears as she drinks one cup of tea after another.

But we sit in silence, thinking about the man that brought us together, wondering where he is now and what he can see.

At 2 p.m., she stands up. "I'm going now."

"Okay. Kiara?"

"Yeah?"

"Why am I here?"

"Because I didn't know who else to call. I needed someone here, and I knew you'd come."

She walks away, leaving me with a multitude of emotions I don't know how to handle.

I'm back the next Tuesday. She's already there, same thing. Silence and tea. After an hour, she gets up, thanks me, and leaves.

The third week, the same thing.

I still make the daily phone calls and voicemail, but the hour every Tuesday is about her, and it's about silence. And I won't say another word until she does.

On the fourth Tuesday, before she leaves, she says, "This Sunday is the deadline for the offer for Watch. Don't forget. Don't not do it because of me. I don't want to be a part of any of your decisions."

For the first time since she left that night in London, my heart sinks to the bottom of my chest, burning any hope of progress to ashes.

During the family Wednesday meeting, I'm the topic of conversation and my love life, or lack thereof.

"You need to make a decision, Kylian. The girl or the company. You can't have both," Matthias delivers his painfully brutal view.

"Yes, you can. I'm evidence of that," Damien adds, only serving to confuse me all the more.

"Kingsley?"

"I have no advice to you, just this, whatever you pick, do it with your whole heart. This isn't something you can half-ass. If you want her, go get her. If you want the company, submit an offer that they can't refuse. We're Baxters, we don't dilly dally."

All three of them makes sense to me, but I know who I'm going to be listening to.

On Sunday 11 p.m., I press the doorbell at the Yin Estate. The newspapers tell me that Nathan is in Singapore and won't be home for a few days, so I don't have to worry about him kicking me out before I've done what I came here to do.

I hear the shuffle of her slippers on the floor as she comes to the door. How had I become so accustomed to the little things that she does in such a short time. How had my mind remembered every little thing and insisted on torturing me with it. My memory of everything about her is so vivid I could create a hologram and it would resemble her perfectly. Except that I wouldn't be able to touch her, smell her, kiss her, hold her, fall asleep with her body against mine.

"Kylian," she says when she opens the door, even though I know she wouldn't have opened the door if she didn't know who it was. "What are you doing here?"

"I came to see you. We don't have to talk. Tonight, I need to ask you to sit with me. Please."

Her brow furrows in confusion for a moment, but then she opens the door wider to let me in.

The house is dark and quiet. She's kept the windows open, she must be cold. As if reading my mind, she wraps her cardigan tighter around her. We walk out to the patio, and I sit in the chairs we'd sat in the day we'd had dinner here.

A beautiful memory.

She chooses the seat across from me.

I lean back, hooking my hands behind my head as I stare up to the heavens. The sky is so clear tonight, the stars feeling like they're so close I can reach out and touch them. But there's something beautiful about them being just out of reach. Something to strive for.

I check my clock. 11:25 p.m.

"Kylian."

"Hmmm?"

"What are you doing here?"

"I'm just here to see you. And show you something."

"What?"

"Patience, Kiara. You were always so impatient."

She exhales and then asks the question I know has been on her mind. "Did you submit an offer to in for Watch?"

"No."

She exhales. "You need to get something now and send it to Nathan. It's due in less than an hour."

I smile at her and then look back up at the sky. "Did you know on a clear day, you can see Mars from here?"

"Kylian! Have you gone mad?"

"No, angel. Not 'gone.' I've always been mad. For you." I pat the seat next to me. "Come here."

She shakes her head. "Kylian, no."

"You said you'd sit with me. So, please, sit with me."

The internal struggle plays out over her face, but in the end, she comes over.

"Lean back," I say. "See that there? That's the Big Dipper. Those seven stars there. Isn't it stunning? That in time and space, those giant balls of fire are nowhere near each other. But to us, they make this funny little shape in the sky."

"Kylian?"

"Shhh, I don't want to talk about work. Please. I just want to sit here with you and watch light from over a hundred light years and trillions of trillions of miles away dance just for us. Sometimes you need to feel like a tiny part of the universe."

She finally gives in and stares up, sighing after a while. "They're so pretty."

I look away from the sky and over at her. "Yes, you are."

This time, she doesn't say anything, just points to the stars in the sky with her finger. Giving them a little wave and hoping someone will see it trillions of miles away.

I close my eyes so I can breathe her in. That scent I haven't properly smelled in weeks.

"You're going to lose out on Watch," she says. "Nathan's not going to change his mind."

"I wouldn't expect him to. I'm not here about Nathan changing his mind about me. He's my best friend, he should know who I am. But he's choosing not to. I never did anything to him except love his sister. If he hates me, that's his own shit showing through. But you, I hurt you. You're the one who needs to see I can change. And that every time I said to you that you are the most important thing in my life I wasn't lying. And if words won't show you, then maybe my actions will."

The galaxy twinkles above us, and we sit in total stillness and silence, even while the earth travels through the cosmos at over sixty thousand miles an hour.

At midnight, the clock on my phone rings. A tinkly little melody.

I sit up and turn the alarm off.

"Midnight?" she asks.

I nod. "Midnight." I get up, sliding my phone into my pocket, and pull out a large envelope that I leave on the seat. "Thank you for sitting with me."

"Why did you come here?"

"I didn't come here to talk. If you wanted to hear the things I have to say, your voicemail is full of messages. Tonight was about showing you that everything that happened between us happened because we both wanted it to. Not because of a business deal, not because of family meddling. Just us." I take her hand and press a kiss to the palm. "And that in a hundred thousand lifetimes, given the choice, I will always, always, always choose you." I drop her hand.

Our eyes lock, and I stare at her like I'm trying to commit every last pixel of her to memory... just in case this is the last time.

And then I ask the question that needs to be asked. "Who would you choose, Kiara?"

I don't wait for her answer.

I leave, and the stars are my witness that, to my word, in the most important choice of my life, I chose her.

>>> ———————>♥<——————— <<<

"We know where he is," Frank booms, strolling into my office unannounced the day after." All the cameras and bugs were bought from the same place. We tracked down where he got the equipment and, er, politely encouraged them to tell us where to find him. Either way, these are the three places he hides out in." He throws a stack of photos on my desk, showing him coming in and out his hideouts. "So what's the next step?"

"I want him arrested and tried and locked away forever. We need to catch him in the act. Follow him. He's got to fuck up at some point. We'll call the police to bring him in."

"And if they don't?" Frank asks.

"He better hope that they do; it's going to better than anything I have planned for him."

His eyes bore into me, but there's no protest. I don't know if Frank actually feels an emotional attachment to the people he's watching or if it's just the desire to do a really good job, but it doesn't matter. I know he's the one person I can trust with Kiara's safety.

"Okay, let me know if he makes a move."

I made her a promise that I wouldn't let anyone hurt her. And the least I can do is keep that promise.

I don't have time to ponder it too long, though. A few minutes after Frank leaves, Odette comes running in, koala slippers on her feet, loudly whispering, "Gerry's here. On the warpath, look alive!"

My door flies open, and I'm greeted by the sight of the person I least want to see.

"Have you suddenly entered the business of fucking up and I missed the memo?" he yells, his face red.

"If you're just coming in here to yell at me, Gerald, I'm busy."

"No, you're not. You know how I know? You've fucked up two big deals in the last few months. The Heracles chip and now Watch."

That gets me to look up from my laptop.

"Yeah, everyone heard about Nathan giving you a window for submitting an offer, and you didn't even fucking bother."

"Wow, looks like your sources are actually getting good information for once."

He stomps his foot like he's a child. "Are you mad? You spend six months trying to convince the board to do this, and now when it's time, you don't even bother?"

"Is there an actual reason you are in Hong Kong? Other than to bust my chops?"

"I'm here to meet with Nathan. See if I can save the deal."

"He's in Singapore."

"He's back tomorrow. I'll see him then. And then we'll see who can actually follow through with bringing this sucker home. The board is going to be very interested in hearing about this. I'd be a little worried about your position."

"Then you have no idea about who I am at all. Threatening me is not something I'm likely to forget. Now, feel free to see yourself out before I get you thrown out."

He slams the door behind him, but it opens again almost immediately. I'm ready for another round of insults, but it's just Odette.

"That went well. Phew." She fans herself with a file.

"About as well expected."

She closes the door behind her and sits in the guest chair, staring at me.

"I don't like to be stared at," I say, trying not to think about how that's true except for one particular case.

"What are you going to do?

"About?"

"Gerry."

"Nothing. If he thinks he can convince Nathan to sell to Baxter, then good. But I know Nathan. If he says he's not going to sell to me, that means he's not going to touch anyone named Baxter. Good luck to Gerry.'

"You really gave it all up?"

"No."

"You gave up the Watch deal."

"I still own 50% of the company, Odette. But I'd give it up right now... for the thing that I really want."

Forty-Four
Kiara

The days have started to kind of meld together in a blur. I'm ready to go back to work, but I also don't want to leave the house. And I don't want to tell Nathan why yet; there are enough things he has to worry about. It's bad enough that Kylian knows. He hadn't gotten in contact again, and now I'm sitting at the table with the documents from the envelope that Kylian left for me strewn in front of me.

The letter that was attached is written in his hand. Explaining that he is not responsible for overseeing the staff and contractor for the casino and that someone called Ronald Gai was in charge. He would manage me and my players, and Kylian would have any access to any employee information. A contract had been drawn up to retain fifteen prop players with a fee 5% over what I had quoted. The players would have access to all staff privileges at the casino, including door-to-door transport to and from their residence and the casino in Macau. It would be a twelve-month retainer with a payout of a minimum of three months.

These terms were so much more than what we'd initially discussed in his little salon. I would have to think about it, but it would be reckless to say no.

I'm still trying to recover from him being here last night. And the things he said. The truth is, I always expected him to submit an offer for Watch. And if the truth is that he didn't and I was the reason, I'm not sure I can handle the guilt that comes with that.

Nathan comes back tomorrow for the reading of Dad's will. With an estate as large as his, the lawyers have to clarify some details as well as update values on some of his assets.

I read over Kylian's letter again.

And then I pull my phone out and find a new voicemail.

I move out to the patio, sit in the chair he sat in yesterday, and listen.

"The woman on the fourth floor got another dog. This one looks like her. It has a perm and wears a lacy collar like an aristo-dog..."

When it's done, I press replay. And again.

I lie back, staring at the sky, and remember what it was like to sit next to him yesterday. Tomorrow is Tuesday, I promise myself that I will only continue going to Amber to be with Dad and not for any other reason.

There's a banging on my front door at some time in the dead of night. Nathan isn't coming until tomorrow morning, so it's not like he forgot the key. I've had the gate closed all day, so no one should be knocking. Maybe it's just a dream.

I try to go back to sleep when I feel rather than see my door handle turn.

"Hello?"

I'm going crazy from being home by myself too long. Tomorrow I'll get Ananya to pick me up and take me over to The House. It's time to go back to work.

I reach for my phone to text her to see if she can come over first thing in the morning, and this time, I definitely see my door handle turn.

"Who's there?" My voice sounds terrified in my own ears and makes me even more scared.

"Hello, Kiara." The door opens completely, and he's there.

I haven't seen him in over a year, but nothing's changed.

"What are you doing here? Get out!" I inch back against the headboard, pulling the sheet around me. My brain feels like it's stuck in slow motion as I try to process what is happening.

"What have I told you about closing your windows? Remember when I used to warn you? I had to wait outside your apartment in New York to make sure you'd be okay."

He takes a step into my bedroom, and I want to be sick. Not here. He can't be here.

"Get out! Don't come a step closer!"

"Unfortunately, I can't do that, Kiara. I'm going to need you to come with me."

My hand closes around my phone, and I launch it at him as hard as I can. In the dark, he misjudges the speed, and it smashes against his forehead.

"I really wish you hadn't done that," he hisses.

He grins, eyes wild, and storms toward me just as someone in the distance yells my name.

Not someone, Kylian. What is he doing here? Am I imagining all of this? "Kiara! Wake up! There's a fire!"

My stalker stops. "Did you call him? He's always where he's not wanted. I'm going to have to do something about that."

"No! You leave him alone," I shout, hoping Kylian can hear me. Come find me, Kylian. Please.

"Aww, so sweet. Does he know that you're just going to turn around and betray him anyway, the way you did to me?" He points at a scar on his temple that I've only just noticed. "Your brother gave me this after you lied and told him that I hurt you. It was an accident. You didn't tell him it was an accident?"

I scramble to the end of my bed and jump off it. There's a faint smell of smoke... but where's fire?

"Kiara!" A loud crash startles both me and my intruder, and there's the sound of multiple people shouting, calling out my name.

"I'll be back. You don't have to worry about that," he threatens and then runs out of my bedroom, slamming the door closed behind him.

I crumple to the ground, feeling almost nauseous from relief.

"Kiara!" My bedroom door flies open, and he's there in bare feet and just a pair of track pants and T-Shirt. His face panicked and pale with fear. "Oh my god, thank god you're okay." He runs up to me and grabs me, hugging me roughly before he takes my wrist.

I don't know what he is doing here, but I don't care. "Kylian... he's here. He was in here."

"I know, Kiara. It's okay, I've got you now." He hugs me again, and I don't know if I'll ever be able to let go. "We have to go, right now."

"He... he said he'd be back."

"Let him try. I'm here now." He grabs my dressing gown at the end of my bed and wraps it around me. "We have to go. You ready?"

I don't understand what he's saying, but I nod anyway. Where are we going? Why wouldn't I be ready?

As if reading my mind, he lifts my chin and looks directly at me as he says, "I need you to trust me. I'll explain as soon as we get out of here. But we have to go now."

He yanks me out of the bedroom and down the stairs. I follow as fast I can, trying to keep up with his stride. As soon I reach the last step, the smoke hits me.

Thick and suffocating.

I immediately cough, my lungs rejecting the tainted air.

Kylian pulls his T-Shirt off and bunches it up against my face. "Breathe through this. You'll be okay once we get outside."

"What is happening?"

He doesn't say anything, just leads me through my wrecked front door and out to the front yard where a firetruck is parked as a burning car is being hosed down.

"Oh my god," I gasp through coughs. "That's my car."

He pushes the T-shirt back up to my mouth as he drags me out to the street where the breeze helps dissipate the smoke, and I can breathe a little easier. Almost immediately, he grabs his side and starts to gasp, a harsh hacking cough that feels like it's stabbing my heart with each one.

"Kylian! Help! We need water over here!" I jump up, waving at the group of firefighters tending the fireball in my driveway.

He grabs my arm. "No, I'm sorry, I'm fine. Just took a particularly big breath of smoke." He takes another breath and coughs it out.

I reach out to pat his back without even thinking. But the moment my palm touches the burning skin of his back, I'm the one who can't breathe. Something lodges itself in my lungs, and no amount of coughing can get it out.

"Kiara. We have to get you to a hospital. I need to get you checked out."

"No!" I swallow and force down the urge to cough. "Tell me what happened here?"

There's a pause as I can see him trying to figure out what to say. But we should be past that. Have we learned nothing?

"Don't sugarcoat it. Don't you dare treat me like a child. Tell me exactly what happened, or I am never ever speaking to you again."

The threat seems to work, and he takes one more breath before he finally speaks.

"We've been tracking him for a few days. It took us awhile, but we managed to find where he bought the surveillance equipment he had in your apartment. He's been here for almost six months, and his tourist visa is expired. He moves from place to place. But we found him. And just in time. Frank was surveilling him and saw him pick up your car from the lot he had hidden it in after he stole it. As Frank was tailing him, he realized he must have been coming here. Frank called me, and I tried to call you, but you didn't answer.

"I was sleeping." I don't know why I feel like I need to explain; we both know that I wouldn't have answered the phone even if I were awake.

"Frank tried to catch up to him, but he must've picked up that someone was chasing him, so he pretty much sped the whole way here, and then he rammed the car right through your gate. I'm not sure what he did, but Frank said seconds later the car pretty much exploded. And he was gone."

It all sounds like it's part of some movie. Except that it's my life. "The explosion is probably what woke me."

"Maybe." He swallows. "Did he hurt you?"

"No. He had only come in there when you arrived."

His shoulders drop three inches from relief. "Good."

"Thank you."

"It's not over yet."

He pulls me into his arms, and I let him. I let him because I want to feel safe again. I let him because I missed him so much. I let him because I don't know what my life is without him in it.

"You're shaking," he says, his mouth muffled by my hair.

"I was scared."

"Me, too."

We're standing there, giving in to everything I've been fighting for the last six weeks, when there's a deafening bang. At the same time, I hear Frank in the distance yell, "Look out!"

Then there's another shot, and out of the corner of my eye, I see my stalker standing at the corner of my house and then drops to his knees and falls face down, forever.

"Oh my god!" I shout. "Kylian!"

"Hmmm?" he says, and I look up, his eyes are glazed, watery. "We got him?"

"Yes!"

"Good. You're safe now, angel."

And that's the last thing he says before he collapses against me, his back drenched with blood.

"Kylian! Oh my god. Kylian! Say something!"

But sometimes it's too late.

And there's nothing left to say.

It should go without saying, but I'm going to say it anyway, I hate hospitals.

The beeping, the fluorescent lights, the sterilized stench.

But the worst thing is the not knowing. The limbo, the half-held breath.

The total lack of control.

The knowing that the lives of your loved ones are in the hands of someone you can't even see.

But I pray anyway.

To anyone who's listening.

To anyone who might have council with whoever is watching over Kylian's life.

"Kiara!"

I don't even look up. The person I want to call my name is lying in an operating room. So what's the point?

"Kiara..."

I look up to see my brother. "What are you going here, Nathan?"

A flash of hurt or confusion streaks across his forehead. "What do you mean, what are you doing here? Kylian has been shot. Where else would I be?"

Based on the last two months, literally anywhere else.

"Can I get you something?" he asks, voice filled with worry.

"I don't know what you're doing here, but if you're going to stay, please just let me sit in silence."

He doesn't move, but he also doesn't say anything.

The hours drip by like a Dali painting, having no meaning. At some point, I hear my name again. But Nathan is still sitting next to me, so it can't be him. Out of sheer curiosity, I look up.

It's My-Linh, Damien, and another man who looks like he could be Kylian's twin.

"Damien. Matthias. Hi, My-Linh," Nathan says, standing up to greet them.

When I don't say anything, My-Linh sits down next to me. She doesn't say anything, just takes my hand and squeezes it. I squeeze it back and sit there in silence. A sisterhood of women who love a Baxter man.

I must doze off at some point because My-Linh is gently shaking me.

"Kiara, honey, the doctor's coming."

I jump up.

And then sit back down again, memories of this exact scenario just a few weeks ago and the outcome, flooding back to me.

"I can't."

"I know it's hard. But... this is the time, if ever, to be strong for Kylian. He would be here for you. He would hound the doctors for minute updates, he would take this time to plan an amazing get well party for you. He would do everything that he could to make you smile. That's who he is. Who are you going to be?"

I get up, wiping my hands the pajama pants I'm still wearing. They still smell of smoke. Still splattered with Kylian's blood.

If feels like a lifetime for the surgeon to walk down the hallway to the rest of us standing there, holding hands, each whispering our own final prayer for good news.

"He's out. He's in critical condition, and we're going to take it by the minute. The bullet entered and exited the lung but grazed his trachea, so we were trying to stabilize the structure, so when he does wake, try not to let him talk too much. He had a lot of blood loss, too."

"Can we see him?" Matthias speaks. It's the first time I've ever heard him. It hurts how worried he looks. I wanted to meet the Kylian-on-steroids version Matthias. Not this one.

"You can see him two at a time. He needs a lot of rest. We'll have a nurse get you when he's ready. Okay? We're staying optimistic. He's young and fit, hopefully he can pull through."

We turn toward each other, each processing what we've just heard.

Finally, Nathan says, "It's probably better he's still asleep. He'd probably just injure himself more when he realizes he can't speak to stop exacerbating his damn bullet wound."

It's silent for a moment, and then everyone but me bursts out laughing.

"When the doctor says, 'you can choose to talk or die' he'd be like, 'got the body bag ready, Doc,'" Matthias adds.

Damien roars with laughter as My-Linh grabs his arm, trying to breathe.

"Bet when they pulled the bullet, he was like, 'yeah, can you give me that, I'm going to need it for the thousand times I'm going to retell this story'."

"Each time adding a little extra drama."

I watch them open-mouthed. How can they be acting like this? Then My-Linh reaches over and says, "What do you think he's thinking? Come on. It'll help you feel better. It can't hurt. It doesn't mean you care any less."

She's so kind, I don't want to tell her I can't think about anything but the way he looked before he collapsed against me.

So I try, thinking about everything about him, everything he ever said and did with me.

And then I know.

"Um, he, uh, he's probably thinking... 'I need to get out of this damn bed. I have to get someone to write a C-Drama about me. It'll be called Blond Billionaire Baxter Bachelor.'"

Everyone's mouth drops open, and then Matthias slaps his leg and guffaws, which sets everyone else off.

We laugh.

We laugh so hard it hurts.

We laugh until a nurse has to usher us into an empty room.

We laugh because if he ever wakes up, we can't tell him that we did nothing but cry.

We laugh because he would want us to.

Finally, a nurse peeps her head into the room and says, "We have him in a room. He can have two visitors now for a few minutes. And then some more in a little bit."

I hang back. His family is here, I can't, I shouldn't beg to see him.

Damien looks over and says, "You go, Kiara."

"No... you should."

"No, it has to be you. He's going to want to know you're here. You go."

Everyone nods, and I have to push back a sob. This is why he's so kind; these are the people he's surrounded by.

Damien follows behind me as we follow the nurse, but when she opens the door, he doesn't come in. "Go," he whispers.

I take a deep breath and step in, bracing myself for what I'm going to see. But it's not enough. He has wires and tubes coming out of every part of his body. And although he's sleeping, he looks pained.

"Kylian, it's me. Kiki." I touch his arm, careful not to touch any of the tubes. "I met Matthias. You're right, he's funny. And Nathan is here. We miss you. Wake up so we can talk, okay? They're teasing you in the other room; you have to wake up and get them all back."

One tear drops on his hospital gown, and I take a step back.

"He's gone, Kylian. Frank's bullets got him right in the heart. I wasn't even really sure he had one. But he's gone. You... you kept your promise. You told me he'd never hurt me again. He's gone. And we don't ever have to think about him ever again."

I wipe away a tear.

"Wake up. Please. Wake up. Don't leave me here. I need you. I need you to tell me that I'm being a brat. And I need you to come to Tuesdays at Amber with me. I can't go alone. I need someone I can tease about their obvious tell. I need you to be here with me. I don't know how to do all this without you. Please. Wake up."

But he doesn't.

So I say it again.

And again.

Until the nurse tells me he needs to rest.

And then I say it in my head and hope wherever he is, he can hear me.

Forty-Five

Kylian

I've been hit by a tank.

Fallen under one of its tracks and every part of my body crushed to dust.

My brain smooshed to a pancake.

That's the only explanation for how I feel.

That and my eyes popped like grapes because they're not working right now. All I can see is white haze. It's pretty, but it doesn't help me figure out where the fuck I am.

"Ugh," I groan. What the fuck? Now I hurt even more. Something inside me burns like I've swallowed a cyanide pill.

But please, that wouldn't happen to me, I'd be an amazing spy. Bond has nothing on me. I chuckle. And it's a big mistake.

"Ahh! Ow!" And somehow making those sounds hurts even more.

"Stop moving. Fucking hell, you're like a child who can't sit still."

Kiara.

Kiara!

I squint, trying to focus. Now there's a Kiara shape standing to my side, and I'll take it.

"Kiara," I whisper. But can't say anything more. Speaking, breathing hurts.

"Don't talk. I know that sounds impossible, but you have to try. Your trachea got hurt, and if you talk too much, you might tear the injury."

"Don't. Talk?" I force out.

"Good job. Sheesh," she laughs. "Matthias was right."

"Ma-tee-ass here?"

"STOP TALKING!"

I pout but obey, reaching my hand out. Somehow that hurts, too, but it doesn't make me want to scream.

She takes it. Even without seeing, I know it's her hand. I would recognize it among a million different hands.

"Everyone's here. All your brothers, your dad, Nathan, Odette, Julie. I don't think Odette and Nathan should be on the same planet, though. Wow, I thought you talked a lot. Oh, and My-Linh, she's the one holding it all together."

"How long?" I say.

"You've been out for about five days. Being a sleepy head."

"Frank?"

"Frank is okay. He wasn't hurt. But. He got my stalker. He's gone."

"Good." That one was worth the pain.

"I have something for you. Our family lawyer gave it to us. It was something Dad left for you. I... read it. I just wanted to make sure it was something you should hear... in case you..."

"Read."

She clears her throat and straightens out the paper so she can read.

"Dear Kylian,

The first time I met you, you came up to me, held out a sandwich you had made from the ingredients in my fridge, and said, "Dude. This ham is amazing. You should eat some. Have my sandwich, I can make another one." And then you poured me a glass of coke and made me sit down while you told me about what you'd learned at school that day. You were more at home in my house than I was. And you made everyone everywhere you go feel like family. You got that from your grandfather. He'd be proud of who you are now. There is no doubt.

I'm not leaving you much in the way of money or assets, you could buy me out multiple times over. But what I want to give you is this—my blessing. Maybe you don't know it yet, or maybe you do and don't know what to do because you're afraid of what we'll say, so let me tell you this: You have my blessing. You two are like sunshine and rain, Kiara and you. It was the same with my wife and I, and our lives were blessed with endless rainbows. Now you know the real reason for my asking you to help me. Love my daughter for me. She has always loved you.

Finally, I wish I could leave Watch to you. Unfortunately, I can't. But I have seen what you have done with it, and if my son sees any sense, then he will make sure that you and only you get it. I look forward to watching you achieve all the things you told me you were going to do that day.

You are one of a kind, son.
Don't waste it.
Be brave.

Love,
Dennis Yin.

Her voice cracks at his name. I don't even know how she made it through the whole letter. My eyes are even more blurry than they were before from the tears.

"So... I guess he had a little idea about us," I say, ignoring the pain.

"Before we did."

"Kiara. I want you to know something, if that letter had said something else, that he didn't want us together, I would have loved you anyway. For the rest of my days." Each word feels like a knife to my chest. But it's worth it.

She leans in, her lips wet from her own tears as she kisses me. "I love you."

"Really?" I say hoarsely, teasing her.

"You're really a jerk. What's wrong with me? I love a jerk."

"Promise?"

"A hundred times over."

"I love you right back."

"Promise?"

"Yes, but just the once. That's all you need."

Forty-Six
Kylian

If there's one thing I know about myself beyond anything else, it's this... well, actually, make that two things: one, I love Kiara with every fucking cell in my body, and two, I fucking hate being stuck in a hospital. And it's worse when your whole family is there, the people who know you best, who know that you can't and shouldn't be talking for a few days.

I'll take a fucking bullet to my right nut before I choose to be stuck in a bed again while my brothers take turns roasting me so hard that I feel like a rotisserie chicken, well and truly skewered on a metal pole.

But that behavior is par for the course. Especially since they were paying me back for being so worried and having to drop everything going on in their lives to be by my side. Well, not Matthias, he doesn't have anything going on in his life. Ever. But say he did, he wouldn't have batted an eyelid to rush to me. That's what we do, that's what we've always done, and it'll be a cold, frigid day in hell before anything will change.

What was surprising was when, after a day of lying there taking the abuse from my brothers, everyone had turned toward the door. Then, as if rehearsed, they'd cleared their throats and made up excuses to leave. When they were all done, someone came back into my room.

Nathan.

"Hey," he says. His face unreadable.

"Hey," I respond, even though it feels like someone is stabbing me in the chest with a rusty fireplace poker. But if there ever was a time to make an effort, it feels like this would be it.

"You look worse than that time we ended up in jail in Tijuana wearing a table cloth as a toga."

I laugh, and it ends up in a hacking cough.

"Stop that. You're not supposed to be talking or coughing or anything like that."

"Then don't make me laugh," I whisper.

"I wasn't, I was reminding you of what happened last time we both royally fucked up."

We had both done our part in that particular adventure almost ten years ago. I shouldn't have thought that I could talk us into a back room poker game, and he shouldn't have tried to hustle them when we got there. That time Matthias had had to come down and save both of our asses. Supposed to. He ended up in that prison cell right with us, having tried to hit on the pretty woman standing in front of the police station who turned out to be the police chief's daughter. One day later, they got tired of the three of us constantly talking and dumped us at the U.S. border in the dead of night. When we finally found a motel to check into, I'd almost fainted at my reflection. It had been one of the best times of my whole entire life.

"Last time?" I croak.

"Yeah. As opposed to this time." He walks up to the bed and bangs the side of his fist gently on the bed rail. "You fucked up. Like, we've had more scraps like Tijuana where I thought we were going to actually die, but this time, this stuff with Kiara, this is the most you've ever fucked up."

I don't have to say anything. I know I did. I was too wrapped up in trying to make it work with her, I forgot how much I was supposed to be trying to making it work with my best friend as well.

"You hurt me. You hurt me because you should've come talk to me. This time and five years ago. I wouldn't have wanted you to date her, I don't want that now, but at least I wouldn't have to feel like you two thought so fucking little of me that you thought I'd try to come between you if you'd given me the respect of talking to me. It hurt, man. It fucking hurt."

"I'm sorry." The pain doesn't come from the trachea this time, it comes from my heart. He's right. I should've known better.

"But I fucked up. I know I did. I reacted... badly. God, you don't even want to know the things I said to her. And... I want you to know, I've talked to her about the stuff I said in London. I don't think it was all... lies, but at least she knows that I said it out of hurt. And that you couldn't be a playboy even if you tried." He ends it with a chuckle.

I don't know how to describe what I'm feeling. Gratitude. Relief. Happiness?

"Thank you."

"Don't get me wrong, I hate to hell and back the thought of you and her... dating. Like I hate it with a searing passion. But that's my own shit. Just... you know... try to keep it to yourselves, at least for a bit. I don't need to see my best friend's tongue in my little sister's mouth."

I give him a cheeky grin. "Deal. And... I'm sorry."

"Yeah, well, we'll see just how sorry you will be. You haven't seen me really play my big brother role yet."

"I expect nothing but the worst."

We look at each other for a moment, and I wonder how things will be for us from now on. Whatever it takes, however much work it needs, I'm going to do everything I can to get us back on track as best friends.

"One more thing..." he starts and pulls a folded piece of paper out of his pocket. "This is for you."

My shaking hand reaches out for it, but I can't hold on, so he takes it from me and opens it up so I can read it.

"Don't sell to anyone but Kylian. But even better, keep it. Build something with your best friend. Make this a joint venture between Yin Tech and Baxter Enterprises. Make a legacy for your children to see what their fathers did together."

Dennis. Sending another message from the grave. I can't see the rest of the letter he left for Nathan. I don't need to. This is the part about us. A piece of advice from the grave.

"So..." Nathan says.

"So..."

"I just thought you should know what he wanted, what he thought. I know it would've mattered to you."

I wonder why Dennis didn't say anything to me. I was the one choosing to buy Yin Tech out; why hadn't he come straight to me to tell me he thought it was a bad idea?

"He wanted me to get you to stay," Nathan says, reading my mind. "It wouldn't have worked any other way. I had to want you to keep this between us. And you had to know I wanted it."

"And do you?"

He takes a long slow breath and nods.

And just like that, everything I thought I wanted wasn't what I wanted. And everything I didn't want was what I needed to have.

"Hey, Kylian, do you need...?" Kiara pokes her head in and turns white, seeing her brother standing here. "Nathan... what are you doing here?"

"I'm smothering him with a pillow," Nathan jokes.

And I laugh, ignoring the pain.

Kiara joins us, gingerly. She touches my cheek and gives me a smile, which fades when she sees her brother watching us.

"Kylian and I have agreed that you're not going to do that shit in front me."

She leans down and gives me a soft kiss. "You didn't take the first offer, did you?"

Epilogue - Kiara

THE OPENING OF THE casino comes before we know it. Kylian has been out of hospital for a few weeks and spent more hours in physiotherapy than I imagine is humanly possible.

I arrange for a bed to be brought down into the living room. At first I ask for another bed to be set up, but after the first night of him trying to climb into my bed with me, I agree to join him in his. As long as he doesn't try to extend himself.

He doesn't listen, and the first night, I wake to him gently kissing me awake and then bringing me to an intense orgasm with nothing but the fingers on his right hand.

But if nothing else, it tells me he's going to be okay.

His brothers, his father, and My-Linh join us for the opening. The men take a limo to the casino earlier in the day, and I make them promise they'll keep an eye on Kylian.

My-Linh and I are picked up and taken with Ananya and my girls on a bus.

There was a soft opening a week ago, so most of them know the lay of the land at Jade Bay, but for many of them, this is going to be an overwhelming night with the number of guests unexpected.

We arrive on time, and My-Linh and I decide to forego our invitation to walk the red carpet with the VIP guests and go in a private door with my players instead. Ananya gives them their assignments and shoos My-Linh and I away to join our counterpart, telling us we'd only be in the way.

My-Linh gives Ananya a hug that subdues the woman and tells her that when she grows up, she wants to be just like her. In the corner of my eye, I see Ananya blush and decide that's as good a time as any to run. She would not want us to see her like that.

I tug on my Dolce dress, wondering if Kylian will like it, but as we descend the stairs into the main game room where all the Baxter brothers are standing, there is no doubt in my mind that he likes what he sees. And I can't help but feel the same way about him. A week ago, we'd gone to get a tailored suit made for this very occasion. Unsurprisingly, he'd picked a midnight blue suit that makes him look like it was fitted to his body by god himself.

He meets me halfway up the staircase, taking my hand and leading me down to the floor.

"You look so hot I might take you right here on this Big Wheel table," he growls into my ear.

"I'm pretty sure I did not sign up to be the star attraction. I'm just a guest here tonight," I whisper back. "But maybe, if you're feeling friendly... and not in pain, I heard there's a little salon upstairs. Maybe you can take me up there while still being able to keep an eye on your big opening night."

"Take you is exactly what I intend to do," he responds before leading me over to introduce me to one of his VIP guests.

"Mr and Mrs Cheswick, this is the love of my life, Kiara Yin."

I try not to react to being called introduced that way and have no recollection of anything they said to me or me to them.

The night is so lovely with everyone in good spirits and Kylian getting to see his incredible project come to life.

We all walk down the shopper's lane to see some of the local businesses' stores, and they are filled with customers leaving with armfuls of bags.

Finally, we make it up to The Light Room, and I'm pleased to see some of my players enjoying themselves even while they work. Some of them with already high stacks of chips in front of them.

Kylian gestures to the pit boss who orders a private table be opened for us.

A dealer sits down and gestures for me to take a seat. "Ma'am," she says as I settle and pushes a stack of chips toward me.

I have no idea what is happening, but I do as she says and then laugh as Kylian sits down across the table for me.

"I'm feeling lucky, how about you?" he says with a grin.

"Oh, Mr Baxter, I hope that the house wins big tonight because you won't be winning here."

He cocks an eyebrow. "Big words, Miss Yin. But can you back them up?"

I don't say anything, just stare at him as the cards are dealt.

He picks his up, and the tiniest of frowns flashes across his face, and then he looks up, a giant smile on his face.

"How many do you need, ma'am?"

Something in his eyes tells me he is going to play this to the end, no matter what cards his has. What does he have to lose? And I have no intention of being topped.

"None for me." I place the cards on the table.

"None for me either," he says, laying his cards down as well.

"You don't have to copy me, you know," I taunt him as I throw in a handful of cards.

He makes a show of counting them before leaning back in his chair. "Wow, $500, you must have an amazing hand. I will raise you…" He pushes all of his chips into the middle.

I knew it. I just grin and push all of mine in as well. "Call. I hope you know, I fully intend on cashing in all of these chips, of course."

He picks up his cards and makes to place them down face up, but then he stops.

"I want to raise."

Everyone watching laughs.

"With what? You're already all in."

"I have one more..." He winks at me and then reaches into his pocket and lays a little velvet ring box on the table. "I raise you one engagement ring."

Everything blurs, and my ears ring.

I close my eyes as hands grab around the table to steady myself. And when they open, he's kneeling in front of me. In the background, everyone is gasping, except for my brother.

What is going on?

"Kiara, I have known you for what feels like my whole life, and in those years we weren't together, not a day went by when I didn't think of you. You have brought out the best in me when I thought to make it in this world I had to bring out the worst. You have changed my life in every way. And you make each and every day new and exciting, and I never know if today will be the day you push me off my balcony."

Everyone laughs around us, but all I can see his face.

"So please, will you marry me? And make me the absolute happiest man in the world. Who, for some inexplicable reason, has been blessed with the most incredible amount of..."

"Luck," I finish for him.

And when I finally say yes, even though the sounds of cheers drown out what he whispers to me as he slides on the ring and pulls me into his arms, I can't imagine anyone else ever feeling happier than I do.

***

This is the end of Kylian's and Kiara's journey for now. But they will show up in the next book in the Baxter Billionaire series, Lust. Which you can click here to get it. Matthias is waiting there to sweep you off your feet.

Also By

Don't forget to subscribe to Daisy Allen's email newsletter to receive information on upcoming new releases and bonus offers just for subscribers!

Click here to subscribe or go to:
http://www.subscribepage.com/b3l2q9
You can also follow Daisy on facebook for ramblings and extras: facebook.com/daibyday/ or TikTok at @daisyallenauthor

All Books by Daisy Allen

Available on Amazon and Kindle Unlimited
Rock Chamber Boys

Play Me

Strum Me

Serenade Me

Rock Me

The Baxter Billionaire

Luxe

Luck

Lust - May 2023

Luna - October 2023

Men of Gotham Series

Kaine

Xavier

An O'Reilly Clan Novel

Once Bitten

Acknowledgements

There are always too many people to thank; and sometimes I can't believe how lucky I am to be able to say that. Writing can be such a lonely journey, and much of the process is done sitting in the dark at 3:12am, the only light from your laptop monitor illuminating your face as you immerse yourself in an imaginary world of your own making. There's nothing else I'd want to be doing.
So those who make it happen...thank you.
Especially, to these people:
Thank you to Ms Queen of the Typos, Kayleigh, for always being up for a chat about Tom Holland, and maybe, even more importantly, bowel movements. You keep me giggling.
Thank you to my sister of the soul, Alicia, you joined me in one of the greatest cities in the world, while I raced to get this book done, and made me feel like, no matter how impossible...I was going to get it done.
Thank you to the countless authors in the countless author Facebook groups out there, that always help me know, whatever difficult thing I'm going through in the writing process, someone else has gone through it before...and survived.
Thank you, K-...you know why.
Thank you to Damien Baxter, the protagonist in Luxe, for jumping into my brain, that fateful day in April 2022, and inspired me to return to romance.
Thank you to my Manperson, who is endlessly supportive, and who bought me about 30 danishes because it was the only thing I wanted to eat in the last week before finishing this book.
And thank you, to the readers, all of you, the ones who love the book, and those who didn't, but for giving me a chance.
Like I said, this is the only thing I've ever wanted to do.
Happy Reading, my friends...

love,
Daisy Allen

About The Author.

First thing you should know about the author, is that she really, really hates writing these About The Author things. Who came up with these things? Cursed marketing people, that's who! Damn you marketing people!

The second thing you should know about the Author is that she has an MBA...specialising in marketing.

The irony is not lost on her, even when many other things are...like going to bed at a reasonable hour or how the economy works.

The Author, other than laughing right now at referring to herself in the third person, currently lives in Maine, USA, although she identifies as Vietnamese, who lived most of her life in Australia, and was born in France. I'm...I mean, she is a veritable one woman international food court.

She likes wining and dining, and whining when she's not being wined and dined.

Is a dog person, and professed not cat person, even though there is a cat currently sitting on her lap right now.

She wants to thank you for reading this book.

Writing is all she's ever wanted to do in life.

Happy Reading.

Also, sorry about the swear words. Her parents told her to write that. No, no they did not, they're the ones who taught her those naughty words, guttermouthed, heathens!

Printed in Great Britain
by Amazon